Her Best Life

Lara Asprey

Little White Door
PUBLISHING

Published in Great Britain in 2022 by:
Little White Door Publishing Ltd
9 Hersonsbrook
Buckhurst Road
Ascot SL5 7QD

A catalogue record from this book is available from the British Library

ISBN: 978-1-3999-1928-9

For my children Elise and Oliver.

Preface

Somebody once told me the definition of hell: "On your last day on earth, the person you became will meet the person you could have become."

ANONYMOUS

CHAPTER
One

Once we accept our limits, we go beyond them.

ALBERT EINSTEIN

SIRENS. POLICE SIRENS. THAT'S WHAT HER ALARM CLOCK sounded like this morning as she gently stretched her body in response to the noise. She opened her eyes slowly to her surroundings, pawing for her phone on her bedside table so she could turn the damn thing off and see just how late she was going to be for work.

Except her phone wasn't there, these weren't her surroundings, and that wasn't her alarm. She bolted upright, fearful, and jumped out of bed letting her senses do their work. The room was dark except for some light shining through the bottom of a heavy curtain covering tall windows. She stood up and pulled the curtains aside, feeling cold marble floors beneath her bare feet, and she squinted as the sun shone directly into her face. Outside she could see a garden with perfectly manicured lawns and floral displays. In the centre seemed to be a water fountain of a girl with wings, water coming out of her mouth, dripping slowly like she was drooling with her eyes open, staring straight at Lottie. The odd serenity of the view felt sinister in the morning light — unfamiliar, uncomfortable. It was silent aside from the tepid trickle of the fountain. The heavy curtains and fabrics that adorned the room muted her every move. Her footsteps were hushed, her frantic movements in search of information were seemingly being appeased.

Anxious now and growing ever more concerned, she looked to her bed and noticed now in the light-filled room that her camel handbag was on an ornate chest of drawers. *Oh, thank god for that.* She darted over to it and found all her usual possessions to be in place. Her phone, although dead, was in there. Her wallet with the little cash she carried was too, along with her bank cards and keys. Beside her handbag, she also found some clothes folded neatly along with some black shoes, her work ID, and her makeup bag. A pang of slight relief swept over her. At least she hadn't been mugged and that whoever had placed these items there had been gracious enough to fold them for her.

It was only then that she noticed the note.

I hope you slept well. We are all so excited about today's meeting. Don't be nervous! See you at the office. Cx'

Standing there, she put her hands on the ornate chest

of drawers to try to regain some composure, heart beating, breath jagged and tried to retrace her events of the night before. *How did I get here? Where the hell am I and who the hell is C?* She swallowed, hoping to deduce how dry her throat was and whether or not she had been drinking. She didn't feel like she had been. In fact, she had no recollection of anything that happened yesterday at all.

She glanced again out of the window; the fountain stared back at her as though watching her. Looking down, she found herself wearing an unfamiliar oversized T-shirt. No clues there. She walked over to the bedroom door and gingerly pushed it open searching for signs that may help her piece together where she was. She saw a large staircase and landing filled with motivational pictures on the walls framed in white modern frames *'Your limitation is your imagination'* followed by *'If you believe in yourself, anything is possible.'* None of this was making very much sense.

Although the house was quiet, her instincts were firing at her, telling her to get the hell out. She got herself dressed hastily, grabbing her handbag and shoes. *No time for makeup. I can do that en route.* She glanced in the mirror and tied up her hair into a messy bun as she walked hastily out of the room and down a large glass staircase that led into a grand and heavy wooden door with cast iron bolts. There was a clock on the wall reading just past 7.45 am, and large mirrors adorned the walls that seemed to follow her every move as she headed down the stairs. She didn't want to look. She found her reflection disconcerting, like each step she took, was one step closer to being found wandering around this large, unfamiliar house or that she might spot someone looking back at her who would see her trying to escape.

She focused her gaze on the room at the base of the

3

stairs where she could see a large open-plan living area filled with three generously sized cream sofas adorned with stylish grey cushions. Surrounding them were book-shelves brimming with brightly coloured books. At the far end of the room, she could make out what looked like an office space. It had a large and impressive desk shaped like the wing of an aeroplane and a selection of silver ornaments lit up within a glass cabinet. Wherever she was, it was owned by someone who lived an impressive life, a life very different to hers, a life full of recognition, but that didn't make her any less keen to get out.

She tiptoed keenly to the front door and was glad to see a key was still in the door beneath the cast iron bolts. She fiddled with the bolts and handles, jostling to turn them but they wouldn't budge and with each attempt to turn the key, it made an ear-shattering creak. Her hands started to shake. She was making too much noise. Surely someone would hear her. Eyes focused, clammy palms fumbling, she knew she had to make this work. Suddenly the key clicked and with another loud creak, the door swept open and fresh air breathed new life on Lottie's face waking her up and making her heart sink to the bottom of her chest with gratitude.

A small but perfectly manicured front lawn with trimmed hedges and purple flowers waved her goodbye and she soon found herself on a pavement. Looking back at the impressive white house behind her she noticed a London Street sign adjoining its exterior corner; *Egerton Crescent.*

Lottie Mortimer didn't know why she hadn't woken up in her own bed or how she got there. She didn't know why someone called 'C' was telling her not to be nervous or who she was. However, at least she knew *where* she was and for that moment in time, amidst all the confusion she had faced that morning, she had enough to give her a sense of security. She was ok. She was confused but she was safe. She was unharmed and she was intact. *This will all make sense soon,* she thought as she made her way along the pretty London streets towards South Kensington tube. *This will all make sense soon.*

AS LOTTIE PACED THE FAMILIAR STEPS TO APPROACH THE large revolving doors to her office, she sensed there was an unusual level of bustle. Clutching at her handbag, she peered in through the exterior glass walls where she could see a crowd standing idly by in the reception area which usually lay dormant. If it weren't for the odd guest needing to be signed in, that area was never anything more than a transitory space where people would hurry through. A few rather uncomfortable looking metal chairs greeted visitors along with overly bright ceiling lights. It struck Lottie as odd that the group were so outward-looking; they weren't talking to one another - instead gazing towards the doors as if eagerly expectant of someone. *Oh God, I have clearly forgotten about something important* she scolded herself. *Please tell me it's not an investor meeting.*

Suddenly acutely aware of the fact that she had taken about three minutes to get ready and was totally unprepared for the day, she tried to proceed unnoticed, intentionally looking down as she circled her way through the heavy doors, focusing on her feet as they moved one in front of the other. *Please nobody see me, please nobody see me.* She was still trying to piece together in her mind how she'd woken up in a strange house and what the note was all about before she was ready to deal with anything else. Besides, she was desperately in need of a strong cup of coffee.

However, no sooner had she walked through the doors when a voice called her name. It wasn't a familiar voice. It was deep and booming and reverberated like an echo in the sparsely furnished office entrance. It was the voice of someone older, someone wiser, someone author-itative.

"She's here guys. That's her. Lottie!" said the voice, "Lottie!"

Lottie looked up from her pacing feet to see one of the men from the group swiftly walking her way. He was wearing a smart-looking blazer with a shirt and jeans and had an angular grin on his face, rubbing his hands together with a sense of triumph as he keenly approached her. The rest of the group, of which he was seemingly the leader, were smiling eagerly too, a vacant expression on their faces. They didn't say anything, but their body language was directed her way. She observed them trying to work out if she had met any of them before, and wishing her memory with faces was better.

"We are so glad you're here," said the man. "How did you sleep?"

It seemed like a rhetorical question as he made no gesture to hear her answer. Instead, he was ushering her further inside, the others deferring to him, letting him lead. They surrounded her, circling her like keen wolves in the wild who were trying to behave themselves, trying to show restraint.

"We are so excited that you made it," continued the man. "This is such a big day. The press is here and everyone is looking forward to meeting you. Now please don't be nervous."

That was the second time that morning that she had been told not to be nervous, which only had the adverse effect. There was also something about the way he said it that made her feel all the more uneasy.

"What do you mean?" Lottie uttered, feeling uncomfortable as if this were all some practical joke that she simply wasn't in on.

Ok, this is all a bit weird.

She was reaching inside her handbag trying to find her work ID as she always did when she got to work but decided against it when the security guard beckoned them open like a bouncer at some overpriced nightclub. There was a knowing nod between them, as though an exchange had been made. It was clear they knew who she was, and besides, she really didn't want to embarrass herself by playing along with this weird joke. Soon Will and the team would emerge with some cake and hats, and whatever they were up to would be the talking point of the day.

"Yes, we know who you are," said the man, who had yet to properly introduce himself, his dark eyes narrowing behind frameless glasses. He glanced at the others in the group who looked back at him knowingly.

"We know quite a bit about you in fact," he said with a sly raise of his eyebrows.

Lottie sensed from the wry smiles surrounding her and their rigid disposition, a sense of pent up adrenaline from them, like attendees at a surprise party who couldn't wait to blurt out the words 'surprise!'

The group moved in unison like herded sheep into open elevator doors and as Lottie reached to press the button to her floor, the man beat her to it, pressing it for her. Standing in the middle of the elevator she could feel the heat of the stares searing into her body from all angles, surrounding her.

Ok, this is starting to creep me out...

"Sorry, but do I know you? Have we met before? If so, I'm afraid I don't remember your name..."

The man didn't answer. He didn't get a chance to. The silent, muted tones of the elevator, with its conservative, constricted air, were suddenly transformed by the opening of the metal doors to what reminded Lottie of a tube at rush hour. A sea of shoulders greeted her, blocking her exit. The noise of morning conversations, distant laughter, screeching chairs, the smell of morning coffee, of warm bodies and musky colognes and bright lights accosted her. Led by the man with no name, she found herself almost crushed by the cattle of the crowd around her as she battled her way through, pushing and nudging away elbows and parting shoulders. She looked ahead to try to see what they were here for. *What's all the fuss about?* She had never seen the place so heaving.

But it didn't take long before she started to hear a trickle of applause following her trail that was getting louder with each passing step. The mass of bodies began parting like the Red Sea, and people are suddenly circling her, staring at her, uttering words to themselves and others as if she were not there, as if she were not real "oh my god no way", "that's incredible", "how on earth..."

They had expressions on their faces she had never seen before. Nobody had ever looked at her like this, with sheer amazement and fascination, with half-open mouths. She had always just blended in, always considered herself fairly happy to not be the centre of attention, and now for the first time in her life, all eyes were on her. Part of her found herself unsure as to whether she should be enjoying the moment, embracing her five minutes of office notoriety. But no — something about this didn't feel right.

What the hell is going on?

Looking at their faces, their gaping mouths, their vacant yet glistening expressions, a dislocated look in their eyes, this certainly wasn't the sort of attention she wanted. Lottie began to feel uncomfortable now - fearful even. She looked around for some familiar faces from her office, for any familiarity at all. She couldn't find it, she didn't recognise anyone. Things felt different. Things looked different. She started to take in everything around her. Did the walls also seem as though they were a different colour?

The current of the ushering man and his group was sweeping her closer to a purpose-built stage at the end of the office floor in a space usually reserved for morning meetings. People were everywhere, but she still couldn't see the faces who could give her the reassurance she craved. Instead, she started to see strangers taking her photo. Phones appeared in front of their faces hiding who they were. They were missing the moment but seemed so intent on capturing her face and her changing expressions. *But why? Oh god don't take my picture now!* She tried to cover her face as she approached the stage, speeding up her pace to free herself from the crowd.

It was then that she began to make out a silhouette of a woman sitting on a perspex chair. She was facing the window. She wasn't looking at Lottie at all. She was facing away. She was looking outward onto the streets of London below calmly taking in the view. In a room full of faces pointed directly at her she was facing away, unaffected and unfazed by the commotion. Something about her demeanour made this stranger feel dangerously alluring.

Keen to make out who she was, Lottie stared fixated on her outline, drawn to her magnetically as though she were pulled instinctively her way. She could see that she was sitting with her legs crossed, still and serene like a morning lake. As Lottie edged closer she could see she appeared to be wearing a white minidress showing off tanned limbs with golden, wavy hair. Distracted, Lottie stumbled as she arrived at the stage, not realising it was raised quite as high as it was.

"Ok," said the man who had ushered her in, keen to assert himself as the man in charge. "Please could you kindly sit here Lottie?" pointing to another perspex chair facing away from this woman. There was excitement on his face now. A bead of sweat started to appear on his pale forehead making his skin shine like buffed shoes.

Lottie obeyed, silenced into inaction, numbed, taking it all in, fearful of speaking too soon, fearful of looking a fool. Perhaps she was being treated to a surprise for her ten-year service to the company. Perhaps she was getting a promotion. She sat down with a jolt onto the chair and could feel the energy of all eyes on her like bees in a hive, swarming, buzzing, eager. Beside the stage, there was a large screen with the words 'The Best Life' displayed in large font. Everyone's eyes were on her, paralysing her into feeling nothing but frozen.

The man leapt energetically forward towards the front of the stage and Lottie scanned the room again for familiarity. She became flooded with relief, she saw Will! He was standing by the window near the back of the office and she waved at him frantically, emotion welling up in her eyes from the joy of seeing someone she knew against this unfamiliar and overwhelming scene. She couldn't contain herself and blurts out loudly, with a fervent laugh.

"Oh Will! What are you up to?"

He caught her eye, raised a solemn hand back at her, not saying anything, he looked down.

He's not smiling. Why is he so far away? Why is he so serious?

The man continued to address the crowd. He was an older man, distinguished-looking but with a youthful edge, wearing casual navy-blue trainers that squeaked as he moved on the stage, and he kept flicking his hair to the side as he transferred his body weight from foot to foot as he spoke.

"Years and years of development have gone into today," started the man proudly rubbing his hands together like he did when he first greeted Lottie.

"I am so pleased you are here in what can only be described as a ground-breaking, Epoque-defining moment, and these are not words I use lightly."

He paced the stage, the glasses on his nose becoming unsteady as he looked at the floor coyly. He pushed them back up onto the bridge of his nose and continued speaking.

"This is the beginning of an incredible time, where dreams can finally become a reality and true potential can finally become realised." Lottie sensed he had the polish of a practised speaker, or that at the very least he had been carefully considering his words. His accent was well-spoken and he enunciated each word slowly, pausing for effect.

"No longer do 'filters'," he said bringing his hands up to create sarcastic quotation marks "have to stay on your phone. No longer do they have to remain aspirational and unrealistic. No longer do they have to be accessed when taking a picture or using an app, and no longer can the industry be accused of creating false hope or of leading to unrealistic standards of beauty. Today we have reached a point of ending the negative nuances that surround wanting to be better than you are, of wanting to be the best version of yourself. Today we are here to unveil the prototype of what we truly hope will become the future — for all of us."

Lottie looked around to gauge the reaction of these words on the crowd who seemed fixated on the orator.

"By combining our cutting-edge technologies. By finally working together as tech companies to merge what we all do well without three core fields, augmented reality, virtual reality and artificial intelligence - we are proud to become first-movers in what we are calling *authentic reality.*"

The crowd began to murmur with excitement.

"Today we are proud to unveil the prototype we have all been waiting for ladies and gentlemen. Today is the day that not just *we* get to meet someone living their best life, but so do they.

Now, before we explain how we reached this point and what was involved, I would really like to let the results speak for themselves. Besides, I'm sure you haven't come here today to listen to me."

The man flicked his wrist and gave a playful smile, hoping for a chuckle from the crowd that never appeared. This was not about him and the audience knew it.

"So, with no further ado," he continued unfazed, "and on behalf of the whole team here at Augmented AI, we are proud to show you — well,… what our future looks like."

He was now looking directly at Lottie, who was still frozen in her perspex chair feeling as though she were awake whilst undergoing an operation. Eyes darting, her body still. She had her back to this strange woman and began to feel the energy from her. She could feel the back of her legs sinking into the sharp edges of the seat and her feet felt cold. She wanted so much to turn around and see who was behind her.

"Lottie, if you wouldn't mind carefully standing up for me," he said patronisingly, gesturing an elbow for her to hold onto.

"That's it nice and gentle to your feet."

Incensed at his offer, she suddenly felt a wave of adrenaline, dismissing his elbow and finding her feet on her own. She was beginning to find this whole charade ridiculous. Who was this man to assume she needed help to stand up? *The bloody nerve.* Feeling her heartbeat quicken she felt the blood rush back into her legs as she stood up, suddenly making her feel weak at the knees. Still, she stood strong. If it were a question of fight or flight, she was certainly finding the strength to fight.

"Now stay standing there for a moment my dear. Don't turn around until I say so," said the man, a pantomime lilt to his voice.

"Now, Charlotte," he said with a proud smile before moving behind Lottie to the woman in the chair.

"Charlotte, please also stand up." *She was not offered help*, Lottie observed. "That's it, now please if both of you could come forward just a little and remain back-to-back, just like that for a moment."

Lottie could hear the subtle scrape of a chair and the staccato of stilettos hitting the stage. She looked down at her own flat, black shoes and noticed a scuff on the side of the right shoe. Cameras started to flash from the front row like a strobe light shining directly in her face. Back to back, these women stood, positioned on the stage like two lonely book-end. The man walked around to the front of the stage to address the crowd once again.

"Here we are, ladies and gentlemen. I am proud to introduce you to our prototype. This is it. We are here!" He laughed with excitement and the crowd joined him.

"Ok, now on the count of three, ladies, I would like to kindly ask you to turn around so you can face one another."

The room fell silent now. Hushed tones vanished. Morning clinks of coffee cups and heels clip-clopping on tiles ceased. Lottie's heart was quick and her senses were firing.

What the hell is going on?

"Three…"

Lottie couldn't blink, her eyes were so dry they began to sting.

"Two…"

Sounds began to muffle and Lottie sensed the room moved in slow motion.

"…and one."

A pause.

Turning around on her rubber-soled heel Lottie pivoted towards the golden hair she had seen from afar. She bolted her stare as fast as she could to lock eyes with this stranger, wishing for the punchline, wishing for the joke to be explained. There was a woman in front of Lottie she couldn't quite understand. This woman was extending her hand to Lottie before leaning in with a hug and smiling at her. She introduced herself to her as 'Charlotte'.

She has white teeth. They look perfect, all impeccably aligned. She is smiling. Her face lights up when she smiles and her complexion is flawlessly sun-kissed, making the whites of her eyes pop out, her green eyes piercing Lottie's heart. Lottie feels winded. She can't breathe. She finds her knees losing strength, they are buckling under the pressure and she grabs hold of the perspex chair for support. It's the only support she has in the room.

This woman steals her hand and raises it triumphantly to the sky as though they are two victors of a figure skating competition. Lottie almost collapsed. If it weren't for the adrenaline she was sure she would have fainted. Lottie can't take her eyes off her. The size of her arms, her tiny waist, her long neck. She has confidence about her, as though know she knows full well how well her features work together.

Cameras continued to pound her senses.

Lottie stared not ahead but at this woman. Cameras and commotion continue to surround her but Lottie is paralysed with fear and self-loathing. Terrified and heart-broken Lottie wants the ground to swallow her up. She doesn't want to keep looking but she can't help it.

This woman she is face to face with is not a stranger. The woman she is face-to-face with is herself.

CHAPTER
Two

A few months earlier...

LOTTIE LOOKED DOWN AT HER PINK-RIMMED COFFEE CUP AND RUBBED her finger over her teeth. *'Oh god, have I got lipstick on my teeth?'* she thought before navigating her way towards the elevator mirrors, where she tried to casually grin without bringing any attention towards herself. Relieved to see all her lipstick was seemingly on her coffee cup and not on her teeth she glanced upwards at the rising floor numbers. Grabbing her pen and notebook in preparation she sprung out of the opening elevator doors upon hearing the ritualistic 'ding' at floor number 8.

"Ah, Lottie. Good, you're here," called Will as he darted towards her like a bullet, grinning widely. He was wearing the pale blue shirt she liked so much and his brown hair was looking longer than he usually liked it. No doubt he would need her to book him for an appointment for a trim but before she could think any further, she was walking to his pace and striding side-by-side with him towards the main office boardroom. He liked to walk and talk, coffee-cups in hand and each morning she tried to be ready.

"Did you send the presentation on the potential productivity levels to Michael Dalton?"

"Yup, I did Will. I sent that yesterday afternoon."

Lottie had spent all evening working on those figures and Will hadn't even wanted to check or read them before Lottie sent them out. She wasn't sure whether to be irked or proud that he trusted her so much but decided she would assume it was the latter. She just wished sometimes he could have recognised she could do it, that she had a brain so that maybe one day she might be considered for a much-needed promotion. She really could have done with the money. Living in London didn't come cheap.

"Good. How many attendees have confirmed today's meeting and do we have a lunch organised for everyone?

"We do" she smiled shyly avoiding eye contact and getting a waft of his aftershave as he walked. We have 28 people coming today and yes, we have a plant-based lunch that will be arriving here at 12.45 pm. I will take care of it. Don't forget you also have a 2.30 pm with Dr Williams to discuss psychological impact, and of course not forgetting your 4 pm tea meeting with a Dr Patel."

Lottie had been doing her job for so long she really did feel she could do it blindfolded and although she found it somewhat easy she also found it very comfortable. She had never really had a clear plan for what she wanted to do so when she graduated from university with a degree in psychology so she just applied for anything that paid enough to survive in London. She loved the idea of a job in marketing or advertising. The idea appealed; all media lunches and glossy photoshoots, but the pay was too low and the experience required was too high — so she started to apply for jobs as EAs or assistants just to get a foot in the door. When she got called for an interview as an EA for some social media start-up, she went along, with the view it would only be until she found something else. Besides, she was organised and it didn't sound too hard.

Even at the interview, she didn't really understand all that much about what the company did. She remembered googling it and reading something about augmented reality data. *Oh god, how dull*. Why couldn't she work for some luxury fashion brand or boozy PR company? *Well, it was only temporary*, she kept reminding herself.

She always remembered that interview. Arriving sodden through in Covent Garden as she'd forgotten her umbrella and couldn't find the right address, she tied up her hair in a tight bun and glancing at her reflection in a nearby shop window she reminded herself of a nun. She chose to wear a black shirt with a white pattern on the collar. *Good choice* she told herself, feeling totally overdressed for this relaxed office vibe, before introducing herself to the receptionist who was listening to Michael Jackson's 'Man in the Mirror'. He had just died that week and his music was on repeat everywhere. The offices weren't terribly impressive, there were papers all over the receptionist's desk who greeted her with a fierce look as though she had been interrupted.

"Hello, my name is Lottie Mortimer, I'm here to see Will Sampson," she said delicately.

"What's yer name?"

Lottie stared at the woman unsure as to whether she'd just chosen not to hear her or whether she just wasn't very bright. Keen to not embarrass the woman she repeated with a smile.

"Oh. Lottie Mortimer."

"Yup take a seat," said the receptionist who avoided eye contact and tapped buttons onto her phone before saying, "Hi Will. I have Katy Mortimer here to see you".

Lottie chose not to correct the receptionist and obediently sat down on a spongy red chair by the receptionist's desk. When Will came out to greet her, her preconceptions were immediately put to one side, all confidence and good looks and everything about him was totally believable; developing augmented reality did seem like the future, he was right, and social media was bound to grow; Facebook had just about exploded all over the world and his passion was contagious. Lottie couldn't really understand what he was trying to do and how it would make money, but she liked him enough to take the job. He mentioned something about research and data driving social media, something about augmented reality and advertising, but her role would be more about organising his diary and office logistics. She couldn't help but notice he wasn't wearing a wedding ring and found herself wishing she had put her hair down and brought an umbrella.

Ten years on and the two of them were walking up to that same boardroom where she was first interviewed. Will opened the door and switched on the light, waking up the empty sleepy chairs and desk from their overnight slumber, with the flicker of a strobe light. He looked directly at Lottie, an earnest expression on his face.

"Good, and thank you Lottie for organising everything so well as always."

The stillness of the air in the room felt at odds with the energy levels they had applied to walking up to it, and all of a sudden Lottie was aware they were very much alone.

Keen to impress him further and in order to avoid a blush that she could feel rising in her cheeks from the fact he was staring right back at her in what seemed to be a slightly awkward silence, she added

"I have also spent some time working on the other model you requested, the one linking social media use to productivity levels. It's not fool-proof but I think I've found a causal link to determine social media users are generating lower levels of productivity and that shows a downward trajectory."

"Have you really?"

He looked at her intensely balancing his coffee cup on his leg as he perched on the large round desk.

"That is quite something if you have cracked it. I certainly couldn't have done that! Put some time in my diary for us to go through it."

"Oh sure, ok" replied Lottie shyly with a smile.

Aware of the fact she had nothing to perch on, she became uneasy with her stance, and moved her weight from foot to foot, clumsily clutching at both her handbag and coffee cup.

"I will do that."

Will smiled back at her, his blue eyes fixed on hers.

"What would I do without you Lottie?" and with that, they were interrupted by the boardroom door swinging open to a flurry of attendees who scurried to find their places around the round table. The silent and still air in the room had been transformed into a flurry of handbags, zips and scraping chairs, competing with hushed and brief morning conversations.

CHAPTER
Three

LOTTIE COULDN'T STARE ANY HARDER IF SHE TRIED. SHE couldn't avert her eyes, a combination of fear, of misunderstanding, of sheer incredulity. How was it possible? How did this person look so much like her? Who was she and why was she there? Terror ran through her veins, she found herself breathless, lightheaded, sure this was all some strange dream. Surely, there must be some explanation for all this. But reassurances were few and far between. Aside from Will, she saw no familiar faces and the intensity of the crowd staring and the scale of this seeming unveiling implied there was more to this than she could comprehend at that moment. The ice-cold and raw fear rampantly turned to question everything. Lottie was trying to find a rational justification for this, an explanation that might make sense. She found herself thinking back to when she was born, questioning her parents, questioning her birth, questioning if she had a twin sister she never knew about. In fact, in less than ten seconds of meeting this 'stranger' she found herself questioning everything she thought she knew about herself.

Born and raised in the pretty seaside village of Weymouth on the outskirts of Dorset, Lottie Mortimer had never really had to question very much. She never really had anything to compare it to, but as an only child, she spent her time resourcefully, climbing rocks or playing with the children of passing tourists who would summer in the town. Her parents, John and Maureen, were busy working most of the time and trusted Lottie not to misbehave. Besides she was a responsible child, a fairly quiet child. She would do her homework on her own without bothering her parents for help, she would read stories to herself at night before she went to bed and she seemed to revel in her own company. Often reading for hours, her parents never worried about her, they just thought they were blessed to have a child who was so easy-going and low-maintenance, not like the other children they would see in the town, all screams, tantrums and snot.

It also meant they could live their lives just like they did before Lottie was born. Her father would often come home late smelling of alcohol, and would routinely fall asleep in the armchair in the living room. Lottie made it her labour of love to cover him with a blanket. Her mother, although she loved her enormously, would often be very preoccupied with making ends meet and was in a constant state of stress and distraction. Never wanting to spend money on frugality her mother and father would often stress over paying bills or when they could afford to buy her new school shoes. She remembered her parents having blazing rows, and preferring to keep out of it she would go to her room with a nightlight and book to read under the blankets. It often baffled her that they were still together all these years later, but she was sure there was a part of them that liked instigating arguments with each other to keep an equilibrium of passion in their relationship.

Lottie often wished for a younger brother or sister to come along but they never did. Somebody who she could share a bunk-bed with and talk to at night, but that was not to be. So, she found comfort in school, her teachers taking a much greater interest in her development and studies than her parents, and she liked the company of the other children, excelling at team sports and sciences. At that moment, standing on that stage she found herself thinking back to those nights. How much her parents argued, how her father slept on his own so often and reminded herself it was highly unlikely she had a secret siren sister and she was fairly sure her parents would not have been shrewd enough to successfully hide the fact she had a twin. Besides, they weren't exactly wealthy so everything they did have went into making sure they could provide for her. It all just seemed totally implausible.

The crowd was still clapping, she could feel the energy around her, standing up, vibrations from the moving hands making the hair on her arms stand and sway, but she could not see their faces. Like a performer on stage blinded by lights, she could not see her audience yet she knew they were there. She could only see one thing, she could only hear one thing, and she was staring at a version of herself she could not quite comprehend.

This person moved differently; she had powerful energy. She was groomed, she was feminine yet dominant. She was beautiful. She was breaking Lottie's heart just looking at her. She was everything Lottie wasn't and more than she could ever have imagined she could become. She was everything she was too scared to confront and every-thing she had denied herself from admitting she wanted-and yet all the while, she was utterly fascinating.

"Now, Lottie," said the man with no name who appeared before her once again. "I know this must be a lot to take in, but I wanted to introduce you to Charlotte. Charlotte is the best possible version of yourself who we have created via our new technology that we hope to soon release onto social media, and who you could become if you truly fulfilled your potential. Lottie, this is you at your absolute best. This is who you could be. Aren't you amazing?"

Charlotte smiled at Lottie warmly with a playful wave. Lottie felt waves of nausea mixed with utter humiliation. How badly had she been living her life? How many wrong choices had she made? For someone who consid-ered herself as fairly un-extreme in most things, she had clearly been kidding herself. The difference between the two of them was notable and Charlotte had yet to utter a word.

Lottie had never been overweight but she was not one of those girls you could describe as naturally skinny. She would loosely watch what she ate, constantly starting a new diet every Monday in a bid to lose those final few pounds only to have fallen off the bandwagon by 'Thirsty Thursday' when she would inevitably go out for one glass of wine which would turn into several bottles and a fren-zied dash for food on her way home. By Friday she would often feel so hungover that she would just give up and promise to start again next Monday. It was a cycle she found herself in week after week despite trying to instil better habits.

Yet this person in front of her was much leaner and

seemed much taller than her. She was wearing a white, sleeveless mini dress showing off her arms and legs — both of which Lottie had never felt confident enough to show off. She had the body of a dancer, slim and toned. Her complexion was bright and she seemed so happy. Natural makeup, she let her radiant skin speak for itself. *No wonder she's so bloody happy* thought Lottie with more than an ounce of jealousy. *I would be too if I looked like that.*

"Yes," replied Lottie meekly aware that the man with no name was waiting for a response. She was amazing, that much was true but that was all she was able to say. That was the one word that escaped her beating chest and she could almost feel a quiver on its delivery, as though by admitting it she had let herself acknowledge she wasn't good enough. That she was a failure.

The man continued "We have been developing this filter for a while now, and you my dear Lottie, very kindly volunteered to be our prototype."

I did? When?

"Everything you see here will feel totally real, it's just you have entered a filter called 'authentic reality'. All other factors in your life are the same, except you can now share your world with the best version of yourself who can motivate you to truly excel. You are so incredibly lucky to have this experience Lottie. To have entered the filter like this, this is an opportunity for you to become great for once in your life, to shine as you've never shone, to become somebody, to achieve something."

Charming thought Lottie, instantly disliking this man who still, as of yet, had failed to introduce himself.

"You're going to live with Charlotte for a little while so she can show you how to fulfil your potential and become the best possible version of yourself. We feel that if everyone could vividly live and breathe beside the best version of themselves, they will inevitably start to emulate them. I mean what a motivator! It will encourage everyone to become so much more productive, just imagine what it could do for our economies if everyone got on board."

All of this was so overwhelming, and Lottie started glazing over, it's not that she didn't want to know it's just she found herself feeling too confused to concentrate. It was as though someone had just shattered her heart into tiny pieces on that stage, and she was on her hands and knees trying to find the fragments.

She just found herself staring at Charlotte while this speech was taking place. She watched her lips as she smiled and her eyebrows as they raised in fascination to the conversation. Charlotte didn't seem distracted at all by Lottie, she was wholly fixated on what was being said. Did she not have the same mutual fascination with her, the substandard version of herself? Perhaps she did not want to see or perhaps it was beneath her to look down.

"You can touch her," said the man laughing at her vacant expression, jolting her back to reality. "Everything is designed to feel real while you're here. This is the biggest technological development of a generation Lottie. You've just jumped inside and what you do over the next few months may well change the world."

Lottie nodded but didn't understand. It all felt like a very surreal dream and she pinched at the palm of her hand to make sure she could feel pain, wincing as she realised she could.

I don't get it. I just don't get it.

"Now, if we can get a few words from you both. Let's

give Lottie a moment to get her head around this. Charlotte if we could start with you."

With that Charlotte confidently stepped forward without hesitation, walked up to the man and began to speak steadily.

"Thank you Michael. A big thank you to Michael Dalton, everyone!" She proceeded to initiate a clap whilst looking at certain attendees in the audience with a bold gaze followed by a lengthy pause whilst she smiled. Controlled, calm and resolute.

Michael Dalton? The man with no name was Michael Dalton?

That name rang a bell. She had never met him face to face but she had organised several meetings with him and had even spoken to him on the phone a few times. In fact, she remembered doing some models for Will as he had mentioned Michael needed them. Why was he standing here instead of Will? What was going on?

"It's really been a privilege and an honour to be a part of this filter and this company, working alongside such incredible talent, and without you all *this,*" she said gesturing to Lottie and then herself with a slightly haughty laugh, "would not have been possible. I cannot thank you all enough for enabling me to put my dreams into reality.

"The filter industry is now worth billions of pounds and we have long been able to record and upload perfected videos of ourselves onto social media via Instagram, Snapchat, TikTok or Facebook stories. Now, thanks to increased technology in augmented reality, virtual reality and scientific breakthroughs in artificial intelligence we have been able to take filters outside of the technology, outside of the smartphone or device we are using, and place our subjects into another world. In other words, we have finally learnt how to authenticate the virtual technology we had for many years but never really knew what to do with."

Lottie recognised her own voice in Charlotte's as she spoke, yet something about her was entirely different. She was fearless. She didn't hesitate in making her points clear. She had conviction. She was articulate. Lottie had always been rather shy and hated public speaking or being the centre of attention. If she ever had to read aloud in school, despite being a very good reader, she would clam up from anxiety, and that continued into her adult life. If ever asked to stand up in a crowd to speak she would blurt words out quickly to get them said, and then spend the next few hours replaying the moment over and over in her mind, wondering how she had come across and what others had thought of her. Charlotte, however, was measured in her delivery, she paced herself like a practised speaker, she modulated her tone and she didn't care what people thought. She found members of her audience and held their eye contact, she conveyed reassurance through her gaze. Her voice sounded different too, louder, with more gravitas, and she stood with poise and grace.

"I am so proud to be living proof that through the world's first authentic reality filter, I am truly living my best life, and what a life I have been living as I'm sure you will all agree. I'm excited to share some of my nuggets and pearls of wisdom that I feel blessed to have learnt about how to be the best possible version of myself, with Lottie."

A rupture of applause erupted throughout the room

before Lottie felt vibrations beneath her feet like a herd or stampede. Charlotte smiled widely and triumphantly.

"Please, please!" Charlotte attempted to lull the crowds like a comedian giving comic timing to the effects of a joke. With a grin, and showcasing her pearly white teeth, "I feel in order to explain how we did this we must hear a few words from the wonderful scientific mind behind this breakthrough. Ladies and gentlemen, I would like to welcome to the stage, Dr Ravi Patel."

A short, quiet man with white hair and glasses and a gentle stoop emerged from where he had been sitting, unbeknownst to Lottie up until that point, and walked slowly to the stage with his head down, carrying a rather ordinary-looking notebook and pen. Lottie couldn't help but find this vision contrary to the seemingly cutting-edge technology surrounding her.

"Hello friends," began Dr Patel looking down past his bifocal glasses to address the crowd "and thank you to the incredible Charlotte for helping us to make all of this happen. For those of you who don't know me, my name is Dr Patel and I have been leading the scientific development of this filter, using my medical background to guide the team here. I would like to say a few words to explain to you all and to Lottie of course, what this filter is all about." He half-smiled at Lottie before continuing.

"Now, I know what you're probably all thinking." Mr Patel began with a chuckle and with a click of his pen. "How is it possible and how can I get one too?" He looked out to the crowd who were laughing and nodding their heads. "It's quite amazing to see these two ladies side by side I'm sure you will agree.

Now the path to perfection, like anything worth having, is never easy to attain. Many people would love to change but lack motivation and a good enough reason. Some lack sufficient willpower as change can be difficult, change can be scary and it's easier and less hassle to just stay as we are. We felt that seeing the best version of yourself in front of you would simply be the most motivating way to achieve real personal development. Imagine a world where everyone can see who they could truly become. As Ernest Hemingway once said, 'There is nothing noble in being superior to your fellow man; true nobility is being superior to your former self.'

This morning Lottie awoke inside this brand-new filter for the very first time. She awoke in Charlotte's house where she will be staying for the next few weeks where she can learn all there is to know about self-improvement. Charlotte will be her guide, her mentor and her confidante. She will be there to show her how she did what she did to get her to achieve such impressive results by giving her a strategy, a plan and a guide to becoming her best self, and living her best life.

During this time, we will be closely monitoring Lottie's biometric body composition, her level of movement and sleep patterns, her calorie consumption and productivity levels by tapping into various data sources. With this microchip in her body," he said pointing to the screen next to the stage which suddenly came to life with graphs and charts, "we will be tracking her daily calorie consumption along with, amongst other things, the macronutrient breakdown and protein intake, calorie expenditure, steps, etc. All of this data gets compiled with other data on the individual including performance data, personality data and innate talents and abilities to generate an optimal version of that person in real-time.

Now we already had a lot of data about Lottie, in

fact, she was selected because she showed promise. We knew she was underachieving based on where she was in her life vs her abilities. Here," he said pointing to another chart, "are the results of pre-filter tests we did to gauge where her strengths and weaknesses lie. She is incredibly academic, a numbers person, yet also very well-read. In fact, our findings showed she had read more books in one month than most would read in a year. Lottie however, lacked confidence, inner belief and a strategy for success. Nobody has ever put their faith in her so she never put any in herself. As a result of this, she had a huge amount of negative self-talk and as a consequence, willpower, meaning any good intentions would be quashed quickly. She never sought to improve herself, having the same job for ten years when she was capable of more, so all in all, she really was an ideal candidate."Lottie was listening to this man recite these facts about her as though she weren't there, as though she were a mere specimen going into some weird experiment. However, try as she might to find frustration with what he said, he was remarkably accurate and she found herself intrinsically fascinated. She was also oddly emotional. Nobody had ever articulated that she had potential before or thought she could be anything other than she was.

"Charlotte is Lottie six years from today. This is what six years of hard work and dedication look like. Not long if you think about how these changes will last her a life-time. She is the result of improvements physically, mentally and spiritually. She is quite literally, the best version of herself, and works hard to maintain these optimal levels of performance in all three of these areas.

Physically, well most obviously we can see that Char-lotte is much leaner. She has lost twenty pounds and whilst she was not overweight before, she was only in the top fifty percent of body compositions, and her body fat was fairly 'average' at twenty six percent. She had a BMI of twenty two point five and now has a BMI of eighteen which makes her bang on healthy for her height with an incredibly lean body fat of just seventeen percent. She has more muscle definition as a result of the exercise regime that she has applied herself to, which is a combination of HIIT and strength training six times a week, with one day for stretching. Each day she works out for between sixty and ninety minutes."

He turned to Charlotte and smiled, and she smiled back and laughed whilst flexing her arm muscles in a Popeye display of humour. Lottie looked at her arms and looked at Charlotte's. Her arms always seemed so wide, as though little pockets of fat were always trying to escape from underneath them. She hated the tops of them, and yet here was this woman with a sleeveless dress and she had definition where Lottie just had none. She couldn't recognise the body of this woman as her own. It almost looked too good to be true, unimaginably good. Even if she had tried to lose those final few pounds, she had never have envisaged getting to this point, of being *that* good.

"Charlotte's lean physique is due to a plant-based diet and at least 2.5 litres of water a day each day, we can see the difference here."

Ravi brings up a slide showing the before and after breakdowns of her height, weight and vital statistics for all to see.

"It's also very clear to see from her complexion, there are no bags under her eyes, her eyes are brighter and less dull, and her hair has grown out to be longer and healthier than ever before, and she has had no health issues whatsoever, not even a common cold in the six years since we started gathering data on her."

Lottie felt so humiliated but this man was right. This woman was doing everything right and the results were clear. Lottie had been kidding herself. She hadn't been honest with herself about how bad things truly were.

The crowds were looking at Lottie now with pitiful faces, *poor-you* expressions, sympathising head tilts.

"Now Mentally," he continued addressing the room with the next slide. "Mentally we can see that Lottie has had a fairly clouded mental state, unable to strive for more, not thinking she deserved more. "As a beloved EA Lottie was always well organised, but she failed to finish personal projects she started. We have records of her expressing her dreams to do something with her life, to be an entrepreneur, to write a book, but she failed to have the self-belief and discipline required despite her innate abilities. Her mindset was fixed and not growth-oriented and she appeared to display very evident insecurities leading to limited beliefs — which I think we can all agree by looking at Charlotte, that she no longer has."

The room gave a collective chuckle and once again all eyes were on Charlotte as she modestly rebutted his claims with a jovial laugh and an 'oh stop' wave of the hand.

"Charlotte has now, thanks hugely to her diet and exercise regime, achieved mental clarity and can focus on one project at a time. Gone are the days of multitasking and failing to start and finish anything. Furthermore, she has found the strength to cut out toxicity in her life by removing friends and family who don't support her or encourage her to live her best life.

And finally, Spiritually," continued Ravi. "Spiritually,

Lottie was in a frenzied state it's safe to say, often failing to live in the moment and have true mindfulness. She was focused on the tomorrow without the focus on today and as a result, suffered from anxiety. Now thanks to a ritual of meditation and relaxation she has reached a point of spiritual enlightenment. She used to make little time for self-reflection due to life and family commitments and was easily distracted. She often participated in excessive Thursday drinking, but now she makes time for herself religiously each day.

And just when Lottie thought her torture would end, Ravi steps back from the screen and turns to the crowd, his head and shoulders square up at this point, before he looks at Lottie directly.

"Lottie, with all this in mind, would you like to see what Charlotte has achieved in the past six years?"

CHAPTER
Four

"WHEN IS THE PROTOTYPE NOW DUE TO LAUNCH?" ASKED THE MAN behind the desk, putting his phone into the right-hand pocket of his blazer and leaning back in his chair.

"We have everything ready," replied Will. "We are just deciding on the right candidate which as you know, is an important part of the process in itself."

Will had been nervous about this meeting all week. He looked the man in the eye as confidently as he could, hoping he wouldn't detect his anxiety. He knew they were delayed that questions would soon need to be answered, but he had hoped he could stall him by reinstating his faith in the bigger picture, reminding him of why they had originally invested in this project to begin with.

"We hope to make the selection this week and then we will be all systems go," continued Will with a smile.

"As we've discussed, it's not something we have done before, so we have to be very careful who we choose to go into the filter. It has to be someone who shows promise, but who we can control, we don't want the prototype to outsmart us before we have even tested it."

"Yes, I quite agree," said the man, a knowing nod.

"Also remember, there is a long-term strategy behind this filter so we might not be able to justify returns right away, but productivity levels will rise, and six years from now the country will hopefully look very different indeed.

Will knew this filter would interest the government but he hadn't quite anticipated their vision to invest in its early stages quite the way they had. Since Brexit and COVID-19, the economy was in a recession, property prices had stalled, unemployment levels had increased and people were generally feeling insecure about their futures. As is typical in times of uncertainly, people were spending more time on recreational activities; more online shopping, more lavish holidays and social media usage statistics between the twenty to thirty-five year-olds continued to rise. This age demographic was spending more and more time on social media and less time in the real world and the government knew, as did Will, that this would not serve the country or the economy well in the long term.

However, Michael Dalton was a bit of a visionary in a world of grey suits within government. Identifying a gap in the market for the UK to expand its technological output levels, and with growing competition from increasingly tech-savvy nations abroad, Michael proposed that a new position be established within government to focus exclusively on making Britain an innovative leader on the world stage.

'A bunch of lazy-arse entitled wannabes,' he had been known to call the social media generation, as he was not one to mince his words, and his feeling was shared by many. *'If only they got off their backsides and stopped expecting the world to give them everything.'* Michael didn't like the way

the future was heading and was keen to do something about it.

His resumé gave him a foot in the door to deal with the Government without objection. The founder and CEO of BizPlay, a music streaming service that was recently listed on the FTSE 250, had successfully launched internationally, and thereafter he had established a chain of technologically advanced fast-food restaurants serving inexpensive but healthy food. This made him not only popular but listened to. The UK was proud of him. He was a success story who represented the nation well. He not only had the vision but the drive. He was outspoken, perhaps some would say a marmite character, but he had made his fortune to prove himself. The fact that he was willing to work for the government unpaid, made his offer to establish himself as 'Minister for Innovation and Digital Output' a no-brainer, in a government seeking more self-starters and certainly more populists.

"Yes, I'm quite aware of the long-term strategy," replied Michael. "I just need something to show the cabinet office. Do we have anything that will serve to demonstrate how this filter will affect bottom-line productivity levels?"

"Not directly," responded Will "as there are so many variable factors that are out of our control. We won't know many facts and findings until we fully launch the prototype, but we have found a link between social media usage and decreased productivity levels, which only shows a downward trajectory."

Michael knew this was the case. Although he was no technical expert, he could see the youth of today hiding behind their smartphones more and more. Whereas the original strategy behind such smartphone expansion had been to equip people with more knowledge, more podcasts, more online courses, more ways to improve their body and their minds - he could see what nobody else wanted to say. More people were spending hours of screen-time on totally unproductive social media channels such as Instagram and TikTok, creating stories and images of perfect lives they wanted to portray they had. Becoming an 'influencer' was becoming more a desirable vocation than law or medicine, and Michael was convinced the future would display its true worth.

'It was all bullshit. Nothing but true hard work creates success in life,' he would say to Will, and *'these bloody influencers are nothing but a generation of entitled, narcissistic attention seekers.'*

Will had presented average screen-time statistics to him, and it was shocking. Some were spending up to fifteen hours on their phones each day and eighty percent of this time was on social media. Michael knew this age demographic was missing the point. They were getting more degrees, but higher education had lost its value, and they were trying to make their lives seem perfect to compensate for large gaps between perception and reality.

Mobilising this age group would be key to economic success, but he hadn't quite worked out how it could be done. It wasn't until he was introduced to Will Sampson at a business networking summit that it clicked. He immediately liked what Will was all about; all charm and good looks, a great leader who came from a powerful family too, which gave him credibility. Will reminded him of himself when he was twenty years younger. A visionary like him, Michael could resonate with his drive. The two clicked immediately and Will had invited Michael over to the office to get his head around their detailed vision for the company and their business plan. It was incredible. They needed money, and that was where Michael could most certainly help.

Proposing the idea to the rest to the government ministers had not been a difficult task. In parliamentary meetings preoccupied with "top-priorities" such as COVID-19, Brexit and immigration, a technology filter that had a long-term strategy behind it to help increase productivity levels seemed harmless enough. Michael had been assigned a modest government budget to develop his department with more to come once the prototype had been tested. But he wasn't worried. If they needed more money, he could make up the difference himself along with money from investors who he didn't doubt would be chomping at the bit to be involved with something like this.

Besides, the fact he would also put his own money where his mouth was, reassured not only the government but also any potential investors that this was a safe bet; that he was onto something. So, they left him to it unchallenged, except for needing the odd statistical model to demonstrate its validity as a concept.

"Yes, well no big surprises there," responded Michael with a half-smile. Ok, send me over all the models you have and keep me posted when we are ready to go with the prototype. I shall be eagerly awaiting news."

CHAPTER
Five

THE MEETING ATTENDEES SETTLED INTO THEIR SEATS AS WILL FIDDLED with the projector, readily awaiting their attention. Lottie found her place at the back of the room, putting the meeting agenda neatly in front of her to try and make herself look and feel more organised. She always found moments alone with Will quietly electrifying and although she knew others were soon due to join the boardroom, she couldn't help but wish they had just had another couple of minutes together alone.

As the crowd settled into their seats, two other men moved towards Will and stood beside him at the head of the boardroom table asserting themselves as speakers. She had been briefly introduced to these men before when they had arrived at the office to see Will. The meetings always had cryptic descriptions like 'viability discussion on project x,' or 'cost-benefit analysis' so Lottie was none the wiser with regards what they were about - but she assumed from Will's instruction to prioritise them above other meetings that they had to be important.

Lottie recognised the man on the left as Richard Myers. He was the founder of AI Incorporated, a company that had been around for a while that focused on developing artificial intelligence. He had been in the news quite a bit over the past few years commenting on how much companies were spending on AI and he always seemed terribly clued up on technology. The other was Mark Ball. He was, she believed, a scientist of some sort, she wasn't entirely sure. All she knew was that from all the covert meetings these men had been in over the past few months, something was certainly going on.

"Right," said Will, keenly trying to switch on the charm and hush the morning conversations. "I think we are all here. Good morning everyone, and thanks for lending us your ears so readily on a Monday morning. I hope everyone has helped themselves to coffee," he said gesturing to the back where there were silver pots and white mugs with pastries neatly laid out very close to where Lottie was sitting. Eyes turned her way as he said this and Lottie immediately began to blush.

"I wanted to call this meeting," continued Will "to update you on a few company developments. As valued employees here at Augmented Minds, I know how much you believe in this company, and I truly thank you for that. A lot of you have been here since we started ten years ago and I'm so grateful to you all for everything you've done. From developing our first augmented reality ads for Sky and Lego all those years ago, we now have the privilege of being at the peak of our industry developing apps and retail experiences for some of the world's biggest brands. Our specialised sensors in this field do not just promise the best quality digital overlays, but we have also expanded to take in more information about the surrounding areas of that overlay than any of our competition — which has really helped us not just stand out in this market but grow exponentially.

Over the past few months, we have been looking at the best ways to help the company to grow even more, and I've personally been in several brainstorming meetings with some very smart people who have endless ideas on what the future looks like not just for us in augmented reality industry but for technology in general.

With so much potential in this space, there is certainly a need to start combining expertise and knowledge with other forward-thinking companies; other companies who see the future the way we do. So many tech companies are making the mistake of only working within their own silos, but I am convinced the magic will happen when we come together. When we bring our technologies together to truly break some ground.

With this in mind, I wanted to share an exciting update for our company. It's something that has been in development for several months now and something that I feel will benefit us all immensely."

Will looked to his two comrades standing like military soldiers by his side, who had yet to utter a word but who gave a knowing nod.

"I'm delighted to announce that we here at Augmented Minds will be merging with AI Incorporated, and Virtual Worlds to do just that. To combine our expertise to create a new technology. Now I know that plenty of you have probably been hearing rumours through the grapevine of a merger...

I haven't thought Lottie suddenly feeling embarrassed and incensed. How had she missed this? Did everyone know about this except her? She scanned the room, trying to read the faces of her colleagues.

Yet, somehow it made sense. All the work she had been doing for Will on the side, all those models he had needed. She hadn't questioned anything as she had enjoyed helping Will with juicer pieces of work, but it was all starting to click into place.

"This merger will be taking effect from next month, where we will start to combine our office spaces and technologies in a way that no one has ever done before. Please rest assured, we will not be cutting any jobs, quite the opposite in fact, as we will only be looking to grow. Floors six and seven will become ours and we will go from having a team of just under 60 to a combined workforce of 250, where we will have a dedicated research lab, a testing suite and a filter proofing facility."

A filter proofing facility? What the hell is that?

"I would like to introduce you to the men by my side who will be helping me make it happen. This, to my left, is Richard Myers he's a visionary leader on all things artificial intelligence and a bit of a data geek!"

Richard laughed yet remained silent, letting Will continue.

"And to my right is Mark Ball, he founded Virtual Worlds and has been instrumental in developing virtual reality backdrops. The backdrops to his virtual worlds are now so lifelike they are on par with our real world".

Suddenly the screen beside Will came to life with a collage of pictures of men and women running at the gym, one was drinking a bottle of water with sweat dripping down their cheek, there was a man with white teeth smiling broadly, children were playing in sun-lit pools with their parents, a beautiful model was taking a selfie.

"Although the potential for combining technologies is endless," Will continued "we have recognised the potential within one key area specifically, and that is a certain hashtag that has taken the world by storm."

The screen beside Will lit up.

#LIVINGMYBESTLIFE

"This hashtag has been used more than any other in the last five years, it's growing year on year and its popularity is tied to a huge number of incredibly profitable industries;

healthy eating plans, juicing diets, gym workouts, wellness retreats, holidays, self-improvement, e-learning, and many more, In fact, the list is endless as you can see from the screen."

The screen changed to show a word cloud full of words and tags that had been applying the livingmybestlife hashtag.

"More and more people are becoming fascinated with becoming the best version of themselves. To some, it's become a lifestyle, to others, it's an obsession.

People are wanting to improve and are finding their own ways to try to do so, some successfully but in truth, the majority of them are not. We know that most people who look to social media using this hashtag, do so to get inspired rather than to proactively adopt this lifestyle. According to stats, only 2% of people are truly successful in sticking to any self-improvement intention long-term, the rest are all living a life hoping that one day they will find the motivation."

Lottie looked around the room at her colleagues who were listening attentively to Will. Their jeans and white trainers, some with beards and haircuts that probably cost a fortune to look slightly dishevelled. The hipsters. She wondered if they felt they were living their best life at this office, in this company. She certainly didn't. Although she wasn't unhappy in her job, she often thought about looking for something else or even asking for a pay rise - but the truth was that she was too scared. She had been doing the same job for so long that she was not only comfortable, but monotony had caused her to lose confidence. She often went home after a long day at work and thought about what she would do if she wasn't Will's EA. She used to have dreams of doing something for herself like starting a company or writing a book and she often imagined what life would be like to be free from the shackles of a salaried job, living life month to month, hand to mouth.

The thought of all the effort subdued her with doubt. Who was she kidding, she was just an EA, she had no game plan, these were all pipe dreams, and as quickly as she had built her imaginary house of cards, she blew them all down in quick succession with a thud of practical reality. Deep-down, she didn't feel she deserved to be in the room when it came to success. Those rooms were saved for other people, special people, people with unique skills and confidence. She also admitted to herself that she often gave up practically everything she started, whether it was a new fad diet (which she would stick to for about three days), or an exercise regime which was always so hit and miss — so what chance did she have of sticking out a new business venture or transforming her life?

"We feel," Will continued, gesturing to Mark and Richard, "that in order to get people truly living their best lives, we have to take the inspiration outside of the phone or tablet they see on screen. We have to make them realise who they could truly become — as we all know how important visualisation techniques are in making your dreams a reality.

So, could you imagine a technology that doesn't just show you an improved version of yourself on the screen through a filter, but that shows you who you could truly become?"

Will paused to gauge the attention of the crowd. He still had it. They were all ears.

"Well, we will be creating this technology. By joining forces and merging augmented reality, virtual reality and artificial intelligence, we will be creating what we are calling 'Authentic Reality'.

With that, the screen changed once again to show what appeared to be a before and after of a human avatar. On the left, there was a slightly overweight and uninspired looking woman with an unhappy look on her face, and by her side was the same woman looking trim, bright and happy.

"Authentic Reality will allow users to enter the world where the best version of themselves live, they can see first-hand who they could become and what kind of life they will live. No longer will 'living your best life' be a pipe dream. It will be an Authentic Reality."

The audience was now starting to murmur. Bodies were turning around to talk to one another, eyebrows were raised, hands were covering whispering mouths. Will took a moment to pause. He was taking in their reactions. What would they make of this idea, would they get behind him?

Raising his voice slightly to hush the rumbling he continued, "I appreciate this is a lot to take in and I know you're probably all wondering how on earth we will make this happen, but rest assured we have given it a lot of thought. The next steps are as follows". Will pointed to another slide with a timeline on it.

"The next thing we will be looking to do is to develop a working model of this filter via a prototype. This prototype will essentially 'soft-launch' the product, and put all our work and findings we have done to date to the test, and only after this has been successfully launched and rolled out, will we do a staggered release of the filter in the territories you can see on screen. We will be starting exclusively in the UK as the government here has invested in its development.

Will was now pointing to another slide called 'Roll-out' with some information on which countries would be rolled out and when, but Lottie was too far away from the screen to see all the details.

"We are currently in the process of selecting a person who could become our prototype. It would be a hugely exciting opportunity for that person to see what and who they could become. They would need to be someone who shows untapped promise or who doubts their own beliefs, and who hasn't established success yet. They would need to lack discipline, yet show aptitude. We are reviewing several people at the moment and are looking for volunteers — if anyone would like to be put forward or could suggest someone do let us know. We have until the end of next week to make the selection."

Will paused once again, aware that he had bombarded these people with information. Many of his team were 9-5 programmers and here he was standing before them with a vision to change the world and a request to support that vision. Even he knew it was a big ask and that there would undoubtedly be questions, doubts, sceptics. The truth was that although he had a plan, it was a prototype they were looking to launch so there were so many unknown factors and questions he couldn't answer. He read the room and the quizzical faces and he tentatively continued.

"I appreciate I have done a lot of the talking," a beaming smile came from his lips, one of his most charming.

"I would be happy to take any questions you may have."

Arms flew up in front of Lottie's view. The team at the office had never been backwards about coming forward, they hired extroverts, they hired opinions, they hired thought leaders. She too, could think of several questions, but not only was she too shy to ask them but she assumed someone else would ask them first.

"What would be required from the person who volunteered to be the prototype?" asked a young developer at the front.

"Well, a lot of hard work," replied Will. "The whole objective of the prototype is so the person can see what they could become, and then set about becoming it themselves. So they will be set challenges to become their best selves, and we will be closely monitoring those challenges. When they leave the filter and go back to their real worlds, we want them to put what they have learnt into practice and make positive changes for real. So it's going to take a lot of hard work and dedication."

"So when will the person leave the filter? What happens to the person in the real world when they are inside this filter?" asked another.

"Yes, that's right, for the sake of the prototype to properly be tested they will remain in the filter until they become their best selves or until perfection has been reached. In the real world whilst all this is going on the person will be in our filter proofing facility here in the office which will be ready soon, so we can keep an eye on them.

The room fell silent. Will looked to his silent allies by his side who hadn't seemed to add much value to proceedings. There was a sense of disbelief mixed with incredulity. To Lottie, this all just sounded a little bit too 'out-there'. How on earth was he going to pull this off?

Several more questions were fired around, slowly and steadily, and Lottie watched Will handle each one like a pro. His body language was open, his energy was trustworthy but despite his best efforts, judging from their expressions, they didn't all seem totally wowed by the idea. Many were looking down avoiding eye contact with one another. Perhaps they were all still taking in the news, she thought to herself. It was times like these when she wished she was privy to office gossip. How she would have loved to have discussed this with everyone to find out what they thought, but being Will's EA she was always kept slightly out of the loop.

"Well, if no further questions," Will continued trying to elevate the energy levels, "I would like to put one to you. Would anybody in this room like to be considered for the prototype?"

WILL SAMPSON FELT A JOLT OF ADRENALINE SHOOT THROUGH HIS veins like a current as he put the request out to the crowded room. Faces that he had known for many years, expectant faces, faces who depended on him, faces who fed their families as a result of his existence. He knew this was going to take some of them by surprise but he hoped deeply that they would follow him as they had always done. Even he knew this was a big ask. At times he didn't even know why they had followed him this far, he doubted himself constantly, and now he was asking them to follow him into a foreign land with something that must have sounded incredulous. He was putting their faith in him to the test, and for the first time in years, Will wasn't sure what the outcome would be.

Not that he wasn't used to feeling tested. Growing up just outside Bath to the son of Sir Maxwell Sampson he had a lot of work to do to climb out from his father's overbearing and impossibly high achieving shadow. Known for most of his life as 'Maxwell's son' he found success in his own right ever elusive. Most of the time people assumed he would have had a foot in the door because of who his father was, or had sizeable family money investment. People didn't take him seriously for most of his twenties, and looking back now at the age of thirty-six he could see why. He played up to being the son of a 'somebody' to make him feel like less of a 'nobody'. The only real job he ever had during his twenties was being a co-founder of KRYO, one of Mayfair's most exclusive nightclubs, which he did with a couple of his friends who were nightclub promoters who were keen to leverage his surname. They didn't ask him for financial investment, only to assist with the promotion and PR, which he was happy to do. Minimal risk and he would look like the big shot. Win-win.

It gave him a sense of importance, a feeling of power and status that he felt was lacking and he played the role of playboy really rather convincingly. This was of course aided by his intolerable good looks and natural charm. He had piercing blue eyes that conveyed trust and honesty that women would find irresistible. He was tall and knew how to dress opting for classically elegant shirts and belts. He knew then as he knew now how to work a crowd, and how to make people love him and believe him, especially women who swarmed around him like bees hoping it would be them who the eligible bachelor would pick to settle down with.

However, as he went through his twenties living the fast life, he found he increasingly started to dislike himself. His reputation as a playboy with the notorious string of beautiful women on his arm, most of whom were models — hence his nickname to the press and society magazines as the 'modeliser' — wasn't helping his cause. Fast living was paying a price on him, and he developed a penchant for the white powder, often disappearing into bathrooms alone or with others to get his fix. As much as he hoped it might, it didn't go undetected by his family. His mother Penny was everything but the soft and maternal mother hen, ruthlessly meticulous herself with a keen eye for detail she knew Will had moments of being loud and chatty, and she knew why. She was a part of the swinging sixties after all.

Nothing was lost on her much to Will's annoyance, and she had an incredible ability to judge character and decipher who the good and bad guys were around her brood. It was what kept the family so powerful for all these years she was convinced of it. As her only son, she adored Will and although not necessarily affectionate and warm, she brought him up with strength and dignity. She tried to show him a moral compass and good education. She encouraged him to read and expand his mind, which he used to do avidly, and now he was changing, morphing into someone else and she couldn't bear it. She couldn't stand the fact he was losing his integrity, and, as a knock-on effect, hers and the family's she had spent her whole life trying to protect. As a doer and a problem solver, Penny was keen to eradicate the negative influences in his life with swift efficiency.

Will was 28 when his mother finally made an intervention and sent him to rehab. The weekend prior was Maxwell's proudest moment, he was being knighted by the Queen for his services to the country as a business tycoon and entrepreneur. He was to become 'Sir Maxwell Sampson' and Penny could not have been more humbled. His renewable energy technologies were far-reaching and had enabled the UK to lead as an example for wind and solar powers all over the world. He was also the patron of many charities giving solar panels to mud huts in Africa so they could have electricity in their homes. He was a remarkable mind, a remarkable man and although he hadn't always been a remarkable husband Penny was proud of him. Nothing was going to ruin their celebratory party that evening. All of her three children were lined up to say a few words and it would be the proudest moment in all of their lives.

That was the plan. However, when Will turned up to the party, rubbing shoulders with royalty, and politicians from all over the world, pissed and high as a kite Penny felt her heart sink. Will was smart, he was handsome but he had lost himself. Where was her beautiful boy? What was he doing to himself? She concluded there, thinking on her feet, that she had two choices to make, either she let him do his speech and deal with the consequences later, whatever they may be. Will did have a habit of just switching on the charm when needed. Or, she stop the bleeding before he made a fool of himself and the entire family in front of everyone. The papers would pick up on it and he would be the talk of the town for all the wrong reasons, totally eclipsing Maxwell's glory. Looking keenly out to the room like a lioness determining the level of danger for her cubs she assessed the room and decided upon the latter strategy, swiftly pulling Will to one side, smelling the alcohol on his breath as he swayed with her out of sight. Up the stairs they went, his body easily manoeuvrable, his movements were slow and his speech slurred. She positioned him in their guest annexe on the top floor, gave him several bottles of mineral water, propped his head comfortably onto the fluffy pillows and locked the door. Her two girls would give the speeches instead and she would find a plausible explanation for Will's inability to be there. Terrible fever, she thought, sick as a puppy. That'll do.

When Will woke up the next morning all bleary-eyed he knew he had royally messed up. He could taste the drugs in his saliva and he could feel the shame in his sinking heart. The weekend after that, his parents wasted no time in escorting him to The Priory, both of whom knew that something drastic needed to be done to turn their son's life around.

Maxwell saw a lot of himself in his son. Like him, Will was bright, but never the brightest in the room, but what he didn't necessarily have in academia he had in creativity and charisma. Both father and son had a knack for surrounding themselves with the best. They were what you might call unassuming leaders, never necessarily wanting to lead but something about them led people to defer to them. Both could think like chess players, strategically able to jump steps ahead in their thought processes and both absorbed new information like sponges. Maxwell just wished his son could find his way. He had offered Will money to start his own venture, but Will had refused. He was too proud. He didn't have a big plan, he didn't have direction and his cocaine addiction was killing his future.

By the time he was on his way to the priory Will conceded it was time. He didn't fight it, he was exhausted, he was depressed and he felt empty, lost and shamefully shallow. His friends seemingly only cared when he got the best tables at the nightclubs, and he was almost positive nobody would notice he was gone until they needed him for something. He too knew he needed to change and was grateful, in part, for the fact that his family cared enough to notice his downward trajectory. Besides, his lifestyle was expensive, the cocaine was costly and although the family had money, Will's parents had cut him off until he got his act together, which he knew deep down was the right decision on their part.

Not that it was easy in The Priory, Will had to deal with issues he had been brushing under the carpet and address needs he didn't even know he had. He had to come to terms with the cold, hard truth. That he had been living a lie all these years and that his life had been an illusion. He was drifting, lost at sea and he had no idea who he was. All the things that he had been surrounding himself with over the past few years were empty and meaningless because it was simply easier not to let himself care about anything too much, and that included himself. He made sound and solid friends during his journey in rehab, and after six months and a 12-step program Will emerged brighter and more positive. He spent a lot of his time reading again as he had always loved to do growing up and discovered new things about himself. He recognised he was fairly shy, despite the exterior bravado, and he understood he was impetuous and creative. What's more, he finally realised that he wasn't here on the Earth to live in someone else's shadow. *"What would you do if your father wasn't alive?"* asked one of the therapists one day, and this question rang through Will's mind constantly. At the time he was unable to answer, never having given it much thought and unable to formulate a valid response, but over the months he spent at The Priory he set himself a challenge to answer that question properly. Not just because he wanted to but because he felt deeply that he should know.

One of his friends at The Priory was another guy around his age called Simon. Simon had also been on the scene quite a bit and although his poison was the alcohol rather than drugs, it turned out they had a lot in common and quite a few mutual friends — however that wasn't what bonded them. It turned out to be a fairly unlikely friendship. Simon was what was known as a 'white-hat hacker', he was a technology whizz kid who infiltrated the 'dark web' to suss out who the bad guys were and stop them from stealing private information about people or companies. He knew his way into any system and seemed pretty clued up about the future. Although during their time at the priory screen time was kept to a minimum, Will and Simon would have lengthy conversations about technology and what the future looked like in terms of companies using peoples data, and what would become more automated due to advances in artificial intelligence. Facebook had recently exploded globally and many questions were being asked about what the implications of such a platform would be in the long-term in terms of advertising, data and privacy. Simon was convinced such companies would only increase in size and scale and eventually they would rely on advertising revenue targeted so acutely to behaviour that they would become a dangerous force in themselves for political reasons. Will didn't understand what he meant at the time, but he would listen intently to him speak with passion and conviction.

He had never really met anyone like Simon before, someone quite so ahead of the curve, and he found him truly fascinating, marvelling at the way he was self-taught to bypass pages that were complexly restricted, not taking no for an answer. Will admired his ability to break down these cyber walls and to spin his own web, surviving on his own. Will had never been restricted from anything in his life, and still felt very much like he had always played the part of the fly caught in the web, rather than the spider who spun it.

Will would read many of the books Simon recommended and enjoyed understanding the way the technological world was constructed. Like spirituality it almost gave him a sense of believing in a higher power, it gave him strength and focus. By the time Will had left The Priory he had read several books on 'The Automation of Technology' and 'What our Future Looks Like'. He was convinced he would find his calling in the digital space thereafter.

Six months later, he had a sound business plan and a vision to develop Augmented Minds, which would become one of the first movers in the augmented reality space. Its proposition; to develop augmented reality ad campaigns and experiences for companies wanting unique ways to sell their products. It was brilliant. He would need an office and some startup technology. He would need to hire in the talent, and from there it was all about getting the clients which he hoped he could do. He would never know if he didn't try and at that point in his life he had nothing to lose. Proud and ever reluctant to walk a step in his father's shadow, Will graciously refused his numerous offers of investment and sourced his own initial backing from the bank, leveraging his flat as collateral. He had to make this work, and having hit rock-bottom he was determined he was never going back to his old ways. His addiction was now ambition and he was on a path he was happy to tread, for as long as he could make it work.

CHAPTER
Six

LOTTIE SAT THERE NEXT TO CHARLOTTE, IN THE ROOM that was usually so familiar to her for so long listening to accolade after accolade being listed off like a shopping list. How had she been able to achieve quite so much in six years? She thought back to what she had done in the past six years, where she had been in her life six years ago and felt ashamed to admit to herself that not much had changed. She still wasn't married, or in anything resembling a serious relationship. Sure, she had a few guys buzzing around her but most of them were deadbeats she didn't want to progress things with. She always fell in love with the ones who buggered off after a few months, and of course, then there was Will. Nobody could ever quite compare to Will. She had no real achievements, she didn't own her own property and had never written anything close to her own book, even though she was always full of ideas. Everything she had ever started had never been finished including getting into a good workout routine. She thought for a moment and wondered why this was?

Was it fear of failure? Was it because she was too shy to ask for much out of life? Was it because she didn't feel she deserved better?

Mr Patel continued speaking and projected yet another slide listing her achievements.

"So after starting to write just one book Charlotte got immediate interest from several book publishers. Her first novel became an international bestseller and positioned her as the new Queen of Chick-Lit. It sold more than any other book worldwide and did particularly well in the US so she quickly got snapped up for a publishing deal to write four more books. Two years ago the series of books was developed into a TV series that Netflix commissioned and her brand has gone from strength to strength. She is the JK Rowling of her genre and with another trilogy already in development, it's amazingly clear that her career has, and continues, to snowball.

Charlotte this year also launched her own app called 'Strength to Success' which gives entrepreneurs practical tools to 'achieve more through believing more'. She is a motivational speaker and has done worldwide tours on how to adopt a growth mindset, attracting business leaders from all over the world. She is a living example of how to turn your life around. She is regularly listed on Forbes. She is on the board of BumbleBee and most recently has been named co-editor of The Huffington Post. All of this has happened within six years. I think we can all admit it's been quite a journey and it's by no means over."

Lottie looked at Charlotte who was smiling modestly yet confidently. She was seated in front of her like she were the expert on Mastermind, about to unveil her special knowledge to the audience. Lottie felt shame, she felt embarrassed, but strangely at that moment, she felt a great amount of pride. This was what she was truly capable of. This was what was inside her to do. She was born with talents and abilities that the whole world could see. She was special, and for the first time in her life, she could do something about it.

CHAPTER
Seven

LOTTIE FELTS THE THUDS OF FOOTSTEPS LEAVE THE MEETING ROOM, whispering, muttering, talking to each other. She would have loved to have been involved in those conversations to gauge what people made of the news. It was pretty big news. She wasn't entirely sure what she made of it herself but she couldn't help but admire Will for just going for it. He had a vision, and if he could pull this off, it did sound pretty incredible, even she could see that. She went about picking up coffee cups and papers left on the large boardroom table and smiled at Will who was still standing near the projector finishing a conversation with his fellow musketeers.

"So…," he buoyed towards her, "how did I do?"

"Well, you kept that quiet," said Lottie teasingly. "I can't quite believe you've been working on all this and didn't think to mention it to me. It all totally makes sense now, all the secret meetings and endless models. I knew you had to be up to something."

"I know Lottie, I'm so sorry." Will tapped Lottie affection-ately on the shoulder. "I was truly sworn to secrecy until today. I hope you realise all the work you've been doing has not gone unnoticed. It's because of you and your endless models that we got the investment we did. I couldn't ask the analysts here just yet due to the confidentiality issue but you have basically been doing the work of an entire team of very bright people."

Lottie blushed.

Is that so? Shame you've never offered me a pay-rise or a promotion.

"Oh god it's fine, I'm so glad I could be of help to you. It sounds pretty exciting! Do you need help going through the volunteers for the prototype?"

"Yes, please," said Will. "I have asked them all to submit their entries to you. I would like you to go through them and look out for anyone who gives a good reason as to why they should be considered. It would be an exciting opportunity for the right person so let me know who shines out to you. I trust you Lottie."

Will smiled at Lottie, his blue eyes making her heart beat a little faster.

He trusts me...

"Sure no problem," replied Lottie with a compliant smile, hoping her makeup hadn't melted off her face already and she didn't look shiny from blushing so much. "Will do."

Lottie returned to her flat that evening and felt a huge wave of exhaustion. She closed the door behind her and walked to her small kitchen ready to pour herself a drink and have a cigarette. She only smoked when she was stressed but the past few weeks had been ridiculous. She had been working pretty much around the clock for Will and it was model after model, with each new piece of information she supplied he needed something else. She looked at her iPhone for the time. 7.05 pm and she was home already. That made a change. Lately, she hadn't made it home before 9 pm and if she had she would often continue working in her pyjamas. Will would usually call her with just one more request, and she would always be available to him, no matter the time.

Honestly, how was she expected to have a boyfriend at this rate? Not that there was anyone she fancied. The men at her office were just awful, apart from Will of course. Not that anything was likely to happen in that department, after ten years of working together he had never made a move. She often wondered if it might spark something in him if she started dating someone else from work, if he would get jealous in any way, and then remembered his recent girlfriends had all been basically supermodels and told herself to dream on. *Yeah right, like he would go for you anyway.* Still, she often dreamt up ways of making him sit up and notice her and imagined some super hot man gallantly arriving at her office reception to pick her up for lunch dates and the whole office turning their heads to look at him and then gossip about it. That would have been fun, but the chances of her meeting any swoony men who fitted such description were few and far between when she hadn't been out for weeks on end, and when weekends came she felt more like curling up with a Netflix and a pizza than a hot man.

She heard the white wine glug into her glass as she poured it fairly full. She was tired. Not just physically but mentally. She had been doing the same job for ten years and although she was starting to feel more challenged now that she was being given meatier pieces of work, she wasn't feeling rewarded for her efforts — and the feeling of constantly 'giving' was leaving her drained. Why hadn't Will offered her more money over the years? Didn't he think she had earned it? Also, the bloody cheek that she had done the work of an entire team. Didn't he think that might piss her off?

She sat and thought about the meeting; the electrifying news, so unexpected, so ...odd. She had been instrumental in getting the investment apparently yet was none the wiser as to what had been planned all the while. There were times when she had tried to guess what was going on but honestly, even Lottie who was a pretty sharp cookie could not have imagined this. I don't think anyone could have imagined quite this. Truthfully though, after all the years they had been working together Will really could have told her what he was up to. She wouldn't have said anything, it could have been a good trust exercise for her to prove herself as a reliable confidante. To find out like the others in the meeting did feel a little dismissive considering the amount she had contributed.

If she hadn't been quite so in love with him, she probably would have asked him for a promotion or a pay rise ages ago, but she couldn't bring herself to do it. She had tried. She had even prepared the night before what she would say when she sat him down to ask — but when the moments came, he looked at her all gorgeous and open buttoned-shirt, and she found herself simply agreeing to do more work for him. She convinced herself that after each workload she would say something as, by then surely she would have earned it, deep down secretly hoping that he would offer it to her based on merit alone.

It was a cruel turn of events really, and for the first time, she looked at the situation objectively. He had been working on all of this without telling her, and actually had been using her to make himself look good. In fact, as she thought back over the years he had done that quite a bit but she had enabled it by continuing to let him get away with it. As she sipped on her wine she was glad she had left work a little early that day. She felt she had done enough. She moved outside to sit on her small balcony overlooking the sights around her enjoying her glass of wine and moment of reflection; there was a large cement wall with graffiti all over it and a supermarket car park beyond that. Hardly inspiring stuff. Despite her feelings of frustration with Will she couldn't help but think of what he had said that day; about living your best life.

Who could she become if she was her best self? She took a moment to imagine it as she saw someone walk past the large cement wall with their dog, who cocked their leg to pee by a weed in the ground. She was thirty-two, she was still renting a flat small flat on her own, she had no boyfriend, no kids and no real prospects. Her boss was taking advantage of her and she was letting him because she was in love with him and all she really wanted was to impress him. She probably wasn't making any effort to meet anyone else either as she just compared everyone to Will, and nobody could even come close to how she felt about him. With him, it was still butterflies and tummy dances. It was still, after ten years, about wanting to give him the best impression of her. She still wanted him to notice her, yet with each passing year felt more and more invisible.

She sighed and raised her eyebrows to the sky. A raincloud was looming overhead and birds were starting to flee from their nests in anticipation. All the while she had been spending time impressing others, she had failed to make any sort of positive impression on herself. She knew she was clever enough, she could do certain things if she set her mind to them. She had good grades at school and she was athletic. So what was going on? Why was she so hopelessly underachieving?

Depressed at the thought she went back inside to pour herself another glass of wine and upon passing her little living room area she caught a glance of her reflection in the mirror above the fireplace. She stopped to look at herself, squinting her eyes as though she were a bug under a microscope, inspecting her angles, her features. Granted she was tired at the moment but her eye makeup was halfway down her face and her skin seemed dry and dull. She hadn't had her hair cut for months and it was so in need of a trim she had become used to tying it up more often than not in a scruffy bun, hoping the fact that she put makeup on every morning would make her look presentable. Her complexion was so pallid as a result of being office-bound that she was almost transparent and her eyes were lacklustre, nothing resembling the emerald green eyes she used to be complimented on. She used to be considered pretty, and now she just felt bland — like vanilla ice cream. Nothing interesting about vanilla ice cream she thought as she looked once again at her face. Nobody glanced her way in the street anymore, she had begun lowering her standards when it came to men as she was sure it was all she could get. She looked at her clothes. Her flat black ballerina pumps shoes were worn at the heels and scuffed at the sides, her burgundy jumper was shapeless and old and she was pretty sure her tummy was growing each week due to lack of exercise.

Unsure of what to do with herself with an evening at home without work she turned on the TV to distract herself from her feelings of inadequacy; news, sitcoms, documentaries. Nothing interested her and she really couldn't concentrate. She felt restless with nervous energy like a volcano with something bubbling up inside her.

Habit and a keen need for distraction led her to open up her laptop and just check her emails whilst just putting on a rerun of 'Friends' for background noise. She knew she probably shouldn't keep working, but she couldn't help it, and besides, she was keen to see who, out of all of the people in the office, had readily put themselves forward as a volunteer for this prototype.

She pressed refresh on her inbox and one after the other, email after email popped in with the various subject lines; 'Prototype' or 'Hello Will' or 'why you should pick me'. She clicked on one from Rowena Clarke, a marketing exec who she had said hello to a couple of times by the coffee machine.

"Hi Will

I am so impressed by you and your vision. My name is Rowena, I'm a marketing exec in your team. I'm fairly new to the company, I joined three months ago but I have such strong ambition that I know I can fulfil! I would love to be given the opportunity to see my best self as I'm only 25 so I have my whole future ahead of me to make it happen.

I attach my CV for your reference, please do let me know if you have any questions.

Rowena, Marketing Exec

Then another...

Wow, Will. What a meeting and what an opportunity. I've always been fascinated by exploring my full potential, regularly setting myself challenges. This year I did a triathlon raising money for disadvantaged children. I think my potential could be amazing as I would do so much more charity work and help people who are truly in need. I think that's as good a reason as any to pick me. I have no dependents and would really make the most of this opportunity.

Adrian Berry, Systems Technician

She kept reading...

Hi Will and team.

It was lovely to meet your new co-founders and hear about the merger and the plans for the new filter. I am fairly shy usually so this is a little out of my comfort zone, but I would love to be considered for the prototype as I've never really had an opportunity like this before. I do feel I could shine if given half the chance. I always had dreams of being in politics and changing the country for the better so this is right up my street.

Madeleine Johnston, Data Programmer

The emails just went on and on, from the most junior to some heavy hitters on the management team. Lottie started thinking about creating a qualifying questionnaire that she would create to send out to all applicants. That can wait, she thought and then she shut down her laptop and went to run herself a bath really consciously trying to switch off for a few hours.

However, as she submerged herself beneath the warm soapy suds she couldn't stop her mind from circling. Why did these people who applied feel they deserved this? These people wanted a unique opportunity, they wanted to see themselves as better than they currently did, they wanted to feel empowered, motivated and driven, they wanted more from their lives.

Well, so did she.

They wanted to do good, they wanted to be better, they

wanted to feel different, they wanted to see what they could become, they wanted to feel special...

Well, so did she.

They thought they had potential that was untapped. They felt they had more to offer, they felt invisible...

Yup.

It occurred to her as she lay in her bath running her feet under the dripping tap and feeling the water spill down her leg that their reasons were just as valid as hers. She had just as much to get out of this as they did. Why didn't she put herself forward? She would actually rather like to see the best version of herself. She knew she had potential as her brain worked pretty well most of the time, and how amazing would it be to see Will's face when she was looking her best? Surely it would hit him between the eyes then and they could finally become the team that she always knew they could be. Besides, it's not like she would be giving up much in her current life, nobody would probably even miss her when she was in the filter proofing facility. She had no kids, no boyfriend, family in Dorset who she didn't see all that often, no siblings. It was perfect.

Lottie felt that something needed to change as her strategy so far (if she could even go so far as to call it that) wasn't working. It was bold and it felt wholly outside of her comfort zone but she was ready to start living life differently, at a different tempo. She would go in tomorrow morning and sit Will down and tell him she had gone through all the emails, and that she found their perfect prototype — herself.

CHAPTER
Eight

LOTTIE FOLLOWED CHARLOTTE INTO A LARGE BLACK four-by-four that was readily parked outside the office awaiting Charlotte and Lottie's descent. A suited-up driver greeted them both with a smile as he hurried around from the driver's seat to open their car doors. He clearly needed no directions or instructions as to where they were headed and Charlotte gave him a knowing nod to say thank you as he closed the door and they set off on their way through the busy London streets.

"Lottie I know this is so much to take in," started Charlotte gently leaning towards her with a warm smile as they settled into the plush leather seats. "Don't worry, we will break this all down when we get home into manageable chunks. I will introduce you to my team who will be on hand to you over the next few weeks to show you the ropes with regards to getting to grips with my schedule. I will be here for you every step of the way".

"Thanks," replied Lottie quietly.

She was looking at the car's interior with a heightened awareness. Everything was being observed in detail. The armrest with drinks holders and USB points in them, the elegantly placed bottles of water in the seat pockets, the hushed classical music. It reminded Lottie at that moment, that it was like she had landed in a foreign country and was looking for clues from passing strangers as to the way people behaved in that foreign land. What did they eat here, what language did they speak? What could she glean from this person who sat beside her, and the life she was living that would piece together what she needed to do? She was acutely aware too, amidst all of these thoughts, that she needed to fill the silence and try to behave somewhat 'normally'.

"So…" Lottie started carefully "that was your house I woke up in this morning? Wow…"

As soon as Lottie made the obvious statement she regretted it and winced. She wasn't sure how to act around Charlotte. Being aware she was beneath her did nothing for her confidence.

"Yes, it was. We're going to head back there now and I'll show you around properly and get you settled in. It's going to be such a fun ride we have together. It's so lovely meeting you Lottie as it reminds me just how far I've come. I hadn't really appreciated it properly until I met you this morning."

Lottie stared blankly at Charlotte.

Thanks, and just when I thought the charm offensive would never end.

Lottie watched as Charlotte held up her phone to start posting a story to Instagram. Before she started recording, however, she spent a good twenty seconds, contorting her body into what seemed like a rather uncomfortable position, seemingly to get the best light and to show her best side.

"Where's the good lighting... Ah, there it is...

Hi guys! So, I'm here with the lovely Lottie. We're on our way home after the big reveal. Did anyone see the live on Insta? I can't wait to see your thoughts! Look at her! She's going to be so amazing in no time at all. Say hi Lottie!"

Lottie waved awkwardly, frowning at the camera, and noticing she didn't benefit from any gracious lighting. Her hair looked horrendous and she had black mascara coming down under her eyes. She wiped beneath her eye with her finger self-consciously.

"When we get home I'm going to show Lottie around. I'll keep you posted with the day of course. Don't forget to send me any questions you have for Lottie!"

Charlotte looked at Lottie as she put the phone in her large handbag that was placed beside her feet.

"It's so important to keep up your social media presence. I try to check in as much as I can."

As the car pulled up outside Egerton Crescent Lottie saw the familiar house from that morning. It looked less sinister now that she could give it some context and although she wished someone could have prepared her for what she was about to walk into that morning, she was wearily glad it was all over now and the big secret had been revealed. She had faced the terrifying truth and the plaster had been ripped off, so she had seen what she needed to see. All that was left now was to work out what needed to be done.

The wild ivy climbing up to the heights of the roof were beautifully contrasted against the whitewashed house. The elegantly placed paving stones led their way from the car to the front door next to perfectly manicured lawns. There was a warmth to the house as the sun reflected brightly against the windows. This was where she could be living. This was the beginning of her future life and with nervous pride, she understood that this is what she was capable of. Why had she never imagined it being this good?

"Welcome home!" Charlotte exclaimed with a smile as she pushed the front door open and let Lottie walk in first.

"Now, let me show you around properly. You can take your shoes off and leave them in the cloakroom if you don't mind."

Lottie looked up and saw a door beside the front door she hadn't noticed that morning. As she walked in, she was astounded to see an entire room full of shoes and jackets, all beautifully displayed in chic, back-lit cabinets. There were umbrellas pointed downwards in a handsome vase intricately painted with what seemed to be Chinese art, and flowers sitting beside some perfume on a coffee table in the middle.

She obeyed and politely placed her shoes as instructed, continuing to follow Charlotte into the main living area she had seen that morning. She could take it all in now in more detail. There were the three cream coloured sofas she remembered, beautifully appointed with luxurious looking pillows. There was a large glass square-shaped coffee table adorned with various oversized coffee table books. Elegant candles were dotted around the room and there was a smell of fresh linen mixed with rose blossom. Behind the sofas and along the long walls was bookshelf after bookshelf overflowing with books.

"This is the living area where you can relax and

unwind after a long day. You'll see there is no TV though, I just don't have time for it and I do love to read. There is a small TV in the kitchen mind you, but to be honest the only thing that's ever on there is the news. I work from home on Tuesdays and Thursdays so I will be in the office area you see here."

She walked further down the long room to an office desk shaped like an aeroplane wing.

"I always liked this desk," she said, "it reminds me to aim for the sky."

"I think I've read some of these. Have you read them all?" Asked Lottie picking up a book from a nearby bookshelf called *Feel the fear and do it anyway*.

"Oh, yes. A few times. That's just a small selection of my favourites. The majority are on my Kindle and Audible accounts. I like to read several new books each week. You'll most certainly need to do the same."

"I love reading too. It's just so hard to find the time when you're busy isn't it?"

Charlotte stared at her with a patronising head tilt as though she had just seen a puppy dressed as a princess.

"Oh Lottie, I don't find the time. I make time. There's a huge difference. We'll go through all of this."

Feeling instantly put in her place Lottie felt thereby compelled to keep quiet, so followed Charlotte into the kitchen where she could see a man in an apron chopping vegetables.

"Hi Nico!" exclaimed Charlotte excitedly as she rushed up to him to hug him warmly on the shoulders. "Nico, this is Lottie who I told you would be joining us for a little while".

Nico put down his large kitchen knife and wiped his

hands on his apron before moving towards Lottie with a warm smile.

"Wow, that iz unbelievable," he said with a strong Italian accent and inspecting Lottie quizzically. "I canna believe it, iz amazing."

Turning back to Lottie, and sensing her discomfort at being stared at Charlotte continued.

"So here we have Nico's turf - the kitchen! Nico is my personal chef and is a total genius. He and Gunter are almost entirely responsible for the body I have today. I must admit I stopped making my own meals a few years ago as it just became a priority for me to have my diet taken care of for me so I can focus on other things. Nico, Lottie, Lottie Nico."

"It's a real piacere Lottie. So nice to ameet you," said Nico. "Mamma Mia I canna wait to get started with you. We'll be sitting down later to develop your food plan. You're going to love it, "he said blowing an Italian kiss her way by kissing his clenched hands.

Lottie warmed to his earnest character immediately.

"Nice to meet you too Nico' she smiled back. 'Wow, so you have *all* your meals cooked for you?"

"Yup, breakfast, lunch and dinner. Nico is truly the best in the business and I'm very lucky to have him work for me exclusively," continued Charlotte "but you must learn the basics of how to cook for yourself so I would like you to use all he can teach you and then you will need to cook your own meals for a while until you have reached what we call conscious eating. When you get there you won't look back as everything will start to feel so much easier, especially when your habits become ingrained. The body and mind move at their peak to optimal food, it's so important and you'll stop getting those cravings for sugar I know you struggle with."

Lottie thought of how nice a cup of tea and a biscuit would be right now and had secretly hoped that someone would offer her one.

"Great," said Lottie, trying to hide her total shock that Charlotte had her own personal chef as if that was normal given the numerous anomalies of that morning. In no part of her existence had she ever contemplated or even dreamt of having a personal chef on hand to design her dream body, but in this unfamiliar house, with these unfamiliar people, Lottie was trying to convey a sense of normality, for her own sake. In some way it allowed her to justify all of this madness to herself.

She thought of what her mum would have thought of all this. Ever keen to save and not splurge she could almost hear her voice in her head. *'She has what? What a load of nonsense! I mean honestly, can't she make her own dinner?'*

"So what's on the menu for Charlotte today, Nico?" Lottie asked inquisitively as she saw Charlotte get out her phone again and start filming what Nico was cooking whilst speaking to her followers on social media enthusiastically.

"Well, for her lunch atoday we have a nice alight Kimchi grain bowl, it's made with black rice, pearl barley, lots of vegetables, kimchi, soya beans, garlic and chilli. It's buonissimo. Today I've made enough for you so you can try it and tomorrow we'll starta with your cooking classes. Iz good for digestion and why she have asuch beautiful skin." Nico was grinning widely looking at Charlotte proudly.

"Yes, I have a plant-based, sugar-free, organic diet. It works for our body type and really helps reduce body fat and inflammation if you do it properly. Oh and it's super important if you want to manage your hormones," interjected Charlotte before repeating it back to her phone so they heard.

"I see," replied Lottie raising her eyebrows. She didn't really know what that meant and just had visuals in her mind of sitting alone eating big green leaves and coconut water whilst all of her friends tucked into pepperoni pizzas.

"Do you ever cheat?" She was half trying to keep the atmosphere light, half genuinely keen to know.

"Not anymore to be honest as it always just makes me feel so sluggish if I do. I really crave eating this way and have no desire for junk. Anyway, let's go upstairs and I'll show you to your new bedroom. I have taken the liberty of getting some clothes ready for you in the dressing room that a stylist has picked out for your body type. I think you're going to love them."

Lottie gave Nico a friendly wave goodbye and walked up the familiar glass stairs from that morning with mirrors following her every move and saw herself reflected next to Charlotte. She looked considerably bigger than her and shorter. She never felt 'fat' so to speak but walking up the stairs next to the best version of herself, she really did realise right there and then how much weight she could do with losing. She walked past the motivational quotes in frames she had seen that morning and into a different room to the one she had woken up in. It too looked out onto the garden with the eery fountain but it was equipped with a desk, a whiteboard, exercise equipment, a mat, a dressing area at the end and a beautifully appointed en-suite.

"So, here is where you will be staying for the next few

weeks. You can make the most of the gym equipment here but also note there is a full gym in the basement. I'll show you that later. I just made a habit of doing workouts and meditation from my room every morning and evening too. In the wardrobe, you'll find a whole load of clothes. Bear in mind I have a combination of sizes to cater for your shrinking physique! You're starting off as a size 12 but when you get to my size you should be a 6/8. I believe it's really motivating to see what you could be wearing in a few short months time so I have left the smaller ones here for you. Come and take a little look at my wardrobe to see what you should be aiming for."

Charlotte led the way into what she assumed was her master bedroom, clutching again at her phone the whole time which seemed to be constantly recording her every move, and upon entering Lottie heard herself gasp. A luxuriously appointed and enormous bedroom greeted her adjoined by an ensuite and a sumptuously opulent walk-in wardrobe if you could even call it that. Such a term didn't seem apt for what this was. As Charlotte glided through the main bedroom as though it were no big deal chatting away to her followers on Instagram, she arrived at the wardrobe. It was a room bigger than Lottie's entire flat with a central island topped with vases of white roses and a suede armchair beside it. Marble floors reflected the light shining off the mirrored cream cabinets that seemed full to the brim with clothes, meticulously and impeccably hung up. An entire cabinet was full of shoes, the back of which were mostly red and there was another wardrobe unit entirely for handbags, which were backlit with soft amber lighting. There was a dressing table with mirrors and a plush white rug beneath it. Lottie couldn't help but notice there were no makeup stains on the rug and wondered how this was possible. Everything was immaculate, there were diffusers dotted around the room giving a breezy fresh scent.

"Perhaps my favourite room of the house,' sighed Charlotte as she swung herself dramatically over the suede armchair that was placed under the window. "Isn't it just heavenly? I worked hard for all of these items and do believe that they are all investments. You can never skimp on making investments in yourself if those investments help you do your job, and I believe every time I put on a beautiful outfit, I feel so empowered like I could rule the world, you know?"

Lottie looked at Charlotte, who was clearly waiting for her to agree.

"Wow, Charlotte this is amazing! I mean, I don't think I've ever spent more than £60 on a pair of shoes in my life, this entire collection is insane!"

"Thank you Lottie. Well, if you work hard you can have this too. This is what you're capable of having Lottie. It's already in you, you just have to find the strength to find it."

Charlotte guided Lottie (and her Instagram followers), proudly through the rest of the house on the 'grand tour' as she called it, and she really didn't leave anything out. She continued walking and talking, guiding and blinding. She showed her every bathroom, explaining where she sourced the stone for the floors and walls, how the kitchen surfaces were imported from tombstones in northern France so they didn't have to cut the slabs, and the basement gym, explaining how she started out doing loads of cardio and now is more focused on weight-bearing exercises. She even showed her the kitchen along with every gadget and the enormous walk-in freezer where she was able to keep everything she needed fresh at all times — all organic of course.

Lottie watched her lips move as she spoke about the 'music room' and let her ears listen as moved her hands across the keys of a grand piano, adorned with photos of herself and trophies she had won. She walked from bedroom to marble bathroom with underfloor heating, to library. She even had a massage room in the garden. Staff were busying around as they walked. In addition to Nico the chef she had also briefly said hello to Gunter her personal trainer and Tessa the housekeeper.

Lottie found herself feeling rather giddy with delirium. It was strange enough to be confronted with this new 'authentic reality' or whatever they were calling it, but her best self was just so far from where Lottie was now it all seemed unachievable, and quite frankly it felt bizarre. If she was being honest, part of her felt a bit confused. She had never really considered herself quite so ambitious, she'd never really been into designer clothes and organic kimchi and was too shy to have a personal trainer just for her. She started to wonder if money and success fundamentally changed people. Perhaps she too would be different if she had made it. Perhaps she too would start wanting shoes with only red soles and expensive designer handbags that she would display on a backlit cabinet in an enormous dressing room. Perhaps she would become more high-maintenance and demanding, and in time would learn to have more exacting standards?

However, she couldn't help but feel like she would just never really be that person. She was a saver, not a splurger; probably thanks to her ever-frugal mother who would repeatedly chastise her for spending too much on just about anything. She often felt guilty for spending real money on herself. Not that she had any money to spend anyway, but did Charlotte really need a personal chef with all the trimmings? Wasn't it all a tad excessive? Was it really in her character?

She also couldn't help but be a little surprised not to see any clues of a boyfriend or children's bedrooms. In theory, Charlotte was her in six years which would have made her 38, so she wondered if a family was going to be on the cards for her. She had never desperately wanted children but, like many women, she would have been delighted if she had met someone special enough for it to happen. However, Lottie noticed that Charlotte hadn't mentioned anything about anyone else, so she did wonder if all of this success had perhaps come at a price.

"So, I hope you settle in well. Feel free to make yourself at home. I have left towels on your bed although the house is cleaned by Tessa every day you will need to learn how to become more organised. Clothes are an investment and if you treat them with respect so will other people. So I don't want to see anything on the floor." Charlotte tutted as she finished this sentence before swinging on her heel with a grin.

It was clear that Charlotte was giddy with excitement about the prospect of a protégée, Lottie could sense it. It was as though she had been looking for someone to show this off to, as though not many people, aside from her social media following, had seen this immaculate house despite it being staged perfectly for guests. It had five bedrooms and aside from Charlotte's room, all the others lay seemingly dormant.

"But anyway, today is all about making you feel comfortable, I can imagine this is a lot to process and you must be exhausted. Tomorrow morning we will start the

'Induction'. This is where you and I will work together to devise your plan for the next few months. I'll guide you through everything with regards to what we are going to do, and how we're going to do it."

Lottie felt her shoulders drop down with a sense of relief. She had not expected a day like today and nothing would be expected of her right now, not right away, and oddly she was thankful for that. She didn't need any further motivation to change, she had that walking around in front of her, but she did need to understand how she was going to do it.

Tomorrow is another day, she thought to herself as she let her body and mind ease into the grand house which was to become her home for the time being.

It might have been too much to process, but this was her new reality. Her pain and shock from that morning were turning into fired-up motivation and although it was terrifying and bizarre, she was most certainly inspired by her own potential. For the first time in her life, she was going to change and she was being given the gift of a lifetime — to learn exactly how to.

CHAPTER
Nine

THAT MORNING LOTTIE FELT MORE SHATTERED THAN SHE WAS expecting to feel after leaving work early and having a relaxing night. She hadn't slept well as she kept replaying in her mind the exact words she would use when she spoke to Will when she got to the office. Part of her imagined a scenario like the scene from Bridget Jones where she boldly wandered in and demanded a little more 'R-E-S-P-E-C-T'. She could hear Aretha Franklin singing along as a soundtrack as she told Will that she had done enough over the years to prove she was capable and deserving of this opportunity — more than anyone else here and he knew it. She was surprised he hadn't suggested it himself.

As much as that filled her with adrenaline each time she played it out in her mind, she knew when it came to that exact moment she would opt for a more diplomatic and professional approach. It would start something like this. Lottie would bring up his coffee as per usual, but instead of handing it to him and telling him what he had on his to-do list and answering any questions he had about his diary, she would start by asking for a word and shutting the door of his office behind her. She would then confidently and assertively stand in front of him giving her reasons for why she should indeed be the one selected for this unique opportunity.

She had thought it all through, and as she collected her regular orders from the Starbucks downstairs, one tall flat white for her, and one grande Americano for Will with one sachet of sugar she found it regrettable that she did not have an extra hand free to pull down the skirt that was riding up on her hip as she walked to the office. If she was going to have an attempt at doing something that could change her life, she decided to do a little power dressing that day. Instead of wearing her usual flat and serviceable ballet pumps and black trousers with the inter-changeable blouse, she opted for a slight heel, (even though one was a bit scuffed as it had recently fallen prey to a 'drain-grate'), and a black skirt with a fitted shirt that made her feel the need to hold in her tummy when she walked. She also wore her hair down so it sat comfortably upon her shoulders. She didn't want to overdo it, but more than anything she wanted to feel as though she might mean business for once. She wanted to be taken seriously, and as she walked out of her house headed for the tube for work, she felt as though she looked good.

Well, better than usual anyway.

Will was already there that morning when she arrived, sitting in his office.

Oh god, here we go. She swung her handbag onto her desk, carefully trying not to spill the coffees and took a moment to pull her skirt down a little and re-tuck in her shirt. She felt her palms hot and sweaty but wasn't sure whether that was from carrying the coffee or from nerves. She was glad he was already sitting down, that made things easier. She didn't like bothering him if he seemed in a rush. He seemed deep in concentration, his two eyes squinting intently at something he was reading. Seeing Lottie near his glass walls he darted his gaze towards her and waved her in with a smile.

"Morning Lottie. Oh, thank you so much, you are a superstar." He said as he placed his coffee cup on his desk and she stepped back to shut the door behind her. This was step one of her plan, so far so good. She was about to start speaking when he got there first.

"Come here. Look at this."

Lottie walked tentatively towards his screen and leant over. He was scrolling through emails at lightning speed. She got a waft of his aftershave and felt her heart race at their proximity. She hoped he might notice the extra effort she had made that morning.

"Can you believe the response we have had to this request for volunteers? I was copied in on quite a few of those emails last night. Wow, I wasn't sure what to expect but this is something else! I think I may have a couple of my favourites. Did you have a chance to see these? You probably know a lot of these people better than I do…"

Well, clearly I don't as nobody was kind enough to fill me in on what you were up to…

"Yes, you're right I do", she laughed coyly. She wasn't about to correct him if he thought of her as popular.

Will was beaming with excitement. His eyes were glistening like thawing icicles. This was going to be his time to shine. For the first time in his life, Will was on the brink of really making a name for himself, not as his father's son but for himself. His people had continued to follow him and he was overwhelmed with an impossibly huge sense of relief. Will leaned back in his chair and looked at Lottie. She bolted upright and although she was focused on his screen could feel his eyes looking her up and down.

"You look nice today," he looked back at his screen awkwardly. "So who do you think is really smart and shows incredible potential? God sorry you haven't even had your coffee yet. I'm just excited. I mean, ideally, we would rather choose someone who doesn't have a family or dependents. Someone who could take over the world if we let them see what they're capable of," Will said with a laugh.

Lottie stood there and thought about her lines. What she had planned to say next escaped her. Will hadn't noticed that she had closed the door behind her, he was too distracted by his own sense of achievement. She hoped that what she was about to say wouldn't make him feel uncomfortable and bring his joyous mood crashing down. He seemed to be in such a good mood.

"Yeah, I must say, Will, I read every single email last night. I studied them all in fact, in quite a lot of detail. Not just the emails but the people, I looked up their professional backgrounds, some of their latest pieces of work, and how they are in the office. I was keen to find out what their deal is. I know you have a big responsibility on your shoulders to pick someone clever and reliable. You want this to work otherwise I'm sure you'll be getting a lot of questions…"

Lottie had caught Will's attention. It was a modest downer on his jovial spirit. He looked up from his computer and half-smiled back at her, and began rocking in his ergonomically designed chair.

"Yes, that's very true Lottie, and there was me thinking you might have had a quiet night" he half-chuckled, flicking his brown hair from out of his eyes and trying to inject the playful tone back into the conversation.

"So go on then, tell me, who stood out to you?"

Here we go.

"Well, Will, I have been giving this quite a bit of thought, I hardly slept thinking about it."

Lottie decided to take a seat in front of Will's desk, pushing her skirt down once again.

"Will, I think you need to select the one person in this company you can trust the most."

Lottie felt herself blush at her own self-confidence in the matter. She hadn't planned to say that and she hoped she wasn't going to have to spell it out for him.

Oh my god, who am I?

Will was looking at her straight in the eyes, it was electrifying every time he did.

"I think you should have full confidence in who the person is, and know first-hand what they are capable of delivering. This is your baby, Will. Why would you risk all of your hard work on anyone you don't one hundred percent know and trust?

"Yeah, you're right," I guess hadn't thought of it like that. I was just thinking we should choose someone who shows the greatest amount of potential."

"Well, you won't know what someone's real potential is unless you know them."

"Lottie, who do you have in mind?"

"I think there's only one person who you really need to consider. Only one truly viable candidate."

"Bloody hell spit it out Lottie."

Really Will?

"Ok Will. Well, I think that person should be me."

Silence entered the room like a breeze through an opened window. Old stuffy air was being replaced and replenished with the new. Lottie wanted to give him a moment to take this in so she stopped talking. She wanted to gauge his reaction. She had imagined him closing his eyes and apologising for not immediately considering her. She dreamt he would slap himself on the head with an 'oh my god' notion and smile and run towards her arms open wide.

That wasn't quite what happened.

Will started to laugh. He was actually laughing. The man was sitting there behind his glass desk, between his glass walls in his proverbial glass ceiling — laughing. Not a mild, moderate half-laugh but a deep belly laugh. There she was in a power dressing outfit, confident and eloquent, assertive and direct, honest and bold – ten years of service to him and his company and there he was leaning back in his chair laughing at her. She didn't join him, she just stared at him, and after a few consecutive chuckles, he stopped, sensing his comedic timing was being monumentally misplaced.

Oh my god. What the hell?

"Oh what? Oh, bloody hell Lottie sorry I thought you were joking."

Lottie felt winded and could feel the blush rising in her cheeks like hot flames. She was mortified with humiliation, she felt like bursting into tears there and then on the spot, but the indignity of it all helped her hold it together. Of all the scenarios she had played out in her mind the night before, over and over, she had never anticipated this. She never really thought, after everything she had done for him, that he would just sit there and laugh. After all these years of hard work and long hours and devotion and loyalty. All the feelings were rising up in her gut like bubbles in a caldron, like a pressure cooker she had reached her peak. This was the crescendo in the symphony, and what's more, it didn't just break her confidence it was breaking her heart.

Lottie brushed her skirt, stood up and pivoted on her heel reaching swiftly for the door handle. She just wanted to get out of there. There wasn't much more to say at that point. Did he really think so little of her? Did he undervalue her that much despite everything she had done for him? It was bad enough that she had to find out what he was up to with the rest of the office yesterday, and now this.

That was it, the next words out of her mouth were truly going to be to give her resignation, she was visualising writing up the letter that morning and handing it to Will by lunchtime.

"Wait!" Will stood up from his desk, suddenly acutely aware of the hurt running through her body. He put his hands over hers as she clutched the door handle, and pressed into her body to push the door back closed. They had never been this close. Lottie shut her eyes to stop the tears from welling up in her body and the two of them just stood there for a moment unsure as to what to say next.

Will sensed there were feelings there for some time but he hadn't acted upon anything as he wanted to keep it profes- sional and he didn't want to mix business with pleasure and lose a damn good EA in the process. So they had been solidly flirting for years and he felt they had a great relationship. He could usually tease her and she respond with suitable witty banter, but this was different. She was different. She was being serious.

He had always liked Lottie, but he knew better than to go there romantically, especially with how much she helped him at work, but he always thought she was one of the good guys. He trusted her, and he certainly didn't want her to feel wounded by his words. He thought more highly of her than he did many of the people in the office, she was incredibly smart, she was shrewd, she was pretty and she was right about most things. He found himself often deferring to her for her opinion, like sound counsel she would advise and rarely if ever, had she ever complained or asked for much in return. It was just so surprising that she would wish to be considered for something like this, she had never really voiced any sense of ambition before. It all sounded so foreign, almost as though she had come in that morning speaking fluent Japanese.

"Sit down", he said quietly in her ear, both of them still standing close to one another. He offered her a chair as he flicked his hair out of his face and composed his facial expression to convey earnest sincerity and concern. Lottie obeyed, avoiding eye contact as he sat on the edge of the desk in front of her.

"Look, Lottie, I'm so sorry. I just never in a million years thought you would be up for doing something like this. It's just it's going to be pretty full-on and you've never mentioned anything to me before about what you would like to do going forwards. You always just seem so cool and laid-back when it comes to stuff like this."

Is this his attempt at a compliment? Thought Lottie incensed. Was he trying to appease her? She raised her eyebrows at Will.

"What? You don't think I can handle it Will? Is that what you mean? The work you've had me doing has been ... what was it...? That of an entire team?

She didn't know where this attitude was coming from but she found herself to be rather enjoying it. Suddenly, she wasn't seeing Will as the dreamy, gorgeous boss she had been trying so hard to please, but as an equal, and someone who had crossed her moral compass with swift aggression.

Will bowed his head, slightly taken aback by her bold assertion, and inwardly very impressed by how she was standing up for herself.

"True," he admitted again, looking her straight in the eyes. Lottie felt he was looking straight into her heart.

He was contemplating what she was saying. The woman did have a point. She had practically done all the number crunching and models on her own for the new company merger, including five projections and analyst level forecasting. Each time they had a new client pitch, it would be her who would put together the glossy decks and absorb information. She would know the ins and outs of this business and she had his back more times than he cared to admit. What's more, he trusted her, he knew she had more potential. He knew deep down, at some point, she would surely demand more.

The truth was that he knew how good Lottie was. He had always known she was way better than she gave herself credit for — but that suited him fine so he played along with it. It was an inconvenient truth that she was easily pleased, because, without her, Will was worried people would see right through him. She made him look good. She put a polish on his work and credibility to his name. If he promoted her, he could lose her and if he lost her, god knows what else he could stand to lose.

However, looking at Lottie now it became apparent that there was damage that had been done. She had been by his side for a long time, and for the first time in ten years, she was asking for more from her life. All the while he had been thinking of himself and how to get what he wanted out of the situation. He wanted to make his father proud, and feel like a success. Lottie was still on a basic salary, doing more work than ever, without any talk of moving up the ladder. Will felt a pang of regret. He shouldn't have let this happen.

"I just meant you might be in for a surprise when you realise what would be required of you", Will continued keen to fill the silence with modest appeasement hoping to sense how serious she was."It's going to be a very serious level of commitment."

"Will, I have made a ten-year commitment to this company. I have been here with you from the very beginning and I have done everything I can to help you grow and succeed. I don't appreciate you talking to me about serious levels of commitment."

Wow, I can't believe I just said that.

She held it together. She was being firm but fair. She could feel her eyes starting to glisten over and a lump starting to form in her throat but a strength inside her pushed it down. She was strong and she wasn't about to start crying in front of Will now she had made it this far in the conversation. She had to admit to herself though, that Will obviously had never seen her the way she had hoped he had. She realised there and then that all the false hope she had been clinging onto, hoping that he would wake up and realise how right they were for each other was just that — 'false'. She had been fooling herself this whole time and letting herself stagnate professionally and personally as a result.

Will looked at Lottie sitting on the chair, her brown hair resting on her slumped shoulders, her eyes gazing to the floor. She was right to want to be considered. She had everything inside her, but she didn't know it. He also deduced he was going to lose her if he didn't do something about it. He couldn't afford to lose her, not now. There were two ways the conversation could go at that point and he most certainly didn't want her to resign. He reached forward and touched her on the shoulder, gently moving his hand to touch her cheek. He took a deep breath before the words came out of it his mouth.

"Lottie you know what, you're right. I'm such a bloody idiot. You're right about most things to be fair. I actually can't believe I didn't think of it myself. You would be perfect for this."

WILL WATCHED LOTTIE WALK MEEKLY OUT OF HIS OFFICE, LEAVING the door open behind her. He stared blankly out to the office floor for a moment. He just wanted to take it all in. What had just happened? He looked beyond his glass walls as he saw her head to her desk and open up her emails. He looked at the hustle starting to form from the rest of the team, the comings and goings of office staff going about their day. Small-talk conversations were happening by the lifts, there was a large hive swarming around the tea and coffee station at the far end of the room and people were chatting, mingling, bustling. Then he looked again at Lottie, sat on her own away from all the activity. Despite what he'd said about her knowing people better than he did, he knew that to be a lie. She was an outlier in this office for more ways than one. She didn't socialise that much with many people, and although they all knew her to say hello and she was friendly back, she rarely seemed to go along to after-work drinks or out for lunch with anyone.

Not that she had much time to join in with the others, mind you. She was always busy working with Will on some project, and often the two of them would stay in the office working late together. Sometimes they would get hungry and Will would order something from Deliveroo for them both, proud that he knew what she liked. "One dragon roll and rainbow roll for you, sashimi and nigiri for me" he would say with a wink. Occasionally he would order a bottle of wine too and they would drink it out of office tumblers laughing at the glamour. He could sense she loved those evenings, those moments of calm and connection together. They would chat and unwind, he would tease her about any dates she had been on and they got to know about each other's families and lives. Mornings after working long nights like that she wouldn't come into work tired and resentful but with renewed enthusiasm for her job and a radiance about her. He loved that glow.

Aside from Will though, she just wasn't on super friendly terms with anyone else, often just sitting at her desk during her lunch break on her own eating something from Pret with her headphones on. She was seemingly often quite invisible. Yet, despite her low profile in the office, the impact of her work was far-reaching. Her effect on the company was, to Will's mind, very evident, and yet her confidence imperceptible. As he looked out at the contrasting undertones from Lottie to the rest of the office, he wondered why this was. What had happened along Lottie's way to make her feel she didn't deserve her right to be at the table or to want or expect more?

Will admired Lottie but he had a slight personal conundrum to face. On the one hand, he liked her, and although nothing had ever happened romantically he simply couldn't imagine the company without her. If Lottie became the prototype what would become of him? Professionally would he still be able to progress and excel? He knew what Lottie was capable of and was very intrigued to see what she would become. She would no doubt do the filter proud, and she was right — he needed someone he could trust.

So, as Will stared blankly out to the office he began to daydream. He imagined her walking in like she owned the place. Glamorous, striding, handbag swaying with her Hermes scarf around her neck, instead of shuffling in with her tired clothes old leather backpack. He imagined her boldly going up to someone to ask them a direct question in the office, sitting on the end of their desk and gesticulating wildly with her hands, not emailing them the details of everything they needed to know with professional competence yet intrinsic shyness. He imagined her being assertive, being bold, being a thought-leader. He then began to look at her body, imagining her toning up and getting her hair done, wearing clothes that accentuated her body, her long legs. To his eyes, she looked good already but he couldn't help but wonder what would happen if she were looking at her absolute best.

Yes, he thought as he narrowed his eyes — considering and conceding that perhaps the best strategy for success had been staring him in the face this whole time. Yes, Lottie Mortimer could do very nicely indeed.

He decided he would call a meeting with the other board embers tomorrow to discuss matters. He didn't want it to look like he was being biased by using his own EA, but the more he thought about it, the more he thought he might well have found the perfect candidate.

CHAPTER

Ten

Lottie awoke in Charlotte's house to the sound of loud music thudding against her walls, the vibrations of which were so strong she could feel the mattress beneath her gently shake. Sitting up, she looked for the time. It was 7 am on the dot. Rubbing her eyes she pivoted her body to rest her feet upon the padded rug and stood up, feeling the muscles of her feet and ankles weigh into the floor as she walked.

Today was the start of her induction and she was excited. It was the first day of a new life for her and, similar to a child on their first day back after the summer holiday, keen to ensure their school uniform was pressed and clean, Lottie was keen to get herself in the right mindset for what lay ahead. She wandered over to the shower in her en-suite and got herself ready for the day choosing from one of the outfits in her new wardrobe. She wanted to feel strong today, ready to take on whatever criticism came her way, and she expected there to be quite a bit. Today would be the day she would look back and say 'wow, wasn't I terrible, look how far I've come', so she looked for something smart and serviceable. Something uncharacteristic that didn't say she was trying too hard. She pulled out a pair of dark-denim jeans along with a navy jumper, size 12 and she was relieved that they fit. Most of the other things looked far too tiny. Looking in the mirror she thought about how much better this outfit would look on Charlotte.

She had slept wonderfully, despite all of the thoughts swirling around in her mind. There had been so much to take in since the reveal yesterday and a great deal of what she'd been told just seemed so surreal. Why was Will so far away and why didn't he say hello? How did all of this come to be? What had happened between the two of them? She couldn't help but wonder if something romantic had finally happened. Her heart started fluttering at the thought. Perhaps he suddenly realised that she was the perfect woman for him, and there had been a stormy and uncontrollably passionate love affair.

Grateful to have charged her phone overnight she looked through it habitually, like she did most mornings. There were all her old photos and some of her messages but it looked like her social media apps were blocked. She also noticed there were quite a few new apps on there, a weight loss tracker, motivational quotes, a range of fitness apps and hundreds of books that had been added to her Kindle account.

She soon found herself walking and moving around her bedroom to the beat of the music incessantly playing through her walls and made herself feel presentable by dabbing some makeup on her cheeks and putting her hair up into a neat bun. There wasn't much point trying to make too much of an effort at this stage, she really couldn't compete with Charlotte on the looks front, and in a way, she didn't want to try. It made her feel less bad about her shortcomings if she knew she didn't make a huge effort to look her best. Along with her phone, she picked up a notebook and pen from the desk in her room and headed downstairs ready to get to work, hopeful that she might well have been the first one to have made it down.

Wandering into the kitchen she found Nico navigating pans on a stove like a pilot preparing a cockpit for landing. Steam was swirling over his head and there was a hive of activity.

"Ah yes! Lottie. Iza time for your breakfast. Take a seat, Charlotte will be down soon."

Lottie took a seat at the long marble kitchen island so she could observe what Nico was up to. Within a few seconds of sitting, she was presented with a fairly unappetising plate of food.

"There you are may darling. We av a simple breakfast today of hot water and lemon which you should drink first, and after dat you can av a green juice smoothie and some coconut overnight oats and berries. Later on, you can have some black coffee donna worry," he said with a knowing wink.

"Thanks". She didn't really like her coffee black but wasn't about to start making demands. Lottie looked at this selection of food Nico placed before her and wondered why Charlotte felt the need to have a chef magically create such a simple meal which basically looked like porridge. She thought about just how much money she had to splurge on such luxuries. She hadn't even had a chance to consider how much she must have been earning to not only live here but have all the added perks. A personal chef, a gym at home, security systems. She could hear her ever-thrift mother's voice in her head saying *'how much did you spend on that?'* Clearly, Charlotte took what she put into her body and mouth much more seriously than she ever had. Lottie had never professed to be much of a cook, but she could certainly whip up some porridge if needed, not that she ever liked it all that much, especially not served cold.

"Charlotte has been working out with Gunter this morning hence the loud music. Eez er personal trainer. You will probably hear that most mornings. Now she's a having her hair and makeup done."

Hair and makeup?

"Oh, has she got a special event today or something?" Lottie asked trying to keep it cool

"No, she just doesn't like to do it herself."

Bloody hell, thought Lottie. She always rather liked makeup and playing with colours on her face. She couldn't imagine ever getting to the point of having a professional do it for her all the time. Lottie picked up her hot water and lemon and took a sip, the tartness lingering on her lips and the heat steaming over her nose. Sensing some motion she looked up and saw Charlotte near the kitchen. She looked immaculately dressed in elegant denim jeans cropped at her ankle along with a white shirt. Her hair was bouncing off her shoulders and her complexion seemed more tanned than yesterday. As she got closer Lottie could see she had rosy cheeks underneath her makeup from what must have been her workout.

"Good morning Lottie, how did you sleep?" Charlotte

was positively glowing as she was handed hot water and lemon by Nico.

"Yes, really well thanks. Super comfy mattress!"

"Good. I'm pleased. Yes, it's so important to invest in the best bed and mattress money can buy as sleep plays such a big part in how we perform during the day and our mental and physical wellbeing. Ok so after your breakfast we will start your induction. If you can meet me in my office at 8.15 am?

"Sure, I'll see you there in a bit," replied Lottie watching the back of Charlotte as she walked away and observing her figure enviously as she did so.

Lottie didn't luxuriate in eating her coconut overnight oats but made out to Nico that she was enjoying it with the occasional 'mmmm' sound. She then helped herself to some black coffee that had been freshly prepared on the worktop and made her way into Charlotte's office, feeling like a slice of toast or two wouldn't have gone amiss or a little honey or golden syrup.

Charlotte was sitting behind her aeroplane wing desk, her legs crossed and eyes focused on something on her large computer screen. On her desk, there were no papers, just a single notebook and a couple of small leather-bound books with post-it notes poking out from the top of them. She welcomed Lottie in with a smile and a shake of her hand which jingled with some expensive looking bangles and watches on her wrist.

"Come in Lottie. This is exciting. Today is the first day you'll be living your best life! This is going to be fun! I hope we can enjoy this journey together and be friends and allies. Remember, what you're about to go through I have been through myself so I'm living proof you can do what you stick your mind to."

Lottie smiled and thought about being friends with Charlotte. She wasn't sure she had anything in common with her. Not yet anyway. If anything, she was intimidated by her, she felt she was out of her league in the friend stakes. She just didn't have friends like Charlotte. Not that she had a huge amount of friends anyway but most of them were broke or still living at home with their parents.

"Ok, so today we are going to outline what the plan for you is while you're in this filter. We are going to be working closely together to learn habits for success that we hope will last you a lifetime.

You will be set three challenges during your time here, and upon completion of all three challenges successfully, you will be deemed to be truly living your best life and can leave the filter. The idea is that when you return to the real world, you will have all the tools at your disposal to apply to become your best self.

I expect each challenge to last approximately a month, but it depends upon your dedication and commitment. This is an intense course in achieving the ultimate so it will take hard work and there will be times when it won't be easy."

"Right ok," muttered Lottie listening intently to her every word. She was keen not to interrupt so Charlotte could relay as much information as she could.

"At the end of each challenge there will be a review, and that's conducted by myself and Michael Dalton. He was the man who introduced us on stage. He's one of the founders and was an early-stage investor in all this. We'll sit down to assess how much progress you've made and whether you're ready to progress to the next challenge.

So today we're going to talk about the first phase of your journey, challenge one."

Charlotte pulled up a screen on her large Mac screen and waved Lottie over to come and sit closer so she could take a look. Lottie could see a whole load of metrics against her name including bar charts and tables. Fortunately for Lottie, she was used to looking at dashboards so quickly understood these were her performance metrics and what appeared to be a weekly timetable.

Lottie scanned her eyes down the long list of metrics and could see these were remarkably updating in real-time. Her heart rate was on the rise and she looked to her body for some sort of tracking device.

"Don't forget, you have a microchip in your body" smiled Charlotte, realising what Lottie was looking for. "That's where we pull all the data on your body composition, heart rate and all of these items here," she said pointing to a long list of metrics. "So we can track pretty much everything about your body at all times including what you've been eating, how much you've been exercising. It makes the data very accurate and that way, we all know when you're sticking to the plan."

"Oh right ok," replied Lottie. She had no recollection of this at all

This was a level of accountability that she had never imagined. One of the biggest reasons her many diets had failed over the years was because if she failed, she only had herself to answer to and blame. Now it would appear, the world and their dog would be watching. Part of Lottie did feel slightly concerned with the all-seeing eyes and ears on everything that would pass her lips but she carried on listening. *Maybe that was a good thing.*

"Here you can see your objectives clearly for this month, you will also see these on an app on your phone called 'Your Best Life which you can refer to anytime. Not only does that app show you your challenges but it also shows you your daily workouts and pings you reminders throughout your day to help you stick to your new habits."

"In summary, the first month is about setting new habits for yourself. We want to press the reset button on your mindset and your limiting beliefs. We also really want to zone in on getting your health and fitness kick-started as everything leads from being healthy. Having a healthy body really does give you a healthy mind and you will need all the mental strength you can muster going forward. At times it won't be easy and you will feel like giving up. Well, I'm not just here to tell you that you can, I'm living proof that it is possible.

Ok, let's go through the objectives. Starting with your physical ones. For this first challenge, I want to see a substantial weight loss of ten pounds through healthy eating and exercise. That's two to three pounds a week which is very much doable with your frame and at your current weight. It's generally easier to lose more at the beginning when there's more to lose. Weight loss always gets harder as we progress but with an overall weight loss challenge of twenty pounds, losing ten in your first month would be an incredible start. Your body fat is currently around twenty-five percent and we need to get that down to twenty-one percent this month."

Lottie felt trepidation wash over her, losing ten pounds in a month just felt like a lot.

"Gunter, my trainer will start you on your first session today and explain what will go into your workouts. Essentially, there are six workouts per week with one day for stretching.

As touched upon yesterday, you will be eating a purely

plant-based, organic and sugar-free diet, and Nico and I will be helping you navigate what that looks like, but you'll love it. It's delicious and after a while, your body will crave eating good, nutritious foods.

Ok so moving on to your mental objectives. Mentally: a huge part of this is about developing a 'growth mindset'. I want to see you becoming open to believing you can do it which will come when you build your confidence levels and when the body and mind are working together optimally. I also want to see that you are continually educating yourself by expanding your mind and reading several books as well as exploring new ideas and philosophies. You will need to write down every book you have read. We will regularly check in with you on this but the key target is to read three books per week. We can discuss them together if you like. I have picked out a couple of books for you to get started with this week. Charlotte handed her two very worn out looking books entitled 'The Magic of Thinking Big' and 'Outliers'.

You'll also need to make sure you're sleeping enough. It's so important and can't be underestimated if you want to reach your peak performance. This will all be tracked in the filter but the goal is to sleep a minimum of eight solid hours each night. It's not as easy as it might sound when you're up against it with your projects and assignments."

Lottie thought back to her current bedtime routine. Usually, she was asleep by around midnight and up at 7 am so she would have to start going to bed earlier, especially as looking at her timetable she was expected to be up at 6 am every morning.

"And lastly spiritually," continued Charlotte "we want to see you being at peace with yourself and so a healthy body and mind need to work in harmony. You will need to meditate each morning and evening before bed and teach yourself the practice of spiritual enlightenment that suits you. It's also important for you to have time for friends and family but you must learn how to distance yourself from non-believers. These are people who are not totally supportive of your quest for the best. You will be surprised how often people find it hard to be around you and you must be ruthless in cutting these people out of your life.

There will be time in your schedule for yoga too and you must spend time outside. Get some fresh air, go for hikes, or runs, explore the world we live in and connect to it. It's so important to recharge and refresh your spiritual system.

Work out who you are, and what you want. I have made my fortune as a chick-flick writer, and I could say that I have been lucky, but a woman makes her own luck. I have fought tooth and nail to get where I am and it's paid off. You can do it too. If you also want to become a writer you'll need to develop a plot outline this month and let me see it for review. It doesn't have to be chick-lit it can be any genre you want, but the idea this month is to create a blueprint for your success.

And finally, give back. Help others and show compassion by forming an alliance with a good cause. Find something you're passionate about. For me it was dogs, I developed such a love for dogs and felt my heart break whenever I saw one hobbling around without legs that I knew I had to do something."

Charlotte touched her hand against her heart and tilted her head empathetically.

Lottie tried not to frown with sarcasm as she wasn't

really buying any of this. If she had such a love for dogs where was her dog? It's not that she wasn't open to allying with a good cause, it just all seemed a bit pretentious.

"Oh right," replied Lottie immediately breaking the rules and not speaking her truth but it seemed too soon to rock the boat.

"You see what this first challenge is all about is habits. We are going to reeducate your current habits and reestablish your belief system. Good habits will need to be learned that will change our behaviour in the future. You need to learn how to stop making excuses for yourself, and how to speak your truth. No more accepting things that aren't absolutely favourable to you. This is the time for you to work out what makes you happy and to go for it.

It might sound fairly straightforward but trust me, this level of discipline you are about to experience will be something so totally against your internal grain and so uncomfortable to you. Any change is uncomfortable but it's that discomfort that gets you the results you want so don't be afraid of it. If you don't change then you can't change. It's all part of the process, and you're lucky that you have me and a full team here to support you.

Lottie, you have seen what your potential is, and it's truly boundless. It's remarkable what the body and mind can achieve when they apply themselves together. Now it's time to get started."

When Charlotte had finished her monologue, she moved away from the computer on the wheels of her chair and sat with her arms neatly placed one on top of the other on her lap, ready for any questions. Lottie didn't even know where to start, she just stared at the list of objectives on the screen before her. Charlotte had recited this list so easily. How they had just rolled off the tongue with ease. Just lose ten pounds, just work on a blueprint for success, just give back — but Lottie had no idea how easy any of it would really be. Could it all actually be done within a month? What's more, some of the goals seemed slightly vague. How could anyone really determine if she was continually educating herself or if she was getting enough 'fresh air'? Surely it would be her word against anyone else's?

"How will we all agree when these have been reached?" Lottie considered her words carefully. "Couldn't some of these goals be slightly open to interpretation?"

Charlotte looked at Lottie coldly.

"Perfection is not open to interpretation Lottie, I will know when you're there. The data will know when you're there. One month from now Michael and I will assess your results and determine if you have progressed to the next challenge."

Oddly, Charlotte's tone changed. She sounded cool and icy, like a saleswoman who had become automated in her response to an objection. Slightly haughty she had very swiftly tried to shut Lottie down. Lottie wasn't sure she appreciated her response or the stare that preceded it.

"So are these the only objectives for this month?" Lottie scanned the computer dashboard again. "I don't have to have earned a certain amount of money? What about my job?"

"Oh no, we can't expect you to achieve what has taken me six years to build right away. Becoming your best self isn't about the immediate results, it's about the journey. It's not about getting wealthy and successful but it's about changing your habits, your mindset, your discipline and doing everything you can to be living at your true potential. We believe if you do all of this the wealth and status will come from all this hard work. So just be patient, that will come."

There was something about the way she said 'that will come' that annoyed Lottie, closing her eyes momentarily and giving her head a gentle shake from side to side.

"And with regards your job. You still have your job at the office, just not for Will anymore. Ideally, though, you need to be resigning as soon as possible so you can learn how to. It's super important to learn how to stand up for yourself and ask for what you want out of life. Nobody can do that for you, and it will give you the time you need to focus on creating the life you want."

"Right," responded Lottie flatly. Although motivated to improve she was finding this grand unveiling incredibly bizarre. She also really wanted to find out about what happened with Will but she sensed this just wasn't the right moment to ask.

Lottie looked again at the screen before her. There was a full timetable of activities. Her day consisted of a 70-minute workout with Gunter, some meditating, one and half hours for reading time, two hours for research towards goals and two hours for actioning those goals. That would take her to the evening when she would have a couple of hours of free time, one hour eating an evening meal and bedtime would be no later than 10 pm.

It was all there, it was all planned out. Lottie felt her throat dry up at the thought of what lay ahead. She scratched her head. It all seemed unfamiliar at the moment, so unbelievable, but she had never felt more motivated to try. She didn't want to be average anymore and this was her chance.

"Ok," replied Lottie "Well I'll give it my best shot."

"Well, you'd better," laughed Charlotte "otherwise you'll be here for a very long time."

CHAPTER
Eleven

"WE HAVE FOUND HER," STATED WILL UNEQUIVOCALLY TO THE GROUP of men gathered in front of him. "We had a huge response from volunteers, but I can safely say we have found the one who's going to be perfect for this".

Richard Myers, Mark Ball and Michael Dalton were sat around a round table looking up at Will as he spoke. Will liked to walk around during meetings, it gave him more energy and he felt he needed to assert himself with what he was about to say.

"Good news," replied Michael rubbing his hands. "It's about time. The cabinet office was getting a bit antsy so we need to get on with it. Ok, don't keep it to yourself. Who is it then?"

The three heads were all ears.

"Well, I have been going through several submissions and the prototype needed to be used on someone who, as we know, shows promise, who is bright and competent but under-achieving, and who we can trust. We essentially would all agree the person needs to be someone will the intellectual abilities to have real success without the risks of using their power against us — god forbid that should happen."

The three heads were nodding along, like apples bobbing in the water.

"Yes," Mark said. "We do need someone who will be on our side and work hard I, quite agree. We can't risk using the filter on someone who's too ambitious in a way as they could turn into a nightmare. It does need to be someone we can feel moderately comfortable we can control. So who do you have in mind?"

Will stopped walking and leaned his arms over the back of an office chair which swung up and down with his weight. He wanted to look them all in the eyes for this one and understood the importance of them all sitting down as he spoke to them from an elevated position.

"Well, actually guys, it's my EA - her name is Lottie Mortimer." Will was smiling broadly now. He knew this was when he'd have to sell the idea to them and he wanted to convey how he felt, that he had never been more convinced about anything in his life.

"Who the hell is Lottie Mortimer?" Michael blurted out. He hadn't ever actually met with Lottie face to face, as she had only ever booked in his meetings with Will virtually, and when her name was mentioned, she seemed too unimportant to remember.

"Hang on, you mean the girl who books our meetings? You want to use our investment and funding on some EA?"

Michael was chuckling with a frown and motioned to the other men to join him. They simply stared ahead at Will.

"Is she really the best possible candidate?" Mark gestured tactfully.

"Actually yes. She's perfect, and let me explain precisely why. Lottie has been working here for me for over ten years and not once has she asked for a promotion, a pay rise or a change in her working hours. She's got very little confidence when it comes to her professional career, but get this," his eyes widened as he spoke, "she is probably the smartest person in this office. Michael, although you haven't met her I can assure you she's the brains behind a lot more than you might think."

Michael Dalton started to laugh even more at Will's pantomime dramatics and looked again to Mark and Richard for a reaction.

"Really? And what proof do you have of her mega-brains then Will?" Michael objected.

"Ok I know how it might sound but just hear me out. Not only has Lottie single-handedly conceptualised all of the models that went into making this filter happen," Will paused for effect and to make this point sink in "but she has done the work of an entire team of senior-level analysts. She works over-time but doesn't complain, she is a hard worker without being confident enough to ask for more. She puts together all our pitches, our decks, she writes beautifully. She's smart but she's underachieving. She's charming and kind…"

Will stopped himself. He didn't want to give them the wrong impression by mentioning anything too personal.

"The beauty of her is that she's someone we can trust. She's been with me from the beginning and has been by my side for ten years. I would trust her to do this filter proud. Quite frankly, I think she's perfect for it."

Will slapped down on the table a wad of papers, some of which escaped their plastic sheaths and spilled out over the meeting room table.

"Stats, models and dashboard, all of which Lottie did herself. She's never had a single bit of training in this guys. There's also new business pitches she put together. She's a smart cookie."

Silence ensued as the three musketeers stared at these papers, unsure as to whether to grab them or touch them or whether this would be an act of conceding to the notion, accepting the idea.

"How come she's just an EA then if she's so good?" Asked Michael objectively. Why hasn't she climbed the ranks? You say she's been with you ten years?"

Will thought carefully about how to answer this. He didn't want to look bad for keeping her down, for stalling her potential. Besides, they didn't have to know about the fact her salary had remained the same all this time.

"Well, she never strived for more," Will responded plainly. "She didn't want more from her life. You see, that's the point here guys. She's an ideal candidate in so many ways because she doesn't see how good she could become. She hasn't been envisioning it. She never dreamt big or had grand plans."

Can we talk logistics and practicalities?" Richard stated pragmatically "Does she have dependents, a family, boyfriend or husband? Whilst we want to get her in and out as quickly as we can, we don't know how long she could be in the filter. We don't know how long all of this could take or how this will affect the individual when they come back to the real world."

"No," responded Will. "Not married, no boyfriend, no kids. She lives on her own in a small flat in Clapham. It's the same flat she's rented for years. She's never been that close to her mum and dad from what I gather. They live down in Dorset where Lottie's from and they rarely come up to London to see her. The same goes for her friends. She has a small group of friends I believe but her age is ideal as most of them are settling down to have kids so she's probably starting to feel more detached from them. There really couldn't be a better life stage for her to do this."

The room was met by hushed tones and shuffling papers.

Mark and Richard glanced through some of the paperwork before them, models, supposed proof of her excellence. They didn't know what they were meant to be looking for or reading from all this, but they did know they were eager to get the spot filled and move on. Investors were battling down their doors in anticipation. This did sound fairly plausible, and her loyalty to the company may well mean she may be somewhat easier to control. Even Michael Dalton, originally sceptical had gone quiet and sat there in pensive contemplation as he fiddled with a pen in his hand. Having someone go into the filter who at least one of them knew and trusted wasn't a bad idea.

"Well," responded Michael speaking on behalf of the others. "Do you really think this Lottie is the best we've got? You know how much is riding on this."

"I do Michael." Will stood firm and proud, a tenseness rising over his lips.

"Well, we have trusted you this far," Michael sighed unsure of what to say. He too picked up some of the papers on the table and idly started to rifle through them with his index finger.

"If you say she's the one, then let's agree to move forward. We do need to get on with it."

"Great, we won't regret this," Will responded, reflecting on his ironic use of words.

"I hope not, but I must ask you Will," said Michael. "Remind me what we will be able to see while she's in there with regards to how it's going and how much progress she's making. Will we need to wait until she comes out to gauge progress? I do worry the cabinet office and our investors will need some reassurance over coming months that we haven't pissed their money up the wall."

Never one to mince his words Michael sat back conceitedly in his chair. Will was well aware he had explained this to him before and often grew concerned about his ability to recall information when it came to this filter. He liked to be surrounded by sharp minds, and whilst Michael was a formidable businessman and entrepreneur, Will did worry he still didn't fully get it yet. Acceding to the fact it was the first time anything like this was going to be done and that perhaps Michael just needed his hand held a little bit he explained it to him calmly once again.

"Yes, so let's be clear. We won't be able to see everything through Lottie's eyes in terms of what she sees, but the technology has been designed in such a way that we can see a limited number of snippets. These are basically going to be clips of what Lottie sees throughout her day. There is simply too much data for us to get a constant live stream where we could see everything. These snippets will be coupled with constant statistical data that we'll be getting from her food and activity trackers so we should get a fairly good idea as to the progress Lottie is making and indeed where she has the potential to go. I'll make sure we are all in the loop with regular updates".

"Ok, good. Well, that settles it," replied Michael, seemingly satisfied with that response. "Let's get on with it then."

"Great".

Will felt a surge of relief and excitement. Lottie was going into the filter. She would be so happy when he told her, he already couldn't wait to rush out and give her the good news, but he tried to contain himself.

"OK. So the next step is to get her synced up to the filter so we can start tracking her data. We'll need her to take some tests so we have a baseline to work from and then we'll insert a microchip into her body so we can have accurate performance measures to work with. Once everything is in place we'll get Lottie into our filter proofing facility where we'll be keeping her under observation. She will essentially be asleep here with us throughout this entire period whilst it's all going on."

"Will she know what has happened to her when she wakes up inside the filter?" asked Michael.

Mark was keen to answer this as he leant forward in his chair.

"We are planning to do a one-month memory wipe as part of the process, so when she wakes up in the filter she will be none the wiser to what is happening. This is intentional so we can get accurate base-level readings. We need the surprise at seeing her true potential to be a huge motivating factor. If she knew what was coming we question whether the results would be quite so good."

"Right ok," replied Michael. "And what about when she comes out and returns to her normal life. What will she remember?"

"Well, hopefully, everything, that's the idea", replied Will. "Remember, she's only going to leave the filter when she's learnt how to live her best life. and has mastered what it takes to be the best version of herself. When that happens we'll bring her back to her old life, back to reality. She'll wake up ready to make the changes for real."

"Guys, we are there!" Will was excited. "We are almost ready to go. The filter has been made, the technology is ready, and we've got a great candidate for the prototype. Everything is aligned. Now we just need to figure out when to send her in."

Will's baby was finally getting off the ground. It was happening and the more and more he thought about it, the more he truly felt Lottie was right. She was the perfect candidate. So much potential, so much good to come out of this and he couldn't wait to see just how she would turn out when she came out.

CHAPTER
Twelve

LOTTIE'S FIRST DAY HAD GONE PRETTY WELL SO FAR. AS IT was a Saturday it felt like she was on some spiritual retreat, jumping into each of her tasks on her timetable with optimism. After her workout with Charlotte's trainer in the basement of her house, where she was eased into exercise with what she felt was relative kindness. *Well, it could have been worse,* she thought as she left feeling pumped and positive.

Gunter took some unforgiving measurements of her arms, legs and waist with a tape measure and wrote them down in a book before getting her to jump on some industrial looking scales. She didn't look down, instead opting to close her eyes and take a deep breath fearing the worst. He then used some clamps to grip the fat behind her arms and on her tummy, which he told her was to measure her percentage of body fat. It all felt rather invasive but she knew it was necessary, and she had conceded by this point they already had pretty much every other bit of data on her, they might as well take it all.

Despite being told by Gunter that she was heavier than expected, even although she wasn't entirely sure what he meant by 'expected', it didn't bother her as much as it typically would have as she knew one day she would look back on all this and smile to herself. She now knew this was the starting point and it would only get better from here.

She thought back to when she had attempted her last diet. The no-carb combined with intermittent fasting diet. It wasn't so much a diet, more of a half-hearted attempt to fit into her clothes better. For whatever reason she had never really envisaged losing considerable body fat, just losing a few pounds here and there. She never really thought she needed to lose *that* much weight, but looking at Charlotte move, and how bloody happy she seemed within herself, she realised for the first time that a few pounds here and there really wouldn't cut it. She wondered why she hadn't aimed higher before? Why was she happy to aim for just losing a few pounds when she could have aimed for more?

"Ok, so we have a little work to do here," Gunter said with a serious tone after taking down her measurements. He was a stocky looking man with short blonde hair that was shaved so close it almost reminded her of a marine. He looked a little bit like the Terminator out of Terminator Two, but more muscly, she thought to herself. His blue eyes were piercing but there didn't seem to be much emotion there.

"We are going to work on getting your body fat right down and really leaning you out. The diet you're on will make a huge difference so what we want to do is work building your strength with weight-bearing exercises. I also want you to incorporate stretching, some yoga and pilates to stretch out this body."

Lottie was impressed by the fully equipped gym that Charlotte had built in her basement, filled with a running machine, an elliptical, a reformer Pilates machine and several machines and bands that she didn't recognise but understood would inevitably target every body part with military precision. She quickly counted what was approximately twelve machines, along with a punching bag and exercise mats stacked up beside a mirrored wall that ran alongside the entire length of the room. There were no windows and adjoining the ceiling were a couple of air conditioning machines and music speakers that looked down upon her as she stood studying the reflection of herself in the mirrored walls.

Thinking a joke may lighten the mood she attempted to get Gunter on side.

"Ah, so you are my new torturer. How very exciting. I shall look forward to working with you."

Gunter did not respond instead opting to avoid eye contact and continue with his rather monotone instructions.

"Each week we are going to build on what we have done, so weights will get a little heavier, sessions will get a little harder and you will get a little fitter. This morning though, I just want to determine your current level of fitness so we know your baseline fitness level."

Right, thought Lottie, not really listening to the specifics. *I guess serious is the new black around here.* She wondered at that moment if people who were serious about their lives could also have a sense of humour. Was it really possible to have both? Then she thought perhaps it's not that they are too serious it's just that perhaps she just wasn't that funny.

Nonetheless, she bit her lip and complied with her directives. She was placed on a running machine and what looked like a large oxygen mask was placed over her mouth and was asked to run as fast as she could for as long as she could without stopping. Gunter had a big screen in the gym which seemingly tracked all the data which was being tracked in real-time from her various tracking devices implanted in her body.

Although running had never been her forte, she did her best to run at a fairly steady pace but noticed Gunter kept turning up the speed and writing things down. She must have run for what felt like ten minutes before she felt like her legs were going to fly off her torso. The next thing she knew was that she had been flung off the machine and had landed on the floor face mask still intact but facing upwards like an elephant who had fallen onto her back after attempting to climb a tree.

Gunter's face appeared in front of her and with a swift gesture of a hand she stood up, catching herself in the reflection of the mirrored wall, she looked bright red and had been sweating so much her black leggings were clinging to her nether regions in a rather unsightly manner.

"OK, so you ran for three and half minutes."

"Three and a half minutes, bloody hell it felt like a lot longer than that. Are you sure?"

"No, it was three minutes thirty-three seconds," replied Gunter, monotone and serious. "We need to improve your overall fitness level."

Yes, I gathered as much thought Lottie as she stood panting, her hands on her hips next to the machine.

"Sorry", she gasped. "I didn't realise you were going to up the speed quite so fast. I wasn't ready for that."

"You can't always be ready for everything. We want to get you ready to be as adaptable as possible and that comes through the element of surprise. The body needs shocking every now and then to improve. We need to tear the muscle to repair the muscle."

"Right," replied Lottie before jumping back on the machine and attempting to improve her performance. *Tear the muscle to repair the muscle. Joy.*

Despite the rocky fitness test at the start, the rest of the session hadn't been too bad. Lottie had managed the weight-bearing exercises just about and actually enjoyed herself towards the end. Her muscles were tired and weary but they felt used and that gave her a feeling of accomplishment. She thought back to when she was at school and remembered how she was always so competitive. When the gun would blast for the one-hundred-metre sprint, she would run as fast as her legs could carry her and the one thing that truly spurred her on was sensing the swift approach from a nearby competitor. She could feel their breath over her shoulder and the thud of their feet and she pushed herself, wanting to win. She was rarely a winner, but if anything, she always felt as though she had given it her best effort. She felt the same way that morning, like catching up to Charlotte would become her new thrill, and she was excited to begin the journey to close in on her competitor.

She spent some time after her session reading. Thankfully she had always been a fast reader and within an hour had made solid progress on her first book *'The Magic of Thinking Big'*. It spoke about the excuses people make in their lives that stop them from achieving their goals. She found it interesting and considered for a moment what her excuses were. Was she telling herself she was too inexperienced, too young, not qualified enough? Yes, probably, and it gave her food for thought that perhaps she needed to have a few more conversations with herself questioning how she talked to herself.

For lunch, Nico had given her a masterclass in making vegan beetroot and lentil tabbouleh which she devoured, along with some fruit and by six o'clock she had completed all of the tasks on her to-do list; working out, reading, meditating (or at least attempting to listen to a meditation track Charlotte had recommended on Spotify which she tried incredibly hard not to laugh at), she had even started looking into what her blueprint for success would be. She decided she too would explore writing, as it was always something she loved doing and it had worked for Charlotte.

Lottie was feeling good, as she sat on her bed she felt as though if she broke this all down it would be manageable. Besides, she had so much support to succeed she really had no excuses now.

She was just starting to wonder where Charlotte was when she heard the front door open and an *"I'm home"*. As she neared the landing she saw Charlotte come in with a brown paper bag under her arm and a warm smile.

"Hi Lottie, how was your day? I thought as a little welcome treat we could have some organic non-alcoholic wine! It is Saturday evening after all!"

Sorry, what? Thought Lottie, *Oh god, it sounds vile.*

"Oh wow, I never knew such a thing existed", replied Lottie trying not to laugh, helping her with the bag and trying not to hide the levels of disappointment in her voice at such a thing.

"Yes, I've had a good day so far. I have made a good start on everything, to be honest. So far so good."

The two women made their way into the kitchen and Charlotte look off her cream wrap coat and draped it over a nearby chair.

"Yes, it will be good to get myself into a solid routine. I'm looking forward to going back into the office on Monday for work," continued Lottie cautiously. "I'm curious as to what happened with Will. I gather I'm not working for him anymore?"

Charlotte pulled out a couple of glasses from the cupboard above the sink as they clinked together, and started opening the rather odd-looking wine bottle.

"No, that's right Lottie. You're not".

Charlotte paused to pour the wine. It was clear from her body language she wasn't all that keen to talk about it.

"I stopped working for him a long time ago, as soon as I realised I had to start putting myself first. The thing is, Will is a very talented man but he was, unfortunately, using me for his own benefit so I had to put a stop to it. It took me a while to realise he was simply keeping me down to keep himself up. He was holding me back. You have to realise Lottie, although he had the initial vision for the company he didn't have the ability to make it happen. You did more than you will ever know to help that man get to where he once was, and it was time things were put back into a logical pattern. How the mighty have fallen huh?"

Lottie was struck by her use of words *How the mighty have fallen…*'

"What do you mean? What happened, was he demoted?"

"Yes, in a sense he was. I told the board I had done

most of the work over the years and he'd taken the credit and they took my side. I tried to get him fired but they couldn't do that as had rights to the idea blah blah blah, so I settled on him being demoted to work somewhere in development. Michael and the others didn't seem that bothered about any of it really. You see, when I worked for him I stopped supplying him with anything that he could put his name to and I called out any work I had done so they knew and understood his value, and more importantly mine. Remember, I don't expect you to work for that company for long, only long enough to learn how to resign as that's a crucial step in learning how to stand up for yourself. One of the most important factors in getting confidence is acquiring it. Nobody is born confident you have to learn how to develop it, and one of the best ways is to make sure you are always standing up for yourself.

"Anyway, tonight is not the night to talk about work, we have the next few weeks and months to get into all that. Tonight, I want us to get to know each other and relax."

Charlotte moved towards her cream coloured sofas in the living room and sprawled herself out comfortably.

"Sounds good," replied Lottie, following Charlotte, rather glad this was on the agenda for the evening. "I have to ask you Charlotte. Did anything ever happen with you and Will?"

"What do you mean romantically? Oh god! I forgot I was totally in love with him wasn't I?" She laughed incredulously at the prospect "All of that feels like a million years ago. Let's just say the tables turned significantly in that department. Will was after me for years but

I would never go there. He was too messed up. Besides, I don't know if you may have noticed…"

Charlotte was grinning and moving her ring finger up and down. How had Lottie not noticed the huge rock that was placed on her hand? In all of the shock from the reveal, she had clearly been distracted. Or perhaps Charlotte hadn't been wearing it until now? It was a stunning emerald cut diamond with a beautifully intricate silver band.

"Oh my god! No, I didn't even…Let me see!"

Lottie admired the ring. It was enormous, and although she knew little about jewellery even she could tell it looked expensive. Watching it sparkle brightly beneath the ambient living room lights she became more and more convinced that she would have noticed had Charlotte been wearing this before.

She must have just put it on…

"Congratulations Charlotte! Wow! Who is the lucky man?"

"Well, you know…a certain someone." Charlotte was being coy. "Ever heard of a Mr Oliver Scarsdale?"

Lottie stared at Charlotte, a stunned expression crossing her face. She wasn't sure whether she was having her on.

"Oliver Scarsdale? The actor?" replied Lottie incredulously.

"Yup, the one and only. We've been dating for about two years now. Honestly, Lottie, he's just so perfect. Just such a gentleman They are so rare these days, you know?"

Lottie nodded trying hard not to widen her eyes and keep it cool. She started thinking back to his accolades.

Oliver Scarsdale had starred in some of the biggest grossing movies of all time and was one of the UK's most successful exports to Hollywood. His ex-wife was the supermodel Pandora White! Not only could he not put a foot wrong in terms of his film choices but he was notorious for only dating the most beautiful women in the world.

Sorry, what? How on earth did this happen? Oliver Scarsdale?

"I can't believe it! How did you meet?" Lottie was shocked but also truly excited and intimidated about the prospect that she had it in her to be dating someone like him, that *he* could fancy *her*?

I mean Charlotte does look good but really?

"Yeah we met at Annabel's one night," continued Charlotte. "He was totally charming and we hit it off straight away. You'll see what I mean when you meet him, he's going to pop over this evening to say hi, he's excited to meet you."

"What? He's coming here?"

Suddenly Lottie went from feeling excited to getting a wave of anxiety. *With me looking like this?* Somehow being cocooned in this house from the moment she had left the office had given her an odd sense of security and the notion of a Hollywood movie star just popping in just seemed so unappealing, especially as he would just be seeing her standing next to the goddess that was Charlotte looking anything but 'ready'.

"Don't worry, he's totally down to earth and cool," replied Charlotte with a wave of the hand. "I wonder what Nico has fixed us for dinner," she said casually changing the subject and pulling out her phone ready for another social media update highlighting what was cooking in the kitchen.

Charlotte really did have everything she could possibly wish for, financial security, a wonderful career, a perfect body, wealth, status and to top it all off she was about to marry a global movie-star sex symbol. Everything just seemed so perfect. Surely this couldn't all be in her future? It all seemed too good to be true.

As Charlotte danced into the kitchen clutching her non-alcoholic vegan wine, whilst speaking to her 'followers' enthusiastically, Lottie took the opportunity to head upstairs. She wanted a moment to herself, or better still to put on a little makeup if Oliver Scarsdale was about to 'casually pop over'. It was clear Charlotte was thinking the same as not long after she had gone upstairs, she heard the familiar noise of a hairdryer coming from Charlotte's room. Lottie was secretly relieved she did do her own hair and makeup *sometimes.*

The doorbell rang calling out throughout the house.

"That'll be Oliver," called Charlotte "Would you mind answering the door, Lottie? I think Tessa's off-duty. I'll be down in a moment."

"Ok", Lottie shouted back, glad to be getting on such familiar terms with Charlotte as she quickly blotted in some under-eye concealer, added a little mascara fluffed up her hair and walked casually down the stairs to open the door.

Fiddling with the fussy front door lock she twisted and pulled the awkward bolts she had remembered from the morning before. Before she knew it the door had creaked open and the one and only Oliver Scarsdale was standing in front her, smiling from ear to ear. He was even more handsome in the flesh, taller than he appeared on screen, his skin soft and tanned with small dimples in his cheeks that she'd never noticed in his films before. He was wearing a brown leather jacket and white shirt with a belt that drew attention to his very flat, very toned stomach.

"Well, can I come in?"

Oliver Scarsdale is here, that's Oliver Scarsdale. THE Oliver Scarsdale. Say something, Lottie. Say something. Anything. Speak!

Lottie found herself pinching her palms again just to check she had feeling there and that she wasn't dreaming. She was clamming up, fumbling her words.

Be cool, be cool, be Charlotte, think Charlotte…

"Uhhh. Oh yes of course," replied Lottie staring perhaps a little too hard at him. She quickly looked to the ground to try to rectify this.

Wait. What would Charlotte do?

She looked up at him as confidently as she could.

You have to acquire confidence.

As Oliver entered the house he looked Lottie up and down too. The pair of them were staring at each other with a huge amount of interest and incredulity.

"Wow," he said as he circled her like an art installation.

"That's amazing. You look so different."

Worse, you mean. I look worse…

"Hi, I'm Lottie" she managed, embarrassed. She reached out a hand for a handshake but he laughed and leaned in for a kiss on the cheek.

"Nice to meet you. You know I have to be honest you're much more beautiful than I was expecting. When Charlotte told me what was going on I thought it all sounded crazy! I mean I wasn't sure what to expect but you are very lovely."

He's a pro. Total charmer, and talking total BS.

"Thanks," she replied knowing full well he meant none of it.

Just as the two of them were done with exchanging niceties Charlotte emerged at the top of the stairs wearing a black and gold mini dress with long sleeves and some cowboy boots looking every inch the glamorous rock chick and totally overdressed. Lottie looked down at her denim jeans and top and felt thoroughly outshone once again. Not that it was a competition in the looks department. There was no competing with Charlotte at this stage if she was being truly honest with herself — but all of this did make her feel about the size of a pea.

"Oh, Lottie. Here's my phone can you film us greeting each other for my Insta followers?"

Lottie did as instructed and stood at the bottom of the stairs with her phone in hand.

"Tell me when you're ready Lottie."

Lottie found this all very bizarre. Oliver stood waiting before he said anything, as though he were used to it.

"Ok. Charlotte, on the count of three."

Without hesitation, as if rehearsed to perfection, Oliver bounded up the stairs two at a time to greet Charlotte, placing a very passionate kiss on her cheek.

"Darling you look spectacular as always. What a dress. I'm the luckiest man in the world."

He took Charlotte's hand and helped her walk down the stairs. Charlotte was grinning like a Cheshire cat, looking into the camera of the phone.

"I can't quite believe how amazing it is to have another version of you here. You're still so incomparable."

Oliver looked at Lottie, who was still filming this bizarre spectacle. She wasn't sure about any of it. They looked as though they were two actors doing a scene from a movie. Lottie stopped filming and handed the phone back to Charlotte who quickly asked whether she had got it before burying her head in her phone to post it. Lottie and Oliver stared at each other awkwardly, waiting for Charlotte to finish.

"So what do you think of my protégée?" Charlotte said, returning the conversation and draping her arm around Oliver's shoulder. "Isn't she amazing? In no time I'm going to have her in ship shape."

The two laughed rather haughtily at each other.

"Well, I look forward to seeing you work your magic on her darling," Oliver said as he took Charlotte's arm and guided her into the kitchen.

Lottie could feel herself frowning at the oddness of the situation. She found herself transfixed on them both as though she were watching a pivotal moment in a movie or some incredibly engrossing reality TV show. This was who she would become in the future? Would her character and personality really change that much? This was who she would date and this was where she would live and this is what she would wear. She still couldn't get her head around quite how odd this all was and for some reason, it wasn't sitting quite right with her. Was it really realistic but more importantly, was it really, her?

"How are you my darling?" Charlotte gushed to Oliver, sounding even more well-spoken than she had been five minutes before. "God, I have missed you. Would you like a drink? Let's have dinner. Nico's prepared us all something delicious and I am starving!"

Lottie followed behind the two lovebirds and watched the two of them sit next to each other on bar stools in the kitchen, giggling into each other's necks as they did, with Charlotte's phone never far away. She had balanced it on the fruit bowl and was filming their entire conversation. They were all over each other which she found surprising considering they had apparently been dating for a couple of years. She thought back to her last boyfriend, Alex. It was a while ago already but she was pretty sure the honeymoon period only lasted a month or two before they both got a bit bored of each other. She wondered how they were keeping things so fresh and how often they saw each other.

Lost for what to say, and feeling tremendously like a third wheel, Lottie started to feel a little uncomfortable at their rather excessive levels of affection and so, keen to distract herself she checked her phone. Looking at the 'Best Self' app she noted that she had only consumed 750 calories today and was starving — and interestingly her heartbeat was at an all-day high.

As Oliver stepped away from the loving restraints of Charlotte he poured himself a glass of non-alcoholic, organic, vegan wine, sensing Lottie was feeling left out.

"So, Lottie," Oliver gestured. "How do you feel about seeing Charlotte? Is it very surreal?"

Lottie was grateful for being included in the conversation at last, and it struck her that nobody had actually asked her that question since this whole bizarre journey began. Nobody had really questioned how she was feeling in the present, it had all been so focused on who she could become in the future.

"Yeah, it's pretty bizarre to be honest, just to see her walking around in front of me, living here, dating you. I mean, wow!"

Keen to not make out like she was flirting with Oliver and sensing an icy stare, she added.

"I mean, you know to have all of this, to see all of this. It's pretty amazing. Charlotte is amazing. All I can do is hope I can do her justice by working hard."

Charlotte was reassured at the addition to that sentence and grinned proudly and leant her head into Oliver's neck as the two of them stood with their arms interlocked. Lottie felt compelled to fill the silence and keep talking. She noticed Charlotte had her phone in her hands again, filming her speak.

"I mean, at first I felt terrible, you know like someone had just punched me in the stomach several times," she laughed trying to lighten the mood "as to be quite honest with you I didn't realise I had been getting it so wrong. I mean, the whole idea behind this filter is crazy."

"Yes," replied Oliver. "Well, we only live once right, we might as well make the most out of it. I wonder what I would be like if I lived my best life," Oliver asked them both while looking at Charlotte.

"Oh darling, you're perfect already I couldn't imagine anybody better."

Charlotte leant over him giving him another slightly over-affectionate kiss on his lips. Lottie stood there slightly weirded out by their behaviour. Oliver seemed too lovely, so charming, so handsome. She still couldn't quite get over how this could happen to her, a simple EA from Weymouth. How on Earth could she end up being engaged to someone like him? Lottie thought of Will once again, how he'd always been the ultimate man for her, so incredibly handsome, and they just had this connection, but even she could admit he wasn't perfect. She knew about his past. Everybody knew it was all over the society magazines; the 'modeliser,' the stints in rehab, his difficult relationship with his parents. He was the eternal bachelor who had yet to settle down, who had yet to find the one, and this led to him being eternally alluring in Lottie's eyes.

Yet Charlotte had stopped seeing him that way. She could barely remember the fact she was ever in love with him. She had moved on. She had replaced Will with this god-like man who seemed to be the full package, and what's more he clearly utterly adored her. *Perhaps*, Lottie thought to herself, as she sat down to observe the two feeding each other their dinner, almost as though she weren't there. *All I need to do is find someone I like more than Will*. She had never really considered it as, to her, he was so perfect, but maybe it was time for her to expect more from her life. Perhaps Charlotte was right, her perceptions had been flawed.

That hadn't stopped her thinking about him though, despite what Charlotte said. Her feelings had been there for ten years they couldn't just disappear overnight, and seeing Charlotte so loved up had only reminded her of how alone she was.

The evening continued with what felt like pleasantries. Charlotte was right, Oliver was totally charming. He paused to listen when she spoke and laughed at her stories. She could see why Charlotte was so smitten but there was something about the interactions between them that felt all too perfect. There was no vulnerability there, conversations were fluffy and light, everything felt very staged. Then there was the fact that so much of what they said was repeated into Charlotte's phone for her followers to see, it was constantly clutched in Charlotte's hand — so much so that she noticed she ate her dinner using only a fork.

Lottie put her head on her impossibly fluffy pillow

that night and thought it all through. As much as she was aware their relationship seemed envious, something about it all just seemed a little unrealistic.

CHAPTER
Thirteen

"How was Lottie's first weekend in the filter?" Will asked the analyst as he put his coat over the back of his chair and ushered the man to enter his office.

It was Monday morning and Lottie had been in the filter a full weekend. Will was keen to see some stats he could relay to the board and was curious to see how she was getting on.

"Really good so far. The good news is that we are pulling the data snippets through as intended, and the quality is fine. The bad news is that we're only getting short clips at the moment, around three minutes each so we can't see much - but we're working on pulling through more.

All her vitals are stable. She went into a slight state of shock for a few hours after the reveal where her heart rate was all over the place, as expected, but seems to have been coping remarkably well since then. We can see she has already started her workout regime, and so far we are seeing a noticeable calorie deficit so if she continues like this she'll soon start to shed the weight. Anyway, I have a full report coming your way but I know you're probably keen to see some of the clips."

"Yes, I can't wait."

The man had his laptop open and balancing on his hand and he walked keenly towards Will's desk where he positioned it in between the keyboard and mouse on Will's desk.

"Ok, here we go. So we have three short clips of what Lottie sees. As you know we also have all the supporting statistical data being fed in automatically from her microchip — but I think you're going to find what you're about to see pretty amazing."

The man pressed play and Will sat beside him with bated breath. He was keen to see not only if this had worked but he really wanted to see if Lottie was ok. He hadn't stopped thinking about her all weekend, wondering what she was seeing, who she was with. There was motion on the screen and suddenly Will saw the familiar interior of the elevator office, Michael was standing next to Lottie and as the doors opened she was faced with a crowd of people, some familiar to Will, some not at all. Lottie seemed to be walking through the office towards a stage towards a woman dressed in a white dress who had her back to Lottie sitting on a chair. Michael was guiding her to a stage and giving a speech. He explained a bit about the filter as Lottie sat down looking out to the crowd of faces.

"This must be Lottie's best self right?" Will asked the analyst. His name was Jed and he was one of the newer members of his team. Super bright, and very conscientious Jed was keen to please as much as possible.

"Yep, that's right. She refers to herself as Charlotte though," replied Jed. "Check out the moment they meet." He was smiling with anticipation.

Then Will watched as the woman in white turned around.

"Oh my god."

He squinted his eyes in astonishment.

"Oh my god. Oh my god. Oh my god".

Could this really be Lottie? The woman was a vision. She had the body of Elle Macpherson, lean and toned, not overly muscly, with a radiant face, natural, with makeup highlighting her more defined cheekbones and green eyes. She was stunning, a beauty, moving with grace and poise. She confidently hugged Lottie before turning around to see the crowd, holding their hands up together as victors of their own championship. They were the winners of their own lives. Charlotte was unshackled by not living in the shadow of her potential, she had become what she could become, and she looked sensational.

Will could see Michael Dalton standing at the front alongside a few other people he didn't recognise. He couldn't see many familiar faces from the office, everyone looked different. In fact, he couldn't even see himself. *That's odd*, he thought to himself. *Where the hell am I?*

"Is that all we've got from the reveal?" Will asked as the clip suddenly stopped playing.

"Yes, I'm afraid so Will. We do have a couple more though hang on."

Jed loaded up the other snippets and pressed play. The second one was of Lottie in a gym with a blonde-haired man pushing some weights. That must be her first workout, thought Will.

Good good.

Then he played the final clip. It looked like Lottie was in a kitchen with Charlotte and the two of them were deep in conversation.

"Anyway, tonight is not the night to talk about work, we have the next few weeks and months to get into all that. Tonight, I want us to get to know each other and relax."

"Sounds good. I have to ask you Charlotte. Did anything ever happen with you and Will?"

"What do you mean romantically? Oh god! I forgot I was in love with him for ages, wasn't I? All of that feels like a million years ago. Let's just say the tables turned significantly in that department. Will was after me for years but I would never go there. He was too messed up. Besides, I don't know if you may have noticed ..."

"Oh my god! No, I didn't even...Let me see!"

"Congratulations Charlotte! Who is the lucky man?"

"A certain someone... Ever heard of a Mr Oliver Scarsdale?"

"Oliver Scarsdale? The actor?"

"Yes, the one and only. We've been dating for about two years now. Honestly, Lottie, he's just so perfect. Just such a gentleman. They are so rare these days, you know?"

"I can't believe it! How did you meet?"

"Yeah, we met at Annabel's one night. He was totally charming and we hit it off straight away. I mean, you'll see what I mean when you meet him, he's going to pop in this evening to say hi, he's excited to meet you."

"What? He's coming here?"

"Don't worry, he's totally down to earth and cool. I wonder what Nico has fixed us for dinner."

The clip continued and a short while later Will saw Lottie move throughout the house in the direction of a bedroom, her bedroom where she was staying in no doubt. The house looked impressive. She was walking away from the kitchen through a beautiful open plan living room stacked with books and up some glass stairs before the clip stopped.

"Wow," said Will looking up at Jed for some sort of reaction.

Jed was nodding with a smile as though he didn't know quite what to say to that or how Will would react. Then Will burst out laughing, impressed.

"Oliver bloody Scarsdale!"

He looked at the desk Lottie used to sit at and thought of her. Beneath the girl who never liked to draw attention to herself was a bona fide force to be reckoned with.

"I know it's pretty unbelievable to be honest Will," continued Jed with a smile. "I don't think anyone could have predicted that. I mean, not just how she looks but did you check out the house! Wow!"

Will thanked Jed and asked him to leave the files with him, he would take it from here and show the board what they needed to see. Part of him was elated with satisfaction at the incredible success of Charlotte, but he couldn't help but feel an inkling of concern too.

Why was he not at the reveal and why had Charlotte dismissed him so unequivocally? He put Lottie inside the filter because she was someone they could trust, she always delivered and because she deserved the opportunity. Yet, something about the way Charlotte was speaking denoted that she had changed. She was not one to live by the rules of others anymore. She was there to be whoever she needed to become, and she would do whatever it took to get what she wanted.

Will sat at his desk playing the clip from the reveal on repeat and pausing it to try to see himself in the crowd. He played the scene when Lottie looked out towards the crowds frame by frame. He couldn't see himself anywhere near the front.

Then he saw himself. There he was. He recognised his shirt. He was standing at the back of the room by the window with his arms crossed.

CHAPTER
Fourteen

CHARLOTTE SAT AT HER DESK FLICKING THROUGH THE newspapers. All very complimentary to herself she was pleased to see. The media had gone wild at the notion that one could live side-by-side with ones best self and that she was the shining example of the ideal. The Daily Mail had gone with the headline *"Beauty and the Reject,"* the Sun had asked, *"Is this the most perfect woman in the world?"* Newspaper after newspaper printed Charlotte and Lottie side by side with their hands up victoriously. Charlotte looked good. She liked the way her arm muscles were so lean in comparison to Lottie's. She liked the way everyone was calling her 'perfect,' 'a miracle woman'. The Times had written in detail about the technology behind the filter claiming it was a *'technological feat, unlike any other in Britain today.'*

The press were proud of this development, the media were hungry for optimism, investors were chomping at the bit to get a piece of the action and Charlotte was aware of what her role in all of this was. She was there to be seen to coach Lottie, to be her mentor, to let her live with her and marvel at her level of commitment and dedication to building a better life for herself. However, Charlotte had doubts that Lottie could really pull all of this off. Looking at this young woman who emerged before her, she didn't remember ever being that way, ever being so shy and keen to please. She couldn't remember how it felt to be so easily manipulated. To think she still asked after Will!

No, Charlotte wasn't really worried Lottie would rise to become the powerhouse and threat they all hoped she would become. Despite being cut from the same cloth Charlotte felt she had such a long way to go before she would even remotely be anywhere near her level. As she sat there, reading all the wonderfully complementary articles on how good she looked, and what an inspiration she was, she smiled at herself conceitedly. No, she wasn't really worried about Lottie one bit, she didn't stand a chance to make it in her world, especially not in the timeframe they are hoping for. It will take months, years to pull this off! She had nothing to worry about.

She thought for a moment as she tapped her fingers on her desk before her phone buzzed before her. It was Michael Dalton.

"Hello darling," she answered coyly. "I take it you have seen our press?"

"Well, all I can say Charlotte is once again, you never cease to amaze me. I mean, I knew the big reveal would make waves, but we have only gone and started a tsunami! We have officially broken the internet. My phone has been ringing off the hook. I know we wanted some hype pre-IPO Charlotte but this is on another level."

Charlotte laughed coyly and shrugged her shoulders.

"What can I say, Michael? I always knew the press would love this story."

"Is this the most perfect woman in the world?" Michael read a paragraph to Charlotte that she had already read. "*Friday saw the unveiling of what looks set to become a technological game-changer, a filter to show you who you could become if you were really living your best life, and the results speak for themselves.* Jemima is going to be on your case today no doubt, everyone is scrambling for the exclusive."

Jemima was in charge of the marketing and PR surrounding the launch of this prototype. She was good as she was easy to control and didn't ask too many questions. Young and inexperienced, Charlotte liked the fact she just did what she was told and seemed proactive enough to just get any press booked in around a tight and well-organised schedule.

"Yes, I have spoken to her already this morning and both Lottie and I have a schedule for press over this coming week including TV and print. It's exciting and great publicity too for my new book."

Not that Michael would care about that, but Charlotte was keen to prove she was still at the top of her field. Still delivering, still dazzling. With so much talk in recent months of this filter, Charlotte didn't want anyone to forget that she was indeed a renowned author, somewhat of a celebrity, and she most certainly wasn't done yet.

She also knew very well how to play the game. Having such glowing press would only mean more copies of her book would fly off the shelves. She was delighted to be seen as the guru in this story, as the expert, as the role model. Lottie would sit there, sheepishly during interviews no doubt, and let her do the talking anyway. She was becoming a master chess player in her own life, carefully managing relationships with those around her to her benefit. Michael was another such character. The two of them had become very close in recent months especially as Charlotte knew how much power and control he had over her life. One call from him and the filter could be shut down completely, so Charlotte was keen to keep him sweet, and he certainly didn't seem to be complaining.

"Let's keep Lottie focused," he said. "We want a positive story when it comes to her doing what she needs to do as quickly as possible. We want her in and out remember. It can't be seen to drag on for months."

"Oh, absolutely Michael; Don't you worry," replied Charlotte cooly. "She's been set her first challenge and seems to be doing well. If she's anything like me I have little doubt she will."

Except that was a lie and Charlotte knew it. As Charlotte checked her eyebrows weren't out of place in a pocket mirror in her desk draw she took a deep breath. She had plenty of doubts about Lottie achieving what she needed, about any of this at all. There was a lot of work to do there, a lot of weight to lose, a whole plan for success to develop. She couldn't pull this off surely, and when Lottie failed, which she would, it would mean ever greater press for her. All of this just fed into a brand image about herself that she liked, that she was perfect and that her levels of success were totally unobtainable.

She certainly didn't welcome the notion that someone like Lottie would be stepping on her toes, and although she never mentioned this to Michael, it's certainly how she felt.

"When am I seeing you?" Michael hushed quietly down the phone.

"Soon," replied Charlotte. "We just have to be careful who sees us. All eyes are on me now."

CHAPTER
Fifteen

It was hard for Lottie to pinpoint when exactly she started to feel better but she had been adopting a new life-style for a little under a month when the results really began to show. Not only did she have more energy from a new and improved diet, but her body had different cravings. She no longer wanted to eat sugary foods or carbs, instead she really wanted the good fuel that came from eating clean. She was exercising six days a week and her body was starting to change. Her clothes felt looser, her muscles felt tighter and she was starting to stand taller.

However, it wasn't all plain sailing. The first few days were a challenge and she could barely walk after some of her sessions with Gunter. In her first week, she felt light-headed, hungry and craving more food for the amount she was working out. She almost passed out one morning when she had to work out on an empty stomach after not feeling like she had eaten much the day before.

"We need to get you in a calorie deficit for the engine

to burn your fat," Gunter told her matter of factly, as he stood over her on the floor and gazed down at her upside down.

"You will feel tired and weak but you have to learn to stop making excuses and to use your mind to your advantage. Tell yourself it's ok and to get up and keep going."

One thing that Gunter was not, was forgiving. He didn't want to hear anything other than the words 'yes' and 'ok', and anything deemed even slightly resembling an excuse would be met by strong words. She was not allowed to say she was tired or hungry or sore from previous workouts. She was simply expected to develop a fighter's mind and get on with it.

"Kickboxing helps Charlotte get the anger out," he would say. "Anytime you feel you want to get it out just learn the basic moves. This is what she does," and he would proceed to show her exactly how she did it.

It had certainly become clear in that month that Charlotte had seemingly become quite the expert in many things. Lottie had not just read her three books a week as per her challenge instructions, but she had been keen to read the books that Charlotte wrote too to see what the fuss was about and whether she had it in her to write well. She couldn't deny that the books were page-turners and that the characters were likeable and funny. In fact, the main character running through all of her books was a lady called Violet De Gaulle who rose up the ranks in certain social circles to eventually marry a prince. It was a real love story, a perfect chick-lit trilogy, and hugely aspirational. Lottie couldn't help but wonder if writing about such aspirational lives only helped Charlotte better envisage hers. Much of what Violet had in her life became 'ideal,' the cook, the trainer, the driver, the handsome boyfriend, the flowers that were always elegantly positioned on every prominent cabinet in the house, the designer wardrobe. She too had it all.

However, she didn't feel as tuned into this sort of fairy-tale life just yet. She didn't understand the designer handbags and shoes and the need for hair and makeup to pop by each day to beautify Charlotte. It wasn't that she resented Charlotte doing it, it's just she couldn't identify with it. It wasn't something that really drove her and she did find herself questioning at what point that changed for Charlotte. At what point would she suddenly desire such things? *Maybe when I actually have enough money to splurge I will,* she thought, but then she would always hear her mother's voice in her head saying, *'you spent how much on that? Oh, that's ridiculous.'*

No, she thought it over and decided she wanted to write about something else. As much as she loved writing, she wanted to find her niche and was much more intrigued by the art of crime writing. She loved reading crime mysteries, trying to work out how the crimes were committed, who was involved, and she would almost always feel as though she had learnt a little something reading a crime novel, even if it was morbid facts related to how long a body took to decompose or how to commit a perfect murder.

It was a perfect way to meet her goal of creating her blueprint for success too. She would focus on crime writing much like Charlotte had become a chick-lit queen. So she read voraciously that month, absorbing as many writing style ideas as she could, and sought to find relatable, likeable characters who could fit into a compelling storyline. By the end of the month, she had developed an outline for her debut novel, and when she had shown it to Charlotte she was fairly disappointed with her subdued reaction to it. She wasn't incredibly complimentary and excited, which in turn, led Lottie to wonder if she was barking up the wrong tree.

In fact, it wasn't just that. Lottie had certainly noticed a subtle shift in Charlotte over the weeks since they met. While her energy and enthusiasm towards her at the beginning had been open and warm, full of encouragement. Lottie had noticed she was slightly more distant lately. She had been colder, curter and less pleased or impressed with her progress. She didn't seem to want to acknowledge that Lottie was already a dress size down and that her efforts had been nothing short of remarkable. She was too busy working on her new book and doing interviews with the press to give Lottie the sort of mentoring she had envisaged getting, and that was fine. It was just, her attitude towards her had changed and around the house, she seemed quiet and withdrawn, with an incredible ability to turn on the charm when talking to her Instagram followers or the press.

The first week they had spent together after the big reveal was really overwhelming. The two of them were being ushered from interview to interview, from radio station to TV network. The brief Lottie was given was almost always the same. A young girl called Jemima would thrust some notes in front of Lottie's face and essentially brief her to "Just let Charlotte do most of the talking. If they do ask you any questions just defer to how amazed you are at Charlotte and that you're so motivated to improve."

Lottie, sitting next to Charlotte at such moments, felt compelled to do as she was told. Charlotte was the star of the show here and this was her time to shine. She was merely a subpar version living in her shadow. Besides, here she was, living in her house, getting the benefit of her knowledge and expertise, the last thing she wanted to seem was publicly ungrateful, even if she did find some of the interviews positively nauseating.

Questions repeatedly fired her way included;

"Lottie, how does it feel seeing the perfect version of yourself?"

"Lottie, did you realise you had quite so much to improve upon?"

"Lottie, what's Charlotte really like at home. Is she always this perfect?"

"Lottie, what's impressed you most about Charlotte?

Each time Lottie had a well-versed response and Jemima would be sitting close by, clipboard in hand nodding attentively at every sentence she uttered, guiding her to adhere to the brief with such ruthless precision it was positively patronising.

'This Morning' wanted an interview to include Charlotte's famous fiancé Oliver Scarsdale, and they insisted he sit in the middle of them on the sofa where they proceeded to ask him all about their different appearances.

"What's it like seeing your fiancé like this?"

"Oliver, is there any part of you that is attracted to them both?"

It was incredibly humiliating and Lottie just sat there through it all, trying to keep a smile on her face whilst Oliver and Charlotte held hands and leaned in towards each other adoringly saying how much they definitely preferred each other. Before each interview, Lottie told Charlotte what to wear, usually something modest and shapeless, and then she herself would then emerge with seven-inch heels, a perma-tan, perfect hair and a figure-hugging dress.

Lottie brushed it all off however like water off a duck's back. This was all part of the process, and in fact, galling as it was this only served to fuel Lottie's motivation all the more, as though the more she were pushed down, the further she wanted to bounce back. The humiliation was something that Lottie was finding herself getting used to and as much as she was encouraged to 'speak her truth', she also just found it made more sense to ignore all of this silly nonsense and focus on getting herself to where she needed to be.

However, there were a few things that weren't adding up in Lottie's mind. She was still not convinced about the relationship Charlotte had with Oliver. If her first impressions had been that it all seemed too perfect, this had only been reinforced as the weeks progressed. It appeared that they only really saw each other once a week on Friday evenings, and usually, that consisted of Oliver popping over to the house to pick up Charlotte and tell her how wonderful she looked, often advising her on her outfit choice, recording a few videos of the two of them on Instagram and then they would then go out to some hotspot in London for dinner or drinks, photos of which would always make their way into the newspapers.

She had also noticed that whenever Oliver would call she would put him on speaker for the whole house to be privy to their phone calls. Lottie would sit reading on the sofas downstairs when suddenly her train of thought would be interrupted by the sound of Oliver's voice. Then when Charlotte would put down the phone she had said on more than one occasion 'Bless Oliver, he's so gorgeous and charming but he's just not terribly bright is he?' Then she would proceed to laugh haughtily as though Lottie were somehow meant to be in on the joke.

Then there were the other mysterious phone calls. Sometimes when the phone rang Charlotte would quickly disappear into her bedroom or take a walk in the garden. Lottie wasn't sure who it was, but she was certain it wasn't Oliver. She was only too proud to let the world know all about their relationship details, and this person was handled privately, discreetly like she didn't want anyone knowing they were talking. Charlotte would say things like "Not now," and "we have to be careful who sees us." Something about her behaviour struck her as off.

As the weeks progressed she, like Charlotte, also started getting a lot of press attention. Lottie found paparazzi hiding outside the house keen to snap either one of them coming or going as proof as to whether this filter was succeeding or not. There were news trucks parked outside the house with satellite dishes on their roofs eagerly awaiting a constant stream of updates, and Lottie wondered how disappointing they must feel on days where nobody even left the house.

With all of this press attention and hype, it really wasn't a difficult decision to quit her job as an EA. Not only was she feeling wholly put down by Charlotte for ever having such a job, but she knew she was destined to quit anyway so why stall things The Monday morning following her reveal she, as per Charlotte's instructions, sent her new boss, Georgie Besset, an email explaining that she would no longer be coming to work nor would she be working through her one month notice period.

"They won't care." Charlotte had told her. "Don't worry about it. It's not the same place there now anyway."

Lottie never heard a peep back from them. It all seemed so painless, so easy. In her mind, the thought of resigning had always been fearful, scary and filled her with such anxiety, especially as it would involve confronting Will directly.

However, Will didn't seem to be a prominent figure in Charlotte's life now, so it would undoubtedly not be the same place there anymore. That was very clear from the big reveal. Will seemed out of the picture and she hadn't had a chance to work out why. After bringing up the topic of Will with Charlotte a few weeks ago, Lottie didn't feel it was a welcome topic to bring up again. She got the sense that she would be judged for wasting her time on someone like him when she really needed to be aiming for bigger and better things. So she had dropped it, but she couldn't shake the ardent curiosity regarding what the full story was. What's more, with Charlotte helping her to effortlessly untangle herself from her previous job via nothing more than an email Lottie hadn't had the chance to go back to the office to see if she could do some digging of her own.

She was due to go back there though. Charlotte had mentioned that her first challenge review was coming up next week and that it would be taking place at the office, so she couldn't help but wonder if she might see Will there and get the chance to talk to him. She was also so incredibly nervous, full of anxious energy wondering whether she had done enough to pass. The sheer humiliation she had felt from seeing Charlotte the very first time had been so public, it had really motivated her, and she'd worked hard, but she had no idea whether what she had done had been enough. In the month following the big reveal she had tried to follow her instructions to the letter, keeping her head down, training, reading, working hard.

She had been meditating and encouraging herself to do better, to be better.

She had no idea what to expect at her review but felt a need to protect herself by preparing for it to be even more humiliating. *It can't be as bad as it was when I first arrived*, she thought. *Anything is better than that.*

CHAPTER
Sixteen

WILL COULDN'T SHAKE THE FEELING THAT HAD BEEN IRKING HIM FOR the past few weeks. Why wasn't he a prominent figure at Lottie's reveal, why was he standing at the back with his arms crossed looking down sheepishly? What had happened in that filter?

As much as he didn't want to admit it to himself, the fact that he was there but on the periphery reinforced Will's greatest insecurities; that he wasn't good enough and the sense of imposter's syndrome he had carried around since he started this company. He imagined his father shaking his head and saying to his mother, "I was right Penny, he just doesn't have what it takes," before writing a cheque to bail him out of what- ever financial ruin he ended up in. Will's determination to succeed could only take him so far in his mind, he needed to be competent too, and that's where Lottie had helped him fill the gaps.

He had checked in on Lottie in the filter proofing facility whenever he could; relieved to see she looked comfortable, her neck propped up on padded pillows and calm as though she were simply sleeping soundly. Occasionally her eyes would tremble as though she were in an evocative part of a dream and he wondered what she was seeing, where she was going, how she felt all alone in that filter. He wondered if he was being a support to her, a friend, or whatever they were to each other — or whether she was just being Lottie and not complaining about anything or seeking help. He thought back to her favourite mug she always had on her desk that said, '*Keep calm and carry on*', and he smiled as he thought how apt it was for her character. She had never really made a fuss over anything and as he looked down on her in her bed, he knew that that was likely to change.

Will had been impressed with her transformation though. Charlotte seemed so dynamic, much more than he could ever imagine knowing Lottie's character. From watching the clips, she hadn't just transformed her life, she had developed her character. She was confident, direct, assertive and bold. There was a fearlessness about Charlotte that just seemed so at odds with Lottie, a glossiness to her exterior, a ruthlessness, and he wondered if becoming better also meant changing who you are. *Could you still be you if you decide to be better or do you lose part of yourself and give it up as a sacrifice for change?*

Despite Jed saying they would only be able to get three short clips per day Will knew he needed to push for more. Now he had seen some of what was going on, he wanted to get a fuller picture. When they designed the filter the main focus had always been on the raw data over the daily clips. Those were only meant to support the data not narrate it. However, seeing through Lottie's eyes had proven more enlightening than any statistical information they could ever have imagined.

"Well, we can't really get a huge amount more without significantly increasing the bandwidth," Jed had replied, a sideways raise of the lip. "And that doesn't come cheap, especially not if you're looking for a 24-hour live stream."

Will knew that any additional costs would have to be run past the board, and at this stage, he didn't want to have to explain why he felt it was necessary.

"Ok, so what can we do within the budget that just gives us more to see? I just want to have more to work with, and in the meantime, I will see if I can persuade the board to go for the fully live stream."

He knew that dangling a financial carrot Jed's way would get him to deliver, and he also knew it was unlikely he would be able to get a penny more out of this project from the board until they had delivered a little more in terms of results.

"Ok. Let me see what I can do. Bear with me, I'll come back to you," replied Jed helpfully.

A week later Jed had managed to increase the clips from three minutes to twenty. It wasn't great, but it was certainly better, and Will could edit these clips down just fine to show the rest of the board what he wanted them to see.

"Thank you, Jed," replied Will. "That will do nicely for now."

CHAPTER
Seventeen

I<small>T WAS UNUSUALLY WARM THAT</small> F<small>RIDAY MORNING AS</small> Lottie got herself ready. Her outfit had been left out for her by Charlotte on her bed, as per usual, whenever cameras may be present, and Lottie was disappointed to see she would be expected to wear long sleeves and long trousers in what looked set to be a fairly sweltering day in mid-July.

Nonetheless, she got herself dressed and sat down to do her hair and makeup. She noticed as she crossed her legs underneath her dressing table, that her clothes were fitting so much better, and although she didn't know exactly how much weight she had lost up until that morning she knew she was on target for the 10lb weight loss that was expected of her in the first month. She had been monitored by Gunter each week and was delighted to see that weight had indeed been coming off. Not that she was all that surprised, she had been in pretty much a constant state of hunger and had stuck religiously to her diet.

Knowing they were tracking and monitoring everything that passed her lips gave her a whole new level of accountability but what's more, Charlotte had almost become somewhat of an obsession to her. It was as though it were a way of shaking that feeling of inadequacy that she'd held onto for so long and of living in the shadow of her own ability. She wanted to unshackle herself now more than ever and found herself surprised by her own self-discipline and determination.

She wondered why she had never found a drive like this before. Whenever she had tried to stick to anything she had always found an excuse to give up. Perhaps it was the stories she was telling herself that she didn't really need to change or the fact she kept asking herself nonsensical questions like 'who do you think you are?' Perhaps she didn't want to draw attention to herself too much by making a stand or having a voice. It takes courage to have conviction and to put your head above the parapet. It takes inner confidence in one's beliefs to really do something about them. Deep down, she just never really thought she had it in her to do anything worthwhile with her life, so she would more often than not, sabotage her own efforts.

Perhaps on some level too, she was worried that if she did lose weight and put in all the work, nothing in her life would really change and she would see who she really was. That even who she was at her best was all she could ever be. However, being here in Charlotte's world, in this filter she realised for the first time that she could do this and that losing some weight was only one component in a long chain of events that she needed to change. She understood for the first time that it was mind over matter, and she got to really taste what a new life for herself could be like. The visualisations for success surrounded her and she lived and breathed them.

That Friday was the day of her first challenge review and she wasn't sure what to expect. She envisaged herself standing once again on that stage, in front of Dr Patel and a wide audience. Will would be there, the audience would be there, she would be told what she had and hadn't done successfully, where she needed to improve — and she tried to prepare herself for what was to come. Anxiety trickled through her body like chilled sand, grinding its way through her nervous system. She knew she had put in the work, she just hoped whatever she had done would be enough.

She squinted at her reflection in the mirror. Her skin was looking good and her foundation seemed to glide smoothly onto her face. She found herself thinking back to her teenage years when she started experimenting with makeup for the first time. All her friends had dabbled with makeup here and there, a little metallic eye shadow was all the rage for a while, some mascara to widen tired eyes. She had always felt like a late bloomer in that sense. Her mother wasn't much of a role model in the glamorous stakes, never really bothering to make much effort for either herself or indeed her father. Her parent's relationship by her teenage years had become so tenuous, hanging from a proverbial and invisible thread that nobody even knew existed bar them. They squabbled, they bickered, they seemed to hate each other, and themselves, more and more with each passing year.

Her mother Maureen had resigned herself to a life of acceptance. Powerless to change the hand she had been dealt in life, and it showed. By the time Lottie was a teenager, lines on her early forty-something face looked deeper, frown marks had become heavy set and a smile behind the eyes that Lottie remembered as a child had been replaced by hardness and a cold, distant stare. She had often been told she had her mother's eyes and grew up wondering if the same would become of her. Would she just end up looking at life through cold, weary eyes and pursed lips that seemed to suppress everything she wanted to say?

It wasn't helped of course by her father's continued drinking which got progressively worse over the years. By the time Lottie was old enough to recognise he was an alcoholic with a serious problem, it seemed too late to do anything about it, at least that was the impression she got from her browbeaten mother who had given up hope of a better life for herself or for any change for the better.

He had started to do a little better professionally though. It wasn't like they were ever even remotely 'wealthy' but by her teens, he was doing ok. Working as a heating engineer, (not plumber as her mother would correct anyone who confused the two), through several cold winters of the mid-nineties had led to a surge in demand for new boilers along with a big trend in fancy radiators and underfloor heating. This meant they always had enough for food on the table and a little left aside for a rainy day. Not that anyone ever touched the rainy day fund, her mother was far too frugal for that, never wanting to spend money on anything unnecessary, including herself. She would very rarely get her hair done or make much effort to look after herself in any way. Besides, who was she trying to impress? She didn't feel her husband deserved it, all that drinking and all, so why should she bother?

Lottie was convinced there was part of her mother

that had kept that rainy day fund safe in case she did decide to up and leave one day. She didn't doubt her mother wanted to, but she had never found the strength and courage to flip the switch, and thus, as a result, went on resenting her father all the more.

As many children do when they become adults, they look at the good and bad from their parents and decide which parts of them their character they wish to adopt, and which parts they want to never become. Lottie found herself drifting further and further away from her mother as a result of her continued negativity. She loved her but just didn't want to be around it, so after she finished her degree, decided to move to London to make a new life for herself at arm's length from her squabbling parents.

She also decided that she would learn to look after herself, and did invest some of what little money she had on skincare products and makeup. Not for any other reason than not wanting to be like her mother in that regard. She often bought her mother pampering gifts for Christmas or a little face cream, but she was sure they all just ended up being re-gifted.

Sitting on that chair doing her hair and makeup she thought of her mother and wondered how she was. They hadn't spoken since she had been in the filter and, despite their differences, she did miss her. If anything, despite her flaws, her mother had been a strength in her life. Her very nature of being ardently pessimistic meant on the flip-side, she didn't suffer fools lightly and would be brutally honest about pretty much everything. She wondered what her mother would really make of all this, all these fancy things, all these indulgences.

Charlotte had told her that she wasn't on speaking terms with her parents anymore and that a big part of her self-improvement was distancing herself from 'non-believers' as she called them. She mentioned her mother had become so unsupportive in her quest for greatness, that she couldn't let her keep on holding her back. So that was it. The topic wasn't brought up again and Charlotte seemingly didn't have a relationship with her parents. They hadn't even been to the house according to Charlotte, so it must have been that way for many years as Lottie understood she had lived there for several years. Lottie could understand, on the one hand, what she meant, as she knew what her mother could be like, but to not have any relationship at all felt extreme. She also knew, due to the nature of Maureen's cool hand that whatever she decided, John would have to do by proxy, so not speaking to her mother, meant she wouldn't have any relationship with her father either.

How proud they would have been though, to see how well Charlotte had done; their only daughter. Surely they would have been brimming with pride. *Or would they?* Lottie wasn't sure.

"Are you ready?" Charlotte had knocked and pushed her door jolting Lottie out of her daydream. "The car is outside, we're excited to get you back in that office to see your results from this month!"

"Yes, I'll just be a minute," replied Lottie with a sighing smile.

Lottie slipped on her clothes took a deep breath before making her way into the black sedan parked outside. She was trying to remember if she had forgotten anything on her to-do list from that morning as she had been so preoccupied with just finding out what these results would be. She went through a mental checklist and nodded to herself as though recounting her steps, that she was indeed up to speed.

Lottie was apprehensive about the possibility of finally seeing Will. How she had wanted to catch up with him this month but hadn't had the chance. She really needed to get to the bottom of what happened but moreover, she just wanted to see him. She wanted to check he was ok, to talk to him in private and find out what was really going on. Something about all of this instinctively just wasn't adding up.

As the car pulled up at the familiar entrance to her old office the two women got out, yin and yang, and they made their way inside. This time, there was no welcome committee awaiting her arrival. This time, there was nobody there to press the buttons on the elevator for her, but despite all that Lottie still didn't feel more comfortable. In fact, if anything she was surprised. When they stepped out of the escalator she was led into a small and slightly dark meeting room with an unlit screen affixed to the back wall. There was no stage, there was no audience. The only person waiting for them both to arrive was Michael Dalton who stood up from behind his laptop as they entered the room.

"Good morning to you both. Please come in and take a seat."

Judging by the expression on her face as Lottie looked around the room he added eagerly, "Oh, don't worry. We have a cameraman coming here in half an hour or so to take some shots for the media, but we thought it might be better we go through your results first just between us."

Lottie felt perplexed as to why she should 'worry' there were no cameramen. Did they really think she enjoyed all the media humiliation?

"Oh ok," replied Lottie as she watched Charlotte confidently take her seat next to Michael. "That's fine."

Although she was pleased there would be no grand unveiling (or public humiliation), she had expected in her mind a team of some sort; scientists, screens, monitors bringing up different data feeds, developers, Dr Patel on hand for any questions. Instead, she was sitting in a room with Michael Dalton and Charlotte with nothing more than what looked like a lonely laptop shared between them. For something at the height of its technological game, this moment seemed incredibly basic.

Nonetheless, not wanting to complain or draw attention to herself, she complied and took a seat beside Charlotte where she took a deep breath and awaited her reckoning.

"Well, Lottie, you are looking great!" Michael gestured, looking down his nose past the end of his glasses. "You are definitely looking healthier and today we are going to find out how you have done on your first challenge. Before we get into that though, I would love to hear from you. How are you feeling and how have you been finding it so far?"

Lottie could see Charlotte turn her body towards her with interest at what she was about to say, the smell of her perfume wafting her way.

"Yes, good thank you Michael. I have been making a solid effort I would say."

It occurred to her at that moment that she had not actually spoken directly with Michael Dalton so far, despite him clearly being a key figure in this project. On the morning she was introduced to Charlotte she had no idea who the man was. It was only later that it clicked that he was *the* Michael Dalton whose name she had heard mentioned so many times, and who she had booked in for several meetings with Will over the years, but whom she had never been introduced to. She vaguely remembered he was a successful entrepreneur and involved in government somehow. Saying his name to his face felt like a long-overdue interaction and she regretted not taking the time to look him up on Google before she came in.

Observing him closely, Lottie deduced Michael must have been in his mid-fifties with grey hair that was making its way out above his temples. He certainly had a youthful air about him though, with a slim physique a classic but laid-back style. He was wearing a classic light blue shirt and jeans, but he seemed more relaxed without the blazer and he did have a charming, charismatic demeanour, like an old-school public schoolboy.

His body language was open, his eyes seemed kind. She noticed he was wearing a wedding ring and had an elegant fountain pen clipped to his leather moleskin on the desk.

"I have been getting into it. The diet was tricky at first but I think I'm now used to eating less, and I'm not feeling anywhere near as hungry as I did at the beginning. I've also been reading as much as I can and trying to stick to everything. I mean, we'll see what the results say but hopefully so far so good."

Lottie didn't want to tempt fate by being overly positive but she felt she needed to fill the silence. She also didn't want to appear weak, she wanted to come across as a trooper, as a fighter, as someone determined to get the job done — just as Charlotte had. However, listening to herself she did wonder if it all sounded a bit robotic. Where she might have previously injected a little humour into her way of speaking, she seemed to have adapted to

Charlotte's tone — by cutting out anything other than what really needed to be said. *"We don't need to waste our breath on silly nonsense, just get to the point Lottie,"* Charlotte had said to her when she was once recounting some funny parts of her day, and that had told her. Humour was a forgotten friend in this filter, as was not taking herself too seriously.

"And how have you found living and working under Charlotte's wing? Quite the role model you have there." Michael nodded with a smile as he spoke through glistening eyes.

There was a moment of sideways glances between the two of them before they both fixed their gazes on Lottie. Michael was jovially smiling, Charlotte more stern and serious.

"Oh yeah, I mean she's amazing what more can I say. All of this has just been a real eye-opener."

That much was true. Charlotte *was* amazing and it certainly was an eye-opener for her. However, she couldn't help but feel she was just starting to scratch the surface. So far, despite living under Charlotte's roof and abiding to a life she had been prescribed, she had yet to really understand who Charlotte *was*. So closely guarded was she, so automatic in her motions and calculated in her pursuit of success, that Lottie hadn't really felt much closer to Charlotte than when they had met four weeks prior. Charlotte had started out being quite encouraging, but over the weeks she had become less so, leaving Lottie to work with her 'team' (Gunter or Nico more often than not) and she'd certainly become less friendly. She hadn't been mentoring her all that much either, just asking if she had done what she needed to do and taking her word for it. That's not to say they were on bad terms, Lottie had been cautious not to step a foot out of line. She had been inquisitive and diligent, asking plenty of questions to Charlotte that flattered her. It's just they hadn't really become fast friends, more arms-length work colleagues who kept it professional.

"Yeah, Charlotte is quite something," Michael agreed. "Well, look Lottie I won't beat around the bush, I know we're all here to find out how you've done on your first challenge.

This is how these reviews are going to work. In order to pass each challenge, you need a score of eighty percent or higher. Your total score is made up of the data from your microchip combined with feedback from Charlotte with regard to how you've been doing against each objective within the three core areas she set you; mentally, physically and spiritually.

Lottie sat forward in her chair, her hands cupped together eagerly. Her hands felt balmy and she felt her spine rigid in apprehension. The black long-sleeved blouse that had been left out for her was sticking to the small in her back.

Michael pressed a button on the laptop which brought the screen on the back wall to life. A green table appeared on it that seemed to itemise her objectives into three columns.

"Now, you must excuse me for not going into all of the detail from your data feed. I'm afraid I'm no scientist!" Michael laughed. "But we can see the specific objectives of your first challenge".

As you know, this challenge was all about getting you acquainted with your new habits and preparing you for what lies ahead. Whilst a huge focus was on your physical objectives and getting you to lose those first ten pounds there were numerous other objectives too.

We needed to get you in touch with your spirituality by learning to meditate and love and take time for yourself. You need to understand your worth if you are to have any impact on this world. You also needed to work on your mental objectives by educating yourself, reading, creating a blueprint for success and being organised with your time. Essentially, it was about pressing the reset button on bad habits and building a new foundation for success. It was about eradicating what you know and replacing that conditioning with a positive belief system."

Lottie nodded, wishing someone had offered her a glass of water before they got started, but feeling too shy to ask for one.

"Now, if we break it down I would like to take you through your results."

Michael clicked a button again on his laptop turning the table she had seen on the screen from blue to green.

"Spiritually and mentally, you have really embraced getting to know yourself. Charlotte tells me you have been meditating daily and finding time in your busy day for calm. This, in turn, has led you to develop some pretty strong self-discipline this month. The data from your chip tells us that you've stuck to your eating plan, well done, and you've established a foundation of good habits, which is so important if you are going to succeed on this journey. You've scheduled in time for exercise, reading, and writing. It seems you have also shown compassion in your own way, as I gather through Charlotte you have reached out to work with a children's charity. All very positive steps forward."

Lottie nodded, keen not to interrupt Michael mid-flow.

"I also gather you've worked on an outline for a new novel. Charlotte has seen it, and she tells me that although it needs work, it's a start. We all know what you are capable of when it comes to writing so you'll certainly need to keep developing that."

Oh god, they hate it.

There was something about the way Michael and Charlotte exchanged glances that led her to sense they weren't very impressed.

Has no one else seen it? Was Charlotte's opinion the only one that mattered?

Michael was about to continue when Lottie stopped him mid-flow.

"Sorry to interrupt Michael, just a quick question. Have you not read it? Has anyone else?" Lottie tried to smile so as not to appear uneasy that the sole judge of her own success was indeed, herself.

"No, I haven't Lottie. Charlotte's the expert on that front so we rely on her guidance."

Michael side-glanced at Charlotte and continued to look down his nose at the screen.

"Anyway, let's move on to the more physical parts of the challenge."

"You have lost the ten-pound weight loss we wanted to see which is an incredible achievement within just one month, and your body fat has gone down to twenty-one percent due to all the exercise you've been doing! Well done! Some days you are sleeping less than eight hours but on average over the month we are happy with the amount of rest you're getting. If anything, going forward, we want you to go to bed earlier so you are waking up earlier ready to start your day. The early bird really does catch the worm."

Michael grinned patronisingly at Lottie who compliantly tilted her head back at him and smiled.

"So onto your total score. By combining the data from your chip with the feedback from Charlotte against your objectives your total score is..."

Michael clicked another button on his laptop and Charlotte leant forward in her chair as though she too, was receiving the news.

"A remarkable eighty-eight percent! Congratulations Lottie! You have successfully passed your first challenge. An incredible start, well done.

Your second challenge will start on Monday, and Charlotte will be sure to take you through what's expected of you then, but for now you can just relax and enjoy the weekend. You did it. You should be very proud of yourself."

Lottie sat there slightly numbed, looking at the screen on the wall displaying the result and she found herself feeling confused. As relieved she was that she had passed, and as proud as she was of herself for sticking to the plan, Lottie felt underwhelmed and instinctively as though something didn't feel right.

Whilst everything Michael had said was true, she had been meditating, she had allied with a children's charity and she had been sticking to her diet and exercise plan — she did wonder how they were measuring everything. Sure, they could track the statistical data through her microchip, but how did they actually know she was complimenting herself daily and learning to realise her own worth. The softer, less tangible objectives were so open to interpretation. It seemed as though it were Charlotte's word at the end of the day that decided whether she win or lose, and something about that filled her with unease. Charlotte hadn't seen her meditating every day, she hadn't watched her read the books she needed to read. If the main judge was to be another version of herself, wasn't this whole process missing some objectivity?

She turned her head to look at Charlotte and gauge her reaction. She was silent and had yet to utter a word so far which also seemed unusual as she always seemed to have something to say. There was no well done, no words of encouragement. Instead, she just cleared her throat, gave Lottie an unconvincing smile and said.

"Great. Good news."

Lottie wondered staring at Charlotte's icy eyes, what would happen if the two of them should fall out. If it became Charlotte's word against Lottie's. Yes, today she would relax and enjoy the moment, but she would certainly be keen to go forward to uncover some question marks that had formed in the cloud around Charlotte's seemingly perfect aura.

"Ok, so Lottie we have a photographer who will be here in just a minute. I want to get some photos of you and Charlotte for the press release. I can't wait to tell the media how well you're doing. They will be so excited to see your progress." Michael gushed enthusiastically.

Thinking on her feet Lottie decided she would take this moment while she got the chance.

"Perfect. Do you mind if I go and freshen up in the bathroom before they arrive? It's just it's fairly hot today and I've been so nervous about these results." Lottie couldn't believe she felt she needed to justify why she wanted to take a loo break but such was her life these days.

"Oh, yes, of course, Lottie. Take your time. The cameraman still needs to set up the lighting." Michael reassured her.

"Great, won't be a minute. Oh, I forgot, I don't have a pass anymore. Do you mind if I borrow yours?" Lottie said gesturing to a white card that was hanging around Michael's neck. She knew the office building well and that you couldn't leave the main doors to use the bathrooms with a 'visitor pass' like the one she was given.

"No problem. We'll be here," he replied with a smile as he circled the pass over his neck and handed it to her.

With that, she stood up boldly, cold trepidation running through her body and she walked briskly to the lobby to call the elevator, hopeful that no one was watching. The coast was clear, and she was grateful to see there was already an elevator on her floor. As she entered, she scanned her pass and pressed 'B'. She knew she had to be quick and was surprised to see her hand was shaking. Probably for fear of being caught, but she also knew this could be the only chance she got to go in search of Will.

"You've been very quiet darling," Michael said to Charlotte after Lottie had left, putting his hand on her arm. "Is everything ok?"

"Yes, I'm just feeling a little tired today. You know there's so much going on and then all this mentoring I have to do. It's a lot, and it's probably just catching up with me."

Charlotte grabbed Michael's hand and gave it a quick

squeeze to reciprocate his gesture, before releasing her grip. She certainly did feel as though something was catching up with her, that was for sure. These results had been impressive. Perhaps she had underestimated Lottie. Perhaps she was capable of more than she had given her credit for. Lottie had been playing catch up with swift aggression and she really wasn't sure she appreciated the feeling of anyone stepping on her toes.

"You're doing a fine job Charlotte. Look at these results! I mean, Lottie will be out of your hair in no time at this rate."

Charlotte smiled back at Michael but she didn't feel at all happy. She hadn't expected Lottie to breeze through this first challenge quite so effortlessly. She had made it look as though the challenge she had been set had been too easy, and the one thing Charlotte didn't like was being made to look like a fool. It wasn't easy being her. All that hard work and dedication it had taken for her to build her life, her brand, her persona and then for Lottie to come along and undermine her. Who did she think she was? She obviously had to make it a little tougher for Lottie from this point onwards.

What's more, there was a bigger issue that had been playing on Charlotte's mind for some time. If Lottie did succeed in completing her three challenges, which she never really thought she could do, what would become of *herself*? Michael had always said that her life would go on just as it had before however, she was starting to wonder if that was really true. It cost money to keep this filter going, and she doubted whether, when they got what they needed from Lottie, they would have much further use for Charlotte - or whether she and her formidable world would essentially just get shut down. She couldn't let that happen.

"Yes, she's doing very well, I'm very proud of her," Charlotte lied.

"Why don't I take you two out for dinner this evening to celebrate? I'm sure Lottie would like that too and besides, it would be nice for me to get to know her."

Michael stroked Charlotte's arm. The two of them had become so close their relationship had developed to more than just friendship in recent months; a strategy Charlotte hoped would keep him close and keep him on side. She wanted to be sure she knew exactly what he was up to. What's more, despite the fact he was certainly older, she liked him. He was good company, attentive and funny, charming and charismatic. The fact that he was married wasn't really her problem. She needed to get information out of him and to keep him sweet. Now he was wanting dinner with them both? No way was that going to happen.

"That's kind, Michael. I'm sure Lottie would love that as would I, but maybe we could just spend some time together you and I?" She leant in to kiss him, conceding that she needed to do whatever it took to remain an active pawn in an otherwise, unpredictable game.

CHAPTER
Eighteen

WILL HAD BEEN DELIBERATING OVER WHAT TO SHOW THE BOARD. HE had been pouring laboriously over the data and had watched the daily clips repeatedly with interest, so when it was time for the one-month review meeting he wanted to be really careful to show them what he felt they needed to see.

Not that the clips were always juicy for that matter, or at all informative. Seeing as the twenty minutes were intentionally designed by Jed to be selected at random (so as to show varying parts of any day), often Will would get a five-minute clip of Lottie sleeping or on an exercise machine. He hadn't been privy to any more talk about himself, and from what he could gather Lottie hadn't even stepped foot inside the office again.

She seemed to be taking her time in the filter seriously and was progressing well. She seemed determined, vigilant and proactive. She was doing what was expected of her. The data feed from her chip were indicating that she had been sticking religiously to her diet and exercise plans and that so far, the concept of this filter very much seemed to be working.

So far so good. So why was Will still feeling an internal pull of unease? Why was he so protective over what the board saw? He sat in his office moving his mouse button over the various files and reports on Lottie he had been privy to over the past few weeks. Despite the merger and the investment, this was still his baby. This was still his idea and his chance to prove himself and he wanted more than anything for this to work.

Nervously, he unplugged the memory stick from his computer and made his way to the boardroom, ready to show the board the results from the first month that he had prepared. He wasn't so worried about Mark and Richard, they were happy so long as the filter was working technologically. Since the merger, they had been concerned with making sure the technology worked, that it did what their respective companies promised they would do. From Mark's side, with a background in virtual reality, he was keen on ensuring the quality of what Lottie saw was realistic and lifelike, that the characters were vivid and believable. From Richard's perspective, he wanted to ensure the artificial intelligence gathered was going back into the filter to make the characters behave rationally and in character. So together they would be delighted today that their efforts had seemingly designed a fully working prototype and Lottie was very fast, becoming Charlotte.

However, it was Michael who worried him the most. He had invested money, his own money as well as Government's money into this to make it what he believed it could be. He was by far, the most vocal on the board and also the most powerful. Yet, he didn't understand the inner workings of this filter, the technology that went into it, or how each component worked together. He didn't feel it was necessary, claiming it was more important to keep selling the big picture as that was what most people would be buying into.

Will had also started to feel that, at times, Michael had

been stepping on his toes. Older and more experienced, Michael would regularly attend meetings with the Government and other potential investors on his own, claiming they wanted to see that someone 'grey haired' was on board as it gave the whole operation more kudos. Will had stepped aside obligingly, be he did start to wonder what was being said in these meetings and how much he was claiming to be the one steering the ship. This made Will all the more cautious with what he let Michael see when it came to the clips. The last thing he wanted, was to give Michael any reason to doubt his abilities and lay more claim to his idea.

Will opened the boardroom door and was unsurprised to see the three men already there waiting for him. He had been running late, and indeed, since Lottie hadn't been around he had admittedly been catching his tail.

"Sorry I'm late boys," he said switching on the charm with a smile. "Wow, are you going to love what you're about to see? I can't wait to show you."

"Yes, we're looking forward to seeing what's been going on. I still don't quite understand why we are only seeing the clips now, I'm dying to see how this Lottie turns out." Michael was the first one to say something and it didn't surprise Will at all.

"Well, you have been seeing the data reports but, as mentioned before Michael, with the clips we needed time to compile what we were getting, into anything that made sense. To weave them into a story. Random clips here and there weren't very informative at first.

So I have taken the liberty of collating and editing everything into something that can take us on Lottie's journey so far. It summarises nicely what has happened this month, and I'm pretty confident you're going to be amazed."

Will was keen to distract Michael from the negatives and focus on the positives.

"Just before I press play, some context. What you're about to see starts with Lottie meeting her best self for the first time at the grand unveiling. Her name is Charlotte. Watch this…"

Will had inserted his memory stick into the laptop and was fiddling with the projector before a big screen came to life. Will pressed play and sat back so he could see the faces of the trio before him.

The three musketeers were silent as they watched. The silence however didn't last for long and the moment they saw Charlotte smile triumphantly at Lottie, raising her hands, they collectively erupted into cheers as though their favourite football team had just scored the winning goal of the world cup final.

"This is incredible", Michael beamed standing up and walking closer to the screen. "This is simply incredible".

CHAPTER
Nineteen

LOTTIE COULD FEEL HER HEART POUNDING IN HER CHEST as she reached the basement level of the office building. She didn't want her microchip to pick up anything out of the ordinary so she took a few deep breaths and tried to compose herself. As the elevator doors opened she was greeted by a receptionist to a floor she wasn't familiar with. She had never been down to the basement and after all of these years even though she knew that's where the development team worked.

"Hi. Can I help you?" the receptionist said with a smile. She was on the phone as Lottie approached and looked slightly preoccupied, phone nestled in between her chin and her shoulder, typing.

"Oh don't worry I work here. I'm just here to see someone for a meeting," and she boldly waived her security pass in front of her and kept walking, hoping she wouldn't get stopped. She had no idea where she was going but she knew the receptionists didn't know everyone in the building so wouldn't ask any questions if she wandered through acting convincingly enough.

Aisles and aisles of desks greeted her, all with incredibly busy looking men and women typing away diligently. Some were on the phone, most were wearing headphones, and all were absorbed by what they were doing. There was no idle office chat, no small talk. They hardly noticed her walking around somewhat sheepishly, which Lottie found relieving. She knew she had to be quick, Michael and Charlotte were waiting for her upstairs for photos and she only had a limited window of opportunity to get in and get out.

She had walked right to the back of the office without seeing Will and felt her heart sink. She needed to turn around and walk back without drawing attention to herself when suddenly a head popped up from one of the aisles.

"Lottie?"

Will was standing up, his modest cubicle was some-what towards the centre of this busy room. Lottie had been looking for the desk at the front or back, the boss' chair, separated from the others. Where he was standing didn't look like anything of the sort, his cubicle was grouped amongst the others. He didn't look the same. The smile lines on his cheeks had started to hollow and he seemed frailer and somehow defeated."

"What are you doing here?" He had walked towards her now, whispering anxiously.

"I was in the office and I needed to see you. Charlotte mentioned you were working in the basement so…"

"Not now, not here Lottie," he said drawing her aside casually so they were out of earshot from the others.

"I can't talk right now. Not like this."

"But I just ..."

"No Lottie." Will reached the inside pocket of his jacket. "Here, take this," and then he looked around before he slid it into her hand before saying loudly for everyone to hear.

"Yes, well good to see you too. I'll work on that."

Lottie played along with Will's performance.

"Great, thanks Will," she said walking swiftly back towards the elevator lobby. As the doors slid closed she looked down to see what was in her hand. A phone with a business card. On the back was a handwritten note.

'Use this phone to reach me, 276772. Text me don't call. Don't let them see.'

THE PHOTOS WERE JUST AS LOTTIE HAD EXPECTED. Charlotte had worn the glamorous dress and was striking poses, and Lottie was instructed to look like a work in progress.

"You're wishing you could *be* her Lottie, you're looking lustful. Now let's see that in your eyes," the photographer had instructed, a twinkle in his eye, before clicking away at Charlotte and Lottie standing back to back.

They had experimented with poses and at one point had even asked Lottie to be sitting down on an office chair with Charlotte sitting on a desk, pointing her stiletto shoe into Lottie's knee, which hurt.

"Oh it won't take long," the photographer laughed. "The things we do for fame ay?"

Lottie had smiled, although she really wasn't that bothered about the fame, especially considering how merciless the media had been towards her, but she was playing along dutifully. No doubt, the papers would print stories tomorrow and they would want another exclusive where Lottie sits next to Charlotte and talks about the work she's been doing to play 'catch-up' as they liked to call it, to a version of herself Lottie could only dream of becoming.

Lottie felt relieved to be home later that afternoon and quickly excused herself, telling Charlotte she was keen to crack on with some reading and mediation so would be in her room.

"Oh sure, that's fine. By the way, Michael invited us both for dinner this evening to celebrate your good work. I presume though, you're counting the calories so won't be keen to join?"

Charlotte was right, she was always counting the calories but there was something about the way it was presumed upon her that irked Lottie. Charlotte was controlling. Surely, that should be up to her to decide either way? Mind you, she really couldn't think of any worse way to spend her evening. The last thing she wanted to do was sit there all evening listening to how formidable Charlotte was and how far Lottie had yet to climb.

"Yeah, I'm pretty tired, to be honest. It's been a busy few weeks and I'm going to try and get some more of that beauty sleep I apparently need to work on! You go and have a lovely time."

As Lottie headed upstairs she wanted to call out after

her, "*Is Oliver going with you?*" but knew there was little point. She had learnt he was unlikely to go anywhere with Charlotte where there weren't photos being taken and hadn't seen much of him in the past few weeks at all, reading more about him through the Daily Mail's sidebar of shame. Apparently, they were planning their upcoming wedding. Well, that was the first she had heard of it as, from what she could tell, Oliver hadn't stayed over once at the house, nor had Charlotte ever spent a night elsewhere. Lottie was perceptively also picking up on the fact that Charlotte and Michael seemed slightly *too* close. There were the phone calls, the glances, the awkward silences. She was sure something was going on.

That aside, getting Charlotte out of the house for a few hours was really just what Lottie needed now she had been armed with a new weapon. A phone. A way of finding out something on her own, of getting to the bottom of what had really been going on with her life.

As soon as Lottie heard Charlotte leave via the familiar clinks and clanks of the front door opening and closing, she got the new phone Will had given her out of her pocket and switched it on. Relieved to see it was an iPhone much like hers, she had the charger to hand and lay on her bed while she plugged it in and it powered up.

"*Enter passcode*"

Lottie entered 276772 that had been written on the back of the business card, and the screen came to life. It seemed pretty much unused, there were no apps on it other than those that come installed on new phones and there were no messages or emails to read. There were, however, numbers saved in so she quickly found Will's and sent him a message.

"Will, it's Lottie. It was good to see you today. Can we talk?"

Within seconds of typing, he had replied.

"Meet me tomorrow morning at Concertos on Walton Street at 10.30 am. Make sure you're not followed."

CHAPTER
Twenty

MICHAEL POURED CHARLOTTE ANOTHER GLASS OF RED wine as the two of them sat leaning towards each other, elbows on the table eating some large and juicy green olives. Scalini's was their favourite and they had almost adopted a ritual whenever they went. Michael would be sure to order one of the tables at the back, where he would proceed to order a bottle of Sassicaia. He would order the lobster linguine and Charlotte would inevitably always go for the crab salad but without the crab.

"No Lottie joining us this evening then?" Michael gestured to the empty part of the table with lonely place settings and an empty wine glass. He had booked a table for three just in case she could come, as he was was keen to get to know a little more about this formidable protégée.

"Unfortunately, no she couldn't make it. She's really trying to stick to her eating plan and to be honest, I think she was pretty tired tonight. Besides, I kind of wanted you to myself remember.."

Charlotte rubbed at Michael's leg under the table with her foot.

"Well, it's all testament to you Charlotte. You're teaching her well, setting the example." Michael wiped his hand on the back of a white linen tablecloth after helping himself to an olive, enjoying his leg rub beneath the table. "How's it been going with her... and be honest."

Charlotte could feel her eyes widen at the question, as though incensed he would assume she had been anything but.

"She is doing well Michael, what you see is what you get. The results are real. She's a remarkable woman with her sights firmly set on the prize."

"But...?", Michael was goading her for information, ushering her to continue.

"No buts Michael."

Charlotte took a pause and considered herself carefully.

"It's just that she does have a long way to go. I mean, I know you want her in and out of here as quickly as possible but I do think it's only going to get harder from here and each challenge might take longer than you think."

"I shouldn't think so," Michael replied confidently sipping on his wine. "You forget yourself Charlotte. All the data we have from you succeeding indicates that when you got yourself into the swing of success and had established the right foundations you were well on your way in no time. If anything, with you as Lottie's role model it should be even more of an incentive for her to change faster."

Michael looked at Charlotte. He knew the woman

before him was as shrewd as she was calculating but he also knew that she was going to be worried about having such a formidable opponent hot on her heels. Never before had Charlotte shared the stage with anyone, and it certainly didn't come naturally to her. However, he also knew that the filter needed to prove itself and the faster it could do that, the quicker he could retire. He loved working, but he was getting tired of the grind and deep down wanted nothing more than to take his kids on a holiday to the Caribbean and to sort things out with his wife.

A relationship with Charlotte was never meant to happen. It just sort of developed that way. They found themselves talking on the phone, developing a rapport. She was incredibly attractive, funny and smart, that body, those legs! But Michael still very much loved his wife and never wanted this to be anything more than just a little bit of fun. He was also well aware of Charlotte's upcoming wedding to Oliver so assumed whatever *this* was would be over sooner rather than later, but he sure didn't want to be the one to end things and piss her off.

He just couldn't help himself. His relationship with his wife had become more like teammates than lovers and as much as they were good friends, the spark after 20 years of marriage just wasn't there anymore. It also didn't help that Charlotte had made the moves on him, which had surprised him at the time. They had a business meeting over dinner one evening to discuss the logistics for when Lottie would be entering the filter, and Charlotte had invited him back to her house for a drink. She poured him a finger of his favourite whisky, and both of them laughing and joking, when Charlotte had straddled him on the sofa and began taking off his shirt. What was a man meant to do?

So, it had become a little secret for them both, one that he very much enjoyed but certainly no more than just a little bit of fun for just a little while.

"We're already one challenge down Charlotte. Two more to go. We need to get Lottie in and out of here as quickly as we can, you know that. We're almost ready to IPO and all of this incredible press is a gift from God quite frankly. I saw the photos from today. Look at this…"

Michael got out his phone and showed Charlotte some pictures from the results meeting. You look phenomenal! The media will go wild. Look out for the headlines tomorrow."

Being the businessman that he was he knew that mentioning the IPO would keep Charlotte in check. As an incentive for her to comply and do her part in mentoring Lottie Michael had offered her a percentage of the company, based on her performance. If Charlotte got Lottie to succeed in achieving her challenges and became her 'best self' as planned, on target, she would get handsomely remunerated.

"We can both retire soon I kid you not."

He knew a big part of this was carefully managing publicity to ensure that demand for the company shares would be high, and a huge part of that publicity would come from Charlotte herself. She needed to play her part, and be on board, and he was pleased to see this progress so far.

Charlotte had agreed to his terms, but she had set conditions. She didn't want Will involved anymore. She realised he had been putting her down for so many years, it was time the tables turned. So, Michael reluctantly agreed, and although he couldn't remove Will entirely from the company board (he still had shares and rights to the idea), he did manage to get him demoted to working some menial job in development. Michael was far more curious to put all his energy into Charlotte. He wanted to keep her focused, he wanted to keep her close and most importantly he wanted to keep her sweet.

CHAPTER
Twenty-One

LOTTIE PUT ON HER GYM KIT AND HEADPHONES AND TOLD Gunter she was keen to do some exercise outside today so was going to go for a run. She hadn't slept very well as she was looking forward to seeing Will, and kept replaying in her mind what she was going to ask him. There were so many questions she really didn't know where to start.

She jogged her way up to Concertos and stood panting with her hands on her knees for a few moments before going inside. She wanted to make sure she wasn't being followed so took the moment to pretend to catch her breath to scour her peripheral vision. The streets were unusually quiet that Saturday morning for a weekend in London, with empty-looking pavements from cars that had taken weekend trips to the country, and as she entered the coffee shop she heard a ding from above the door and quickly spotted Will sitting at a small table in the far corner.

He stood up as she approached his table in what seemed to be a rush to greet her, but instead, he darted right past her and looked behind her, checking to see if there was anyone or anything in her trail. Nervous at his energy Lottie stayed standing up, unsure as to whether or not to sit down before an overly jovial waitress came up to their table.

"Everything alright? How can I help?"

"Oh, just a peppermint tea and a glass of water for me," said Lottie.

Lottie could see Will had already ordered himself a coffee, not that he looked as though he needed any more caffeine. He seemed shaky and unsettled, eyes darting, nervous energy permeating from every pore on his body.

"I checked Will," Lottie whispered as the waitress walked off. "I wasn't followed."

Will seemed to calm down at the sound of her voice. His shoulders relaxed — and for a moment there it was. There was the Will she knew. He reached his hand out towards hers which took her by surprise.

"It's good to see you, Lottie."

She tried to act cool but found herself smiling broadly, butterflies flying around in her chest.

"You're looking incredible."

Lottie could feel herself starting to blush.

"I'm so glad we can finally meet, Will. I've been trying to work out what's been going on. I honestly don't know where to start."

Will was biting the inside of his lip. He spun his coffee cup around on the wooden table, looking down nervously. Lottie noticed he had been picking his cuticles as all around his fingernails the skin looked chewed.

"I know. We have a lot to catch up on. I'm glad you came to find me, I was hoping you would. We just need to be careful. They really don't want me talking to you. You don't know what they are like."

"What do you mean Will? What *who* is like?"

Will paused as though carefully considering his words. He leant in towards her to speak in a hushed tone.

"The thing is Lottie. She won't let you win. Whatever she tells you, she won't let anyone beat her. She's designed to be the best. Don't expect to just breeze through this and go home, you need to know that. I know that's what they are telling you, but I know what she's capable of."

"What do you mean? Will, what happened?"

Lottie waited earnestly for Will to keep going. She needed to find out what it was that she wasn't being told. What did he mean about Charlotte? What had happened between them? What was the big issue with them talking?

"It's not that you're not capable. You're incredible. I mean, you know…"

Now it was Will's turn to blush which surprised Lottie. She had never seen him quite so vulnerable, so open.

"You have seen what your potential can achieve. It's not a question of that. It's just that Charlotte doesn't want you to beat her despite what she might say now."

Lottie was taken aback, confused. That was the very reason she was there? Her thoughts were interrupted by the waitress returning with her peppermint tea. The two sat silently facing one another while she made space on the table for the teapot.

"But why not?" Lottie whispered as the waitress walked away. "I thought that was the whole point."

"The thing is Lottie, the filter is flawed. Charlotte strives for perfection but who's to say when you're ever good enough? Charlotte? In other words, yourself? She'll just keep changing the goalposts as the more you improve, the more Charlotte will seek to improve. Eventually, you are going to humiliate her and when that happens you need to be careful.

Don't trust her Lottie. She's manipulative and will use you to her advantage and dispose of you when she's done with you."

Dispose of me? What does that mean?

Lottie sat there taking it all in. She thought back to Friday when she went in for her review; how Charlotte sat there so quietly. She *had* been acting off with her lately too, not checking in with her regularly and not being as encouraging as she had envisaged. She had also been so controlling over the media and what she was going to wear and then there was the strange relationship she had with Oliver and indeed Michael. Still, Lottie wasn't sure what to believe. She had been on such a positive journey over the past month trying to self-improve, and this news hit her like a steam train.

"Listen, Lottie, I know you're confused, but trust me on this. She got me demoted, she tried to get me kicked out of the company entirely but legally she didn't have a leg to stand on.

Think about it. What do you think is going to happen to Charlotte when you leave the filter? When you're deemed 'perfect' and theoretically go home? You think Charlotte is just going to go on living her perfect life here?"

Lottie hadn't really thought about it. She had assumed that the filter would continue to go on like it seemingly had before she had arrived.

"Lottie you have to realise, Charlotte and all of this would be shut down. It wouldn't need to exist anymore. The filter wasn't designed to go on after it's achieved what it's designed to do. What would be the point? In theory, the very nature of you leaving the filter would mean it had done its job.

Look, Charlotte hasn't been told any of this, but she's smart and Michael knows she's going to start to get suspicious if she isn't already, so he's been cosying up to her and keeping her sweet. The two of them are pretty much inseparable. He even offered her shares in the company to incentivise her to follow things through to the end. I know he's just guarding his investment but it's all a bit much for my taste. Michael should have just shut her down ages ago but he can't stand to see his money pissed up the wall. He wants the company to IPO, he wants the government to roll it out and he wants to retire.

It's yet to be known whether she'll stick to the deal for as long as you're here. It's all very well for her to agree to this in principle, another is to see you stepping on her toes. I don't think she's going to like it."

Lottie sat there in silence staring at her peppermint tea bag floating around in her watery mug. It swirled around and touched the edges before floating back, like a fish trapped in a tank wishing for somewhere further to swim. What if Will was right and whatever she did would never be enough? What if Charlotte did start to see her as a threat and everything that she had led to believe wasn't quite as it seemed?

"So when you say cosying up... do you mean Michael and Charlotte are having..." Lottie couldn't quite get the words out without clearing her throat, "an affair?"

"Yes, Lottie. For many years now. All this rubbish with Oliver is just good PR for them both, they are both represented by the same agency who wanted to up their profiles. It's bullshit. Don't believe a second of it."

"Wow." Lottie sat stunned at the whole spectacle of it all, but it did seem a bit too good to be true and her instincts had been telling her something was off between them.

"Will, can I ask you a question?" Lottie felt herself feeling bolder now, more like equals for the first time as they sat across from one another.

"What happened between you two? I mean, did anything ever happen... you know?"

Will looked down at the floor as though mulling over what he was about to say. There, she had asked it. It was out. Will raised his eyebrows to the ceiling and then fixed his gaze at Lottie.

"Charlotte and I? Well, something was going to happen between us eventually wasn't it Lottie?"

Lottie could feel her heart beating at the rate of noughts.

"I didn't know you thought of me... like that."

"Of course I did. I just didn't want to ruin a good thing. We made a good team..."

Lottie wanted Will to go on, to find out all of the details. How had it happened? How long for? Will shrugged and continued.

"A few years ago, Charlotte was on her way up. We worked together and had a great relationship as we had always had but she started being a bit more ballsy and assertive. She started looking after herself, working out, getting fitter and she got more confidence. You know, she was feisty and fun to be around. She had good energy and I found her attractive. I guess there had always been a soft spot there but it all came to the fore. I was single, she was single. She was sexy, and just had this incredible aura about her that said she was in charge of her own life - and

I liked it. I wouldn't say we were an official couple but we did spend some time getting to know each other in that way if you know what I mean.

Then she started to go too far. She changed. Whenever I would ask her to do something she started just saying 'no' or claiming I had been passing off her work as my own. She became obsessed with the notion that she felt I had been holding her back and started telling everyone that she should take all the credit for how the company was so successful. She started sending out pieces of work to the shareholders that she had done that I put into company pitches, claiming I was a liar and basically an incompetent leader. She wanted me off the board so she could take my place.

Michael had no choice but to go along with it as, without her, we have no filter. He got me demoted and conceded to her demands, but thanks to her, years and years of my hard work have basically been wiped away because I didn't comply with her ego. It was so scary to see. She was amazing at first. Just like you, she was so sweet and hardworking, so charming, but soon after it all went to her head and she changed."

"How long were you guys, a thing before this happened?"

"A few months I guess. We were pretty crazy about each other. I mean I guess if I'm being honest, there was always some truth in what Charlotte said. I did use a lot of the work she did to my advantage but I always just thought we worked well together. But she was right, you did deserve more recognition than you got over the years. It's just the way she tried to publicly humiliate me and basically get me demoted was so vindictive, I have never understood it."

Although still confused, Lottie found herself agreeing with much of what Will was saying. They had always been a good team even if she had felt held back professionally for a long time. However, she also had to acknowledge that it couldn't all be blamed on Will. She never asked for what she wanted either. She had never taken responsibility for pushing for more out of her life. That wasn't Will's fault — and to publicly humiliate him like that! So much of Charlotte's behaviour just seemed so at odds with her own, so out of character.

"Lottie, I know this is a lot to take in, but you need to tread carefully. Play the game and do what you need to do, but keep your wits about you. The filter was supposed to make people the best version of themselves but she's just become so self-obsessed and ruthless in her pursuit of success that she'll step on anyone to get where she wants.

Don't draw too much attention to your victories, and play down the times you beat her. It sounds like she might be about to make things much, much harder for you from now on."

CHAPTER
Twenty-Two

WILL HAD BEEN DELIGHTED WITH THE REACTION FROM THE BOARD TO the results of Lottie's first challenge. Michael had tears of joy welling up in his eyes, and Richard and Mark were stoic in their self-admiration, giving each other cordial handshakes and pats on the back. So far, the filter did seem to be working and Will was keeping everything crossed that this really would be the game-changer he and everybody was hoping it would become.

They all agreed that the sooner Lottie came out the better, so she could start to apply what she had learnt to her real life. That was when the results would really speak for themselves. For now, though, they would all be keeping a close eye on the next two challenges to see whether Lottie could do enough to improve.

After that meeting, the four men had celebrated. It was Friday evening and they decided to make the most of the mild evening weather and head out to a nearby pub to spend the evening congratulating themselves on what remarkable progress had been made and what formidable men they were. Michael was excited to get some results over to the cabinet office however he agreed to wait until Lottie had completed her challenges.

"Honestly, the young kids today are addicted to their phones! They never look up! I would love to see what would happen to them if they really saw what hard work was. Can you believe being an 'influencer' is such a lucrative career?"

Whilst never shy and retiring on the subject after a few drinks Michael really found his voice in his annoyance for the youth of today. Richard and Mark spoke about the trends in AI and virtual reality and Will came away from the evening a little tipsy, but somehow reassured that perhaps he had been over-reacting about this whole thing. Perhaps there was nothing to worry about after all. He had misjudged the situation. Lottie did seem to be performing well. There was nothing indicating anything untoward was going on from anyone at all. Surely he was just being paranoid and this was all in his head.

He shook off his hunch and went into his weekend feeling more positive and optimistic. This filter would be a success and Lottie was doing well. He had always trusted her before so why should that change now?

It wasn't until he opened his laptop over the weekend to see the latest clips in his inbox from Jed. It looked like he had met up with Lottie for a coffee, but he didn't like what he saw and most certainly didn't like what he had to say about Charlotte.

CHAPTER
Twenty-Three

THE PAPARAZZI AND THE MEDIA HAD GONE CRAZY FOR THIS story. Since the press had seen the pictures with the results from Lottie's first challenge with *those* photos (they had used one of Charlotte's heel digging into Lottie who, in turn, was wincing from the pain), they had been constantly surrounding the house. They were desperate to get the money shot of Lottie and Charlotte together. The media were getting hungry for more. They wanted something unpolished; they wanted something real; they wanted a scoop.

Lottie was fairly certain she hadn't been followed on her jog when she went to see Will, but of course, she hadn't noticed the long lens camera hidden in the car across the road from the café.

As Charlotte sat at her desk on Monday morning getting ready to take Lottie through her second challenge, and deliberating on what she would task Lottie with that month, she was keen to see what they had to say about the results unveiling. The Daily Mail had led with, *The path to perfection never runs smooth but Lottie's looking better than ever.* The Sun had gone with *Lottie's gotta lotta promise.* One thing was clear; the media were starting to want a comeback story. They were beginning to root for Lottie in a way they hadn't done a month ago. When all of this started Charlotte was the 'golden girl' and represented all that was unobtainable, aspirational, glamorous and inspiring. Now the press was focusing on the fact that Lottie was already hot on her heels, and there was a sense they were shifting who they were rooting for, cheering for the underdog for the very first time. The tides were beginning to change.

Feeling hot and bothered, the blood pouring through her veins, Charlotte was just about to stop reading and close down her computer, keen to focus on setting the next challenge for Lottie when she saw another article in the sidebar of shame. *'Lottie meets up with new beau for a coffee in Kensington,'* and it had Lottie in her gym gear leaving a coffee shop with none other than Will Sampson looking sheepish and unnerved.

The article focused on how sporty she was looking, how toned she was getting and asked how long she and Will had been dating. *Dating?* This was certainly news to Charlotte. How on Earth had this meeting happened? She hadn't even realised they had seen each other, let alone that they were dating. Surely, it wasn't true. It couldn't be. Lottie had hardly been out of the house since she had arrived, and she knew not to believe everything she read. But a meeting had taken place judging by the photos, and Charlotte knew that meant only one thing. Lottie was keen to find out what was really going on behind Charlotte's shiny façade and that soon if she hadn't already, she would begin to ask questions.

CHAPTER
Twenty-Four

LOTTIE FELT EXHILARATED AFTER SEEING WILL OVER THE weekend. Now armed with some information and answers to her questions she had a newfound perspective on her current situation. She felt clued up, and more confident about how to deal with Charlotte. She had a strategy and her antennae were switched on to the fact that she needed to be careful. To think that Will had also had a soft spot for her after all these years filled Lottie with more happiness than she knew what to do with. She found herself floating around the house, humming to herself and full of the joys of spring.

However, as much as she was excited, she was also saddened to see Will like that. He just seemed to be a shadow of his former self with his stooped disposition and nervous energy. Although she saw flickers of the old him, she wished she had seen a few more. It seemed as though he had been bruised by life, disillusioned by his business and most importantly broken by Charlotte.

Yet, it was still Will, and Lottie knew that beneath the

knocked-down exterior he would come back fighting eventually, he always did. He was just biding his time, treading water. They had been in touch since Saturday via WhatsApp on her secret phone and Lottie felt so relieved to have a friend on her side who could give her some context into her bizarre life. She found herself surprised by how excited it made her to be on such close terms with Will, as though the two of them were in on a secret together and, for the first time, she felt as though they were developing a relationship that was breaking new ground.

As Lottie headed down the familiar glass staircase on Monday morning, slightly nervously, to find out what her second challenge would be, she wasn't surprised to see Charlotte already sitting at her aeroplane shaped desk reading something through narrow eyes. As she approached her, she hardly seemed to notice Lottie, she was so deep in thought and appeared to be reading whatever it was with interest. Lottie assumed it must have been some press.

Probably about her.

"How has the press been since the results were announced on Friday?"

Lottie spoke delicately, keen to find an excuse to flatter Charlotte's ego, conscious of Will's words.

"Oh good morning Lottie," and then turning away from the screen to look at her coldly in the eyes,

"Yes, it's been remarkable.

Charlotte gestured for Lottie to take a seat.

"So, are you ready for your second challenge?"

Lottie wasn't keen to dig deeper into what the media had said, especially if it wasn't one hundred percent favourable to Charlotte.

"Yes, ready as I'll ever be."

Charlotte clicked a button on her mouse and pulled up a presentation on her screen.

"Ok Lottie, let's get straight to it. We have a busy week ahead of us.

So your first challenge was really about resetting your inner foundations to establish better habits. We focused on getting you on track with what you ate, and your exercise habits and you nailed it. We're very impressed. You really embraced the process so far and put yourself on the right track to take you forward.

Now, this month will look a little different. You will need to continue with everything you did in the first challenge but now it's going to get harder as we're going to add to it.

Lottie looked at Charlotte's screen as she spoke, but noticed it was moving. Looking down, Lottie was surprised to see Charlotte's right leg was shaking slightly.

Ok so starting with your physical objectives. You still need to be focused on your health and fitness. Your objective this month is to continue with your diet and exercise plans with the goal of losing another eight pounds. It's a little less than last month as it gets harder the less you have to lose, meaning you're going to have to get even stricter. With that, we want your percentage of body fat to drop from twenty-one to nineteen. It might not sound like much but trust me, you're going to really have to zone in on everything that passes your lips. Nico will help you with regards showing you what you can eat, but it's up to you to do your own food prep and resist any temptations. You'll also need to work on getting more sleep as discussed in your review."

Spiritually, a lot will remain fairly similar to the last

month except you will need to extend the amount of time you spend meditating to forty minutes per day, and during that time I want you to focus on visualisation techniques for what success looks like to you. This will help you develop self-discipline and willpower. The charity work you've been doing is a wonderful start so I want to see more of that."

Lottie sat there silently. She was surprised at just how quickly Charlotte was reeling off her objectives. It was like she just wanted to get them over with so she could get on with her day.

"Lastly, your mental objectives; I want you to really make your brain work this month. Last month you created an outline for your first novel which we said was ok but needed a little work. By the end of this month, I want you to finish the first draft of your book and I want you to send it to me to read."

Charlotte pushed herself away from her desk on her roller chair and sat looking directly at Lottie.

"Ok," nodded Lottie, sensing that Charlotte had finished. This was exciting and would give her some-thing to sink her teeth into. She mulled over everything that she saw before her on Charlotte's screen. It didn't seem that bad. Lottie was about to say her thanks and that she understood everything when Charlotte continued.

"There is just one more thing Lottie. Another of your mental objectives is that I also want you to remove anyone around you who might be giving you negativity. I call them non-believers," Charlotte continued. "They are people who aren't supportive of your journey for what-ever reason and who will do what they can to keep you just like them, on their level of pathetic mediocrity. You need to make sure you're keeping your distance from them."

Lottie stared at Charlotte, wondering what she knew.

Surely she couldn't know about Will?

"Ok," Lottie replied, trying to read between the lines.

"Look Lottie, you really don't have time for distractions right now. You need to keep your head down and keep yourself focused. Make sure you keep away from anyone who might derail you on this journey, anyone who speaks negatively about what you're doing, anyone who's not fully supportive of this filter."

Charlotte's eyes narrowed as she spoke.

She knows.

CHAPTER
Twenty-Five

NOTHING WAS CLEAR TO HIM. WILL SAT AT HIS COMPUTER AT HOME on a warm Saturday morning and played the scenes he had received from Jed on repeat, stopping and pausing the frames, rewinding the repeating. There was Lottie in a coffee shop, and Will was explaining things to her about Charlotte. He looked awful, scared, and as though he hadn't slept in months.

"She won't let you win. Whatever she tells you, she won't let anyone beat her. She's designed to be the best. Don't expect to just breeze through this and go home, you need to know that. I know that's what they are telling you, but I know what she's capable of....

The filter is flawed...She'll just keep changing the goalposts the more you improve...Don't trust her Lottie...she tried to get me kicked out of the company...What do you think is going to happen to Charlotte when you leave the filter? When you're deemed 'perfect' and go home?

Do you think Charlotte is just going to go on living her perfect life here?... All of this would be shut down. It wouldn't need to exist anymore. The filter wasn't designed to go on after it's achieved what it's designed to do....

...are Michael and Charlotte are having an affair?

Yes, Lottie. For many years now. All this rubbish with Oliver...Don't believe a second of it."

"Will...What happened between you two? I mean, did anything ever happen... you know?"

Well, something was going to happen between us eventually wasn't it Lottie?"

Will felt like he needed air, so stood up to open the large bay window of his living room, but warm air wafted in, disappointing him as he wished it were cooler; something to blow the cobwebs out of him, something to jolt him out of his current state of mind. He had a hunch something wasn't right about all this. He knew he should have trusted his instincts.

Furious, Will hated the feeling of disappointment, of disappointing himself, of disappointing the people around him who had believed in him. There was a sense of dread and doom that came with things not working out the way he had hoped, and so many hopes had been placed upon this filter becoming a beacon of success. Then there was Michael. The two of them were having an affair and were in cahoots to try to get him kicked out of the company! Was this him showing his true colours? Was this what the future had in store?

Moreover, was this who Lottie would become? Someone who would be on a mission to destroy him, to show him up, to take him down? Was this really the sweet Lottie he had loved working with for all these years and was that what the future looked like for him? A future of embarrassment, of shame, of bitterness? Will felt the hair on his arms stand up on end with terror and wished for the first time in a long time, he could have a stiff drink.

He watched himself sitting there drinking his coffee, a bag

of bones he looked older and pallid. The skin on his face had thinned and dark circles had formed under his eyes hollowing out his features. There were no more toned shoulders, he had a stooped disposition, hunched over the table as though he were covering his coffee cup with his body. He stared at the man. Was this really what his hard work had led to?

In his mind, the filter was to become a game-changer, and Will would be notorious like his father had been, for doing something that made a difference; a force for good. He would be renowned for driving change, for bringing out the best in people. People would stop him on the street to thank him for changing their lives. He would become a motivational guru espousing how to live a full life, and he would become the talk of the town, the toast of the world. However, looking into the filter he saw for the first time that it all came at a price. Did one person's success lead to another person's failure? Charlotte became someone at the expense of Will, and perhaps, as he mulled things over, he had been doing the same to Lottie. Could there really be a population of high achievers grouped together or did society need all levels of achievement for people to be able to stand out?

Will began to question everything. Was allowing everyone to see who they could become and then improve themselves, questionable and flawed. Had he missed a trick when thinking this through? Was the very nature of success based on the fact that it came from a drive to be different, to do things differently, to be better than the rest? Surely, if everyone was bettering themselves then the entire playing field would change?

What had he created here? What was Charlotte capable of?

He looked at Lottie in the clip, all alone in the filter, trying her best to be diligent and positive, but finding out that whatever she did might never be enough. How scared she must have been, all alone, trying to navigate her way through this unfamiliar world. He hoped he was being a support to her as she had always been to him, and wished he could help. He should never have let her go into the filter as the prototype! What was he thinking? He obviously cared about her more than he had ever admitted to himself. The fact that something had happened between them didn't surprise him. It was one piece of welcome news amid the horrors of what he was hearing.

Will tried to regain some perspective, to calm himself down. He took some deep breaths and paced around his living room, reassessing the situation. This was not the real world and perhaps he was overreacting. It was way too soon to judge long-term results, she was only one challenge down. Besides, it wasn't necessarily indicative of what would happen. No, he wouldn't raise any alarm bells with the board just yet. He would keep this information to himself however, in the meantime, he would most certainly be keeping a closer eye on Charlotte.

CHAPTER
Twenty-Six

LOTTIE WASN'T SURE WHAT TO MAKE OF HER SECOND challenge objectives. Although it certainly sounded difficult, it did sound fairly doable if she put in the work. But when Charlotte had mentioned that he had to distance herself from *non-believers*. That was odd. It was the way she said it. It was as though she had just added it on the end like an afterthought. What did she know?

She knew things were only going to get harder, but she had also begun to feel prepared for the tough stuff to make her stronger. At least that's what the majority of the books she had been reading had drilled into her. That, to break out of your comfort zone you have to do things that make you uncomfortable. So Lottie accepted that it was ok to go through hard times if it meant something good would come out of it.

It's just that now she was armed with a certain amount of information about Charlotte that she couldn't shake off. She found herself looking at Charlotte differently, as though she were trying to find reasons to justify what she now knew. What was behind what she said? It was as though she was constantly thinking about how best to manage Charlotte and her sense of self-importance. If everything Will had said was true, that Charlotte would only feel increasingly threatened by her in time, then how would she achieve what she needed to achieve to progress without making an enemy out of Charlotte on the way?

She decided that this month her strategy would be not to bother Charlotte at all. She would focus on getting what she needed from Gunter and Nico, and from reading books, and writing on her own, but that questions to and for Charlotte should be minimised. She would essentially observe Charlotte from afar, and keep her head down, agree with her, not rock the boat.

Her behaviour began to get weirder too. Charlotte had been so focused on finishing her new Chic Lit book that she threw herself into some of the characters a little too much, occasionally blurting out some lines as though she was acting out some of the scenes. "It helps me get into the characters," she would say behind her desk before burying her head into writing again.

Then there were the phone calls. Lottie would often hear her sitting giggling into her phone and knew she had to be speaking with Michael.

She still couldn't get her head around her affair with Michael Dalton. Not only was he married, but he must have been twenty years older than her. She considered how ruthless she was in her pursuit of success that she would stoop to having an affair with an older married man, and wondered what had happened to her morals? Wasn't she meant to be an improved version of herself? She was also bizarrely baffled by Charlotte's ability to act so effectively.

It was like she had several personalities. She played the role of the wealthy and successful celebrity author, engaged to dreamy god-like Oliver Scarsdale so well. She was the captain of her ship and had built up this grand illusion of perfection like a faultless pyramid, all sides equal and supporting the rest. Even if Lottie did change her habits and achieve success, could she ever really play along with these alter egos Charlotte had created for herself?

Lottie took heed of Will's words though now and saw through the facade of Charlotte's world. What she needed to do was work out how best to succeed so she could get out of the filter as quickly as possible. She needed to knuckle down and write her book this month, and at the end of the month, Charlotte wanted to see it for review. However, as hard as she tried, she was finding the writing aspect of the second challenge much more difficult than she anticipated.

Having never written a book before she really needed to find the time to hone in on what she wanted to write, to develop the characters and build suspense in the storyline. She needed to do research into how to commit the perfect crimes, what goes through the mind of a murderer. It was fascinating, but equally much of her time went into research and reading other crime novels, so she began to feel concerned that she wasn't writing as much as she needed to in order to finish the book on time. It felt rushed, part of it felt light, devoid of feeling or description, but she ploughed on each day typing through tired and weary eyes.

Working out, therefore, became more difficult, she felt hazy and exhausted mentally from pushing herself. All of the writing was making it difficult for her to get her required sleep too and she could feel herself getting more sluggish.

Two weeks into her second challenge and she found her progress had slowed right down.

"No weight loss this week," Gunter had said with what seemed like a grunt before he wiped some sweat off the back of his forehead. "What have you been eating?"

Lottie had been sticking to her plan but did agree she hadn't found herself feeling as though she was losing weight. Nico had been helping her by leaving out the foods she could eat with recipes next to them for her to follow. Maybe it was that she had built up muscle and she was getting more toned?

"No, we still need to be seeing more weight loss," Gunter replied categorically. "Check your calories and reduce them by 500 a day."

Lottie was confused but acceded that it was part of the journey. She understood that success never happened linearly. Some days she would do better than others but it was what happened overall that month that would make the difference. It's just that she couldn't help but link her self-worth to the numbers on the scale. Even though she knew it was arbitrary, those days where there was no progress, she would always feel a little more negative as though she had failed in some way.

Vowing to eat less, she went up to the kitchen and saw Nico preparing Charlotte's lunch. He was always wearing his blue apron and a warm smile that made Lottie feel better. The two of them had nice chats after her workouts and she would ask him all about what went into the food she was eating. She loved learning about how best to fuel her body and tried to make the most of having a resource like Nico at her disposal. They had almost become, what she would call, friends. Nico would recommend places for her to go to in Italy on holiday when she got the chance and even the exact restaurants in the small towns that she had to try. He was a walking example for the food he cooked. His skin was radiant and glowing, and although Lottie didn't know his age she guessed he was in his early 40s despite looking much younger.

Lottie also got the sense from some slight micro-expressions that Nico found Charlotte a bit much. He would make the odd comment to Lottie.

"Izzz her ladyship having her hair blow-dried again? Ow iz it going with Charlotte?"

Coming up from the basement to see him after her latest training session she found herself slumped on the kitchen bar stool watching Nico chop parsley for a tabbouleh salad. She stared at his fingers working over the knife, removing the stalks and chopping the green herb finer and finer with each crunch of the knife.

'Whazza matter with you?' Nico laughed looking at Lottie's disposition.

"Did Gunter give you a bit of a hard time in training atoday?"

Lottie looked up and smiled. She didn't want Nico to see her so downtrodden. It's just she was feeling weary. As though everything she had been doing just wasn't enough.

"No, I'm ok. It's just I am two weeks away from results day and I'm not losing weight. I have been doing everything but I just haven't lost more this week."

Nico stopped chopping and looked puzzled.

"But you have losta so much weight already Lottie. You have been doing so well I thought."

"Yes, I started out well but I really need to lose more to progress to the next challenge! I don't get it".

There was a silence in the kitchen and Lottie could have sworn she saw Nico blush under the kitchen lights. Nico leant over the kitchen island and spoke quietly.

"Izzz just she atold me you were a doing so well that you were allowed a few more calories these weeks."

Lottie looked up and felt cold blood rush through her veins, waking up her senses, as though she had been jolted back to life.

"She said what? She told you I should eat more?"

"She just said that you were doing so well that I didn't need to be azz strict and you could eat some more. So I left out recipes with more calories in them. I thought you were appy wiz that and zat and that you knew."

Lottie thought back to all the food that Nico had left out for her, the recipes, the guidance and she heard Will's voice in her head. *Don't trust her Lottie… She won't let you win.*

Lottie was going to need to take action into her own hands from now on if she was going to stand any chance of beating Charlotte and getting out of the filter. She needed to up her game on her own without help from anyone else.

Later that evening Lottie told Will what had happened.

"Well, it doesn't surprise me, Lottie. I told you she would make things more difficult for you. I'm surprised Nico let it slip out, to be honest."

Lottie had formed a good relationship with Nico, she too had started to wonder where his loyalties lay. She'd noticed the raised eyebrows from him when Charlotte left the room and the diva dietary requests getting more and more specific, as though she was inhibiting him from creating true masterpieces. Nico also didn't need Charlotte as much as she probably hoped he did. He was a critically acclaimed chef, who had written several best-selling books. If he wasn't working as a personal chef for Charlotte he knew he would still be busy working somewhere else, and he would probably be more fulfilled too. *Perhaps he did it on purpose,* Lottie mulled over to herself. Perhaps he wanted her to know who she was up against.

"You just have to find your own way out of here Lottie. Do whatever it takes," Will said. "We have two weeks until the results day and we need to get you into the final challenge."

Lottie found herself surprised at Will's use of the word 'we' like they were in it together, and she liked it.

"How's the book going?"

"Good, I'm getting there, although it's taking me a little longer to write than I had hoped. I have two weeks to finish it and I'm nowhere even close at the moment."

"Oh, Lottie," Will sighed down the phone sympathetically. "Just know that you have it in you to do this. Keep your head down and it will happen for you. Is Charlotte home this evening? Why don't you come over tonight for dinner?"

Lottie realised it was Friday, and that usually Charlotte and Oliver headed out somewhere to be 'seen', photos regularly appearing over the weekend. As much as she knew she had to be careful with what she ate she couldn't resist the opportunity to spend time with Will. What was she going to wear?

Keep it cool Lottie, keep it cool.

"Ok, sure; text me your address. I'll aim to make my way over to yours as soon as she leaves."

CHAPTER
Twenty-Seven

MICHAEL DALTON HAD BEEN DOING HIS BEST TO KEEP Charlotte sweet. He was aware of how important it was to keep her doing her end of the bargain, motivated to help Lottie progress, but he also knew she was no fool. He knew she would cotton onto the fact that once Lottie had attained the level of perfection she needed to attain, Charlotte's role would become redundant, and her seemingly perfect world could no longer go on to exist.

Nonetheless, there was just too much riding on this for anything to go wrong. He needed Charlotte to stay motivated and to help Lottie to achieve everything she had achieved for herself. She couldn't see Lottie as competition, they needed to be allies. But how long could this go on before Charlotte started to see things differently? He knew she was shrewd so part of him was grateful if not slightly apprehensive that he had managed to get her to comply thus far.

He was regularly checking in with Charlotte on the phone, asking about Lottie, and as keen as he was to not seem too interested in her new protégée, to keep his energy and focus on Charlotte, he knew that was getting harder and harder. The media were changing. Once hailed the pinnacle of perfection, her star power was on the wane in the wake of a rival, and Michael knew that Charlotte's ego needed careful nurturing if he was going to get this over the line.

The company was almost ready to IPO. All they needed were the results of the final two challenges to complete the circle, and give the Government and investors the reassurance they needed that this filter would change the world. It did have the potential, but it was fragile, like a china vase being passed from pillar to post in the hope it didn't get dropped. Michael had already seen how Charlotte reacted to the threat of Will; how she had dismissed him, publicly humiliated him and encouraged everyone around her to do the same. Michael felt obliged to play along for the sake of his investment, but he didn't like it, and he saw first-hand a side of Charlotte that he wished he hadn't. She was certainly capable of greatness, but in pursuit of that greatness came some very unappealing characteristics. She was selfish, self-obsessed, and unforgiving. She was vain, she was vengeful. She could be merciless with anyone who threatened her, and these parts of her nature worried Michael. He was concerned that all it would take would be one moment and she would flip, change her mind and decide she didn't want to help Lottie anymore, that she was tired of being her mentor, and the whole filter could be jeopardised.

Michael didn't like the level of control she was starting to demand either. He had asked her several times for details on what the second challenge entailed, and each time he asked he would just be told the bare minimum; that Lottie was doing well and he would have to see for himself at the results day, as though it would be some exciting surprise for him. However, the fact that Charlotte was so key in determining whether Lottie succeeded worried him. Although a great deal of data was pulled in from her microchip, she was never meant to have this level of control over Lottie. It was never what was agreed upon. She was meant to be fully transparent with everything she was challenging Lottie with, but she had been keeping more and more information to herself and Michael didn't like it one bit.

He needed to broach the subject of the two of them judging her upcoming challenges together. He needed to make sure that what she was tasking Lottie with was fair and realistic. Why was she holding back from letting him know what the second challenge entailed? What was she hiding?

Michael decided that he needed to plan an impromptu visit to the house, perhaps under the guise of a romantic gesture, he wanted to get a grip on things. He was worried that, at any given moment, the house of cards that he had been carefully balancing, could be blown over with the slightest gust of wind.

CHAPTER
Twenty-Eight

ARRIVING AT WILL'S HOUSE, LOTTIE NERVOUSLY PULLED down her blouse and rubbed her finger over her teeth hoping she didn't have lipstick on them. *Some things never change.* She was curious to see where Will lived. In her mind all these years, she had pictured him in the ultimate bachelor pad, a flat with panoramic city views and large open plan spaces. She thought Will probably had a trendy brick wall in his kitchen and some deep, grey kitchen units that were probably empty aside from some chopsticks and sauces. He probably wouldn't cook and would order most of his meals from delicious local restaurants that knew him by name. The sofas would be some Italian designer space-age ones, probably made of leather or suede, and he would have a no-shoe policy when you walked in.

However, as Lottie neared a pretty Victorian terraced house in Chelsea she was surprised that her impressions of Will had been wrong. It was a suburban street, full of neat looking houses with well-maintained front doors. Knocking on the heavy lion-shaped knocker she was grateful for the camel mid-season jacket that covered her thighs. It was August and already there was a chill in the air but that hadn't stopped her from deciding to walk to try and fit in her daily exercise. She had been so nervous about what to wear and had tried on almost all of the clothes in her wardrobe before reverting to the first thing she picked out; a pair of skinny jeans and heels with a pretty yellow blouse. She didn't want to seem like she was trying too hard, which was why she had spent an hour and a half trying to look effortless, with newly blow-dried hair and carefully applied makeup. She felt good getting slightly more dressed up than usual and wearing fitted clothes that highlighted how much her body had changed.

It was lucky that Charlotte had been out that night. Lottie didn't have to explain where she was going or what she was up to and just crept out of the house after she had left. She wasn't a prisoner of the house, but didn't want the raised eyebrows and concerned glances from anything that was deemed to be taking her away from the task at hand; her second challenge. Especially as it was fairly evident that she hadn't been nailing it as effortlessly as she had her first.

But she needed to let off a little steam. She missed having real conversations. She missed laughing. Her sense of humour felt like it was disappearing and being replaced by all things steady and serious, her life was about no-nonsense now. All the pawns in her constructed reality game meant business, Gunter was hardly a barrel of laughs, and Nico despite being her only real friend in the house always went straight home when he had finished his work so their time together was limited.

What would Charlotte have made of the two of them

meeting up like this? The fact that she had specifically told her not to associate with 'non-believers' did make her wonder what she knew. Was she aware of the fact she had met up with Will already? She didn't want her to find out about any of this, she was sure she would use it against her at the second challenge review.

Lottie decided it would be her little secret, or better yet, *their* little secret. Will agreed they had to be careful not to be seen, and she found it exciting to be in on something with Will even if it was against the rules. It felt like it bonded the two of them and brought them closer.

After a couple of knocks, the door flew open and Will was standing there, a big smile on his face. He looked bright and handsome. His brow didn't seem weighed down with worry, and his eyes seemed more expressive. He was happy to see her.

"Come on in," he gestured. "It's a bit chilly, isn't it. Here, let me take your coat."

Lottie thanked him and took a moment to take in her surroundings. There were no panoramic views or designer leather sofas. Instead, Lottie was guided through to a beautiful living area with large bay windows that looked out onto the street. It wasn't the bachelor pad she had in her mind. It was a comfortable feeling and cosy house. Two grey fabric sofas were bursting with large, comfortable pillows in various colours, and there was a wooden coffee table between them appointed with magazines and candles. A large metallic floor light bent over the area filling the space with warm light and Lottie noticed a fireplace with some abstract looking artwork hanging over it.

"Let's go into the kitchen and I'll get you a drink. What would you like?"

"Oh, just some sparkling water with lemon would be amazing."

Will handed Lottie her drink and the two of them sat down next to one another at a marble kitchen table. Will's kitchen seemed well equipped, he had several appliances lined up against the walls as well as bottles of olive oils and spices. Lottie could see a glass cabinet full of beautiful crystal glasses and she found herself surprised by the number of home comforts he seemed to have. It felt like a family home but for someone who didn't have a family.

"So how's it been going, Lottie? How're things with Charlotte?"

"To be honest we have been keeping out of each other's way. She's been a bit off with me lately so I've just been keeping my head down and getting on with it."

Will nodded slowly as she spoke and she could feel his eyes glancing down toward her chest. She began to fiddle with her necklace.

"She wants to read my book and I have literally two weeks to finish it. I'm so worried I won't get there!"

"Do you want me to have a read too? Sometimes two eyes can help and all that..."

Will was being kind, and Lottie was starting to see more and more of the old him. She pictured him at his desk in the office, smiling and joking with her. She felt nervous sitting there at his kitchen table talking about herself, her book, her life. It was all so self-indulgent, but perhaps letting him in was what she should have done all along.

"That would be great." Lottie smiled at Will as if to say thank you and his eyes softened.

"You're going to be fine Lottie. We'll get through this I promise. I'll make sure of that."

We?

"We just have to make sure nobody sees us. If Charlotte knew about this..."

Will laughed softly and turned his chair towards Lottie. Suddenly, she felt his hand reach for hers. She looked at him nervously expecting him to take it away but he didn't. He just held onto it tighter and began to draw her towards him. She blushed, feeling the strength of his arm tighten around her back as her chair screeched. Feeling hot, her palms began to feel clammy, blood rushing through her body she could almost hear her heart beating in her chest.

"I have wanted to do this for some time," he said as his hand smoothed some hair away from her face. Gazing into her eyes, his hands gently brushed the side of her cheek causing shivers to run down her back. She breathed him in, smelling his aftershave, his neck, trying to hold onto the moment. She closed her eyes and let the moment happen as he leaned in towards her and kissed her.

CHAPTER
Twenty-Nine

ARMED WITH SOME GIFTS, A BEAUTIFUL HERMES SCARF HE had just collected from Harrods and a jaw-dropping Cartier necklace, Michael arrived at Charlotte's house hoping nobody would spot him and report back to his wife. He surreptitiously looked around, being careful to hide the gifts in his briefcase to not draw attention to himself and as he led himself up the pretty front path, walking away from Egerton Crescent, he could hear music coming from inside the house and felt glad that someone was home.

Tessa the housekeeper opened the door after making several clicking noises with what seemed as though she was having difficulty. She looked flustered and exhausted, as though she were partway through a rather arduous task.

"Oh hello," he announced. "My name is Michael, I'm a friend of Charlotte's. Is she home by any chance?"

"Yes, yes Mr Dalton I know who you are, but I'm

afraid Charlotte isn't at home at the moment. She is doing her speech at The Savoy."

Michael suddenly remembered she had mentioned something about an empowerment speech she was planning to hold for women in business that related to her 'Strength to Success' app.

"Ahh right Ok," and just as he was about to thank Tessa before turning on his heel he thought for a moment and decided to make the most of the fact he had made the journey.

"I don't suppose Lottie is home is she?"

"Yes, she's here. Just a moment, come in" and with that Tessa stormed off back to wherever she had come she shouted Lottie's name.

Lottie was confused by Tessa's announcement that Michael wanted to see her and not Charlotte. She was in the middle of writing a murder scene where the victim was thinking about where to hide the weapon. It was all getting a bit heavy, so in a way, she was grateful for the break.

She saved her work and headed downstairs where she saw Michael had made himself at home and was sitting calmly on the sofa facing away from her. Something about his body language implied he had been there before - like that was his spot.

"Michael, hi," she said confidently. "Not sure if Tessa told you but Charlotte's not back until a little later today."

Michael stood up and put his hands out to greet her.

"Lottie, Lottie, well would you look at you! You're looking fabulous."

He inspected her from head to toe, his eyes wide.

"She just told me but I thought that whilst I'm here I might get a moment with you to see how you're doing.

How are you getting along? How is the second challenge going?"

"Oh I see ok," and Lottie sat down tentatively on the cream sofa opposite him conscious she must have looked a mess, and wishing she'd had a shower after her training session that morning instead of diving right into writing as she had.

"I'm doing ok thanks. We've got the results day next week so I'm really busy keeping my head down."

"Yes, I know. Are you feeling confident? Remind me again, what is on your to-do list this month?"

This was what Michael really wanted to know. He wanted to sense how much Charlotte was sticking to the plan. How much she was guiding, coaching and mentoring and whether Lottie was set feasible tasks she could complete on time. He got out a small leather notebook from his lapel and was ready to take notes.

"It's going ok, few ups and downs. A lot of it is the same as last month but Charlotte added a few more things. The weight loss has been harder this month but I'm working on it. I had to lose another eight pounds and I'm pushing myself to get there. Other things included me writing a book, which I need to send to Charlotte to review before next week, and really developing myself; continuing to keep fit and healthy, continuing to read and self-improve. The main goal is to focus on writing my book and developing my path for success."

"Oh yes that's right," lied Michael, as though he knew all about it. He was glad that the challenges sounded reasonable. There was nothing too contentious about them.

"Yes, and not associating myself with non-believers,"

remembered Lottie. "I mustn't have any ties to anyone who could hinder my progress."

Lottie sat across from Michael hoping her answers would suffice so she could get back to work. It was certainly all true, she had been giving it her all, especially now she was making her own recipes up and counting her own calories, the weight loss was happening again. Her book was taking shape too. If anything, she wanted to prove to herself that she could do it. Except now it wasn't just about proving it to herself. Will and she were in it together.

Their night together had been more than she could have ever wished for. It was beyond electrifying and she hadn't been able to stop herself from thinking about him. It had been distracting. She kept pinching herself that this had happened, that Will had felt the same way about her.

That kiss. It was so overdue and so fraught with antic- ipation, with a passion that had been simmering under the surface. One thing had quickly led to another and Lottie found herself falling asleep in Will's bed, comforted by his warm body still wrapped around hers. As much as she had wished she could have stayed there all night, she knew she had to get back before Charlotte came home.

It gave her more confidence to know she wasn't in this alone, and whatever Charlotte had said about 'non-believ- ers', she was sure she could manage to keep this a secret.

"Non-believers?" Michael smiled at Lottie. "Do you know who she could be referring to with regards to that?"

Lottie sat puzzled. She wondered why Michael was here and why he was asking about the challenge and making notes in his pad. Surely he would have been well aware of what was expected of her this month?

"She didn't say anyone specifically," Lottie responded flatly. "I think it was just a general thing, to be honest."

"Ok, well I'm glad to hear it's all going well and you're happy. You know Lottie, if you have any concerns about anything, you just be sure to give me a call," and with that Michael handed Lottie his business card before leaving what looked like gifts for Charlotte on her desk and walking out.

It had been a strange and abrupt interaction. The conversation hadn't been friendly or formal. It had seemed quite awkward, and as Lottie mulled it over as she walked up the glass staircase to her room, it was clear that Michael was just after one thing, and that was that he was wrangling for information.

CHAPTER
Thirty

Those who think all the time have nothing to think about except thoughts so they lose touch with reality and live in a world of illusion.

ALAN WATTS.

LOTTIE TOOK HER SEAT IN THE SMALL MEETING ROOM IN the office ready to find out her results. It was the same one as before although this time it felt colder, as though the air conditioning had been left on full power for days before she arrived. She had been left out an outfit for the day which consisted of dark green trousers and a white short-sleeved blouse and felt the hairs on her arms stand up wishing she'd had the freedom to take a jumper. She was frustrated at her inability to choose her own outfits now, clothes were fitting her much better and everything was looking better, but still, Charlotte insisted on leaving out something for her to wear whenever there would be cameras present.

Lottie had really gone for it too over the past week. She'd pushed herself so much, she felt constantly hungry and felt light-headed that morning as she got dressed. Charlotte still had no idea she wasn't following her recipe guides anymore and was probably expecting her to have failed today based on the weight loss alone. She could see her looking her up and down as the two of them made their way to the black sedan once again, trying to determine whether indeed she had been outplayed.

It was also time for a new hairdo, so that week Lottie had made time to pop out to the local hairdressers to refresh her colour and give her a new look, which motivated her into action. She had gone for something totally different to Charlotte's long hair and had opted for a sleek light brown bob that felt contemporary and fresh. She loved it and wished she'd dared to experiment with her hair years ago. Will had loved it too, he couldn't stop running his fingers through it when she last saw him. They had hardly been able to keep their hands off each other over the past few weeks and Lottie was so happy to have an ally by her side in what felt like an otherwise uphill struggle. Feelings between them were blossoming she could feel it. For the first time in her life too, she felt glamorous, not different inside or more complete, but more glamorous. She was dressing for her new shape, she was feeling stronger and arriving at the results day she felt as though she was ready for battle with Charlotte, whatever was thrown her way.

She had spent the past week writing non-stop and had met her deadline of sending Charlotte her draft the day before. Pressing send on that email had been like lifting a huge weight off her shoulders and she sat back with a sigh of relief. Overall, she was pretty happy with how it had turned out. There were twists and turns and Lottie had surprised herself by how much she enjoyed getting into the minds of the characters and seeing where they would go.

Lottie hadn't told Charlotte about the odd conversation at the house with Michael. She didn't think there was much point, and it wasn't like the two of them had had much interaction lately. Charlotte had been keeping her distance from her. There was no friendly chit-chat or asking about her progress, and Lottie felt as though she was being sent a very clear message. *I'm not holding your hand you have to work this out on your own.* That was fine by Lottie as she preferred just knuckling down and getting on with it, especially now she knew what she was dealing with.

Feeling confident she had done everything she could she sat before Michael and Charlotte and awaited her fate. Michael spoke first.

"Well, Lottie, we all know why we are here. It's time for us to see your results for your second challenge. Charlotte and I have talked, and we are going to handle this slightly differently this time as we will be judging you together.

I'm going to be reviewing the raw data from your microchip, so your weight loss and fitness goals, and Charlotte is going to review the other aspects of the challenge including your book. The data will be collated as per before. Remember the pass mark is eighty percent."

"Ok, fine by me," Lottie replied perkily. She was pleased to hear Michael would be involved in the judging and sensed that a conversation had been had between them both before they entered the room which had irked Charlotte. She seemed disgruntled and annoyed, as though the two of them had just had a row.

"Great, I will kick things off," Michael beamed enthusiastically before clicking a button on his laptop which brought the screen on the back wall to life.

"So, starting with your raw data, your weight loss and fitness goals…"

Lottie looked at Charlotte who seemed keen to hear these too. She wondered if she knew the results already or if she was hearing them now for the first time.

"You have lost an impressive eight and a half pounds this month Lottie! Quite remarkable as we can see you have been really honing in on what you're eating and how much you're training. Your self-discipline is remarkable, especially considering you lost six and a half pounds in just two weeks. Your body fat percentage has also dropped to nineteen percent. There's now only a couple of pounds between you and Charlotte can you believe it?"

Lottie looked at Charlotte who was now sitting on the edge of her seat leaning forwards.

"Sorry, Michael," Charlotte interjected coldly whilst trying to manage a smile. "Are we certain?"

"Yes quite certain. The data doesn't lie. Isn't it remarkable Charlotte?"

Michael was trying to lighten the tone but it wasn't working. Charlotte bit her lip. He was right to have been concerned. She was getting jealous, and Lottie was getting closer.

Michael went through all the data metrics they had, showing Lottie screen after screen of how her progress had been monitored. Aside from her score from weight loss, she had been attributed points for meditating daily.

She still wasn't getting in quite as much sleep as she could have but there was a slight improvement on the month before. Lottie didn't know what score she was being given for all of this, but the news that she had done well up until this point, led her to take a momentary sigh of relief as she felt her body ease into the chair.

It was then time for Charlotte to review her new book. That book had taken over her life over the past month but little by little, she had chipped away at writing it, and then rewriting it, of loving it and hating it, until she had completed what she hoped would be deemed a complete and entertaining first draft of a novel.

Charlotte cleared her throat before she spoke and looked down at her iPad. She had only received the book yesterday afternoon and Lottie wasn't sure how much of it she would have read. She tried to gauge from her body language what she was about to say.

"Well, I have read your book Lottie," she started with a wry smile. She looked tired today, thinner than before, grey bags had formed under her eyes making her seem to have aged a few years since she met her all those weeks ago.

"Whilst the novel itself is well laid out, the characters are believable, it lacks any plausibility or motive. Why would these characters feel compelled to behave this way? How could they not have realised who the murderer was? None of it made any sense to me. The story was jumpy and the scenes didn't fit together.

I'm sorry but I would have liked to have seen more from you with this. You are capable of being a great writer but instead what you've handed in is lazy and rushed. I'm surprised at you Lottie."

Lottie felt as though she were being scolded by a

school teacher. She was well aware it had been written in a rush but overall she was proud of it. Had she actually read the book? The whole story was entirely plausible in her mind.

Charlotte looked at Michael and said quietly, "I'm sorry Michael, but I'm afraid we have quite a way to go on this."

"Ok," said Michael, slightly impatiently. He knew exactly what Charlotte was up to.

"I have something else I want to raise too. As we all know, another of Lottie's objectives this month was to distance herself from non-believers.

Uh oh…

Michael shot a stare at Lottie who so far had sat there meekly and mildly taking it all in, keen not to jostle the flames of the fire.

"I have reason to believe that Lottie has been spending some time with Will Sampson. We all know what he thinks of this filter, spending time with him can bring on nothing positive at all. It's completely against the rules, so unfortunately I have had to deduct points this month for that too."

"Lottie is this true?" Michael looked earnestly at her, hoping there had been some kind of mistake. He knew that if the rules had really been broken, it would most certainly mean Lottie would not have passed as hoped.

Charlotte threw her iPad down in front of them both and opened up the article she had seen in the Daily Mail where the two of them were having coffee all those weeks ago. It was the only proof she had.

"How do you explain *this*?" Charlotte asked Lottie, a sense of speed and energy had entered her body as though she had been waiting to see the look on Lottie's face.

Lottie had to think quickly. She needed to play Charlotte at her own game now if she was going to win. She decided that she had two choices, admit to everything and accept that she would have failed this challenge, or deny it based on a technicality.

What would Charlotte do, What would Charlotte do?

Lottie decided on the latter.

"I don't know what you mean Charlotte. I happened to bump into him in my local coffee shop that's all. Besides, that was over the weekend before challenge two had started. I haven't seen him since."

Lottie really hoped there wasn't any more proof of the two of them together that would come back to bite her. She sat firm and bold in her lie. Who had she become? She wasn't proud of herself but something told her to just do whatever she needed to progress, to get the hell out of here.

Michael looked at the article. The pictures did seem fairly harmless. The two of them had been coming out of the nearby coffee shop at the same time, but they were looking away in different directions. The article had said he was her new beau, but Michael knew better than to believe everything that he read. Besides, Lottie was right. The second challenge hadn't been laid out until Monday and the date of this meeting was the weekend before.

"I can see the date here Charlotte. It was before you defined the objectives for the second challenge. We can't blame Lottie for bumping into Will...

Charlotte gave Michael a look as if to say *Are you seriously not taking my side on this?* She was flummoxed and humiliated and shook her head at Lottie in disdain with a passive-aggressive smirk.

"I know you've been seeing him, Lottie. You and your boyfriend seem so cosy together these days. I don't know why you don't just tell the truth."

And there it was, the venomous side that she had been hiding from everyone. There was the real Charlotte. Angry, bitter and jealous, Charlotte was showing her true colours and it was as though hell hath no fury. Lottie kept her cool and acted indifferently, knowing that not getting a rise out of her would annoy Charlotte even more.

"I don't know what you mean Charlotte."

Charlotte was frustrated. She had nothing else up her sleeve, no more proof up her sleeve, nothing to pin on Lottie. She crossed her arms like a petulant child and sat back in her chair, making Lottie raise her eyebrows and look at her in disbelief. Michael tried to regain composure amongst the trio, even though two out of the three people in that room were being extremely composed.

"Ok. So let's get to the scores. Starting with you Charlotte. What scores are you giving for Lottie's book?

Michael looked down at his laptop as he spoke, keen not to look Charlotte in the eye. He was treading carefully, but something about their changing dynamic told him it wasn't careful enough.

"I gave her sixty six percent for her book. I was planning to deduct an additional twenty for rule-breaking…" Charlotte shrugged. She clearly wanted Lottie to know she would have failed.

Michael furiously typed numbers into his laptop, his eyes narrowing as he did.

"Ok, well that is disappointing I think we can all agree but it's only a first draft. I'm sure Lottie will make tweaks to it this month and it'll be to the standard we would all expect. Ok, so let's combine that with your other results from the raw data Lottie."

Michael paused before clicking the return key and sitting back in his chair, a sigh of relief passing over his body.

"Well, it's lucky that you did so well in all other parts of your challenge Lottie. You scored amazingly well elsewhere, the data says you've been outstanding and your mark is ninety-six percent bringing the average score to... eighty percent on the nose. It's a pass, but only just. Congratulations are due all the same. You passed."

Michael looked at Charlotte who sat there with her shoulders rounded with the same fixed wry smile on her face. She couldn't believe it.

"Congratulations to Charlotte too. Some incredible mentoring by you. If you ladies would like to step outside for some photos for the press, they will be delighted with this story and how it's progressing."

The two ladies stood up and Michael watched as they walked out side by side, standing awkwardly next to one another. Michael knew that getting media photos would annoy Charlotte no end, but she had just shown her true colours. She was deliberately trying to stop Lottie from passing these challenges and her behaviour in that room had proven that. Whatever niggling doubts he'd had before, it was now very much clear as day what her agenda was.

She wasn't on side, quite the opposite, and thank goodness Lottie had passed — if only by a whisker. If she had bumped into Will a few days later things would no doubt have been very different. He couldn't help but wonder what the truth was behind Lottie and Will. It was convenient that there was no proof of any further meetings, but was that really all there was to say on the matter? He closed down the computer and turned off the lights in the office room. He needed to make sure Lottie got through her final challenge, and to do that he needed to keep Charlotte under control.

CHAPTER
Thirty-One

WILL WAS WELL AWARE THAT THE PERCEPTION GIVEN TO OTHERS WAS that the filter seemed to be working. Lottie had successfully passed her first two challenges, the board were delighted with her progress. Yet, he knew that beneath the surface of what Charlotte was portraying herself to be was a very different reality indeed. In fact, over the past month watching Lottie make her way through her second challenge, Will had become fascinated by the Charlotte vs Lottie dynamic.

So much so, that after seeing those clips of Lottie and Will meeting up for a coffee, he had become so alarmed that he had pushed Jed for more and more data. He couldn't just be satisfied with only short clips each day, he needed to see absolutely everything via a live twenty-four-hour stream seven days a week, and he didn't care what it cost. He would pay for it himself if he had to, he just needed to get hold of as much information as he could with regards to what was going on inside that filter, for Lottie's sake.

"We can," replied Jed "But it's not *just* about the cost. It's also fairly risky. If we overload the data servers the system could crash and not having done this before we just don't know what will happen. I will do my best though. Just be aware if it crashes we could lose the lot."

Will considered the risks but deduced he needed to make sure Lottie was ok, so having a careful eye on everything would be essential. He gave Jed the green light and behold a week later, Will was luxuriating in an endless stream of data without a glitch. He had access to it all via his phone, tablet and laptop and it was remarkable. He could see the details of Charlotte's house, the equipment in her gym, how long she was training, what she was eating, what she was writing. It was truly gripping.

Then there was no mistaking the love story that was developing between them. He had asked her over for dinner at his house, pleased to see that he was there for her, supporting her, being her ally, her confidante. Then it happened. A kiss. Emotive and full of angst, a passionate long-overdue moment. One thing had quickly led to another and he was soon watching scenes that felt private and forbidden. Will tried to stop himself from watching, but he felt compelled. She was so beautiful - so graceful. Nothing angered her, nothing riled her, she was poised, she was funny. He wondered why he hadn't made a move before and found himself imaging what their life would have been like now if he had done it all those years ago.

In the weeks following the kiss, things only seemed to intensify between them. There were constant messages, Lottie had a cute new haircut which Will found irresistible. He had laughed at some of the things she had done too, especially when she started making her own food after finding out Charlotte was trying to jeopardise her progress. Or when she was confronted by Charlotte in her second challenge results about whether she had seen Will and she categorically denied it. She had such a poker face too. Through it all, she had stuck religiously to her goals despite being physically and mentally exhausted. She was a real trooper, a keep calm and carry on type of character just as was written on her favourite office mug.

Will knew he had to be careful with what he shared with the board. He couldn't have them privy to the fact a love story had been developing. It wouldn't make either of them look very professional. He also wasn't ready to let them see who just who Charlotte had become. Someone so power-hungry, ruthless and intent on ruining his life. Each day he would rifle through hours of footage to handpick the clips that would show things in the best light; Lottie training, her progress writing her book, her meditating, that kind of thing. He needed to carefully manage what they did and didn't know about her until he could decide what he was going to do with all this information. Lottie was doing well so far, she was holding her own, if only she could pass her third challenge and come out, everything would be ok.

He decided he would go to the filter proofing facility to see her, just to check she was ok. Even just to sit next to her and look at her. He realised how much he missed her. Could this woman really wake up to shake up his world and everything he had created? As he sat by her bed, looking at the tubes and machines beeping around her, keeping her stable, keeping her alive, he stroked her cheek, she looked so harmless, so powerless. He gently kissed her forehead and whispered. "You're going to be ok Lottie. I promise you."

CHAPTER
Thirty-Two

CHARLOTTE HAD WONDERED WHY MICHAEL HAD LEFT HER expensive gifts at the house last week. Tessa had said he had popped by with them when she wasn't home and, whilst it hadn't made much sense to her at the time, she understood it perfectly now. It was to sweeten her up before the second challenge results when he was planning on making her look like a total idiot. Who did he think he was not taking her side when she mentioned that Lottie had seen Will? It was obvious that she was seeing him. Michael was deliberately deciding not to see the facts because he just wanted Lottie to succeed.

She looked at the scarf and necklace that had made its way onto her dressing table. It was beautiful, but she had so many beautiful things it really didn't do the job that Michael had clearly been hoping it would. Nothing could take away the taste of humiliation and embarrassment she was feeling from Lottie having passed her second challenge, and showing her up like that. She had been outplayed. It was positively galling.

At least this time it wasn't a slam dunk. She had only passed — just, but it was still a pass, and that hadn't stopped the media from practically launching into a frenzy with the story that Lottie was indeed *almost there*. Charlotte couldn't deny that Lottie was indeed looking good, they were now wearing the same size clothes, and although Lottie had a very different new hairstyle, she did wonder if Lottie's now looked better than hers.

Charlotte didn't like it one bit. She put the necklace and scarf on a shelf in her walk-in wardrobe, out of sight, and hoping it would all go out of mind. She didn't want to be reminded of Michael's betrayal, especially after how close they had become and the lengths she had gone to, in order to keep him happy. No doubt, he would want to go for dinner later and say sweet nothings into her ear again, but she had no desire to hear anything from him. Part of her was so incensed with how she had been treated, she was tempted to call it quits on this whole project and with Michael too.

However, she couldn't help but worry what kind of life she would have if she did that. If the filter was shut down, would her world and everything she had worked so hard to build no longer exist? Regardless of what Michael had said, she certainly knew she couldn't trust him now.

It would just take one phone call from him, and everything could be over. He could just flick a switch and turn everything off if he wanted to. She was torn between a political game of stringing him along for as long as possible, all the while dragging out Lottie's ability to beat her. Or she could turn the tables on him and Lottie and fight back. She thought things over carefully. It was like a game of chess and each potential move needed to be calculated and well thought through. Sitting at her dressing table she brushed her long hair, sweeping it away from her face and looking at her reflection in the large mirror. Her life was great. From the outside looking in, she had everything, a beautiful home, a gorgeous fiancé, a booming career, an enviable body. Everything was going amazingly well. At least, it was until this Lottie came along to threaten it all. She wasn't ready for it all to end.

Charlotte knew she needed to do something. She couldn't bear the media stories all-singing Lottie's praises. Everyone wanted to talk to Lottie now. She was the new 'it' girl, the new cover girl, the person selling newspapers. Everyone wanted a piece of her success story. It was time to set her third challenge, and this time, Charlotte was about to make things much, much harder.

CHAPTER
Thirty-Three

Michael Dalton was walking on air when Lottie passed the second challenge, even if it were just by a whisker. The IPO was progressing well and with all the media attention it was just a matter of time before this whole filter was a proven concept. Another month to go, one more challenge, and he was keeping everything crossed that he would be well on his way to making history.

Lottie was nearly there and everyone was starting to get excited.

Everyone, it seemed, except Charlotte. She was positively incensed after the second challenge results and had been avoiding his calls over the weekend. He had wanted to take her out for dinner to Scalini's again to celebrate their success, but she wasn't having any of it. It was a cold and blustery Monday morning and Charlotte was due to set the third challenge for Lottie, and he wasn't sure exactly how things would play out from here. Would

Charlotte play fair? Or would she set Lottie some unsur-mountable task she simply couldn't pass?

Michael had often wondered how long he could keep Charlotte going like this, how long he could get her to buy the story that nothing would change once Lottie had succeeded, without her realising the truth; that she would of course be shut down. The truth would be a bitter pill to swallow and he knew Charlotte was onto him. She was no fool. Nonetheless, that didn't stop him from wanting to try. They just had one more challenge, one more month. He just needed to manage things very carefully and he was sure he could push this over the line.

Having had success with a previous house call he decided that he would pop over once again that evening, armed with a nice bottle of wine, and he would try to talk to Charlotte about her fears and concerns, play the confi-dante, the ally. It was a cold September evening and leaves were falling from the trees covering the path to the house. The previously very pretty summer flowers looked wilted and the strong winds had blown away some of the colourful petals leaving a swirl of foliage on the ground. Michael fixed his shirt collar before knocking once on the door, somewhat trepidatiously.

He knew what he wanted to say to Charlotte but he wasn't sure what mood she would be in and how much of the charm offensive he would need to apply. Tessa opened the door again, looking solemn and unsatisfied with life. He frowned as she stared at him blankly, wondering what could possibly have been so bad.

"Yes?"

"Hello Tessa…"

"Mr Dalton. Yes, I am just on my way out actually. I will inform the ladies you are here. Please come in."

Michael nodded politely before deciding to stand in the hallway instead of making himself at home on the sofa, he didn't want to be too presumptuous. He wished Tessa farewell, watching her grab her coat and umbrella and soon after Charlotte emerged from the basement covered in sweat and with a towel around her shoulders. He had clearly interrupted a training session, and walking into this house he felt as though everything was on a strict schedule and run like a tight ship.

She looked at the watch on her wrist dramatically as if to show him she was checking the time.

"Michael, what are you doing here? I am in the middle of a workout."

Michael jumped into his charming character, his voice dropped down and he put out his hands in an 'I'm sorry' shrug.

"Darling, I thought I would surprise you. How stupid of me. I should have known you would have been busy. You do so much. It's just I had tried calling and I couldn't get through and happened to be passing so…"

He let the 'so…' linger in the air for a few moments hoping Charlotte would bite and tell him it's fine, and that she had almost finished, that he could wait a little while. Instead, she stood firm, hands-on hips contemplating her response. She had half-opened her mouth and looked set to speak but nothing was coming out. It was as though she was considering very carefully her words.

"I can come back another time," Michael began turning on his heel before trying one last time to appease. "Unless of course, you don't mind if I wait. I've always wanted to have a good look through your library of books. Besides, I'm dying to hear how the third challenge went today with Lottie.

"Yes, speaking of the devil, you do realise she's just gone out. Probably with you know who, but you have your head in the sand about all that don't you, so as far as you're concerned it's fine."

Michael bit his lip. He hadn't wanted to bring up the Will conversation just yet, not like this. It's just they had no proof aside from that Daily Mail article, and he certainly wasn't about to follow Lottie to try and find some dirt on the poor girl. She'd been working so tirelessly, so what if she wanted a little company along the way? Despite what he told Lottie, Michael had no real issues with Will. He just played along with Charlotte's wishes to get him out of the way to try to keep her sweet. He had been grateful that Will had stepped back so easily, without causing a fuss. No doubt, because he was still very much entitled to his money when things launched as planned. But Michael didn't mind Will so much, underneath it all he still greatly admired him. He didn't see him as a threat, or as someone who could prove to be a negative influence on Lottie. He just thought that on that front, it was best to let sleeping dogs lie.

"Well, let's talk about that, shall we? I never meant to upset you. I brought a bottle of wine, I thought we could talk things over."

Charlotte stood there, eyes on the floor, contemplating his offer.

"Fine, give me an hour and I'll be with you. Don't make yourself too comfortable."

Michael smiled giving Charlotte a soldier's salute before heading into the living area with his bottle of wine.

Closer to two hours later Charlotte descended, clearly making a statement by the fact she was keen to keep him waiting. She looked as though she had just had her hair professionally blow-dried and her makeup was perfect, wearing natural brown lipstick and jeans. She had a nautical blue and white striped blouse on and looked very much the quintessential English rose. Michael, who'd had his head buried in 'How to Make Friends and Influence People' felt his heart skip a beat as she approached him.

"Well?" she said with an air of attitude. "You wanted to talk?"

"Ahh, here she is. My golden girl. Looking nothing short of sensational as always." Michael stood up to kiss her on both cheeks but she sat down on the opposite sofa, crossing her legs.

"Listen, Charlotte. I know you're upset with how things went on Friday. I understand you have set a high standard for everything in your life, including Lottie."

"The book was crap Michael and she's practically been dating Will right under our noses and yet she still passed the second challenge. I'm all for her progress, but only if it's fair. We can't just be passing her if she's cheating."

"Well, she's hardly been cheating. She's been working out and dieting non-stop for the past two months, plus working on that book day and night. I have to admit, after your comments, I took the liberty to read the book too, and if I'm honest, I thought it was great. She's got writing talent just like you do Charlotte."

That was true, after Charlotte's harsh critique of Lottie's new crime thriller, Michael had taken a copy to see what the fuss was all about. He couldn't put it down and found it to be a thrilling read, nothing like she had described it to be.

"Charlotte, we want to give Lottie the credit where it's due. She didn't deserve to fail that challenge…"

"And what about Will?" Interrupted Charlotte. "What do you have to say about that?"

"We don't have any proof anything is going on between them. All we have are some photos of them in a cafe, taken before the second challenge was set. We can't deduct points for that."

Charlotte sat back on the sofa and looked up to the ceiling, clearly wanting to demonstrate to Michael that she wasn't happy before welling up, tears forming in her eyes.

"I just thought you would have shown me some loyalty Michael, after all that we've been through…"

Michael felt compelled to go over and sit with her, to console the wounded cat and reassure her. This was his chance. This was how he was going to get Charlotte on side. He would play the saviour, the one person she confided in. He would rescue Charlotte from her feelings and make it all better.

"Oh darling, of course, I am on your side." Michael cosied up next to Charlotte and handed her a tissue from his pocket. "We are in this together aren't we, you and me."

Charlotte stared blankly out to the coffee table in front of her.

"Well, I suppose we might as well crack open that wine," she said keen not to give in to him too quickly, and off she hurried to the kitchen. After some scurrying and clinking, she soon returned with two full glasses. Michael took a glass thankfully and found himself surprised at her vulnerability. She had always been so tough and impenetrable but somehow he felt privileged to see a very unique side to her that humanised her. He took a sip of his wine, letting the acidity linger on his lips.

"Well," he said trying to change the subject slightly. "Why don't you tell me about the third challenge you set for Lottie today? How did it go? What's in store for her this month?"

Michael was so excited that there was only one month to go, but he tried to contain himself and focus on the fact that Charlotte was upset and needed consoling, whilst being desperately curious to find out what the challenge involved.

"Well, after the second challenge, I have decided I had to reevaluate how I set the challenges."

"Reevaluate how you set them? What do you mean?" replied Michael cautiously.

"It's just, she's so close now we've got to make things a little bit harder. It all seems a bit too easy don't you think?"

Michael stared at Charlotte hesitantly. Anxiety filled his face.

"I don't' know, I don't think it's been particularly easy for Lottie. She seems to be working pretty hard to me."

"Well, this month I have decided to really push her to do what she came here to do."

Charlotte paused and looked Michael dead in the eyes.

"I don't follow," Michael uttered cautiously.

"Her objective this month is quite simple Michael. She simply has to beat me."

CHAPTER
Thirty-Four

LOTTIE HAD DECIDED IT WAS BEST TO HEAD OUT THAT evening. She had already done her workouts and everything else on her to-do list, and after her conversation with Charlotte earlier that day, she could do with clearing her head. Not that she was at all surprised by what had happened. She had a feeling Charlotte would pull something like this, but now setting her third and final challenge to be so ambiguous and open to misinterpretation that it was essentially impossible to win.

Besides, Michael Dalton had just popped over. He had been sitting in the living area for ages waiting for Charlotte to go downstairs. The last thing Lottie wanted was to be invited to join in with their celebratory drinks or whatever they were doing. Lottie didn't get the impression they were on the best of terms after the second challenge results. Charlotte had been fuming at Michael so she wasn't terribly surprised if she were intentionally keeping him waiting.

She had said a polite goodbye to Michael before

explaining that she was popping out for a bit, he hadn't asked questions. He didn't care to know details and she was grateful for that. He merely congratulated her once again on her achievements in the second challenge and wished her luck for the upcoming month ahead. She had thanked him before setting off on her regular walk to Will's house.

"Beat her?" Will replied when she told him about what the third challenge entailed after arriving at his house and relaxing on his sofa.

"Yes, she basically said that the final challenge this month was to beat her on all counts. So I have to be thinner than her, my fitness efforts have to be greater than hers, my book has to be better than hers and I need to perform better than her on everything. It's impossibly vague whilst being so open-ended! There were so specific KPIs, nothing specific at all. Also, when I arrived in this filter, I was told I wasn't expected to achieve what has taken her six years to amass; in terms of wealth and success.

Now I'm not sure that's the case. It's almost as if I have a month to catapult myself to be at her level which was never part of the deal. All of that takes time. It could take me years!"

"She's just trying to do all she can to survive," Will responded as he put his arm on her shoulders. "She knows her time is up and she's trying to keep you in your place for as long as she can. I don't think she probably expected you to do so well so quickly. She's scared."

"Yes, but what do I do now? How do I go into this month intending to win? She's years ahead of me in terms of what she has amassed. Besides, she'll probably just keep changing the goalposts. When will it ever be enough? When do we say, ok I'm good enough now, I'm happy with myself, let's stop?"

Lottie sighed, shoulders slumped down as though a weight or pressure was bearing down on her body from above. She was a fighter, but for the first time since she had arrived in this filter, she was beginning to feel as though she may have no way out. If this was the way things were going to be going forward, she could be living in Charlotte's shadow forever.

"It won't ever be enough," replied Will stoically. "But that's the point though, isn't it? We can strive and strive for perfection — to 'live our best lives', but when we think we've got it there's always another level we haven't reached. You can never win if your goal is to be perfect, you can only really win if you go into life trying to be happy.

You know, it's funny. I always thought less of people who just had a goal of being happy. I thought they must have been weaker, less ambitious, less driven or alive. Like there was something about them that was fundamentally wrong with them that didn't make them want for more.

What this has made me realise is that pushing yourself without stopping to appreciate where you've come is pretty pointless. You've got to live for the journey not the destination."

Lottie sat there, on Will's sofa, her arms wrapped around his and she kissed him. He was wise and she liked the way he put things in a way that made sense. Charlotte was so driven with getting somewhere, with being somebody unique, someone who outshone the rest, that she had no idea who she was or what made her happy. Her relationships were all for show, she didn't have friends or family around her, and she could never be satisfied with her lot. All of it just made her so vain and self-obsessed.

"Look, Lottie. I think we need to start thinking about a plan B here. We need to consider getting you out of the filter before it's too late."

CHAPTER
Thirty-Five

Will wasn't sure exactly how or when it had happened. He had fallen asleep in front of his screen eating sushi, one hand still holding the chopsticks, the other arm was straight ahead of him on his dining table being used as a pillow. He was so tired and weary. Watching the live stream had taken over his life for the past few weeks. He'd barely gone out. He'd hardly seen friends and yet he found himself feeling a sense of comfort at seeing life through Lottie's eyes, just seeing she was ok. She was doing so well and the romance between him and her had been utterly engrossing. He had never seen himself so caring and tactile, not like this. Looking around him at his empty house, with empty sushi boxes and messy plates and mugs by the sink, he started to wonder what it had all been for.

As he awoke, however, wiping away some spilt soy sauce and wasabi from his wrist he realised the screen before him was scrambled. The feed had stopped. It wasn't working. He blinked to make sure he wasn't imagining things. When had this happened? What had he missed? He got up to check his laptop was connected and the WIFI signal was working. Everything seemed ok, but the signal to the filter was no longer coming through.

"Shit... Shit."

He checked the time. It was 3.10 am, far too late to call Jed, but this was an emergency. He needed to get this feed back up and running. Someone had to keep an eye out for Lottie in there.

There was no answer. He let the phone ring and ring before a croaky Jed answered, clearly half asleep.

"Yeah?"

"Jed we've lost the feed. It's gone. It's scrambled. I don't know what happened but we're not getting anything through."

There was a muffled silence and Will could hear the sound of movement from Jed as though he were sitting up in bed and switching on a light.

"Jesus Will, what time is it? It's three o'clock in the morning. Can we look into this first thing tomorrow?"

"No, it's an emergency, Jed. We need to get it back up and running. Lottie is about to be set her third challenge. God knows what could happen."

Jed signed heavily down the phone, intentionally audible.

"Right... ok, give me a moment to load up my laptop. I'll take a quick look, but to be honest I don't appreciate calls at this time."

More rustling noises followed, and the sound of footsteps padding around. Jed was silent as he checked things over, buttons were clicking on his laptop. Will waited patiently, grateful that he had managed to reach him, and hopeful that the news would be good.

"Hmm, that's strange," he managed after a few minutes of clicking noises. "I can't see any reason from here as to why we've lost the feed. Everything seems connected as it should be. I mean, we always knew there was a risk that the data servers would get overloaded..."

"But there's a way to get the feed back right? Even if we just see a bit less each day?"

"Well, no Will. Not necessarily. As I told you, overloading the servers is likely to have severed the feed completely. I'll need to check things over when I go into the office but I wouldn't hold out for much hope we'll be able to see anything from now on in. To be honest, we are lucky that we even managed to get as much as we did."

"No, there must be a way! Even just some short clips each day?" Will pleaded. He was sounding desperate like he needed his fix to his new addiction. "Come on Jed. If it's a matter of cost..."

"It's not about that, Will."

Jed was calm in his response. Everything about his energy was at odds with Will's.

"Once we have lost the feed it's gone. It's almost like it's been burnt or severed. Nothing we can do at the moment can bring it back. This is only a prototype anyway. I guess it's not the end of the world. We'll just have to make sure that when we build the full model we account for more bandwidth."

Jed didn't get it. He wasn't privy to why it mattered so much, how much was riding on this, and his flippancy annoyed Will. Everything about this filter mattered. Every minute detail mattered. Lottie was in there.

"Shit!" Will hung up the phone abruptly before throwing it at the wall in frustration. Without the feed, he felt like he had lost control of the situation. Without the feed, he had no idea what would really happen to Lottie from this point onwards.

CHAPTER
Thirty-Six

CHARLOTTE KNEW EXACTLY WHAT SHE WAS DOING WHEN she handed Michael the wine. She had made sure the house was empty, sending Nico, Gunter and Tessa home so she could 'have some peace and quiet' as she called it. She was grateful Lottie was out with her boyfriend. *That bitch, acting like there was nothing going on with Will.* No doubt she wouldn't be rushing home after hearing today's challenge anyway.

Who did she think she was? She couldn't just come in here and humiliate Charlotte like that. Well, the battle was about to really begin as now she meant business. She knew that setting her a challenge to 'beat her' wouldn't make much sense to anyone but that was the point! She didn't want it to be something tangible. She wanted to make it open to misinterpretation so it would be easy to justify why Lottie had failed. And she would fail. She had to fail.

As for Michael. The man now repulsed her. Looking at him leering at her on the sofa, pretending to console her and not realising these were all crocodile tears. *What an idiot.* She didn't want him asking questions anymore. She didn't want him piling on the pressure, pushing her to make Lottie succeed. She knew the one person standing in her way in this filter was Michael and it was time to do something about it.

She had thought it all through, how she was going to solve the problem at hand. Besides, that's what she was trained to do now; to solve problems and to come out on top. The same logic applied here. Michael was the problem and she needed to do something about it, especially now he was taking Lottie's side. He was the one person who could switch off this filter in a heartbeat so she owed it to herself to stop that from happening. She owed it to herself to survive.

Handing him the wine, she watched as he took each sip, wondering when it would take effect. He'd had two glasses already and Charlotte couldn't help but wonder when his body would start to break down from the inside out. It just took a few drops, that was all it takes to kill someone apparently. So easy considering the weight of the man and how many years he had been alive for it all to be over after drinking just a few glasses of wine.

"Beat you?" he said, still with a confused, wry smile on his face after hearing Charlotte recount her day. "What do mean Charlotte? Beat you how?"

"Well, you know," she responded calmly, feeling very in control of the situation. "We want her to be the best version of herself, and so I have set her the challenge of beating me this month in everything she does. She needs to be thinner than me, exercise more than me, meditate more than me, read more than me and publish a book that does better than me. She needs to be more successful too. Basically, she needs to totally overshadow me — that would be ideal don't you think Michael? To make me look like a fool? Isn't that what you wanted after all? Perhaps, after all, it's time for the protégée to become the mentor?"

Michael chuckled, half disbelieving, half hoping it wasn't true and this was all some joke. He took a large gulp of wine and Charlotte readily topped up his glass, a passive-aggressive smile forming taught lines on her face.

"But Charlotte... The whole point of this filter is to become you, not to beat you. We can't move the goalposts like this, especially when they are so vague. How would we even measure that? I mean, her improvements will be never-ending if we ask her to beat you. When would she ever be enough? We need to set her tangible KPIs, there needs to be an end in sight for this."

Michael began to cough. Charlotte stared at him, her green eyes were narrowing as he spoke.

"And why is that Michael? What end do you foresee? Do you just want to get Lottie over the finish line so you can shut me down? All the while, lying to me and pretending life will just carry on for me as normal when she has succeeded in publicly humiliating me?"

Charlotte sighed sarcastically.

"After all this time. After all we've been through Michael! I thought I meant something to you. I thought you were different!"

Michael, still coughing although trying not to, backed away from Charlotte on the sofa as she spoke in response to her raised voice. He wasn't sure how to react and she could see his mind working with regards to what his best next move was.

"Oh god, I've got such a splitting headache...."

He fumbled under his breath, the colour in his cheeks

running down past his shirt collar. A grey tint had formed to his complexion, his eyes were starting to yellow.

"I mean, do you really think I'm an idiot? Why don't you just tell me, Michael, what's really going to happen to me when Lottie completes her challenges? Why don't you tell me the truth? All this time I believed you. I trusted you. I thought you were in it with my interests at heart. It's all bullshit. I mean at first, I had my doubts. Michael would never do that to me. He cares for me. He *loves* me — but then I saw it for myself. When you took her side at the challenge results. You have no intention of keeping any of this going once Lottie completes her challenges, do you? You thought you were playing me all along, didn't you? You thought I would be happy with some stupid dinners and some expensive gifts and romantic gestures?

God, you are a pathetic excuse for a man. I can't believe I ever wasted a single breath of my precious life on you."

Michael sat there on the cream sofa, speechless, motionless, sinking slightly deeper into the cushions. A look of shock and distortion crossed over his face. His eyes looked dislocated, unattached. He didn't say a word but there was fear written all over his face. Charlotte stood up and walked right up to him, looking down on him and watching his eyes writhe around.

"Well, Michael, I'm afraid you have underestimated me. You, my dear, are a parasite. You survive off other people's blood. You always have. You, my dear, are about to be outplayed. There's one person who is sure as hell going to survive in the filter and you can bet your bottom dollar it's going to be me."

Charlotte paused to stare deep into his eyes.

"Do you understand what I'm saying to you?"

But Michael couldn't speak. He was gazing at Charlotte, startled like a deer in headlights, trying to express what he wanted to say through his eyes, choking on his own air. Something was wrong, and he was pleading with her through his eyes that he needed help, that he wasn't feeling well. He pushed air through his voice box but no sound escaped and when he tried to move his body it was clunky and disjointed. He tried to reach out his hands — but they were clumsy and limp and his jerky motions knocked over his empty wine glass, smashing it onto the table and floor.

"Oh Michael, look what you've done. My finest crystal glasses too! Would you please be more careful? Now I have to go and clear it up as Tessa's not here. Honestly, what a nuisance you are!"

Walking away into the kitchen to fetch a dustpan and brush, Charlotte looked back at Michael, squirming on the sofa like a worm who had been cut in half, his body was starting to shake. His limbs were flat before him as his torso convulsed before collapsing on the floor with a loud thud.

Then silence. She grabbed her phone, checked into social media and uploaded a video she had recorded earlier that day of her trying on clothes ready for a night out. She had to have a good alibi if anyone were to ever ask her any questions.

Her plan was working. She went about her business humming a tune under her breath, keen to clear up this mess. When she returned to the living area, it was fairly evident that Michael Dalton was indeed, well and truly dead.

CHAPTER
Thirty-Seven

LOTTIE HADN'T REALISED SHE HAD FALLEN ASLEEP AT Will's house when she awoke to the dawn light streaming in through his shutters. Will was next to her, still sleeping, his body curled against hers. In the light of the morning, he looked so peaceful. She looked at her watch, it was around five-thirty. The last thing she wanted was Charlotte asking questions about where she had stayed last night, so she hastily stood up, grabbing her things so she could get home.

Will stirred at her movements and she kissed him gently before whispering "Go back to sleep, I've got to go. I'll call you later."

She walked back briskly in the cool autumn air, grateful that the roads were quiet, and that only the chirping birds seemed curious as to where she was going. Arriving at the front door, she gingerly opened it, turning the keys so gently that the usual clanking sound was practically muted, and she hurried straight up to her room, padding carefully along the floor so as to not make a sound. Relief swept over her as she made it to her room without being seen. Charlotte was clearly still in bed so, she too, decided to take an hour or two to rest before heading downstairs to start her day. She really could do with the sleep at the moment, she was so exhausted. Not just mentally, but physically. The pressure to constantly perform was affecting her and now without a clear end in sight, she felt less urgency. She would have to take her time, as what Charlotte was suggesting she needed to do to win, couldn't be done overnight. It could take months, if not years. As she lay her head on the fluffy pillow, she closed her eyes and tried to tell herself that she would take this challenge one day at a time, but for now, it was time to sleep.

When she did awake, it wasn't to the regular sound of music thudding against her walls. The house was quiet. She rubbed her eyes and stretched, taking a deep sigh before putting one foot in front of the other and heading into the shower to get ready for her day. Looking at the clock she was surprised it was gone eleven in the morning. She had really needed that sleep. Her whole body just wanted to stay in bed and disappear under the covers with Will, to recharge before the start of the upcoming week ahead and the start of her third and final challenge. However, she was doubtful she would be going home as quickly as planned.

That was unless Will had something to do with it. He had mentioned there might have been a way to get her out of the filter, but he needed to check a few things out to see if it would be possible.

She craved a sense of normality now though. She wanted to be in her own house, to sleep in her own bed and live life on her terms. She no longer wanted to compare herself to others. She felt happy with what she had done, she was sharper mentally, she had certainly retrained her mind to believing she could stick to a healthy eating and fitness regime, and she had done it. She was looking and feeling so much better, armed with tools she would gladly embrace when she did go home. She had also become much more self-disciplined and believed she could achieve more than she had ever thought possible before. In fact, surely just seeing Charlotte and getting as far as she had could be enough. Did she really need to go that one step further and 'beat her'?

Eventually heading downstairs, she was grateful to see Nico chopping vegetables and herbs behind a large wooden chopping board. She hadn't seen him for a few days, Charlotte had sent him home for some time off, and the kitchen and indeed house had seemed so quiet without his energy and flair. He was watching the BBC News as he chopped. He often liked to be kept abreast with current affairs and would often ask Lottie what she thought about whatever was going on in the world over her morning cup of coffee.

"Hello, sleeping beauty! Buon giorno!" he beamed at Lottie as she entered the kitchen. He seemed genuinely pleased to see her and this couldn't help but cheer her up. She smiled half a smile and sat down at the kitchen counter to watch Nico delicately and speedily chop.

"God, I can't believe I slept so much. I was so tired." Lottie yawned. " How are you? What are you cooking?"

"Atoday I am making a vegetable tagine for lunch. Nice an helfy and delicioso."

Nico looked at Lottie, and read her body language. Everything about her was slumped into her stool.

"Whattsamatter with you? You seem a bitta down? Everything ok?"

Lottie looked at Nico, wishing she could tell him everything and just have a bit of a moan, but she knew she had to be careful. It wasn't that she didn't trust him, it's just she couldn't help but feel as though the walls had ears and every move she made needed to be well thought-through and calculated. Keeping quiet would inevitably be a safer strategy than sharing her feelings with Nico, as much as she would have loved to have let him in.

"Yes, I'm ok. I guess it's all just catching up with me a little. You know I passed my second challenge last week. I guess it's just taken it out of me a little bit."

"Oh wow I didn't know!"

Nico put down his knife and wiped his hands on his apron before walking over to her to give her a congratulatory hug.

" That's agreat news no? Well done. That wasn't easy, especially after the confusion on your food. You must be aso pleezed!"

"Yes, it's good. I'm really pleased. One more challenge to go..." Lottie stood up to help herself to some black coffee from the coffee machine.

"Oh my god."

Lottie could hear that Nico had stopped chopping.

"Lottie, isn't that the guy who iza involved with your filter?"

Lottie spun around coffee in hand and saw Nico waving his knife at the TV screen. The headline across the bottom read '*MICHAEL DALTON, TECH ENTREPRENEUR HAS GONE MISSING*'.

"Can you turn that up, Nico?" Lottie said as she

neared the screen, trying to decipher what they were saying.

Seconds later the sound became more audible and Nico and Lottie stood back as they listened intently to a lady standing under an umbrella outside a pretty house.

"Yes, James, reports are just coming in on this developing story but what we know so far is that police were called to the home of Michael Dalton this morning after his wife called up in the early hours after he had failed to come home, and she was unable to reach him. Now as you know James, Michael Dalton has been heavily featured in the press over recent months due to his association with the Best Life filter that has been causing quite the headlines due to its revolutionary claims to enable people to live life to their fullest potential. The company is expected to IPO soon and there has been a tremendous amount of buzz circulating around the concept. The Government have also expressed interest with Michael Dalton at the helm, who was keen to push it out to the youth of today. As you may know, Mr Dalton is a well established and well-liked businessman and entrepreneur. Many of us would know of him from his previous business endeavours. His wife is saying such a lack of contact is 'out of character' for him, especially as there have been futile attempts to reach him. Police are appealing to any witnesses or anybody who might have seen Michael in the past few days to come forward with information as due to the high profile nature of the case, they are treating his disappearance with suspicion."

"Thanks, Sandy. More on this developing story later..."

Before Nico and Lottie could utter a word to one another there was a heavy knock at the door. They looked at each other in shock and apprehension. The house seemed quiet. There was no Tessa to open the door and there was no sign of Charlotte. Nico put down his knife and headed for the front door, keen to see who it could be, Lottie standing beside him.

The door swung open to three, very tall policemen looming over them both, blocking out any rising morning sun from her eyes and creating a shadow around her from their presence. They were dressed in their full bobby regalia, with white shirts and walkie talkies attached to their chests.

"Lottie Mortimer?" Asked one of them, directly. Lottie nodded.

"We would like to ask you a few questions related to the recent disappearance of Michael Dalton. If you wouldn't mind coming with us to the station."

"Err, well yes sure. I've just seen the news. Why do you need to talk to me though?"

Lottie looked back at Nico as she put on her shoes and coat and headed into the police car waiting outside the house. Paparazzi were ready to pounce and a news reporter was throwing herself in her face as she was led away from the front door.

Lottie said nothing and kept her head down looking at the paving stones and her feet and trying to drown out the sound of clicking and the rays of light coming from the flashes from all the cameras. This wasn't how things were meant to go. What was going on? What did the police think had happened exactly?

As she bundled herself into the back of the police car, relieved to be away from the glare of the cameras she leant herself forward earnestly within the constraints of her seatbelt.

"I think there must have been some misunderstanding here," she said. "What exactly do you think I have to do with Michael's disappearance?"

"We will discuss it when we get to the station ma'am" replied one of the officers sitting in the front, who didn't turn around to look at her with his response. The next thing she knew, she was ushered into a gloomy red brick building with two big wooden entrance doors with the words 'Kensington Police Station' written above them.

CHARLOTTE HAD WATCHED EVERYTHING FROM HER bedroom window and had laughed to herself as Lottie got escorted away in a police car, paparazzi swarming around her, eager and ready to see her impressive fall from grace. She had made sure as many news crews as possible would be waiting, tipping some of them off first thing about the upcoming activity. It wasn't difficult to get them there, many of them had been parked outside for weeks anyway just waiting for some sort of scoop.

So far, her plan had gone just as she had hoped. Michael was dead and as much as it was an arduous task dragging his body all the way into the freezer room located at the back of the kitchen. She did it fast enough so rigour mortis hadn't set it. It seemed to have affected his face though, that look of shock was set firm on his features and Charlotte couldn't bear it, so she closed his eyes. It took her a while to drag that body though, every few times she would heave him a little further she would have to stop and catch her breath, or she would fall and trip over her own feet. So instead of pulling the body from his legs, she decided to grab him by the arms and yank him where she needed him to go. That seemed a little easier, but the body was heavy, and although she had good upper body strength, he was heavier than any weight she was used to, and certainly over twice her own body weight. The house had a wooden floor in the main living areas and tiles in the kitchen and Charlotte found that by placing some tea towels underneath Michael she was able to drag him much more easily, and as there was no blood, thank goodness there was no clear line of evidence leading anyone to find him in the freezer. Not that she minded anyone finding the body there eventually, but obviously she wanted everyone to think it was Lottie who was responsible, and in the meantime, she had a job to do to make sure all evidence pointed her way.

After she had successfully sorted out the body, closing the freezer room with a hefty padlock, the packaging of which she had been careful to leave under the bed in Lottie's room, she removed any food items that were in there and transported what she could into the smaller fridge-freezers in the kitchen. Luckily there wasn't an awful lot in there as Nico was due to do a shop, so it was only a few frozen beans and tofu along with some questionable looking herbs. In fact, despite thinking a freezer room such as this would be hugely useful in her house, it was rarely used to its full capacity. She then wiped her forehead with her latex-gloved hand and proceeded to wrap the body into large black bags. It took more than she realised it would to get the whole body in, shoes and all and midway through she felt Michael's phone vibrate in his pocket. She took out the phone and switched it off, thinking all the while where she could plant it amongst Lottie's personal belongings.

The whole ordeal was tiring but more than anything it had been a nuisance. Michael had clearly been trying to bring her down. It was evident through how he was taking Lottie's side and trying to twist things. What choice did she have? It was self-defence. Him or her? Live or die? She really did feel as though she had been pushed into a corner so there was no sense of remorse or empathy. She was convinced that any sane person in her position would have undoubtedly done the same to protect themselves.

Putting the used gloves in her handbag she snapped herself out of her mini daydream and back into action. She didn't have long to get ready, she was due to meet Oliver soon and really did need to get herself glammed up for the occasion. She had booked for the two of them to have a romantic evening at the Mandarin Oriental Hotel in Knightsbridge. She often stayed there when she fancied treating herself to a night away from the house and so as a result was very much considered a popular regular. They all knew her name, they all loved Oliver. The two of them would certainly not be forgotten if they walked through their doors. After reapplying her makeup and sorting out her hair, she ordered a taxi to take her, and upon arriving saw Oliver standing in the foyer looking deliciously dapper. White shirt, blazer and dark blue jeans. The two of them did their usual routine of being all over one another, feeding each other dinner at the busy restaurant, not making much conversation, and of course, Charlotte being sure to tip the waitress generously so nobody could forget they were there. That, and of course, filming the entire evening so it appeared on her Instagram account. Each story being time-stamped as a good alibi as to where she had been. In the morning, after a night of passion followed by a delicious breakfast, she had been booked her regular facial before her return back to the house.

In essence, if anyone asked as to her whereabouts she could simply show them her phone. It would be very unlikely they could determine the exact time of death anyway, and besides even if they could, she was sure Oliver would vouch for her regarding any small discrepancies, and those little Instagram stories would be sure to lead a dog away from the scent.

She thought through the timings of the evening. Tessa the housekeeper had answered the door to Michael at the house when he had arrived, so the police would have known he had popped over that evening. However, Charlotte had sent her home shortly after for some much needed time off, so she wouldn't be able to confirm or deny *who* he had come to see. Everyone else had been sent home; no Nico, no Gunter.

Lottie's motive was clear too. She was fed up with living in Charlotte's shadow, she crumbled from all the pressure. She couldn't bear it anymore and she lashed out. Charlotte on the other hand was always cool and composed. She would never behave in such a manner. It would be totally out of character against her controlled persona and public image. Lottie wasn't so trusted, and she was still a 'work-in-progress' and so surely anything could go wrong. Her temperament would be called into question.

Charlotte had called the police that morning as soon as the news broke of Michael's disappearance, and she told them he had indeed been at the house but that she wasn't sure for how long as she only saw him briefly before heading out to her evening at the Mandarin Oriental. She told them that he had come to see Lottie to congratulate her on passing her challenge and that the last thing she saw was Lottie and Michael having a drink together on the sofa before she went out. That was all she knew. They would no doubt investigate the rest.

It made Charlotte chuckle to herself as she thought it all through. Of course, Lottie would have been with Will, but if she admitted to being at his house, she would also have to admit she was seeing him, a win-win scenario for Charlotte either way. Beating her could take her a lifetime if she ever managed to beat her at all. At least, if she was locked inside a prison cell she wouldn't have to bug her all the time by living at home, and with Michael out of the picture, Charlotte could go on and have a normal life, forgetting all about these idiots who thought they could outsmart her. Will was a slightly loose end in all this, but he was so pathetic these days. What threat did he really pose? What harm could Will Sampson do? She rolled her eyes. He hadn't stopped her so far and there wasn't much chance he could do anything now. All he could do was watch his little 'girlfriend' get taken in for questioning. It was all so beautiful. Everything was going exactly as planned.

CHAPTER
Thirty-Eight

WILL HAD TO TELL MICHAEL AND THE OTHERS THAT THE DATA FEED had been severed. Arriving at work on Monday morning, looking far from his perky best, hair unwashed for a few days and with shirt creased and partially tucked in, he felt exhausted. He didn't want to explain why the feed had been lost and that the servers were being overloaded, as questions would inevitably get asked that would attest to the fact he was getting more data than they were privy to. Instead, he merely told them that these things happen with prototypes and it's unfortunately, the way it goes. He hoped no further questions would be asked. In fact, when he told Michael he didn't seem terribly surprised or bothered by the news.

"Oh well, we're still getting the statistical data through with regards to everything else right? We're just not seeing the clips?" He had asked.

"Yes, we can still tap into everything else," Will confirmed. "But Michael, we can't see the clips of what Lottie sees. I mean, I know Lottie *seems* stable but we won't know what her third challenge involves nor whether or when she passes it. I really think it's a bit of a risk leaving her in there unmonitored. We don't know how long it might take her to complete it."

Michael looked at Will slightly baffled.

"What do you mean? We have no reason to be concerned. So far, she's proven herself to be remarkably resilient."

"Well, yes she has, but I just think it's risky. Anything could happen to Lottie and I just think we need to be keeping an eye out for her. We have a responsibility to do that."

"Nonsense, Will. We have no reason to doubt Lottie. It's only a filter, after all, look at how well she's performed so far. Besides, we only have one month to go and this whole filter will be proved to be the success we all know it can be. We are so close now! If she carries on the way she's been going we'll be sipping champagne a month from now."

"Michael, I think we've done well but now we should get her out and apply our learnings to another prototype. We don't need to rush it. We need to get this right."

There was a change of energy in the room that was palpable. Michael's disposition went from jovial and playful to serious and unequivocal. He looked at Will sternly in the eye, clasping his hands together across the boardroom table.

"This is absurd. Absolutely out of the question."What on earth are you talking about? Do you have any idea how much money and investment is riding on this? You do realise that investors will pull out if we rock the boat now? This is long overdue, we need to get it over the line. You know all of this Will! I'm shocked that you would even suggest such a thing at this point?"

Michael looked at Will with confusion. His eyes narrowed and he began to shake his head in disdain. He deferred to the other two men for support.

"Don't you see, Will? If we don't see this through now there might not be another chance? Who is going to pay for it? Do you think we are magically just going to come up with more money to do this all again? We knew we had one shot to get this right and we're not backing out now."

Will didn't know what to say, nor could he back up his rationale, so he stood silently staring at the floor contemplating his moves. He couldn't justify why he wanted to get Lottie out so much because, if he did, it would be clear he had been hiding information all along.

He was stuck, torn between getting Lottie out somehow or letting her come out on her own upon completing her final challenge? Would she inevitably turn into Charlotte, intent on ruining his life? He was torn. Was he overreacting about this whole thing? It didn't mean that Lottie would turn out to become exactly like Charlotte. Perhaps the filter was exaggerating character traits and he was blowing this whole thing out of proportion.

He felt weary. Perhaps he just needed to step away from all of this for a little while and clear his head. He decided he would just pay Lottie a quick visit in the filter proofing facility, just to check on her, and then he would take a little time off for a few days. He might go and spend some time at his parent's house in the country and get some fresh air, regain some perspective on everything. Maybe Michael was right. Maybe he was too close to everything.

He took the elevator to her floor and cleared his security card over some double glass doors that swiped open. There she was, so listless, so peaceful. A tube was coming out of her mouth and wires were plugged into her from all angles. It was all such a contrast to the beautiful Lottie he'd seen in the filter, but Will didn't care, it was still Lottie. There was a young doctor on duty in her room sitting at a nearby desk looking at a screen with constantly changing data, her heart rate, her temperature, her blood pressure.

"How has she been?" he asked the doctor wearing a white overall who was sitting in front of the screen clicking a green pen in his hand. His expression seemed vacant like he was bored and disinterested, and that this job was somehow beneath him.

"Well, we're seeing a few changes," he replied.

Will pulled up a chair and sat down next to Lottie taking her hand into his. He really just wanted her to come out of this process unscathed. He felt so responsible for her and so guilty for stalling her potential all these years. He started imagining all the things he would say to her when she came back. How he'd regretted taking her for granted, and how he had undervalued her. God, he was such an idiot.

"She's obviously been having some very vivid dreams or something's going down in that filter," the doctor smiled and frowned at the same time. "She's been displaying some signs of stress, her eye movements have been rapid and her heart rate has been climbing, she's also getting an occasional temperature. Either she's going through some very demanding training or something is causing her to show signs of stress."

Will looked at the doctor, instantly trying to deduce if this young man was qualified enough to know what he was talking about. He hadn't seen him in the facility before and he didn't look old enough to be in there on his own.

"Stress or distress?" Will asked cautiously.

The doctor stood up and hovered over Lottie, clipping his pen to his overall. Standing up, he wasn't much taller than the bed and there was something about him that made Will feel this level of responsibility was above his pay grade.

"It's hard to say. The stress seems to come and go, so hasn't been consistent, but we're keeping an eye on her."

"How often are these episodes occurring?" Will was starting to get worried. "Has she ever displayed anything like this before?"

"Not that I can see from her records. They only just started within the last few hours actually, but they might be getting more and more frequent."

Suddenly Lottie's hand went stiff, her whole body convulsed and her eyes trembled right in front of them both before relaxing into the bed once again.

"There - she's just done it again. You see how she relaxes again shortly afterwards?" The doctor explained to Will half excitedly.

Will looked at the screen next to Lottie's bed. He was no medical expert, but he could see her temperature seemed to be rising along with her heart rate. He touched her forehead, panic starting to set in.

"She's burning up! Why wasn't this flagged before? How long has she been like this? Have you given her any medication?"

Lottie's body was convulsing again, the bed she was on was shaking. It was as though she was fighting with herself. Both men stood beside her trying to restrain her flailing arms.

The young doctor bit the inside of his lip before pushing a mask over her mouth.

"What's that for?" Will was screaming now. He couldn't help it. "What are you doing?"

"It looks like she might have stopped breathing. This deterioration has been very rapid but until we know what's causing it there's not much we can do but wait and see what happens. I will continue to monitor her."

Will wasn't having any of it though. He wasn't waiting

around to see what happened. He wasn't leaving Lottie in there alone, it was clear that Lottie was in distress. Something was wrong. He picked up his phone and put it straight to his ear.

"What are you doing?" The young doctor asked nervously.

"I'm calling an ambulance!"

CHAPTER
Thirty~Nine

EVERYTHING ABOUT THE POLICE STATION WAS SUCH A stark contrast to the sights and sounds Lottie had been used to in the past couple of months. Charlotte's house was a plethora of beautiful flowers, serene interiors, designer clothes and scented candles. Everywhere she looked in that house was something intentionally uplifting, whether it be a motivational poster on the wall, or the delicious smells wafting from Nico's kitchen. However, sitting in this cold, dark and dank police station behind a metal table, surrounded by three burly policemen, her environment couldn't have felt more different. Damp patches were poking through the ceiling accompanied by flaking walls. There was a loud water cooler in the corner of the room making an obnoxious buzzing sound that seemed to become quieter whenever anyone stood closer to it and a smell of lingering curry in the air. The first policeman, a middle-aged man with a beer belly and sarcastic eyes spoke first. Judging by his disposition Lottie assumed he was the boss of the other two.

"Now I want to make it clear to you Lottie. You're not under arrest here. We've merely brought you in for questioning. We're looking to talk to anyone connected to the recent disappearance of Mr Michael Dalton. You have been closely connected to Mr Dalton and we have reason to believe you were the last person he saw before he went missing."

Lottie frowned in confusion, whilst trying her best to be gracious and helpful.

"You are welcome to ask me whatever you like Mr…"

"PC Whitstable…"

"PC Whitstable. Yes, you are welcome to ask me anything you like but just to be clear, I wasn't the last person Michael saw last night…"

"Right, and why is that?" PC Whitstable raised his eyebrows in an expression of *oh here we go, we've been here before.*

"Because I went out last night and left Michael at the house with Charlotte. He came to see Charlotte. The two of them have been…well, seeing a lot of each other lately. They are close."

"What do you mean by close Miss Mortimer?"

"You know. They are close. They work together, but to be honest I'm pretty sure something else is going on between them too. Romantically I mean."

The three police officers looked at each other before giving a collective chuckle.

"You mean to tell me, that Charlotte Mortimer, who is due to get married to Oliver Scarsdale, the Hollywood actor has been having a passionate affair with Michael Dalton, a married man twenty years her senior?"

Lottie hated seeming like a snitch, but she might as well tell them the truth, especially as it looked as though they were angling for her having more involvement in this situation than was the case. She also didn't particularly appreciate not being taken seriously.

"Yes officer, that's exactly right. I mean, stranger things have happened..."

"Do you have any proof to back up this statement? Have you ever seen them together in that way? Has Michael Dalton ever stayed the night?"

"Well, no but..."

"Anything at all that would support that claim?" interjected another officer coldly.

"They do dinners together sometimes. They speak a lot on the phone."

"Oh well then!" Replied PC Whitstable sarcastically with a smirk whilst leaning back in his chair. "Let's lock her up now boys!"

The three policemen laughed together collectively once again making Lottie feel even more uncomfortable.

"It's true. I'm fairly sure something is going on. They are always on the phone with one another. I've seen the looks they give each other."

"Aren't they in business together? That seems fairly normal to me, especially as they no doubt have a lot to talk about with regards to everything that's been going on? A lot of which involves you from what I understand."

"Yes, but, I live at the house, trust me, I see what's going on."

"Right, let's move on," said the PC clearly losing interest in this line of questioning.

"We have reason to believe Mr Dalton came to the house yesterday evening. Can you confirm that? What time was that?"

"Yes, he did. Probably around five pm or so. I think Tessa let him in."

"Tessa?"

"The housekeeper" She opened the door to him and Charlotte kept him waiting in the living room. He came to see Charlotte."

One of the policemen scribbled down the word Tessa on a notebook in front of him in practically unintelligible handwriting.

"And what was your contact with Mr Dalton that evening?"

"I had a quick chat with him before I headed out. Just small talk really, niceties. I had just completed my second challenge and Michael was congratulating me. He is always pretty pleasant around me, to be honest. I have never spent that much time with him though."

"And then what happened?"

"Well, then I went out for the evening."

"And where did you go?"

Lottie had to tell them the truth. It didn't matter at this point if they knew she was seeing Will or not. She had a very odd feeling about all this and it was making her very uncomfortable.

"What is this about?" she managed. "Let me guess, Charlotte has tipped you off with something and it's leading you all up the garden path?"

"Where did you go Miss Mortimer?" PC Hardy continued.

"I went to see Will Sampson. He lives in Chelsea. I walked there and we watched a film together and had a bite to eat."

One of the other police officers wrote a note in his

notebook before walking out saying something into his walkie talkie.

"Was anyone else there other than Mr Sampson?"

Lottie paused for a moment to consider whether she had stopped anywhere on her way there, or passed anyone she knew, but she'd kept her head down and headed straight there.

"No, not that I can recall."

"And what is the nature of your relationship with Mr Sampson?"

"What has this got to do with anything?" Lottie was getting agitated. She felt more and more pushed into a corner with this questioning. "We are old friends…"

"Right. How long were you with Mr Sampson? What time did you go back to the house?"

Lottie paused again. This was feeling more and more uncomfortable.

"I accidentally fell asleep there. I must have woken up at around five-thirty in the morning so headed straight back. I've been really tired lately."

"Seems like a very early hour of the day to be walking home wouldn't you say? Why did you leave so early? Lovers tiff?" Chuckled PC Whitstable.

"No, I just wanted to head back to get on with the day."

The policemen looked at each other, each one waiting for another to comment.

"Can I ask what all of this is about?" Lottie was growing impatient now and was keen to determine what they thought had happened.

PC Whitstable cleared his breath. Her responses had seemingly satisfied him enough to warrant an explanation.

"Michael Dalton's wife called up the station this morning claiming she hadn't seen or heard from him since yesterday morning. Given the high profile nature of this case, we have to treat his disappearance as suspicious. We are talking to everyone who could have any information as to his whereabouts. So far all we know is he isn't contactable and nobody seems to know where he is."

"Are you concerned that something might have happened to him?"

"We don't know that for sure, but we have reason to believe his behaviour is out of character and due to his profile we are exploring all possible scenarios at the moment. That's all we can say on this matter."

"So you have obviously spoken to Charlotte then? Seeing as she was the last person to see Michael last night."

"That's funny," PC Whitstable said as he leant forward on his elbows across the table from her. "As she says the exact same thing about you. Claims you were the last person to see Michael before she headed out for the evening. It's just it looks like we're going to have a whole host of eye-witnesses who can corroborate her whereabouts as she and Oliver Scarsdale were having a cosy dinner for two at the Mandarin Oriental before staying there and heading back this morning."

"Well, she saw Michael before going out? Surely you have considered the timings?"

"We are considering everything thank you Miss Mortimer. At the moment though, all we know is that one of you is lying, and we are sure as hell going to find out which one it is."

CHAPTER
Forty

THE POLICE DETAINED LOTTIE FOR SEVERAL HOURS WHILE they corroborated her statement with other witnesses or people who knew Michael. They finally released her due to insufficient proof and told her she was free to return home, but not to go too far. However, Charlotte's house was the last place she wanted to be at the moment. What exactly was she up to? What had happened to Michael Dalton? As she opened the big wooden doors of the police station, relieved to get some fresh air into her lungs, she had a very dark and ominous feeling in the pit of her stomach. Something was wrong. She called Will right away.

"Will, listen, I don't know what is going on but I've just left Kensington Police Station. They detained me for questioning. Michael Dalton has disappeared. Do you know anything about this?"

"Yeah, I heard," replied Will. "They just sent someone to my house too to ask me all sorts of questions. Obviously, our stories will match, but Lottie, this is getting weird. I have the feeling this isn't the end of it. I don't know what Charlotte is up to but I do know what she's capable of."

"It's weird. What do you think has happened to him?"

"Well, I don't know, and I'm not sure I want to."

"You don't think Charlotte has done something?"

"I don't know what to think Lottie...Nothing would cease to amaze me with Charlotte, and not in a good way."

There was an agitated, pent up energy on the phone, as though they were both frantic in trying to get out what they needed to say, without saying anything really at all. Both were dancing around the ominous doom, not wanting to admit that the worst-case scenario could be anything quite so bad. Surely it couldn't be that bad? Michael may well return home soon enough. There must be some mistake.

"Listen Lottie. I am worried about you, I think we need to get you out of here. You can't go back to the house now, I don't trust Charlotte. I don't trust any of this."

"Yeah agreed. That's probably a good idea, I can come to yours for a bit until this calms down."

"No, I don't mean that Lottie. I mean, we need to resort to plan B. We need to get you out of this filter as soon as possible, and I think I may have worked out how."

CHAPTER
Forty-One

CHARLOTTE KNEW THEY WOULD WANT TO SEARCH THE house. It was only a matter of time. Luckily, she had bought herself some of that when Lottie was taken in for questioning. It gave her just enough time to let her get everything ready and to make sure there were no loose ends. She had cleaned up the kitchen, making sure to remove any traces of the poisonous concoction she had poured into Michael's drink. The beauty of all of this was the technique she had used to murder Michael was one she had learnt about reading Lottie's book. There was a particular scene where a body had been found in a beautiful country pile, leading the detectives to investigate what had happened. It turned out he had been poisoned using a clever mixture of antifreeze found in the garage mixed in small doses into alcohol. Lottie had clearly researched this method of murder as part of her novel so it would make even more sense when detectives were looking for where to point the finger. Charlotte had been surprised at how quickly the poisonous concoction had worked. It only took Michael two glasses of wine before he began appearing disoriented. It wasn't long before he was collapsed on the floor bent over like some primitive ape with drool forming in the corner of his mouth. It had all seemed a bit too easy. If anything, Charlotte was expecting the whole ordeal to take a bit longer as according to Lottie's book, such poisoning usually took up to twelve hours. Not with Michael Dalton, within forty-five minutes he was a decomposing mess of a man on her living room floor.

She had also been careful to place some strategic evidence around the body, again such tips were also gratefully received from Lottie's book. So she took some of Lottie's hair from her hairbrush and placed it in the freezer room with the body, specifically between the bags and tape that she used to wrap the body up. At least as much as she could. She then made sure the padlock packaging to the freezer door was strewn nicely under her bed. Then of course there was his phone, and she had put that in her coat pocket. It was all going perfectly.

So when the police did turn up at her door, it was early evening and she was ready. Charlotte Mortimer was always ready, and she liked games. In fact, she was pretty good at winning them.

"Charlotte Mortimer?" PC Whitstable was at her door accompanied by the same two men she had seen that morning who had escorted Lottie away in a police car.

"Yes."

"We would like to ask you some further questions if we may in relation to the disappearance of Michael Dalton."

"Yes, of course. I just can't believe all this. I mean, what a shock…"

"Would you mind if we stepped inside and asked you some questions? We would also like your permission to conduct a search of the property. You do not have to oblige but if any evidence…"

"Oh no of course," interrupted Charlotte. "Please do come in. Feel free to take a look around as much as you'd like. Of course, I'll help in any way I can."

Charlotte led PC Whitstable inside where the other two policemen quickly split up. One went upstairs and the other remained on the ground floor, muted faces behind white gloves on and face masks. They moved swiftly, but something about them seemed amateur, as though they weren't convinced they knew what they were doing. Perhaps because they didn't know what they were looking for. PC Whitstable sat down on the sofa, in the same place Michael had sat the day before.

"I need to ask you a few more questions Charlotte. I know we spoke this morning on the phone but we have since chatted to other people who know Michael, or who might have seen Michael and we have had varying reports on several things. It would be good to clarify a couple of things once again. Could you reconfirm the last time you saw Michael?"

They were testing her now she was sure of it. This was the part where they repeated the same or similar questions back to her to see if her response differed. To see whether what she was about to say would match what she had said before.

"It must have been around five-thirty to six. I only saw him briefly before I headed out to meet my fiancé, Oliver Scarsdale. Michael had come to see Lottie and the two of them were having a cosy little drink right here when I left."

"Ok, do you have any idea what the meeting was about? Why Michael would have come to the house?"

"I'm afraid I don't know. It was probably to congratulate Lottie on passing her second challenge, but I don't know."

"Has he come to the house before?"

"Oh yes. Michael and I work together. He's been over a couple of times."

"Your housekeeper Tessa mentioned he had been over just last week. She claims he brought gifts."

"Oh yes, apparently he did pop over last week. That's true. I wasn't here though…"

"And the gifts? Could we ask what they were?"

Charlotte hadn't anticipated this question. She hadn't planned for an answer to it. Revealing that Michael had bought her romantic gifts would not look good.

"Yes, he bought Lottie some gifts but asked me not to give them to her until she passed her third challenge. He is very generous like that. Very thoughtful."

"Why would he bring these gifts to you last week instead of giving them to Lottie when she had passed her challenge?"

"I mean, you would have to ask Michael. He's always been very organised."

Charlotte shrugged with a smile. She hadn't even opened these gifts, they had been put to the back of her wardrobe and her mind and she was really hoping he hadn't written a note. The PC moved on.

"Can you describe what Michael was wearing?"

Back to the questions she was expecting, she had been asked that already.

"Yes, I'm afraid I really can't remember. I only saw him so quickly."

"How would you describe your relationship with Michael?"

Charlotte wondered what Lottie had told them and what she knew.

"Oh, well we are close work colleagues. We both have a vested interest in this filter and making it a success, but Michael has been a good friend to me over the years too. He's been very supportive of my career. Almost like a mentor to me really."

"Have you ever had a romantic relationship?"

That little bitch, how did she know! She was clearly more perceptive than she had given her credit for.

"Absolutely not! Michael Dalton is a married man," and with that Charlotte crossed her arms as though such a question were an insult to her integrity.

PC Whitstable looked down the rim of his glasses as he made notes in a small notepad. His handwriting was so bad she wondered how any of what he wrote made any sense.

"We have had claims that you were the last person to see Michael last night and that you were, in fact, romantically involved. What would you say to such claims?"

"Oh for goodness sake," Charlotte replied. "Yes, I would probably profess the same if I were being accused of something and I was trying to snake my way out of it. What a load of rubbish."

"Guv…" Interrupted one of the masked policemen who had been searching the ground floor. "We've got something back here that's locked. We are going to need access."

PC Whitstable looked at Charlotte who was relieved

at the interruption. She nodded and stood up following the young policeman through the kitchen and into a room at the back. Both of the men were now standing in front of the freezer room with quizzical expressions on their faces.

"What's in here ma'am?" The young policeman asked politely.

"That's just the freezer. I'm not sure why it's locked though, I don't usually come back here. It's Nico's domain, he's the chef."

"So you don't know the combination then?" PC Whitstable looked at the padlock, deferring to Charlotte.

"No, I'm afraid not. In fact, I've never noticed that lock before."

"Do you mind if we open it with some of our tools?"

"Please... be my guest," Charlotte replied gratefully. It was all too easy.

A few moments later a crowbar bit off the small chunk of metal that had been connecting the two worlds and the door swung open, bringing with it a cloud of freezing cold air. The trio stepped back, waiting for the precipitation to die down so they could see what was inside. Turning on the light to the side of the room, caused some of the condensation to dissipate and the two men stepped cautiously inside.

It wasn't long before they found it, black bags against the white fog. At first, it looked like a piece of meat, but then it was clearly too big, too long. It was most certainly a body.

CHAPTER
Forty~Two

WILL KNEW WHAT HE NEEDED TO DO. THERE WAS A system override function that had been programmed into the filter when it was built. Enabling it, would essentially shut the filter down, and eject Lottie back into her real life. It was always meant to be a last resort, and only for the strictest of emergencies but Will considered this now a situation that most certainly qualified. Will had raised it with the others over a round table meeting, and it was agreed that they should plan for an exit strategy just in case it was to be required. At that meeting, it was also agreed that such a function would remain highly confidential, so Will felt quietly hopeful Charlotte knew nothing about it.

However, access to it was something Will no longer had. He would first need to get into the office with a security clearance level but since his demotion, he doubted it would work. If, and only if, he did get inside would he need to get access to the main computers and manually override the filter to shut it down. He was no technical expert though, nor did he have the required credentials to log in to the servers. Michael Dalton was probably the only person who currently knew the correct username and passcode, and Will knew it was likely he would only get one shot at this before security escorted him off the premises.

One thing was for sure though, and that was that he needed to think fast. He might not have known how to access the servers, but he sure knew someone who could help. He decided to reach out to his old friend Simon who he had known since his stint in rehab. As a white-hat hacker Will was confident he could hack into pretty much any system in the world, and he was fairly sure that if he explained what he needed, and the urgency for it, Simon would be able to help.

He was glad they had stayed in touch all these years. He would have hated to have called him up out of the blue, asking for favours, when they hadn't spoken in forever; but Simon and Will spoke regularly. Simon was his sounding board for so many technological queries, he had sound opinions and the two of them loved discussing complex and futuristic digital trends. It was clear to Simon immediately though that this incoming call was not a casual catch-up. Will sounded frantic and breathless down the phone. He was speaking quickly, trying to relay information speedily. Thankfully, Simon was already clued up with several details to do with the filter already. He knew about Lottie going in as the prototype, he knew about the technology going into it, and as much as he had never really agreed with it conceptually, he was always there for Will.

"Why do people need to feel they have to live their best lives though?" He had asked Will in the past.

"Why would they not want to?" Had been Will's response. "If someone gave you a crystal ball and told you to look at yourself in the future, and how differently you could be living your life, wouldn't you want to see it?"

"Not really" Simon had replied. "It sounds terrifying…"

Simon never really understood why Will was so convinced the world needed to see who they could become if they fulfilled their potential, but he did enjoy talking about the groundbreaking technology that went into it. Will had explained to him that the merging of virtual reality, augmented reality and artificial intelligence would create something very powerful for the future, and Simon agreed. He just wasn't sure that using technology in this way was the smartest way to do it. He couldn't fathom why people would feel encouraged by looking at how inferior they were to the person they could become. If anything, he felt it would create more depression and anxiety and certainly more mental health issues.

However, now was not the time to tell Will 'I told you so' or to discuss the viability of the filter. Will needed help and it was clear from the way he was talking, that there wasn't much time.

"Ok, yes I think I understand what you're trying to do. Right, so I'll need to get access to the servers via the main computer, which I presume is based in the office?"

"Yes, it is."

And with that Will had arranged to meet Simon and Lottie at the office reception area as soon as possible, hoping that he would indeed, be able to get everyone successfully inside the building and past security as promised. However, as he was about to hang up on his phone call, he heard sirens in the distance that seemed to be fast approaching his street. They were getting louder and more specific in their destination, honing in on their target. Will didn't hesitate. He jumped in his car just in time to see three police cars pulling up outside his house in his rearview mirror. As he drove off, he watched them getting smaller in the distance. Men got out of the cars and headed up to his front door hastily. This wasn't right. Something had happened to Michael, he was certain of it, but he sure as hell didn't want to wait around to find out what.

———

RELIEVED THAT WILL HAD A PLAN LOTTIE, HEADED straight over to the office, hailing a cab without a beat and hoping the London traffic would be kind to her. Like many places in London getting from A to B was not about how far somewhere was in terms of distance, it was all about how bad the traffic would be. Grateful that the black cabbie didn't seem to recognise her or even seem to glance her way before accepting the route, she sat back in her chair and kept her head down from passing tourists who glared in as the car slowed in traffic. Since Michael's disappearance, the story had been on the news constantly along with photos of Lottie and Charlotte. The last thing she wanted was to be recognised and for there to be any distractions to her getting where she needed to go.

It was then that she heard the radio, quietly at first but then as she tuned her ears in more and more to the sound it became clear.

"Police have searched the home of Charlotte Mortimer and a body has been uncovered of Michael Dalton who was found in the freezer of her home. We are waiting for further reports on this breaking story but police are speaking to any potential corroborators who may be involved."

Lottie felt her skin tingle, it was ice cold and the blood had rushed from her head as though she were about to faint.

Oh my god. She killed him! No. It can't be true.

She sat up in the taxi, tears welling up in her eyes, keen to hear more but she got jolted out of her state of shock when the taxi driver had stopped and was pressing buttons on his meter.

"Whereabouts can I drop you, love?"

Lottie gestured to the front door where she was relieved to see Will's car was already there. She paid the cabbie, jumped out and ran straight into the familiar revolving doors glad to see Will standing in the reception area. He looked concerned but smiled as she approached him.

"Simon should be here any minute." Will looked over at the security guard who was seated at the reception area.

"Will, I just heard on the radio."

Lottie was trying to keep her voice down and her emotions flat although every bone in her body was filled with angst and fear. Surely this wasn't true. Surely, Charlotte didn't have it in her to do anything so callous as to kill someone. Lottie would never dream of doing anything of the sort. The filter got it wrong. The data was all wrong.

"I couldn't hear it all but police have searched Charlotte's house and found Michael's body in her freezer. Will, I think Michael's been killed."

Will closed his eyes as though he had just received a blow to the chest and all the blood drained from his face to his shoes. This was turning into a nightmare. He was shaken but knew they had a job to do, and they had to act fast.

"I had a feeling something was wrong. Charlotte's going to try to frame you for this. The police had just turned up at my house. I saw them pulling up as I left. We don't have long. It's just a matter of time before the police come looking for us here."

"Sorry I'm late" Simon was standing there with a big smile on his face, and warm eyes. "London traffic is a bitch."

The two men embraced, warm greetings were made along with quick introductions before Will walked up to the security guards and asked to sign in two guests. It was a weekend so a fairly unusual request, but the guard on duty didn't seem to notice.

"What's your name?" he asked.

"Will Sampson. I'm a co-founder. I'd like to bring in two guests please." Will did his best to sound as confident and self-assured as possible.

The guard looked impressed, as though he were only temping or on weekend duty. Keen not to make a mistake by not letting in the co-founder he obliged.

"Yes, just sign them in here."

He handed Will a form to fill in which he did with such speed it surprised the guard. He slowly and deliberately tore off two pieces of paper and opened the gate without a fuss. They were in. Now they just needed to get Simon into the main servers. Will led Lottie and Simon up to the top floor and showed him where the main servers were located.

Simon surveyed the machines before taking a seat in front of the largest screen and taking out a laptop from his bag which he proceeded to plug into the main computer. He worked fast. He had already started typing something onto his screen and pressing buttons connecting systems to systems.

"Simon, you know what we need to do, don't you. Is it possible?"

"I can try…"

Simon continued pressing buttons on his computer. A login screen kept disappearing and popping up. He didn't say much, just kept entering code and clicking enter several times. After several minutes of non-stop and furious typing, the computer on the main screen pinged to life lighting up the room with white light.

"Ok, so I found my way into the main server. I can enable the override no problem but Will the files are huge. I can't just shut it down instantly I'm going to have to delete things file by file. Getting Lottie out of here is going to take time."

"How much time? We don't have long." Will replied.

"Hard to say but a good few hours at best if not more."

Will turned to Lottie earnestly, taking out his keys from his pocket.

"Look, Lottie, you need to get out of here. This is the first place they will look. Go and hide somewhere until the override has taken place. Simon and I will take care of this. Here take my car, it's parked out at the front. Go and find somewhere safe to hide. If anything changes. I'll call you."

Lottie took the keys and looked at Will, scared. She wasn't sure when she was going to see him again and she could feel her eyes filling with emotion, but he was right. It would be safer for everyone if she got out of there. She kissed Will and squeezed his arm before turning on her heel and heading to the landing to press the button for the elevator, waiting impatiently as she did. Her heart racing, a green button appeared above the elevator and she jumped in, eagerly pressing the button to the ground floor. Tapping her heel she watched as the floors descended one by one until she heard the familiar ding of the doors opening. The doors opened on the ground floor, and standing right in front of her, seemingly waiting to enter the elevator was Charlotte.

"Well, well, well. Who do we have here?" Charlotte said coyly "and all by yourself too. Where is your boyfriend?"

Lottie stood startled in the elevator, frozen like a deer caught in the headlights.

What is she doing here? What did she want? Standing there, unsure as to what to say and whether there was any point in confronting Charlotte Lottie decided instead to simply nudge her out of the way and kept walking swiftly toward's Will's car, with every intention to just leave Charlotte behind and get out of there as fast as she could.

All she needed was some more time. Just enough time to let the override take effect and all of this would be over, but Charlotte followed her, nipping at her heels like an excitable puppy as she walked towards the revolving doors towards the car parked right outside the entrance.

"I thought I would find you here. It's such a shame it's had to come to this Lottie," she said keeping up with Lottie as she walked.

"It was all going so well for you, and then you had to go and murder Michael in cold blood and ruin it all…"

Lottie was taken aback by the brazenness of Charlotte. She had lost her mind.

"What are you talking about Charlotte? I know what you did."

"I don't know what you mean Lottie. Me? I haven't got anything to do with any of this?" Charlotte retorted haughtily with a laugh. "I think you'll find the police are looking for you. In fact, they will probably be here any minute. I told them you might be here. Anything to help the police with such a tragic, tragic story."

Lottie circled her way out of the office doors unlocking the car in her fumbling hands as she did so. Grateful that Charlotte had waited her turn before entering the same doors, she ran as fast as she could towards Will's car and jumped in, but she wasn't fast enough. Before she could drive off Charlotte's hand was on the door handle and her body had flung itself into the passenger seat. Sirens were wailing in the distance. Lottie didn't have time to wait. She started to drive.

"Hey! What's the rush? Where are you off to? I mean, not that it makes much difference, they will find you anyway. It's not really the best getaway is it? Driving off in your boyfriend's car? Very original. Would have expected more from such a prolific crime writer such as yourself, but it was very good of you to describe your murder scene the way you did. It was really descriptive, helpful if you know what I mean…"

"Charlotte. You think you're so smart don't you…"

Lottie managed whilst speeding her way away from the office building and through busy London streets."

"Well, Lottie. I play to win. Always have, always will."

"I know you who are Charlotte. All of this, everything you do is a lie. I don't know how you can live with yourself, how you can look at yourself in the mirror. You're not an improved version of anyone, you're a sad person pretending to the world that you're something you're not. The truth is you have nothing. You might have money, but you're lonely. You have no friends, no family, nothing."

"I have a hell of a lot more than you Lottie. Did you really think you could waltz in here and humiliate me and I would just lie down and take it? I always warned Michael not to underestimate me but he never listened…"

Lottie sped her way towards the embankment. She didn't know where she was going but just knew she just had to keep driving.

"So you killed him? Charlotte what kind of a monster are you? All to save yourself and your stupid reputation. What did Michael ever do to you?"

"I don't know what you're talking about Lottie," Charlotte replied conceitedly and sarcastically. "It's your padlock they found locking the freezer door along with some of your hair and just you wait until they search you and find the phone. Ouch."

Charlotte shrugged and smiled passive-aggressively, irritating Lottie with her haughtiness. Lottie felt a pang of panic. *His phone?* She felt all over her body and noticed an unknown bulge was in her inside coat pocket. *Oh god!*

"Listen, Lottie, I don't know where you're driving to, but if I were you I would just drive myself straight to the police station to hand yourself in. They have found the body, and let's just say all evidence points to you.... It's not looking good if you know what I mean."

That was when she started hearing the sirens. They were in the distance but fast approaching what seemed to be her car.

"Charlotte, you think you're so clever, don't you. You think you've got this all figured out! Well done Charlotte, well played! Yes, check-mate by the mighty Charlotte."

Charlotte smiled triumphantly, but any previous beauty this woman had once had, any enviously white teeth, or long golden hair now looked so ugly. She was a monster and the efforts she had made to improve her appearance did nothing to mask her character.

"Well, Charlotte, it might surprise you to know that Will is currently in the office as we speak. He has hacked into the servers and is shutting down the entire filter, deleting every single file one by one. It's started already. It's just a matter of time before you and everything you stand for will be gone."

Now it was Lottie who was smiling. She had swiftly turned the tables.

Charlotte's whole body language and demeanour changed. Her shoulders drooped downwards, her smile turned upside down, she looked visibly hurt, as though the words of Lottie had wounded her deeply. If Charlotte's ego and world had been a balloon Lottie had just taken a proverbial prick to it, shattering her energy and everything about her seemed to be turned on its head.

"Well, he can't be. That's impossible. Michael was the only one who knew how to. There's no override function."

"It's very possible. You might remember before you publicly ruined Will's life he was the brains behind the whole thing and he developed it with an override function. I guess Michael never told you about that? You are over Charlotte. It's over".

"No..." Charlotte seemed shocked, disoriented. "That can't be true. That can't be true. We have to turn around."

"No Charlotte. Your ridiculous, pretentious world is over. Did you really think you could keep up this illusion forever?"

"Turn the car around right now!" Charlotte was screaming, her seatbelt taught by the side of her bulging neck muscles.

Lottie ignored her and kept driving, checking for the police in her rearview mirror. They were getting closer, so close that she could feel the vibrations fill her body from the sirens. Suddenly, she felt Charlotte's hand grab the steering wheel and swing, a sharp right as swiftly as she could. She was trying to turn the car around. She was trying to force Lottie to drive back to the office. Desperation washed over her. The car spun violently. Lottie braked but the car kept spinning. Suddenly there was an ear-shattering crash. Loud and jolting. Water submerged Lottie's senses. She felt as though she were falling. It wasn't long before she blanked out.

CHAPTER
Forty-Three

As a bee gathering nectar does not harm or disturb the colour and fragrance of the flower; so do the wise who move through the earth.

BUDDHA.

SIRENS. POLICE SIRENS. A BLACK SKY AND A FULL MOON, but the moon was in the distance and looked more like a golf ball, glowing. The sky was so dark, and the golf ball was so far away but it was getting closer, the craters and indentations were getting more visible. A force was pulling Lottie towards the little white ball. It was so white it was almost dazzling. She followed the light and then someone was hovering over her face. She was breathing through a mask, each breath loud and purposeful. Oxygen flowed into her lungs like a cool breeze.

Then nothing. She drifted off again to see the golf ball, floating in the darkness, it didn't want to go away again, so it waited for her, patiently. She reached out it grab it. Then she felt like she was moving, something was jostling up her up and down as though there were bumps along a road. Time was undefined, it was lost on her. Sleep felt comfortable, she felt cocooned, as though an alarm clock had sounded but she didn't want to wake up.

"Oh my god, she just moved!"

There was a shuffling, a commotion around her and although her eyes were closed she could sense someone close to her breathing on her face.

"Lottie love, can you hear me? Lottie, it's your mum. Lottie love, move your finger or blink an eye if you can hear me."

Lottie could hear this voice and her instructions, but her body wasn't responding to the sounds. They seemed so far away, as though they were underwater, muffled. There was a beeping sound. Regular. Steady. Smells were coming into her nose as though each breath brought new, distinctive air. It smelled clean, sterile and plastic. There was still a mask on her face. The smells were unfamiliar. She didn't recognise them. They didn't belong to her.

"Her finger just moved. I just saw it twitch! Doctor, we need a doctor. Where is the doctor?"

The shuffling sounds retreated as the sound of footsteps receded backwards in search of medical help. Lottie had felt her finger move as this voice breathed life into her body, switching it on somehow. She tried to open her eye. Bright light dazzled her. Too bright. Not yet.

"Doctor, I just saw her move." There were two sets of footsteps now. "Her finger moved and her eye twitched."

There was hope in this voice, desperation almost, angst. How long had this voice been longing like this?

Someone with colder hands was touching her hands now, then her feet. Tapping. Saying words very slowly and precisely.

"Lottie. Can you open your eyes for me?"

Lottie could feel her eyes twitch. She was now really putting effort into it, real effort. She focused on one eye, one at a time. The left eye. She tried to peel it open slowly, blinking to keep it moist. The light made it so dry but it was opening. Shafts of light shone to the back of her head, dazzling her. Then the right. Her pupils needed a minute to catch up, let in the light and then they would let her eyes do the work and take in her surroundings.

With one eye ajar she was able to see blearily. She was lying in a bed, a hospital bed. There was a mask on her face that made her breathing sound heavy and exaggerated as though she were snorkelling, and tubes and wires seemed to be coming out of various parts of her body. Lights were shining down above her and a small table was in front of her with flowers on it, some water and grapes along with a few magazines and books. A man was hovering above her head, looming with a white coat on and badge. Dr Ravi Patel. He looked familiar. She had seen him before somewhere. Then a woman. She was holding her hand and crying, tears were forming in her eyes. Tears of joy. It was her mother. She felt herself relax into the bed with comfort at the sight of her mother there. Although she looked tired, it gave her such comfort to see her beside her bed. Familiarity at long last.

Lottie tried to speak but the mask was still on her face thwarting her efforts.

"Can we take off her mask?" Her mother asked with a sense of urgency.

The doctor was making notes about something or other but he quickly put down his pen and proceeded to take off Lottie's mask, putting something smelly under her nose. The smell went right through her veins, lifting her, flooding her senses. It was cool and refreshing, tickling her features, making them itch. Feeling was coming back into her face. Pins and needles.

Lottie tried to speak, looking directly into her mother's eyes, hoping she would understand, but no words came out. She was mumbling, incoherent. It was slurred as though she was drunk.

"Maaa…"

The doctor stepped in.

"Lottie, just take it easy and do not worry. You are in the Royal London Hospital being well looked after. My name is Doctor Ravi Patel.

Unfortunately, you became very unwell at work and developed a nasty fever which turned into what is known as autoimmune encephalitis. It's when your brain swells up. It caused you to be in a coma for over three weeks. Three weeks and nineteen days to be precise, but we are optimistic you will make a full recovery. It's very common for your speech to take a while to come back so don't panic."

There was something about the way the doctor told her not to panic that sent anxiety through her, especially at it was clear she simply couldn't get the words out. She tried again but her body wasn't connecting to itself yet. Her mind was ordering instructions that weren't being obeyed. She tried to move her arm, nothing. She tried to kick. Her legs felt heavy, sedated. She was unable to move.

"Maaaa… maaaaum…Chhhhalut."

"Yes, darling! It's me. Don't worry, we are going to take good care of you and get you home as soon as we can."

"Shhharlotte…ffffittter."

"There, there dear. Just do as the doctor says and take it easy."

Lottie tried to force her lips together to speak but nothing was making any sense. Baffling sounds were coming out that sounded almost primitive and tribal. She was impatient and growing anxious. It was terrifying. She wanted to speak. Her mother looked at the doctor for reassurance, as though he may have the answers as to what she was trying to say.

"It's very normal for there to be some disorientation and confusion for some time upon coming out of a coma. Speech doesn't come back right away, often there is some memory loss. I wouldn't worry at all, it's very much to be expected. Once she's stable we'll get her out of ICU into a rehabilitation hospital specialised in coma patients who will help with her recovery."

Lottie's mother smiled and gripped Lottie's hand tightly.

"You see. You're in safe hands. I am so happy to hear you're trying to talk love. I can't tell you how much we've been worried about you. Your father will be back any minute, he just popped to the loo. Typical John, he waits by your bed all night and then the moment you come to he's not here."

There were tears in her mother's eyes, and she wiped her nose with a tissue. Her mother and father had been waiting by her bed. Although she had never been on bad terms with her parents they had drifted. They weren't close. There was never any emotion from either of them, they were ever stoic with their feelings — yet clearly, they cared more than she realised. She wanted so much to reach out to her mother and hug her, to tell her she was ok, that this would all be ok, that she would be a better daughter to her from now on. That family was going to become more important in her life. She wanted to warn her about Charlotte. She wanted to tell her to reach out to Will and see if they switched off the filter. She wanted to say so much but all she could do was just lay there looking at her mother, terrified by her paralysis and grateful that she was by her side.

Days passed and Lottie spent time drifting in and out of sleep. Movement in her body became more frequent and expected. It started with her fingers and hands, she then found she could move her arms, followed by her legs. One day, she couldn't remember which, she was wheeled into an ambulance and transferred to a different hospital. She remembered the bed felt more padded and comfortable there, and she was grateful to be able to move it up and down with her fingers. There was also a bookshelf in the corner of the room and her mother and father sat at either side of her bed, taking it in turns to read to her. Often one would disappear to fetch cups of tea and snacks from the vending machine. Not that Lottie was up to eating much, she was on soup and fruit juice for a while, as per doctors orders as apparently her stomach was not up to eating solid food just yet.

She found her speech began returning to her too, and when it did the doctor wasted no time in asking her questions. Each day, for what felt like weeks he would come with a clipboard and sit on the chair beside her bed, where he would ask her the same set of questions over and over. He said it was to test her memory, but she couldn't help but wonder if there was something wrong with *his*. Why was he asking her the same things over and over? It was as though each time he asked her something he somehow hoped for different answers.

One morning, however, his questioning felt as though it were more conclusive somehow.

"Lottie, it's Doctor Patel. How have you settled into your new hospital? We've moved you somewhere with a more specialised rehabilitation unit which we hope you'll find more comfortable. Unfortunately, you suffered from some seizures and convulsions when you were unwell, so it's quite likely you have some damaged nerve endings. That's why I need to ask you some questions to see what you remember and what you don't."

It was the same doctor who had been beside her bed when she first woke up and she still couldn't place where she had seen him before. She nodded at him and kept trying to work it out. Trying to place his face into different scenarios in her mind to piece together where recognised him from.

"Ok," she managed, squinting at him through bleary eyes.

"Can you tell me your full name?"

"Lottie. Lottie Mortimer."

"How old are you?"

"Thirty-two".

"Do you remember your birthday?"

"Yes, it's in June. June the 8th."

The doctor seemed encouraged and smiled broadly at her parents who were still sitting at either side of her bed looking eagerly at him.

"Good. That's very good Lottie. Now, do you remember anything about what happened to you?"

Lottie paused. There were still so many pieces of her memory swirling around disjointed in her mind. The order of time on them was confused as though they were painted with broad brush strokes in no logical manner, but she remembered them all vividly.

"Yes, I was in the filter. I think Charlotte was going to try to kill me too. She already killed Michael. Will was trying to turn it off. We had to stop her. Did he manage? Is he ok? Where is Will?"

The doctor cleared his throat and continued with his questioning.

"Ok. Let's move on. Where do you live?"

"At the moment I live at Egerton Crescent with Charlotte, but I can't go back there. Not now…"

The doctor was scribbling in his notebook with a concerned expression on his face. Her mother and father were looking at each other exchanging glances that were not lost on her.

"What do you do for a living Lottie? What's your job?"

"I just finished my first crime novel. I'm working on becoming a bestselling writer."

Her mother then nudged her arm and smiled at her, seemingly impatient at Lottie's recollection of the facts and protective over her level of potential humiliation.

"No Lottie," intercepted her mother. "You work as an EA for Augmented Minds. Remember? You've been there for a long time now. Probably about ten years or so."

Lottie went quiet and frowned.

"But that was before, doctor. Before I went into the filter. You do know about the filter, don't you? It showed me who I could become. It made Charlotte. Charlotte killed Michael. Doctor, you have to tell me. Did Will switch off the filter? Is Michael dead?"

Lottie looked at her mother and father who were no longer looking at her with encouraged faces. They were looking down to the ground as though they were deeply disappointed, as though she had said something wrong.

"That will be all for today," the doctor said before he smiled briefly at Lottie and walked away indicating to her parents through a gentle hand gesture to follow him. The three of them were gathered away from her bed talking in hushed tones. They kept looking back at Lottie with concerned expressions on their faces. Her mother looked so sad, what was he telling them. She was looking down to the ground in a daze. She could hear only the odd words. What were they saying?

"Psychiatric… mental health… close observation".

Her mother and father were nodding now. They stopped looking at her at all now, solemnity taking over their bodies like an imposing dark cloud.

As the days passed Lottie began to attempt to walk. She was so frustrated with being in her bed she was keen to get up and become more mobile. She felt as though her mind was sharpening up but her muscles had atrophied at such a pace that she was beginning to feel as though she were alive in someone else's body. She wanted to see her reflection and to clean her teeth herself.

With the help from a nurse, she began taking steps forward one by one, but after a couple of what felt like minuscule strides, her body gave up on itself and she wasn't able to walk any further. Not one to quit, she fought each day for a little more strength, a little more distance. She knew she could do it.

By her tenth day, she had talked all the way to the bathroom with the help of only a frame and by day fourteen, she had done it on her own. That's not to say that the effort came with any real sense of reward. Upon seeing her reflection in the mirror she barely recognised herself. Pale and gaunt she had lost so much weight that the skin on her face seemed to be so thin she could see veins on her forehead. Dark circles has burrowed beneath her eyes. Her green eyes were grey and bloodshot, her hair greasy, tied back in a messy bun and her teeth were yellow and stained. This was not who she was? Who was this person looking back at herself?

The nurses and hospital team were impressed with her physical progress but she felt none of this joy. Being able to walk should have been a given, a bare minimum for how she lived her life, not a congratulatory achievement. She was capable of so much more and she wanted to get out of the hospital so she could move on and put all of this behind her. She needed to find Will and find out if he'd turned off the filter. She needed to find out what happened to Charlotte. She would talk to her mum, her dad, the nurses and anyone who would listen about the filter, asking them to please reach out to Will and find out what was going on. She would plead that she needed to get out of the hospital as she was worried about what Charlotte was capable of next.

Such conversations were never reciprocated, she felt as though it was a constant one-way dialogue where whoever was listening would avoid eye contact with her and then ignore her as though she were crazy, as though they were essentially blocking her out. Nobody seemed to believe her which made her survival instincts ignite all the more. She needed to get better so she could get out.

She knew her stay at the rehabilitation unit wouldn't last forever provided she continued to improve and just when she thought she was about to be released Dr Patel sat down on the chair beside her bed looking solemn.

"Lottie, how are you feeling today?"

"Much better. Keen to get out of here now, to be honest."

"I understand. The nurses and team here have been amazed that you're walking already, and you're getting so strong. It's quite some progress you've been making."

"I've been trying. I need to get out of here so I can make sure the filter has been switched off. I need to find Will. Has he been to see me?"

"No Lottie, I'm afraid not."

Then after a pause, Dr Patel took a deep breath.

"Lottie I'm afraid we're not quite ready to release you just yet. Whilst you're doing very well on your physical development you're not yet ready to go home from a mental point of view. You seem to be displaying signs of confusion."

"I'm not confused, doctor. Why do you think I'm confused?"

"It's very common for seizures and convulsions to cause lasting nerve damage which, in turn, can lead to psychiatric conditions and confusion. We would like to transfer you to another specialised unit that can make sense of your memories."

"A psychiatric hospital?" Lottie was shocked. She wasn't crazy. Did everyone around her just think she had lost her mind?

"I suppose you could call it that. It's really another rehabilitation unit very similar to this one, but they are specialised in helping you deal with any confusion or disorientation as part of your recovery."

"But I don't want to go there. I just want to go home. You can't force me can you?"

"Well, unfortunately, we would worry you may inflict harm to yourself or others if we release you now so we have a duty of care to ensure you are looked after. We also have consent from your parents who agree."

Lottie became agitated now, standing up, shouting.

"But I'm not crazy doctor! Do you hear me! I'm not crazy! You have to believe me. You will see. Let me out and I'll prove it to you. I'm not crazy."

———

AFTER WEEKS OF FEELING AS THOUGH SHE HAD AN incentive to improve, her admittance to the psychiatric hospital came as a heavy blow, and one that she wasn't expecting, nor was ready to deal with. Of all the scenarios she had played out in her mind, being admitted to another hospital was certainly not one of them. She didn't even know where she was. She was bundled once again into the back of an ambulance and driven to a destination she wasn't privy to. The next thing she knew was she was inside what felt like more of a bedroom than a hospital. The room was painted a dusky pink and there were old fashioned flowery curtains hanging over a small window with a view to a peaceful garden. There was carpet underfoot that was thin and threadbare, the colour of which was indistinguishable and there was a flickering lamp beside a single bed placed near a wall. There was a smell of dried urine wafting in from somewhere, lingering as though it belonged in the room much more than she did.

Lottie walked to the bedroom door and pulled on the loose brass door handle to see if she was free to leave her room and explore her surroundings. Grateful that she was allowed to roam the building as she pleased she walked past other similar looking bedrooms before wandering to a downstairs area. There was a large living room with a TV on and several patients were staring at it, zoned out expressions on their faces. They were a variety of ages, a couple of very young girls probably in their early twenties, and some middle-aged women, one who had concerned expressions fixed upon her face and downward shaped frowns. The men all sat at the back of the room. Some played chess, some read in silence.

Adjoining this room was a large canteen area that had double doors at the back that led to an outside area. Basic looking, wooden tables and chairs were arranged neatly and from the canteen came a smell of school dinners; warm and undistinguishable. Newspapers were dotted around on the tables, no doubt leftover from breakfast. Lottie picked up a newspaper and decided to sit with the others in the communal area to watch TV and read.

A nurse had greeted her that morning and showed her to her room. She wasn't going to pretend to be grateful. She didn't want to play along with this as she wasn't expecting to be there for long. The nurse mentioned something about a timetable for when they served lunch. She said she would begin her therapy sessions tomorrow and today she was welcome to just settle in and make herself at home.

Home. She had forgotten the meaning of the word

lately. What did it mean to her? Where was she comfortable calling home? She couldn't go back to Charlotte's now, nor did she want to. She just wanted to go back to her flat and start building her life up again. Slowly and steadily, brick by brick under no illusion that she should aim for perfection. She saw right through that facade. Nobody was perfect or living a perfect life. Nobody had it all. It was a fallacy, a myth, created by so many to make others feel so little. As she sat in the communal area on a brown leather sofa, looking around her, she knew she had a long way to go to rebuild her life, but if each day she could just be better than the day before, then things would inevitably be ok.

As she started her therapy she began to get into a routine for which she was grateful. It gave her a sense of purpose to her day. After breakfast, she would have a two-hour conversation with a psychiatrist called Dr Wandle about her memories. She had told him all about her experiences in the filter and he had listened. She was glad someone had taken the time to listen and ask her questions about what she recalled. Indeed, it helped her remember more and put things into sequential order. Yet the more she talked, the more he had made her question her memories, asking her why she felt what she had. Whether she had been truly sure this was real or whether she might have been dreaming, imagining the whole thing when she had fallen ill.

For the first few weeks, she was sure her memories were real, they were vivid and conceptual. She was wholeheartedly convinced. She relayed specific conversations with Charlotte, what Nico would cook in the kitchen and what her challenges involved. However, as their sessions continued and Dr Wandle asked more and more poignant questions she too began to question what was real and what wasn't. Besides, her life in the ward had a routine, it was a haven of calm normality conducive to a tranquil appeased mind. She began to feel her mind reaching out within itself, grasping at the questions as they approached her and gripping them with tenacity like small tentacles reaching out for the truth. Perhaps she had been unwell after all, and this was her new reality now.

After her sessions, she would spend time in the communal area. She had found it hard to make friends as many of the patients weren't chatty and kept themselves to themselves but Lottie did enjoy reading and occasionally she would play a game of chess with another young woman named Trish. Trish had some sort of schizophrenia but was incredibly bright, not needing to spend much time at all contemplating her next move, she would always appear to be playing one step ahead of Lottie. The good sides of Trish were endearing and charming, she would often tease Lottie about her book reading, asking her what she was reading and whether she ever put down her books. However when she felt frustrated she would begin hitting herself across the head repeatedly and Lottie had watched a few times as she was ushered away by the nurses, away from prying eyes.

Perhaps this was why so many stayed so quiet. It was easier that way. It was easier to live a life of complacence than revolt. Nobody caused a fuss because what was the point? They could all see that opinions or frustrations would get them nowhere so there they stayed, comfortably numb. No doubt from the medication they were all on. Lottie often wondered what was in the little pills she was handed twice a day with her breakfast and dinner.

Lottie's parents continued to visit, although much less

frequently, clearly the commute from Weymouth was getting difficult to justify with their work schedules and she knew they didn't have an awful lot of money. She looked forward to their visits though, and as per her therapist's instructions, she had made a real effort not to talk about anything to do with the filter. She made a conscious effort not to appear unwell or to worry them any more than she had. It was clear she had caused them a lot of distress. Besides, perhaps Dr Wandle was right. Perhaps she had been imagining the whole thing after all. Perhaps these seizures had caused her to be confused. She hadn't heard from Will, he hadn't been in to visit her at all and as far as she could tell there were no indications that what she had remembered was real. Nobody seemed to know what she was talking about.

After several months the doctors were pleased with Lottie's progress. Dr Patel came back to check on her asking how she was doing. She had replied to him, as she had replied to the others, that she was feeling much better and that the confusion she'd clearly been suffering from had shifted away. Now that she could see things clearly and was grateful for all the help she'd received, she just wanted to go home.

Dr Patel smiled broadly at Lottie and seemed pleased. He told her he was happy with her progress and would prepare her release paperwork for early next week.

Lottie was overjoyed, she had arranged for her parents to pick her up and they agreed she would go and spend some time at home with them in Weymouth as getting out of the city would be a good thing for her. They mentioned they had her bedroom all ready and she was happy at their efforts and that she wouldn't be alone.

That afternoon she settled down to delve into her

latest book with a cup of tea, a crime novel, in the communal area, and excitement welled up inside her that she was finally going to be able to be released. Although the weeks and months had been a blur, she was sure she had been there for some time. No phone, no contact with anyone from the outside world, no autonomy to make her own decisions. She was ready. The TV was on in the background and the news was playing quietly and inoffensively.

Then she saw him.

It was definitely him.

The shape of his face, his features, the way he spoke. He was on the news.

"Could someone turn up the volume?" Lottie said frantically, raising her voice above her normal range already.

From somewhere one of the patients obliged and Lottie found herself moving closer to the screen, the warm tea spilling over her wrist. A caption appeared below his face. 'MICHAEL DALTON - TECH ENTREPRENEUR'.

"Yes, John we are incredibly excited about this too. It's going to be quite a game-changer in the world of social media, so much so that many people are calling this the biggest industry disruptor of a generation. Essentially, what it will do is enable the user to vividly see who they could become if they were to live their best life by letting them step inside a filter that shows them who they could become. We believe that by seeing one's true potential, it will be a hugely motivating factor to change, and the idea is that the person would come out of the filter equipped with

all the knowledge to self-improve to their maximum potential."

"Gosh" replied the TV presenter. "Quite some claims."

"Yes. A huge amount of development has gone into this but we are confident it can change not just our lives, but our economies."

"And when is this filter planning to be launched, Mr Dalton?"

"It's ready to go. It's been through rigorous testing and it will be launched on all major social media platforms next week."

Lottie heard muffled sounds again. She was underwater, swimming with her eyes open. She closed her eyes. Her mug of tea dropped to the floor and a crashing sound sent jolts of electricity through her. It was real. It was all real. She got up, frantically, looking for help as though the eyes of her companions could potentially aid her but she knew they couldn't. They hardly reacted.

"It's real!" she screamed. "It was all real all along and you have all been letting me think I've gone crazy! I need to get out of here. That's Michael! He's on the TV! Please someone just listen to me!"

Before she could say any more the nurses in white coats arrived. They took her away, they drowned out her screams for help. They lulled her into submission. One injected something into her arm, the others carried her. Faces looked at her from sunken sofas, gormless, helpless as she was carried away, extracted from the situation and the room like an unwanted virus.

It was real after all. Everything she had been made to doubt was real and to make matters worse, it was soon due to be released upon the world.

CHAPTER
Forty~Four

Three months earlier…

WILL HAD CALLED MICHAEL WHEN HE KNEW AN AMBULANCE WAS ON its way. It was an obvious decision to get an ambulance there when he did. Something was wrong. Lottie's seizures and convulsions became more frequent and more pronounced and it was clear the doctor on duty didn't have all the equipment nor wherewithal required to deal with it. Michael, who had been working on a lower floor, came up right away, a frantic expression on his face.

Sidelining Will, Michael went straight to the young doctor.

"What's happened?"

"It's not clear I'm afraid but it looks like Lottie may have developed some sort of virus or infection in her body. I've tried giving her antibiotics but her body is not responding. It's been a few hours and she seems to be getting worse."

"You're here alone?" Michael asked the doctor, clearly sharing the same concerns as Will with regards to his level of seniority.

"Yes, sir."

"Will, a word?" He gestured for Will to join him outside, glancing briefly at the concerned looking young doctor as the two men closed the door behind them and stood talking amid the bright lights of the hallway.

"Will, let's just take a moment here to breathe and think this through ok. What will happen to Lottie's progress if we get her to a hospital? Will she forget everything when she wakes up or will she manage to retain everything up until now?"

Will looked at Michael with a blank expression on his face, shocked that he was asking such a question at a time like this.

"I'm afraid we just don't know Michael, but Lottie's health is more important. We have to get her to a hospital!"

Michael looked to the left and right of him to check he was not being overheard by passing ears in the hallway.

"Yes, I agree Will. It's just have you considered what you will tell the ambulance when they arrive and see her hooked up like this? What are you going to say when they ask what happened to her? You're going to explain she was in a filter proofing facility where she's been for several months because we're testing out a filter?

Look, Will, I've been very careful about how we manage this and we need to keep it that way. Think, Will think. God forbid, if anything were to happen to Lottie and it came to light that she was in any way related to this project, there would be serious consequences for us both."

Will hadn't considered this. He only wanted what was best for Lottie. He couldn't believe any of this was happening.

"Look Will, this is unfortunate and I agree that we need to get Lottie to a hospital, and we will - but might I suggest we get this young doctor to unplug her from here so we can take her downstairs where we wait for the ambulance. You can leave the rest to me, ok? I'll explain everything to the paramedics."

Will was in such a state of confusion and shock that he conceded via a subtle nod.

Upon reentering the room it was Michael who was calling the shots. He pointed at a stretcher next to her bed that had been lying dormant except for when Lottie needed turning over.

"Doctor, can we get Lottie on the stretcher and save time for the ambulance by taking her downstairs ready. They should be here any moment."

The young doctor agreed without asking questions and began unplugging Lottie's devices and pulling out wires connected to her body. He put a portable mask over her face as they began wheeling her frantically, towards the elevators. Upon reaching the ground floor the ambulance arrived, blue lights flashing through the office reception and Lottie was pushed out into the daylight, where two paramedics jumped out hurriedly to help.

One of them flung open the back doors of the ambulance and Will went straight towards him, keen to get Lottie inside as soon as possible. The other stood next to Michael, keen to assess the situation, asking him questions as to how she came to be in this state.

"What happened?" Asked the paramedic close to Michael.

"Thank you for coming so quickly. It would appear the poor girl became rather unwell. Lottie Mortimer is her name. She works here. It seems she suddenly developed a fever and then started having seizures. We called the onsite doctor who's been with her until now."

Although this wasn't entirely untrue, there was no mention of anything else and as Will sat down in the ambulance taking hold of Lottie's hand watching Michael speak to the paramedic, he knew this was getting into dangerous territory.

"Does she have any medical conditions? Any allergies?"

"Not that I know of…"

Before Will had the chance to hear much more, the ambulance doors were creaking to a close. Will caught Michael's eye just before the two doors clinked together, and Michael gave Will a knowing nod.

WILL HAD BEEN WAITING AT THE HOSPITAL FOR SEVERAL HOURS. THE last he had seen of Lottie had been when she had been wheeled out of the ambulance in a flurry of activity. Doctors and paramedics surrounded her stretcher like bees to a hive, keen to get their honey into safe hands. She disappeared into the main hospital and Will had been waiting for news. He didn't want to leave her until he knew she was going to be ok.

All this time waiting had exacerbated his feelings of guilt and remorse. What had he done? What had he enabled with this creation? He had no idea if Lottie was going to be ok but the sense of regret cut into him like a deep wound. For the life of him, he couldn't remember why he was so convinced that seeing the best version of yourself would be such a good idea. Simon had been right all along. It was clear it was a dangerous prophecy that nobody needed to live by. It didn't bring out the best in people, it brought out the worst. It brought to the fore their insecurities, their jealousies, the fact they felt as though they were never good enough, and they could never be good enough because perfection was so flawed a concept. It was so obvious, yet he was blinded by the desire to do something good, to be something or someone, he hadn't considered what adverse effects it could really cause.

He thought so much about Lottie, as he sat there on a metallic chair in the busy waiting area, watching the comings and goings of the hospital waiting room, and how he had tried to help her in the filter, warning her about Charlotte, and he wondered what had happened to her when they lost the feed. Had something caused her to react this way? Had something been the catalyst for her becoming so unwell? Clearly, she had been in distress. He so wanted to sit beside her and hold her hand. He didn't want to make the same mistake as before. This time, when she came out of this, he would be there for her, he would tell her how he felt and that he thought she was remarkable. She really was. Whatever he thought he had been searching for, whatever that was, wasn't real. He had changed, he wanted more from his life in more ways than he ever realised before.

After asking the frantic and impatient looking receptionist for updates several times during his wait, he was relieved when a woman doctor stepped out to ask if he was with Lottie Mortimer.

"How is she?"

"She's stable in ICU for now, but unfortunately she is in a coma. It would appear her body is fighting something and until we do tests we won't know what it is for sure. Was Lottie displaying any symptoms that she might have been unwell? Complaining of a headache or running a temperature?"

Will shook his head.

"Were there any changes to her personality in the last few days?"

"No."

We will need to keep her under close observation. As I said, until we run some tests we won't know for sure but I suspect what she has contracted is a form of encephalitis."

"What's that? Will she be ok though? Do we know what caused it?"

"It can be caused by a variety of things, if it's bacterial it could be that she contracted a virus. However, if it's autoimmune it's something the body is very much doing to itself. Its own antibodies are essentially trying to attack the brain. As I said, at the moment we don't know for sure what it is but we are investigating everything."

Will looked down, forlorn. Disappointment flooded over him that this wasn't something that could be fixed quickly. The doctor read his body language.

"The best thing I can suggest is that you go home, get some sleep and we will contact you should anything change. We're not allowing any visitors now until tomorrow."

The doctor smiled sympathetically. Will nodded, grateful to have had an update but his sense of worry unappeased.

"Thank you."

With that, the doctor turned on her heel and walked back through the mysterious double doors Lottie had disappeared through a few hours before.

CHAPTER
Forty-Five

Will went to the hospital most mornings to check on Lottie. Not that there was much change. Each day seemed just like the one before, she would be lying there listless, hooked up to all these machines. So helpless. The only sounds coming out of her were beeps of machinery, letting him know she was still alive. If it weren't for those, nobody would know just by looking at her whether she was alive or dead. Her body hardly moved to breathe, not even a gradual rise of the chest to even so much as hint that she was fighting to wake up.

He prayed for some movement, a finger, a smile. He imagined her sitting next to him and opening her eyes, squeezing his hand in hers. However, he was always disappointed. The doctors were as helpful as they could be, updating him on all the tests that she'd undertaken, but were unable to really shed much light on her recovery. They had no idea if and when she would come out of this coma, all they could say was that they hoped it would be soon. What's more, nobody knew what state she would be in when she did come out. They explained memory loss and disorientation was common, and this often included basic functions, such as learning how to walk and eat. Will prayed she would be ok and that by some miracle, none of this would apply to her.

He would spend the mornings sitting beside her bed reading to her, or giving her the latest scoop of office gossip. He would tell her all about what the two of them would do when she got better. He had such big plans for how they might disappear for a few months onto a private island. It would inevitably be somewhere hot and sunny where he would spend the time painting and she would do whatever made her heart happy. He would talk to her as though she were his therapist, explaining that he no longer wanted what he once felt was so important to him. How the whole concept behind the filter had been crazy and he really just wanted nothing to do with it anymore. He was going to walk away from it all, and leave it all in the past.

By lunchtime, he knew Lottie's parents would normally arrive, likely right off the train from Weymouth, and that was Will's cue to leave. He had seen them once hurrying over to her bed while he had got himself a snack from the vending machine. He didn't want to have to explain himself or why he was there. He didn't want to have to look them in the eye and tell them what he had done to their daughter. The shame and guilt were eating away at him from the inside. What started as a project with such good intentions had turned into a living nightmare.

Weeks went by and Will hadn't been into the office. He couldn't face it after what had happened, and he finally called Michael to tell him that he was stepping down.

"I can see you've become too close to this Will. You're too emotionally invested. It's probably for the best that you step back now."

"Yes, to be honest, Michael after what's happened I want

nothing more to do with this. The whole idea was crazy. We need to pull the plug on this whole thing."

"I couldn't agree more," Michael replied sensitively. "Don't worry about a thing. I'll take care of it. You just take some time out."

"I want everything canned. I want to make sure this whole idea gets dead and buried."

"I understand. Don't worry I'll get the paperwork started Will. I'll get my EA to get some documents over to you to sign. Just get them back to me and we'll consider this all in the past. A lesson learnt."

"Good." Will breathed a sigh of relief. He was going to draw a line under it all, and that gave him momentary comfort.

"How is she, Will?" Michael asked delicately.

"The same. The doctors have no idea whether she'll make a full recovery which is terrifying. I just keep hoping and praying she'll wake up soon."

"Of course. Well, if it's any consolation. From what I under-stand, it was autoimmune encephalitis, which means it had nothing to do with the filter. From what I'm told it's very likely Lottie would have contracted it anyway, so don't blame your-self. Just bad luck."

"Yes, possibly." Will accepted this statement but he couldn't shrug off the feeling of guilt and responsibility none-theless. He also didn't know what had happened when the data feed had been lost. He couldn't help but feel as though some-thing in that filter had caused this to happen.

Michael was sympathetic.

"Let me know if there's anything I can do Will. I mean anything."

Will decided to spend the weekend with his parents in the country. He needed to get away and clear his head. He wanted some home cooking, he was getting sick of vending machine rubbish. However, when he came back to visit Lottie early Monday morning there was someone else in her bed.

He asked the nurses if she had been moved and where she had gone.

"Oh yes, she was transferred to another facility" replied a busy looking nurse he had seen on the ward on and off.

"What do you mean? Why? Can you tell me which one?"

"Are you family?"

"No."

The nurse raised the corner of her lip and flicked some blonde hair away from her eyes.

"I'm afraid we're not at liberty to tell you her whereabouts unless you're family."

And just like that Lottie Mortimer was gone.

CHAPTER
Forty-Six

It really was music to Michael's ears that Will was stepping down voluntarily. What a blessing. The man was clearly not thinking straight. *Poor chap got too close. Mustn't get emotionally attached to the product,* he recited to himself with a wistful tut. He didn't realise what potential this filter still had as all he had been able to focus on was the downside. *One small hiccup and he got scared.*

However, Michael was sure that with the right tweaking, and some precise development work, the filter could still be fine-tuned to be the superstar it always had the potential to be.

More and more twenty-somethings were addicted to their phones, yet were unable to use the time spent on their phones resourcefully. They were connected to thousands of 'friends,' but had genuine connections with so few. There was a huge gap in the market for a company to come up with a product to fill this gap, and this filter was it. This would enable that demographic to do something with their lives if they mobilised themselves. If they learned actual skills, real skills, vocational skills that would lead them to make a difference. It had to be a hit, and Michael Dalton felt a real responsibility to the world and others, not to let it all go because of a minor setback.

As far as he was concerned, Lottie Mortimer had been a superstar. She had successfully passed two challenges in two months, exceeding expectations. She had seen Charlotte and found her to be such a motivating factor that she essentially pushed the accelerator button on her life and off she went like a missile, honing in on its target. So they missed some data at the end. Big deal. Michael felt that the work she had done would have been enough to prove that this filter does what it's meant to. It motivates people to change.

Mark and Richard were keen to plough on too. None the wiser to any real setbacks all they could see was an upside in going ahead with a launch date. Social media bosses were clambering for updates as to how things were progressing. Mark Zuckerberg had requested a meeting with Michael as had Evan Spiegel. Michael didn't want to disappoint them. Besides, after some heavy criticism of their involvement with politics and fake news, they were looking for a positive news story. Something that made them look ethical again. Something that positioned them as change-makers for the better.

Michael wasted no time in getting some paperwork over to Will as promised and was surprised by how easily he had signed it all away, rescinding all rights to the idea and his share of the company. He clearly wanted nothing to do with it, and whilst Michael was aware that Will was under the impression the company would be shut down, he didn't feel it necessary to correct him. If he hadn't read the paperwork properly or called in a lawyer to guide him that was his problem.

Besides, with Will out of the picture, it had been much easier managing the situation. As far as everyone in the office was concerned, Lottie had already come out of the filter after completing her challenges and was happily taking some time off at home. Nobody had asked any questions. In the meantime, the development team were already working on fixing some bugs in the prototype to make sure it would be smooth sailing for the big launch.

Because from Michael's perspective, the big launch was coming and nothing was going to stop him. He just needed to keep Lottie out of the picture for the time being while he got all his ducks aligned, and with the help from a friendly doctor, he had the perfect plan to do just that.

WILL HAD SEARCHED FOR LOTTIE EVERYWHERE. HE CALLED UP EVERY hospital in London to ask whether she had been admitted as a patient and nobody was able to confirm they had ever had a Lottie Mortimer. Some were just unable to divulge private information regarding their patients due to patent confidentiality. It was a nightmare, yet somehow it gave him hope. She must have woken up, there must have been some progress, some change, otherwise, why would they have moved her anywhere?

After what felt like weeks of dead-end calls he finally connected to a helpful nurse at a rehabilitation unit of a private hospital in Surbiton.

"Oh yes, Lottie Mortimer."

Will could feel his heart race with anticipation.

"Yes, she checked out of here a few days ago. She was being transferred to another hospital. I'm afraid I don't have any further details."

CHAPTER
Forty~Seven

Michael was delighted by how fast the development teams were able to work on improving the prototype. There were little tweaks here and there and promises of superior performance and a bug-free system. Of course, it had helped that there had been another sizeable injection of money into the project from investors. Michael had updated them that things were going swimmingly, that the prototype had been a success and that he was now looking to go ahead as planned with a full-scale launch.

Such investors had assigned a modest budget to the project already but had waited for news that the prototype was a success before they released the second phase. They didn't seem to need proof that it worked well, simply just that it worked from a technological perspective. So when Michael spun the news that it performed beyond expectations, he had more money thrown his way than he knew what to do with. It was the classic tale of hype over substance and of investors wanting to believe in a concept so much they placed greater value on it than it was truly worth.

However, within weeks there were bigger filter proofing facilities, more bandwidth for the data and more servers. In fact, the entire first two floors of the office became mass warehouses for storing servers brimming full of memory and algorithms, and staff, ready for the next batch of willing participants to enter the filter to experience their fate.

Michael was ready. The filter was ready. A launch date had been set and so far all he had to do was to share this news with an eagerly awaiting press.

CHAPTER
Forty-Eight

SHE KNEW SHE HAD TO GET OUT OF THERE AFTER THAT. LOTTIE SAT on the unfamiliar bed in the sparsely decorated room and mulled over her options. This wasn't her usual bedroom. They had moved her to a different one, probably far away from the other patients so she would contain herself. So she wouldn't spout her lies upon them, she wouldn't spread her toxicity elsewhere. Because that was how she was made to feel, as though she were toxic in some way. Except, it was all true. Everything she had remembered had been real all along, and the worst part of it was, she had been made to feel as though she were crazy.

They had injected her with some sort of drugs too after the outburst. She could feel the warm feeling of relaxation going through her veins like a soothing hot chocolate in the middle of winter. She could feel her responses were slower too. Looking from the bed to the door handle, she felt she was dragging one image along to the next one, blurry and in slow motion. She knew she couldn't get out like this, she needed her wits about her. Besides, there wasn't even a window in this room or a

341

clock. Whatever the logic was that this room was meant to calm her, it did very much the opposite making her feel as though she were indeed growing a seed of insanity in an otherwise sane mind.

Michael Dalton had seemed so brazen and self-assured on that news clip. Why on Earth were they going ahead and launching the filter? Didn't they know enough to realise this was dangerous? Didn't they see who Charlotte had become? She also couldn't understand why Will hadn't visited her. Something wasn't sitting right with her. Maybe she had been naive, and he had been just out for his best interests. He just wanted to launch this filter and claim the glory, leaving Lottie very much in the wake; surviving in a psychiatric hospital, convinced she was going mad. It just seemed so at odds with the Will she'd grown to love, so out of character.

He'd been kind and compassionate. He had looked out for her, and he must have managed to switch off the filter if she had ended up here. Not that she ever envisaged ending up like this. What was she missing? What was it that she didn't know?

Lottie knew she needed to get out of there, but she needed to do it properly. She needed to get herself organised. She needed to stop taking the mediation they were giving her, she needed to get hold of some money, some clothes and she needed to time it perfectly so nobody would know she had gone. As she lay her head on the pillow she knew exactly what she needed to do, but right now all she could think of was sleeping. Tiredness swept over her body like a continuous wave, rising her up with its strength and sending her off to a peaceful slumber as it lulled against the shore. Tomorrow she put her plan into action.

When she awoke the following morning the room was spinning slightly. Lottie felt her eyes bleary and wiping away the crusts she stood up and reached for the door handle. She wanted to have a shower and get changed, and grateful that the door was open she headed into the hallway bumping into a nurse on her way.

"Oh, you're up early."

Lottie had no idea what the time was but she played along.

"Well, the early bird catches the worm."

"How are you feeling? You feeling a bit better after yesterday. Poor you, what an outburst."

"Yes, so much better thank you. I honestly don't know what came over me. It's all nonsense. I must be a bit more confused than I thought."

"Ah that's ok," replied the nurse. A relieved look formed over her face. "But yes glad to hear it. Ok, feel free to go back to your room now if you like. I'll pop in and see you again in a bit."

Lottie smiled and made her way back to her room. She saw the clock on the wall. It was 6.45 am but she didn't feel tired. She had no idea what time she had fallen asleep so for all she knew she was fully rested. She started immediately on figuring out how to enact her escape plan; looking outside her window at how far she would need to jump. If she could even get out that way at all. It looked too high, even if she was just on the first floor. She remembered somewhere that tying together bedsheets made for a good alternative to a ladder in times of fire. If she could tie one end onto the bed frame she could probably just about jump from there. Then she looked through her small wardrobe. She didn't have many clothes but she had a few things her mother had brought her. Some jeans and T-shirts mostly, a hoodie, some cosmetics and as she rummaged through her things she was pleased to find an old backpack. She hadn't noticed it before. Her mother must have brought it up with some of her things in it. She sat on her bed and desperately went through all the compartments, hoping for a few old coins or keys. Turning it upside-down with all the compartments open she began to shake it vigorously, watching as some objects flew down upon her bed. An old packet of chewing gum, a few old coins, maybe three or four pounds max — and then it appeared. It looked like an old receipt at first, crumpled up into a ball, but as she unravelled it Lottie was delighted to see it was a twenty-pound note. She didn't know how far she was from London or how far it would get her but it was enough. She would find a way to make it work.

When lights went out that evening, she would make her way to Will's house, hoping to God he would be there.

The nurse had been in to see her a bit later as promised, this time accompanied by Dr Patel who approached her bed with a concerned look upon his face. Lottie did her best to appear calm and accommodating, smiling at them as they walked in, putting to one side the book she was reading. Quite the picture of morning tranquillity.

"I'm sorry to hear you weren't feeling very well yesterday Lottie," Dr Patel said cautiously, the nurse biting her lip behind him. "I gather you're feeling better today?"

"Oh, yes thanks, Doctor. I must have just been a bit over-tired, I don't know what came over me. It's silly really. I must have had a dream with that man in it from the news and I got all confused. I'm so sorry for worrying everyone. I feel so much better after a good night's sleep."

The doctor eyed up Lottie, his glasses falling to the end of his nose as he looked down upon her. Clicking his pen in his hands he wrote some notes to the nurse that looked like a prescription of some kind. She clutched at the prescription before looking slightly worried and leaving the room.

"Good. I'm so glad to hear it" he finally said. "You just take it easy, won't you. We're going to keep you in for a few more days just to be on the safe side."

"Ok, yes of course." Lottie smiled and raised her eyebrows as if to say *"Will that be all?"*

He was clearly suspicious but Lottie didn't care. She was getting out of there as soon as she could. It was also obvious that he had given the nurse some sort of prescription. Probably to keep her sedated, to have no surprises. However, Lottie would find a way to make sure she didn't take whatever she was given.

Evening came and Lottie waited for everything to go dark and quiet, for the nurses to do their final checks before they clocked off for the night, usually around ten. Then it was time for Lottie to get into action. Nerves of adrenaline pumping through her body she put a towel at the foot of her door before switching on her sidelight. As quietly as she could, she got herself dressed and stripped her bed, tying the sheets to the duvet, the duvet to the pillowcases and a spare towel she had left out earlier on intentionally.

Packing her bag she zipped it up slowly under the duvet to muffle out any noise and attached the tied up sheets to the bed with a double knot, pulling it as tight as she could before switching off her sidelight. She hoped it would hold, she hoped she wouldn't set off any alarms. Easing her body through the small window it was a tight squeeze, clearly designed not to let anyone escape but she was so slight these days, she was surprised by how easily her limbs fit through. Her bag didn't follow quite so easily but after some gentle tugs, it came too. She pulled her body slowly down towards the ground, holding onto a bedsheet, then duvet before finally her feet reached the ground. No alarm had gone off. No sirens. She clutched her bag tightly and moved close to the walls of the house, heading for the gates.

She had made it just to the end of the driveway before a bright light came on. Dashing into a nearby bush she waited, holding her breath. *Please don't find me now. I'm so close.* She heard no noises, so moved carefully further until she was at the gates. They were too high to climb and even if they weren't there was nothing on them to grip onto, completely flat wood. She frantically walked to the side of the gates hoping for a gap in the bushes, pushing her way through the foliage as quietly as she could. The grounds were larger than she realised and she kept walking until she found a clearing. Pushing her body through a bit of broken fence she found herself confronted by a road. She had escaped with nothing but the bag on her back and a little bit of money, and she started to run.

It wasn't long before she saw found street-lit roads with street signs on them giving her some indication as to where she was. Roehampton. She was in London. That meant getting to Will's shouldn't be too hard. She just needed to find a taxi. She began walking towards signs towards central London, keeping an eye out for a passing cab, but hours went by and there were none with their lights on. Finally, when she reached Wandsworth bridge she saw one coming towards her like an angel in the night. The black cab stopped and she jumped in, instructing the driver to take her straight to Will's house. Relief and exhaustion swelled over her entire body and she shut her eyes. She had done it. She was out. She found herself repeatedly looking back, hoping to God that she wasn't being followed.

CHAPTER
Forty~Nine

WILL HEARD THE KNOCK AT THE DOOR LIKE A DISTANT THUD IN HIS mind. It was the middle of the night, it must have been to next-door's house. He wasn't expecting visitors at this hour, or any hour for that matter. Nobody had come to see him for months. He tried to ignore it and go back to sleep, but there it was again, thudding on his door like a persistent mosquito, flying around the room waking him up. He went downstairs, putting his robe on as he got closer to knocking, which only got louder and more resolute. What in God's name was going on?

Fumbling with the locks, he pulled back the door. Disbelief took over him, blinking repeatedly he squinted in the dim light.

"Lottie?"

There she was, standing there right before his very eyes. Pallid and gaunt, she looked exhausted but as beautiful as ever.

"Hi Will. I'm sorry. I didn't know where else to go."

Will pulled her inside urgently, emotion taking over. Any professional relationship they once had was gone. He knew they meant more to each other than that. He reached his arms around her and held her in the hallway of his house breathing her in. He could feel Lottie's body relax in his. He pulled her away to look at her face.

"I can't believe it's you,' he whispered gratefully. "I've been looking everywhere for you, I've been so worried."

Lottie began to cry. Will took her face in his hands. He pulled her hoody down away from her head and wiped the tears away from her eyes with his hands. He couldn't help himself, and he began kissing her so desperately, so relieved that she had somehow just walked back into his life.

"It's all real, isn't it? Everything. The filter? Tell me I'm not crazy Will."

Will guided Lottie inside and ushered her to a comfortable sofa.

"Lottie, where have you been?"

"They put me in a psychiatric hospital Will. They tried to convince me I had imagined the whole thing. I almost believed them. I really thought I was just confused and it had all been some sort of effect of being in a coma. That's what they told me it was. But then I saw him on TV. I saw the news.

"Who put you in a psychiatric hospital, Lottie? What did you see on the news?" Will was even more confused. What was she talking about?

"I saw Michael on the news Will! I saw that he's going ahead and launching the filter and …

"What?"

Will hastily grabbed at his nearby laptop and started to google Michael Dalton. Surely he couldn't have actually gone ahead with any of this without him. Surely he didn't have the right to do anything with this. This was all being shut down. This was all behind him. That's what he thought. Will scratched his head, he was still waking up. This was all such a sensory overload and he didn't know where to begin.

"Why didn't you come and find me? Why didn't you stop him?"

Will was busy speed reading through the news articles, published yesterday. It was recent news but how had he missed it? Why had nobody told him about what was going on?

"Bastard!" Will shut down his laptop and stood up enraged, pacing back and forth and then realising the concerned confusion on Lottie's face he walked towards her earnestly.

"Lottie, I had no idea about any of this I swear. I've spent the last few months looking everywhere for you. I went to see you as often as I could in the hospital, and then I go in one day and you've been moved and nobody would tell me where you went! I tried to track you down but it was as though someone was trying to make it very difficult to find you."

Lottie frowned, taking it all in.

"I wanted nothing more to do with this filter when I saw what happened to you. When you ended up in hospital in a coma it was the final straw for me, so I told Michael I wanted out and we agreed to shut this whole thing down."

"Except he hasn't Will. He's just gone ahead and done it anyway."

Will was shaking his head in disbelief. How could he have been so stupid?

"Doesn't he know how dangerous this is? Didn't he see what happened to him the filter?"

Will stopped pacing and looked at Lottie, a serious expression on his face, the blood seemed to drop from his cheeks.

"What do you mean? Lottie, we lost some of the data feed towards the end. We never saw what happened after you passed your second challenge."

"Oh my god Will. You don't know?"

Lottie sat down on the sofa her head in her hands.

349

"It got serious. Charlotte killed Michael and tried to frame me for it. It was a nightmare. You tried to get me out of the filter by shutting it down, and then the next thing I remember is waking up in a hospital and everyone's telling me I'm crazy."

———

THEY HAD TALKED FOR HOURS. IN THE STILL OF THE NIGHT, WHEN ALL around them were fast asleep when the world was silent and the roads were resting, Lottie and Will sat catching up on everything. She told him all about what happened after he lost the feed, filling in all the blanks that he had lost.

Will sat there listening, just taking it all in. His head would shake and his hands would go to his temples as though trying to reclaim a distant memory. Except, these weren't his memories, they were Lottie's. What happened in that filter wasn't a success story, it was a disaster but, through no fault of Lottie's. If anything the filter proved she had greatness in her, but the problem was that who she became wasn't an improved version of herself. The person she became was the extreme of all of Lottie's characteristics. What started as a competitive nature turned into a ruthless obsession with winning. What was before a sharp level of aptitude and intelligence turned into a dark need to control. What was a desire to be healthy and look good turned into jealousy when others threatened that part of her identity. Charlotte desired so deeply to be the greatest, that she would do whatever it took to ensure nobody would stand in her way.

The irony was, in Will's mind, that this was what happened with sweet, kind Lottie; a woman who previously wouldn't hurt a fly. Kind and smart — yes. Unfulfilled potential — absolutely, but a ruthless narcissist and killer? The filter, when used on people who were already fiercely competitive, impossibly vain or ruthlessly driven would inevitably be far worse. To Will, that didn't even bear thinking about. What's more, social media already highlighted peoples' insecurities. It exacerbated a need for social acceptance through 'likes' and 'comments'. It validated egos, becoming an addictive force. What would a filter like this do to those with insecurities? Wouldn't it just add fuel to an already seething flame creating a world of people who simply don't feel good enough — because now they have a valid reason to prove that they weren't?

How Lottie had handled herself. Will had always admired her, but she really was a fighter. To escape from a psychiatric ward in the dead of night, comforted only by her convictions was an incredible testament to her character. He had missed her. He felt such overwhelming relief seeing her sink into the sofa, safe and sound. What's more, her mind worked, there was absolutely nothing wrong with her mentally. He put his arm around her and comforted her when she spoke of Michael's murder, and she didn't flinch or react as though it were unfamiliar territory. If anything, they both knew it felt right.

After several hours her eyes began to close and it was clear tiredness was taking over her body. Will let her fall asleep on the sofa before carrying her upstairs to his bedroom where he propped her head on comfortable, fluffy pillows, and covered her with the duvet before turning off the light. They had so much ground they needed to cover, but at that moment Lottie just needed to rest.

The following morning Lottie padded downstairs, appearing bleary-eyed in Will's kitchen. A smile formed over her face when she saw Will making breakfast.

"Good morning," she said as she wrapped her arms around his waist. It felt so familiar to be so close. As though this was where she was meant to be. "Something smells good."

"Well, I figured you might be hungry. Your coffee is ready." Will pointed to a coffee sitting beside the kettle.

"Thank you. That's so sweet." Lottie pulled up a stool beside the kitchen island and snuggled her coffee between her two hands gratefully.

"Listen, Will. We need to come up with a plan. We have to stop Michael. He can't get away with this and go ahead with launching this filter. He doesn't know what Charlotte is capable of…"

"Don't worry Lottie." Will interrupted. "I may have a little plan up my sleeve already."

CHAPTER

Fifty

IF MICHAEL DALTON WERE A SUPERSTITIOUS MAN HE MAY HAVE called it fate how all of the stars had been aligning for him lately. He always knew he was destined for greatness and everything that had been happening lately really did reinforce that notion in his mind.

Will had conveniently stepped aside just at a time when things began to get interesting. He obviously couldn't handle the pressure. Michael was an experienced entrepreneur, he'd seen it all before. He had been there, done that. He'd had successes and failures and felt he was adept at adapting to them much like an old leathery chameleon. Nothing fazed him anymore, and the more successful he became, the more grey hairs that seemed to appear on his head, the fewer questions he seemed to get about his ability or judgement. People just trusted him, they let him do what he wanted because they assumed he knew better, that he had greater experience and that he must be successful for a reason. After the ordeal with Lottie going to hospital, Will had just been ready to pack it all in just like that. He didn't even know if her illness was related to the filter or not. It was so hasty!

He just needed to keep Lottie out of the way now that they were so close to the launch. The last thing he wanted was her coming back now to throw any spanners in the works, telling everyone she hadn't even completed the full challenge, telling everyone she became unwell and no doubt blaming the filter, telling everyone she had been in a psychiatric ward or whatever rubbish she could potentially spout. Yes, he knew exactly what was going on with her recuperation of course. He had a doctor friend on the inside who was giving him regular updates as to her progress, and when he suggested keeping her in until everything was ready to launch, he had obliged, by moving her from hospital to hospital, for a small fee of course.

Everything had aligned impeccably, and since the announcement that the filter would be launched within a week, there had been monumental interest from the press. By the time it was launch day, several news crews were parked outside the office ready for live coverage of the launch 'event'. They were tipped off that Michael would be giving a speech on how 'The Best Life Filter' could change the world, before officially switching on the filter for real and inviting the first participants to take part. Michael had then invited a whole host of celebrity friends and business tycoons to join for a celebratory party afterwards. They were all going to drink champagne and eat canapés in the filter proofing showroom, whilst having their photos taken. As people who had done well in their lives, they were the perfect spokespeople for the value of achieving greatness, and Michael knew the power of the 'influencers' within his target demographic, even if he didn't particularly like them.

Michael had put on his sharpest suit, and he waited for the attendees to take their seats in a newly built office auditorium, designed with the latest injections of capital. It could comfortably seat several hundred heads, theatre style, and Michael was convinced it would be crucial for the ongoing show and tells they would have when people demonstrated their success stories. He envisaged people coming out of the filter to tell their tales, speaking to hundreds of eager ears about who they used to be, how they had changed and motivating others to do the same. Cameras were situated on the front row, live streaming everything to a willing public who could watch from the comfort of their homes or offices.

The audience took to their seats and soon conversations hushed as they waited for action upon the gradual dimming of the stage lights. Michael Dalton strode on the stage, all dazzling smile and designer suit. A slight tan, he looked the picture of health and much younger than his fifty-something years.

"Ladies and gentleman. Welcome. Well, what can I say? We are finally here on probably the most exciting day of many of our lives. A day we have been building up to mentally and technologically for years, and a day I'm sure many of us will never forget.

A very gracious thank you to those of you who are joining us today, and who have helped us get to this point. We wouldn't have achieved any of this without the help and expertise of some incredibly sharp minds, who have worked tirelessly on developing this filter that I'm proud to announce is now ready for the world to enjoy.

Many of you will still be wondering how this all works. How this will really benefit you? Why you should consider doing it? If you should consider doing it at all. Many of you may think this is just another filter. There are so many of those right?

Well, not quite like this one. For those of you who don't

know. This filter is unique and is a rare technological feat. For the first time, we can step inside a filter, and see who we could really become if we were the best version of ourselves. We could live beside our better self, we could learn how to become them, we could see what habits they have adopted and how they have achieved greatness. Because, after all, within each of us is greatness. Most of us just don't dream big enough to achieve it or have enough self-belief to feel we deserve it.

I'm here to tell you that you do deserve it. You all deserve it. You all deserve to see who you could become and I believe I have a duty to show you. Ladies and gentlemen, I am proud to announce today is the day we launch "The Best Life Filter."

The audience, some of whom were still shuffling in their seats when Michael started talking, had become fixated, began to clap, many got out their smartphones and began recording. A sea of phones appeared like silent bobbing heads in the audience, trying to capture what was about to be a monumental moment in history.

Michael's EA, Lizzie sat in the wings with a laptop, ensuring the presentation ran smoothly. Next up would be a motivational video explaining the filter, and why others should get behind it. Lizzie, upon receiving a gentle nod from Michael, pressed play.

A warm smile took over Michael's face. He had been practising this speech for several weeks, rehearsing the order of events for the reveal, and he felt comfortable it was compelling. The audience was lapping it up so far, and after they saw the video he knew they would all be amazed. Images appeared on the screen behind him of some of the team at work building and developing the idea, of the state of the art filter proofing facilities, of what would happen to participants who took part. How they could change, who they could become. It was all so slick. Michael was inexplicably proud.

Then it changed to clips from Lottie's reveal. There she was coming out of the elevator on her first day in the filter, walking up to Charlotte and meeting her face to face. The two of them were side by side holding up their arms triumphantly. The audience was then taken on a sequential montage of her progress, losing weight, working out, there was upbeat, motivational music playing throughout. The audience was witnessing her transformation and it was compulsive viewing.

Suddenly, however, something was wrong. The stream began to buffer, as though they were losing internet connection. The video then paused before it disappeared from the screen completely.

The audience started to murmur and Michael looked at Lizzie for some idea as to what was wrong. However, she just shrugged before shaking her head and clicking on her laptop frantically, hoping that she could somehow fix the issue at hand.

"I'm so sorry about this ladies and gentleman. It would appear even the mighty fall at the odd technological glitch!"

Michael looked once again at Lizzie who still looked perplexed however he was keen to continue unfazed and was relieved something appeared to be playing once again on the screen.

"Ah-ha. There we go. It would appear we have something playing again."

A video started again and Michael stood back, smiling a slightly more forced smile, trying to ride it out with professionalism. However, before he could compute what was happening he felt all the blood rushing from his legs, his face went white. Lottie Mortimer appeared on the screen. She looked pale and gaunt, and nothing like the filtered images he had just seconds before he played to his transfixed audience. She seemed to be sitting in a kitchen somewhere. How was she out of the hospital? What was going on?

"Hello. My name is Lottie Mortimer...

Michael ran over to Lizzie screaming "Get that off, will you! Shut it down!"

"I can't, it's playing on its own I don't know how!"

Soon a team of people had appeared from behind the wings, trying to help stop the stream. They even switched off the laptop entirely but it just kept playing. Lottie's face was speaking straight to the camera. Her hair was tied back in a bun and she looked serious and forlorn.

"I was selected to be the prototype for the Best Life Filter. I went into the filter for several months to see my best life, and I met her. Yet, I'm fairly sure, what you're being told about me and this filter, isn't the full story.

Three months ago, I came out of the filter and found myself awake in a hospital. I was awake, but I couldn't speak and I couldn't move. I couldn't even scream. I was told I had been in a coma for months. I was told I would be confused, disorientated and it would take me some time to get better. I was told a lot of things.

I remembered everything about my experiences in the filter, but as soon as I was able to talk, and explain what had happened, everybody thought I was crazy and nobody believed me. I was admitted to a psychiatric hospital and was put on a cocktail of drugs to sort out my supposed mental condition and my confusion. A mental condition I soon started to believe was real too. I started to think I must have imagined everything. That Charlotte was a figment of my imagination, and that living beside the best version of myself must have been all in my mind.

Here is the truth. And this is coming from someone who was motivated to succeed and give her best. I mean, I really tried. But you can never beat yourself. My best self didn't want to be beaten, she felt threatened by me and she turned into a ruthless narcissist and a psychopathic killer. She turned into a murderer!"

Lottie tried to let these words sink in. She didn't want them to be taken lightly or lost amidst the shock of her revelation. Sitting on Will's kitchen stool she had no idea just how her words were being received in the auditorium, yet she wanted to be as articulate and to the point as possible.

"Don't try to be perfect. It's a myth, a fallacy as it doesn't exist and lurking beneath every exterior of perfection lies a myriad of sadness."

The audience started to murmur. This was a shocking turn of fate. Michael ran off the stage to watch with Lizzie from the wings. He couldn't face the humiliation of just standing there. What was happening? Why couldn't anyone shut this bloody thing down?

"Michael Dalton knew that I was in a coma. He knew that I was admitted to the psychiatric ward because he himself, instructed me to be placed there. Interestingly the same doctor who was in charge of my recuperation, Dr Ravi Patel, is also the medical counsel for the filter. Together, they drugged me and let me believe I was crazy. This filter has been one big cover-up and it needs to stop.

There are so many of us who strive for more. We want things faster, we want to be better, but when we get what we think we want, it's not enough. The goalposts keep moving. In my case, Charlotte became so obsessed with being the best, she did everything in her power to stay in that way and control her life, even if it meant having no friends, no family, and murdering the one person who stood in her way. Is this really what we want? To create a world of unbalanced maniacs keen to destroy everything in their path to greatness? There was nothing great about Charlotte, I can assure you. And nothing great will come from unleashing a filter unto the world that will permeate fears, insecurities and a need for validation.

This filter must not launch and I'm here today to do everything in my power to stop it."

CHAPTER
Fifty~One

Sirens, police sirens — but this time for a very different reason. It wasn't long before there were several police cars lined up outside the offices. Michael Dalton was unceremoniously taken away in handcuffs in the back of a police car, his expensive watch shining brightly against the flashing cameras, keen to capture his every move like preying vultures. They were all screaming out his name asking for comment, but he just looked down at his feet, unable to show his face to the world. It was all over the news. All Lottie and Will had to do was turn on the TV and it was on every channel.

'Michael Dalton was arrested today following a shock announcement at the launch of what was set to be a groundbreaking new filter that could show users who they could become if they lived their best lives. Lottie Mortimer appeared mid-way through his presentation with an explosive account of what she had experienced, exposing what had

*happened when she was used as a prototype,
claiming she was drugged and put in a psychiatric
hospital. Plans to launch this filter are quite unsur-
prisingly, being put on hold and there will no doubt
be quite a few question marks from those
involved.*

Will's plan had worked, perhaps even better than expected. With some help from his friend Simon, he had managed to hack into the presentation that Michael was doing, and override all of the systems to stream the video of Lottie, who was sitting at his kitchen table. They had an outline of what she was meant to say but she just ran with it on her own. She knew better than anyone what needed to be done and as Will sat there, watching her speak so articulately, he couldn't have felt more proud.

Days later, the police had asked them both to provide statements and accounts into what they were terming a 'conspiracy to defraud'. Lottie told them everything she could and the police sat listening attentively. It was the first time she felt able to tell her story without being made to feel as though she were crazy, and it felt like such a relief to get it off her chest. Will too, provided as much background into the idea behind the filter, along with any of the data and footage from Lottie's time there. All in all, it was a pretty bulletproof case, that Michael had proceeded to try to launch a filter, knowing full-well that Lottie's results from it had been far from favourable. What's more, he'd proceeded in taking huge sums of money from investors and the government, claiming the filter was foolproof, when it was far from it.

It was all over, the filter was under police custody and Michael was likely to go to jail for a long time.

Lottie knew she had to rebuild her life, but there was no

illusion to it now. No magic lustre that she needed to aspire towards. Her life was thankfully all within her control, and for that, she felt truly grateful. She knew she had to move on from this but she also felt that now she wasn't doing it alone. Will was by her side, and since she'd turned up on his door in the middle of the night, he hadn't let her out of his sight.

The two had a long way to go together, but being together, conscious that they wanted to move in the same direction was enough for her. She didn't want to live in the future, imagining the life they could have, she just wanted to live in this moment. Will reached for her hand in the taxi on the way home from the police station and squeezed it tightly. It was a start, but Lottie knew she had to start somewhere.

When you realise nothing is lacking. The whole world belongs to you.

LAO TZU.

Printed in Great Britain
by Amazon